Sophie Cousens

This Time Next Year

arrow books

8 10 9 7

Arrow Books
20 Vauxhall Bridge Road
London SW1V 2SA

Arrow Books is part of the Penguin Random House group
of companies whose addresses can be found at
global.penguinrandomhouse.com

Penguin
Random House
UK

First published in Great Britain in 2020 by Arrow Books

www.penguin.co.uk

A CIP catalogue record for this book is available from
the British Library.

ISBN 9781787464940

Typeset in 10/15.2 pt Palatino
by Integra Software Services Pvt. Ltd, Pondicherry

Printed and bound in Great Britain by Clays Ltd, Elcograf S.p.A.

To dear Aunty Em, who would have loved to read this

New Year's Eve 2019

The Night Jam was rammed. Pounding music pulsed through the club and the walls felt sticky with sweat, alcohol and likely worse. Minnie held tightly to Greg's hand as they jostled through the crowd near the door.

'We're never going to get to the bar,' Greg shouted back to her.

'What?' Minnie yelled back, her ears adjusting to the heavy bass.

'We won't be able to get a drink before midnight. I don't even know where Lucy's party is,' said Greg.

He pointed upwards, indicating they should try to push their way upstairs to the terrace on the mezzanine above. Minnie looked at her watch – it was ten to midnight. So far, this whole evening was only validating her hatred of New Year's Eve. Why hadn't she stayed at home and gone to bed early? Then she remembered that her heating had been cut off – she'd come out to keep warm. And Greg had been determined to go to his work friend's party; she would have felt like a bad girlfriend if she'd made him go alone.

Minnie let herself be dragged through the throng of pulsating bodies. Finally, they emerged from the crush, stepping out into the cool night air where the thumping bass from the club settled to a more manageable decibel.

'Watch it!' Greg said, pushing a drunk guy out of his way. Greg glared at the man, trying to make him notice he'd spilt his beer on someone, but the man was too far gone to care.

'I did warn you about spending New Year with me,' said Minnie.

'Will you stop with this jinxed stuff?' said Greg, shaking his head.

'Honestly, it's a thing; bad things happen to me at New Year's. I wouldn't be surprised if this whole building went up in flames before the night's out. Or perhaps a very small asteroid lands right where I'm standing.'

'I don't think we're having a terrible night because you're jinxed; I think we're having a terrible night because you dragged us to dinner at weird Alan's house on the other side of the galaxy. Now we're arriving at a party two seconds to midnight when everyone's high on moon juice and ... come in Star Command?' Greg lifted a finger to his ear, pausing to listen to an imaginary transmission, 'Mission control says we're not even at the right party.'

'Permission to abort the mission?' Minnie asked hopefully.

'Denied,' said Greg.

Minnie and Greg had been dating for five months. They'd met at a march outside City Hall, protesting the lack of affordable housing in London. Greg was the journalist covering the story and Minnie was there supporting Mrs Melvin, a lady she had been delivering food to since the early days of her business. Minnie and her friend Leila had made a sign for the march that said, 'HOUSING IS A HUMAN RIGHT', but they'd used too much paint on the first 'H' so it looked a bit like an 'M'. On the march, Minnie, Leila and Mrs Melvin found themselves walking next to a group of people dressed as large cats wearing monocles and top hats. One wore a T-shirt that said, 'SAY NO TO THE FAT CATS!' Greg ran over to take a photo of Minnie's sign with the fat cats in the foreground. He shook his head laughing as he snapped away.

'Why are you laughing?' Minnie shouted crossly.

'Maybe the cats are so fat because of all the mousing?' Greg said, pointing to her sign. Leila looked and laughed. Minnie rolled her eyes.

'It doesn't say mousing,' she said, hand firmly on her hip.

'It does look like it says mousing, Minnie,' said Leila.

'Minnie Mouse, this photo will make a great front page,' said Greg with a sly smile.

'You'd better not,' said Minnie, trying not to laugh as she chased him down the street, playfully prodding him with her sign. Minnie liked men who could make her laugh. She was instantly drawn to Greg's sarcastic manner and his angular features. He had a neatly trimmed brown beard and distinctive, dark-rimmed glasses. Once they started dating, Minnie discovered that it wasn't just for work that Greg liked to make up headlines – he enjoyed captioning everything she did. When Minnie tripped on a step he would say, 'Stunner trips on stairs – Stairs seek legal advice; chances are they're going down!' Or when she took the last banana in his fruit bowl, he'd pipe up in an American drawl, 'Fruit bowl homicide still unsolved – Did victim go bananas? Cross the lime? Or was it simply a case of sour grapes?' Puns were his thing. Greg wasn't making any jokes this evening.

'Look, you stay here,' he said with a sigh, looking around the balcony, 'I'll go back through and try to find this private room.'

'OK, well, if an asteroid lands in your absence. I can only say goodbye, I told you so, and Happy New Year,' Minnie replied, trying to sound upbeat.

As Greg walked away, Minnie turned to look out at the London skyline and shivered. The city exuded a sense of serenity in sharp contrast to the atmosphere of the club. The buildings were bathed in silver moonlight and the night sky was still and cloudless. Minnie wished she could transport herself to the top of another empty skyscraper just to lie down on the flat roof and gaze up at the stars, unfettered by other people.

'Ten, nine, eight …' People were starting the countdown. 'Seven, six, five …' Minnie looked at all the couples pulling together in anticipation of the midnight kiss. She was glad Greg wasn't there to kiss her. She never understood why the end of the year had to be marked with the ridiculous convention of everyone locking lips in unison. People behaving like lemmings, following the herd. 'Four, three, two, one, HAPPY NEW YEAR!'

An explosion of fireworks erupted in the sky, illuminating the city beneath in a shower of multicoloured lights. Huge bursts of energy ignited in the darkness, miniature universes flaring into existence only to fade to extinction moments later. Minnie wondered at all that effort for such a fleeting display of brilliance. The city buildings below looked still and stately, unmoved by the frenzy of activity above them.

On the balcony of the club, the fireworks cast ugly shadows onto the spaced-out faces of intoxicated people, as they swayed and swerved through the crowd. Light shone into grimy corners, full of cigarette butts and discarded plastic glasses. A group of girls tottering about in high heels pushed into her and Minnie had to grab the railing to stay upright.

'Happy Birthday to me,' Minnie said quietly to herself. Then she felt a warm, wet sensation as one of the girls vomited down her back.

By the time Greg returned, the terrace had thinned out and Minnie was sitting on the floor by the railings waiting for him.

'What are you wearing? Where's your top?' asked Greg. Minnie had folded her sodden shirt into her bag and was now only wearing a grey vest top with frayed spaghetti straps.

'Someone was sick on my shirt,' she said, hugging her arms around herself.

'Oh dear. Well, it's a bit X-rated like that.' Greg cupped a hand in front of his mouth to make a pretend microphone. 'Weather report in – there's a storm in a D-cup presenting itself.'

'Well, it's this or vomit-couture,' Minnie said, pulling up her top self-consciously. She'd never dream of wearing an outfit this revealing in public. She felt very exposed. 'Did you find the party or not?'

Greg nodded. He led her back through the club, up another staircase and then through a double door covered in red velvet, pillared by two bald security guards.

'I was here just a minute ago – we're here for the birthday party,' Greg explained. The security guard waved them through, glancing at Minnie's chest as she walked past. Minnie folded her arms in front of her.

The party on the other side of the red velvet door was everything that the room they had come from was not: the music was at a normal volume, the crowd looked beautifully dressed and sophisticated, waiters were topping up champagne and nobody was being sick over anyone. The exterior curved wall of the room was floor-to-ceiling glass, giving an incredible 180-degree view of the city of London beyond. Minnie immediately felt intimidated. This was a rich persons' party, a black tie one at that – she couldn't look more out of place. Minnie had cooked for enough rich people to know how they reacted to people like her; they would patronise her, or worse, look right through her. If she had been wearing the right armour she could have done a good impression of someone who didn't care, but her skimpy vest top was not it.

'Greg! You didn't tell me it was black tie?' she hissed.

'Black tie is a bourgeois construct, Minnie. I wouldn't wear it to my own funeral.' Greg scanned the room and then waved to a tall blonde girl in a tight red dress. 'Lucy!' The girl turned, gave a smile of recognition, then started making her way through the crowd towards them. 'Better late than never, hey,' Greg said, reaching out to touch her arm. 'This is Minnie. Someone was sick on her shirt on the way in.'

'Hi,' said Lucy. Her pillowy lips closed over perfect straight teeth into a sympathetic smile. 'Sorry about the sick.

It's ridiculous they make you wade through all the plebs to get up to the VIP suite.'

Minnie shook her head, shrugging it off.

'Quite a party,' she said, looking around at all the free-flowing booze. How much would a party like this cost?

'It's my boyfriend's birthday on the first. We thought we'd use it as an excuse to throw an excessive New Year's Eve bash,' Lucy said with a flick of her hand. Then she turned to Minnie with a beaming smile, 'Hey, didn't Greg say you were a first of January baby too, Minnie?'

'Oh, Happy Birthday,' Greg said hurriedly. Lucy turned to look at him wide-eyed.

'Greg, you didn't even say Happy Birthday to her yet? Dump him, Minnie!' Lucy laughed and nudged Greg in the ribs. Greg blushed and looked at his feet.

'I'm not big on birthdays,' Minnie smiled weakly.

They stood in silence for a moment.

'So, um, Lucy is the food columnist at the paper,' Greg said. 'I'm queuing up for a jammy gig like that. I saw you were at La Petite Assiette Rouge last week. So bloody jealous, Luce.'

'It has its downsides, darling. I'm getting fatter and fatter the amount of Michelin-star dinners I'm being forced to eat. I feel like a foie gras goose being stuffed to bursting,' said Lucy.

Minnie glanced down at Lucy's svelte, gym-toned figure in the skin-tight look-how-thin-I-am dress.

'Oh diddums, such a hardship,' said Greg, nudging his elbow into hers. 'Smart, beautiful girl force-fed fine food – Human rights campaigners on standby!'

Lucy threw her head back and gave a half-snorting, half-silent laugh, then she clutched Greg's arm, as though she might fall over.

'You must have an absolute hoot with this one, Minnie.'

Minnie nodded, though she wondered if Greg's hilarious newspaper headlines might be starting to get annoying.

'Mins is in the food world too,' said Greg, standing a little taller. 'Runs her own catering business in the charity sector.'

'That sounds interesting,' said Lucy, looking over Minnie's shoulder and waving to someone behind her.

'I don't think making pies for the elderly counts as being in the "food world", but thanks for bigging me up, hun,' Minnie said, rubbing Greg's back.

'Do you cater events? Maybe I've come across you?' asked Lucy, turning her attention back to Minnie.

'No, we just do pies for the elderly. The company's called No Hard Fillings, it's a bit like Meals on Wheels.'

Lucy blinked her eyes a few times.

'No hard feelings?' she said.

'No,' said Minnie, 'No Hard *Fillings*, as in pie fillings. It's um, supposed to be funny.'

'Oh, I see. Ha-ha,' Lucy said, wrinkling her nose and giving another silent laugh. 'Well that must be very ... fulfilling.'

Greg let out a snorting cackle. 'Good one Luce,' he tapped his elbow to Lucy's. 'See, the thing is, Minnie's company would be a lot more successful if she didn't keep giving stuff away for free and employing a load of time bandits with zero work ethic.'

'I don't, and that's not true,' Minnie said, bowing her head.

'Well, it sounds jolly rewarding,' said Lucy. 'I find old people so sweet, don't you?'

'Some of them are sweet, some of them are total knobs, same as the rest of us,' said Minnie. Greg coughed loudly and Minnie gave him a firm pat on the back.

'But you're planning to branch out, aren't you Min?' Greg said, recovering his composure. 'That's her current customer base, but she could easily expand; do weddings, corporates, high-calibre events, all sorts. Maybe Lucy could hook you up with some contacts?'

'Sure, sure, happy to help,' Lucy said, waving at someone across the room and starting to move away. 'Listen, I must go mingle. Make yourselves at home; drink our champagne – we ordered way too much. And don't worry about arriving late, the party's hardly started.'

Lucy cocked her head and flashed them both a well-rehearsed hostess smile, then with a swish of long silky hair she turned to go. Minnie watched Greg's eyes follow her across the room.

Seeing them standing empty-handed, a waiter came over to offer them champagne. They both took one and went to clink glasses but missed, Greg's champagne flute bumping into Minnie's wrist. He quickly retracted his hand and took a large swig of drink.

'Happy New Year,' said Minnie.

'Happy New Year,' said Greg, then after a pause, 'and Happy, er, Birthday. I, um, I have a present for you back at my flat. Sorry, I didn't have a chance to wrap it.'

'Don't worry. I said not to get me anything.'

Greg shuffled his weight between each foot, his eyes flitting around the room.

'She's a useful person to know, Lucy Donohue, I told you it would be worth coming tonight. She knows everyone who's anyone in your sector. You should never underestimate how far good contacts will get you in life, Minnie.'

'I doubt she knows everyone who's anyone in the pie sector,' Minnie said, then, affecting a posh voice, 'unless it's pastry chefs making choux pie-ettes out of foie gras at la petite rue de la frenchy french.' She stuck out her tongue and then laughed.

'I don't know why you always do that,' Greg said. 'I'm trying to help you.'

'You're right, I'm sorry,' said Minnie, feeling chastised. She didn't need Greg to point it out. She could always hear herself sounding bitchy when she felt insecure and ultimately it only made her feel worse. She bit her lip and fiddled with the pendant on her necklace. Greg pouted, a muscle twitching in his jaw.

'Well, you appear to have made it to midnight without turning into a pumpkin, or whatever it is you were worried about.'

'The jinx doesn't end at midnight, it's the whole of New Year's Eve night and New Year's Day. And I'm not worried about "turning into a pumpkin" – it's the little stuff like getting puked on or losing my coat on the bus on the way here. I'm just unlucky around New Year.'

'Well, someone spilt beer on my shoes, and I missed most of my friend's party because I was stuck at your eccentric friend's house. Maybe I'm jinxed too?' Greg finished the sentence with an overly animated smile, a smile that said, 'I'm joking so you can't get offended.' His eyes dropped down to Minnie's chest.

'Is the vest top really obscene?' she asked with a wince.

'Well, you know I love that view, Min, but maybe the rest of the room would rather look at something else,' Greg nodded.

'Right, I'll go to the bathroom and try to salvage my shirt.'

On the way to the bathroom, Minnie checked her phone. She had a text from Leila.

'Just checking on you. What's the damage? Do I need to rescue you from a hostage situation/pothole/worse?'

Minnie smiled and tapped out a reply, 'Not too bad so far. Lost only coat and got vommed on. ;)'

Leila was Minnie's best friend and business partner. They'd set up No Hard Fillings together four years ago and invested all their time, money and energy into it ever since. If it hadn't been for Leila, Minnie doubted she could have kept it going for as long as they had. They'd faced so many hurdles along the way, it would have been so easy just to give up and go back to working for someone else, somewhere you knew you'd be getting a pay cheque at the end of each month rather than scrabbling to balance the books and give yourself any kind of salary.

'So surprise – I've spent New Year's Eve preparing pies so we don't have to work tomorrow. I'm taking you somewhere for your birthday. You need to wear a dress,' said Leila's text.

Minnie smiled. She sent back a dress and sick face emoji.

Leila sent back a screen full of pie emojis and then a screen full of sick faces. Minnie laughed out loud and then replied, 'You are the best. Thank you Pieface. For you, and only you, I will wear a dress xxx.'

Minnie looked up from her phone and walked straight into a waiter carrying a tray of canapés. A flurry of goat's-cheese tartlets rained down on her.

'Oh god, I'm so sorry,' she said, falling down onto her hands and knees to help the waiter retrieve the debris.

'It's not my night,' said the waiter, miserably.

He couldn't have been more than seventeen. Minnie saw that his glasses had been spattered with soft cheese. She gently took them from his nose and wiped them on her top before returning them.

'I know the feeling,' she said.

Once she'd helped the waiter clean up as best she could, Minnie walked around the back of the bar and found the toilets along a dimly lit corridor. She peered around the door of the ladies' loos. Half a dozen women were chatting at the mirrors, touching up their make-up. She didn't want to wash her vomity shirt in front of them. Walking further down the corridor she found a unisex disabled toilet with its own sink and hand dryer – perfect. She pulled the black silk shirt out of her bag and started rinsing off the worst of it. Luckily, it was mainly sticky rather than anything too globular, but the smell of stomach bile mixed with vodka and Coke made Minnie pinch in her nostrils. She couldn't imagine Lucy Donohue ever finding herself in this situation.

She looked up at herself in the mirror, instinctively pushing her curls back behind her ears. Her hair disobediently sprang back the moment she let go. She'd just had it cut and the hairdresser had gone an inch shorter than she'd asked for. Now she couldn't tie it up or keep it out of her eyes. She drew the back of a finger beneath each eye to remove some smudged eyeliner, then reapplied the plum lipstick Leila had given her as an early birthday present. She would never have chosen something so bold for herself, but it complemented her skin tone, and she wondered that sometimes Leila knew what suited her better than she knew herself.

Minnie dried her shirt under the hand dryer as best she could, and then put it back on. She stood for a moment, staring at her reflection wearing the damp, creased, misshapen shirt. It was the nicest item of clothing Minnie owned; a fitted black silk blouse with white scallop cuffs. It was an expensive brand she had found in a charity shop. She'd been so pleased when she'd found it. Now it was as though even the shirt knew her to be an imposter and was wrinkling itself up in protest.

'Come on,' she said firmly, motivating herself to go back out to the party.

Minnie exhaled slowly. She needed to stop being a killjoy. Greg wanted to be here and she wanted to be with Greg. Maybe her bad luck was over with, for this New Year anyway.

Minnie went to open the door, but as she pushed the handle down it came away in her hand. She tried the door again – it wouldn't open. She tried reattaching the handle, but it wouldn't go on.

She banged on the door with both hands. 'Hello! Can someone help? I can't open the door!' At that moment the music outside notched up a level. It sounded like a live band had started playing and there were whoops and shrieks from the party. No one was going to hear her now. She would just have to wait until Greg came to find her.

Minnie sank down to the floor and looked up at the ceiling. The whole room was decorated with dark blue wallpaper, imprinted with tiny silver constellations. Well, she had got her wish; she was now alone, staring up at the stars. She pulled out her phone to text Greg – the screen was dead.

'Of course it is,' Minnie said, shaking her head with a little laugh. If she could say something for this New Year's jinx, it certainly had a sense of humour.

Minnie woke up feeling disorientated, her throat painfully dry. She remembered banging on the door for hours, but then she must have fallen asleep. She had no concept of what time it was. It was quiet outside, the music no longer playing. She got to her feet, rubbing at the crick in her neck.

'Hello, hello! Can someone let me out?' she called.

What if everyone had gone home and the place was shut for the night? She'd read stories about this kind of thing; people being stuck in toilets for days before they were rescued, people who drank cistern water to survive and wove blankets out of toilet roll to keep warm. How long would she have to be trapped before she resorted to eating the soap? She banged on the door again, this time with more urgency.

'Help! Help me!'

'Hello?' came a man's voice.

'Yes, hello! Oh, thank god. The door handle is broken, I can't get out,' she called through the door.

'How long have you been in there?' said the voice, rattling the handle from the other side.

'Long enough,' Minnie said.

'OK, hold on, I'll go find someone,' said the voice. She heard footsteps walking away. She couldn't believe Greg hadn't come to find her. Had he gone home without her? Three or four minutes later the voice returned.

'OK, I'm back. I have Luis here. He's got a thousand keys in his hand.'

'I don't know how this happened,' came another voice, an older man. Minnie heard keys being rattled in the lock.

'Here, let me try,' said the first voice. More clinking of keys and then the door swung open. 'Look at that, first key and I nailed it. What are the chances?'

Minnie squinted into the light of the corridor. The voice belonged to a tall, broad-shouldered man with sandy-coloured hair and distinctive eyebrows a shade darker than the hair on his head. He grinned at Minnie, a warm, guileless smile. He was dressed in formal black trousers and a crisp white shirt. A black bow tie hung undone around his open collar, revealing a glimpse of tanned skin. Next to him stood a short, rotund bald man with a blank expression.

'What time is it?' Minnie asked, looking between the two men.

'Seven forty-five,' said the man in black tie.

'I go now,' said the shorter man, taking back the huge pile of keys and plodding off down the corridor muttering to himself.

'A man of very few words,' said the man in black tie.

Minnie followed him along the corridor back to the main room. The place was empty. Tendrils of party popper paper hung from the light fittings, and an army of half-empty champagne flutes lined the bar.

'Am I the only one left? I can't believe I slept that long.'

'Sorry, I don't think we've met,' he said, holding out his hand for Minnie to shake.

'Oh right, I'm Minnie.' The man smiled at her, but looked as though he was waiting for more. 'Greg's girlfriend. He works with Lucy. She invited us.'

'Oh sure, everyone's welcome. I think I heard Luce mention a Greg. Funny Greg, right?'

'Funny Greg,' Minnie raised an eyebrow, amused Greg would be called that. The man reached his arms above his head and the stretch turned into an enormous yawn. 'Sorry, it's catching up with me. What a great night, though.'

'Not for me,' Minnie said wryly.

'No, not for you.' The man gave an exaggerated grimace at having said the wrong thing and Minnie couldn't help smiling.

'So, I'm assuming it was your party then, Lucy's boyfriend, right? Thank you for having me, I guess,' Minnie said, clasping her hands behind her back.

'You're more than welcome. In theory it was my party, Lucy invited everyone.'

As he was speaking, the man's phone began to ring in his pocket. He frowned briefly as he pulled it out to look at the screen. 'Will you excuse me for one minute, I'm sorry, I have to get this, Minnie.'

'Sure, no problem,' Minnie shrugged.

He turned his back and walked a few paces away from her.

'Hi,' he said. 'Are you OK? No, I'm still out … I'll come around later … I checked all the locks last night before I left … No … OK.' Minnie could see the profile of his face. He had closed his eyes while he was talking. 'Fine, I'll come and check, just give me a few hours, *please.*'

Minnie watched him hang up the call. He noticed her watching him and gave her a tense smile.

'Is everything all right?' she asked.

'Yes, sorry about that,' he shook his head. He walked across the rest of the room towards the huge glass windows.

'So, how come you're the only one still here?' Minnie asked.

He turned to look at her for a moment, assessing her. Then he said, 'It probably sounds cheesy, but I always try to see the first sunrise of the year. I thought if I left with the others, I'd be in a cab somewhere and I'd miss it.' He held out his arms towards the windows. 'Is there anywhere you'd rather watch the first sunrise of the year from?'

'Plenty of places,' said Minnie. 'The desert, a beautiful mountain top, on a TV screen from the comfort of my bed. Ideally pre-recorded so I didn't have to get up so early.'

The man tilted his head to one side, his eyes creasing with amusement, the stressed look gone.

'Well, you're awake now, no pre-record required. Come on, come over here.'

Minnie walked over to the window and pressed a hand against the glass. The light was beginning to creep over the horizon. A high layer of cloud glowed a deep rusty pink, creating an aura of warmth over an otherwise cold, grey city. Skyscrapers stood silhouetted against the sky, their sharp straight lines in stark contrast to the softness of the clouds above.

'Pretty impressive,' Minnie said. 'I can't think when I was last awake for a sunrise.'

'This is my favourite day of the year,' he said. 'A chance to start everything anew, don't you think?'

'Funny, it's my least favourite day of the year,' said Minnie. 'I hate it.'

'You can't hate it, it's my birthday. I won't let you hate it,' he said, his tired greyish-blue eyes temporarily revived, dancing with energy.

Minnie turned to look at him, she blinked slowly.

'It's my birthday too,' she said.

'It is not.'

'I'm not joking. I promise you it is.'

He squinted at her, his chin retracting towards his neck, a look of scepticism. He turned back to the window just as the whole sky began to glow red.

'Will you look at that?' he said. 'Glorious.'

Minnie glanced sideways at him as he looked out at the morning sky. She couldn't pinpoint one feature that stood out, but there was a sort of synergy about his face; everything came together and just worked. He seemed so comfortable in his own skin, something Minnie had rarely experienced. He looked over and saw her staring at him and she quickly turned her attention back to the other view.

'You know, I don't think I've ever met anyone with the same birthday as me,' he said.

'It's a very elite club. I'll make you a membership card.' Minnie paused, nervous for some reason. 'Look, I'm sorry, I know I should know your name since I'm at your party, but I came with Greg and he didn't say. I guess I'll need to know it if I'm going to make you a membership card.'

'Sorry, I'm Quinn,' he replied.

'Quinn?' Minnie's mouth fell open. 'Quinn Hamilton?'

'Yes, Quinn Hamilton.'

'Quinn Hamilton, born at Hampstead Hospital in 1990?'

'Yes,' said Quinn, his brow furrowing in confusion.

'You,' Minnie said, clenching her teeth. 'You stole my name.'

New Year's Eve 1989

Connie Cooper lay in the hospital bed looking over at the woman in the bed next to her. Specifically she was looking at the woman's legs, which were long, glossy and as smooth as a Barbie doll's. How was that even possible at this stage? Connie looked down at her own short, stumpy legs, covered in half an inch of black hair. She probably should have shaved her legs before coming in – well, at least the bits she could still reach.

Connie watched as the other woman dabbed her forehead with a lacy cream handkerchief. Connie's hair and hospital gown were soaked with sweat; using a handkerchief would be like trying to dry off the decks of the Titanic with a kitchen roll. The other woman's shiny blonde hair was tied back with a delicate yellow ribbon – a ribbon! Who even owned ribbon? Connie's own dark wiry nest was pulled back with one of the elastic bands Bill used to keep his tools together. There was one feature that Connie did have in common with the woman in the bed next to her – they both had enormous round bellies protruding beneath their hospital gowns.

'It's like the overflow car park or something in here; the whole of north London must be giving birth tonight,' said Connie. The other woman didn't respond. She looked pained

21

and exhausted. 'Are you crossing your legs till midnight then?'

'No,' said the woman wearily. 'I want this baby out, I've been in labour for two days but the contractions keep stopping and starting.'

'I thought you might be holding out for the prize money,' said Connie. 'I'm Connie, by the way.'

'Tara,' said the blonde woman, but it came out 'Ta ... raaa ...' as another contraction took hold. She started puffing out short little bleats of breath.

Connie was about to say something else but then had to pause to focus on a contraction of her own. She stood up and walked across the ward in her hospital gown, bending over one of the empty beds opposite until the pain had receded. Then she turned back to Tara and said, 'You're doing it all wrong. Your breathing's too shallow, you sound like a little sheep.'

'A sheep?' said Tara. She looked mortified.

'Yeah, you want to breathe from your gut, sound like a cow, or better yet a hippo. Try and make a hippo noise.'

'I'm not going to make a hippo noise.' Tara gave a sharp headshake. 'Ridiculous.'

Connie shrugged. She started lunging back and forth on her front leg, while holding onto the end of the hospital bed.

'You really never heard about the prize money for this nineties baby then? You must be the only one.'

'Oh right, that,' Tara nodded. 'I think someone mentioned it at one of my prenatal appointments. I didn't know there was a prize involved.'

'It could be one of us,' Connie grunted. Then she gave a low, guttural moan. 'You'll have to get on your feet, though; babies don't come if you lie on your back.'

'I'm just so tired. I can't walk any more,' Tara said quietly.

'There's no getting round it,' said Connie. 'You gotta get up, get walking, let gravity do her job.'

Tara reluctantly sat up and swung her legs off the side of the bed. Every movement looked to be a monumental effort.

'Oh, not again, I don't ... I can't,' Tara sank to the floor, her body consumed by an invisible, agonising force.

'Try and stand,' Connie said, taking her hand. 'Trust me, it's better.' Connie held Tara up, encouraging her to push down on her forearms for support. Tara rocked back and forth, huffing and whimpering through it with her eyes closed. 'OK, we can work on your breathing but you're standing at least.'

The double doors of the ward swung open and a midwife wearing light blue coveralls marched in.

'How are we doing, ladies? I'm sorry we had to put you in together but I've never seen so many babies want to come in one night before. Lucky I didn't have New Year's Eve plans, hey?' the midwife chuckled.

'They're all after the prize money,' said Connie. 'This one claims she didn't even know about it.'

Tara's pain had passed, her eyes were glazed over and she was staring off towards the window. Connie watched her; she knew that feeling – she'd been in labour for four days last time.

'Oh, you didn't hear?' said the midwife. '*The London News* went and offered a cheque to the first nineties baby born in the city. We're all desperate for someone from Hampstead Hospital to be the first. Though the paper must have more money than they know what to do with, if you ask me.'

'Fifty thousand pounds,' said Connie.

What Connie couldn't do with fifty thousand pounds. She could pay back Bill's parents the money they'd loaned them. They could rent a bigger place. She could even buy the baby some clothes of its own – clothes that hadn't already been worn by three older cousins and a brother. She couldn't get her hopes up. There were thousands of other women all over London probably thinking the same thing.

'It's sponsored by some nappy brand. I think you get free nappies for life too,' said the midwife.

'She's definitely going to cross her legs till midnight now,' Connie laughed, but the laugh turned into panting as another wave of pain rolled down into her belly.

'Right, hop up onto the bed, Mrs Hamilton,' the midwife said to Tara. 'I need to see how far along you are.' She drew a cubicle curtain around the bed and pulled on some rubber gloves. A few minutes later she stepped away from the bed and shook her head. 'You're not having the baby tonight at this rate, you're still only six centimetres. You need to get moving, get walking up and down.'

'That's what I told her,' Connie shouted through the partition.

'But how much longer?' Tara whimpered. 'I'm so tired, I just need to sleep.'

An alarm rang out in the corridor. The midwife quickly pulled off her gloves and washed her hands at the sink.

'I'll be back to check your measurements shortly, Mrs Cooper.'

The midwife swept out of the room as briskly as she had arrived, the double doors swinging noisily back and forth in her wake. From behind the plastic partition Connie heard slow, childlike sobbing. She pulled herself off the bed and drew the curtain back so she could see Tara again.

'No, no. No time for tears. We got work to do,' said Connie.

'I can't do it any more, I haven't slept for two days.'

'Where's your man?'

'I sent him home. He hasn't slept either, I thought one of us should.' And then the pain came and she curled instinctively into a ball. Connie felt her own starting. She took hold of Tara's wrist and gently drew Tara's face up towards hers. Tara started mewing, pained little mews like a cat being strangled.

'That's a cat, what did I say? Did I say cat, did I say sheep, or did I say hippo? You got to go lower, come on, copy me.'

Connie started mooing big, heaving moos from the depth of her diaphragm. Tara's whole face blushed red, her eyes darting to the door. 'Don't be embarrassed. No one here but us, come on.' Tara gave a tentative 'mur' sound. She scowled with concentration. 'Lower, bigger, much bigger, MAAHOOOOOOOOOOO ...' Connie thundered. Tara stared at her in bemusement. She tried again, copying Connie. Connie nodded silent encouragement. At first Tara's breathing was self-conscious, still clinging to some urge to be ladylike, but gradually she let herself go and started imitating Connie's heaving moans.

'It helps, don't it? Now get down here like this.'

Connie dropped down onto all fours and swayed her bulk backwards and forwards on the matt. Tara copied obediently. Connie's contractions were getting more intense now. She felt like screaming but she wanted to stay in control for Tara, to show her how to command the breath and ride it out. The women rocked backwards and forwards together silently.

'Did you get a pre-labour manicure?' Connie asked, looking at Tara's perfectly polished nails.

'Yes,' Tara said, stretching out her palm. 'Why?'

'Did you get a bikini wax and all?' Connie asked with a grin.

'That's a bit of a personal question,' said Tara, frowning.

Tara was still rocking slowly back and forth when an involuntary loud trumpet sound erupted from her rear end. Tara took a moment to register what had happened before clasping a hand over her mouth. Connie chuckled, a long, hearty chuckle.

'There's far worse going to come out down there, so you best get relaxed about a bit of wind, prissy missy.'

Tara covered her face with her hands and then started to laugh herself. She had a musical, high-pitched laugh.

'Oh my days, is that your laugh?' said Connie. 'Even that sounds uptight.'

The two women got hysterics laughing at each other; they couldn't stop.

'Yes, that's my laugh, what's wrong with it?' Tara snorted, her eyes streaming.

'Oh, don't make me laugh, don't make me laugh, it hurts worse,' said Connie, clutching her stomach with one hand and fanning her face with the other.

Over the next few hours, Connie taught Tara to relax, to let go. She taught her to move her body in the way it needed to move to get the baby out. She taught her to breathe and moo and growl and shriek and not care what it might look or sound like. The contractions started to get more regular, then more frequent. Things were finally happening.

'So, you know what you're having?' Connie asked, as they finished breathing through another contraction together.

'A boy,' Tara said.

'Got a name sorted?' Connie asked.

'It's too much, it's getting too much Connie ... I can't,' Tara started whimpering.

'Don't waste energy crying,' said Connie. 'Come on, stay with me, do what I'm doing, we'll get there. What are you going to call him then?'

'My husband likes John, after him. I don't know, maybe Roger?' said Tara, wiping sweat from her forehead with the back of a hand. Connie wrinkled up her nose. Tara laughed. 'Not Roger then.'

'Sorry,' Connie laughed too.

Another contraction, both women's bodies were now strangely in sync. They held hands, squeezing hold of each other, breathing in unison.

'Where are the midwives?' Tara wailed. 'They need to call John.'

'Trust me, I've only done this once before, but men just get in the way,' Connie said, panting through the last pangs. When she looked up, she saw Tara had crawled over to the bed and was banging her head against the foot rail. Connie waddled over and stroked her back.

'Hey, this'll be a bad memory tomorrow. Look at me, you want to hear the name I got planned for mine?' Connie pulled Tara away from the bedstead. 'I had this name planned since I was little.' Tara turned to look at her. 'Quinn. It's a family name goes years back. My grandma was a Quinn; she used to say it held the luck of the Irish, said she never knew a Quinn who didn't lead a charmed life.' Tara continued to rock back and forth. Connie couldn't tell if she was listening. 'I had a boy first, Bill insisted on William after him. I said, whatever we got next, boy or girl, it had to be Quinn.'

The midwife returned to find both women kneeling on the floor, holding hands.

'You're going to have these babies at the same time by the look of it,' said the midwife, guiding Connie back to her bed. 'Come on, let's see where you've got to now, Mrs Cooper.'

Connie and Tara laboured together for four hours.

Tara's husband, John, came back to the hospital, but Tara said he could wait outside until she was further along.

'I just need Connie,' she told the midwife.

Private rooms freed up but Tara didn't want to move. When Bill finally made it to the hospital, Connie said he too should wait in reception until he was called for.

'So let me get this shipshape,' said the midwife, 'you want both your husbands to wait in reception because you're being each other's birthing partners?'

Connie and Tara both nodded.

By half past eleven they were both ready to push.

'Right, it's time to get you into the delivery rooms,' ordered the midwives, finally insisting it was time for the women to separate. Connie and Tara were loaded onto beds and wheeled from the ward. They clasped hands one last time.

'Good luck,' Connie said, her voice hoarse.

'Thank you,' mouthed Tara.

'Well, I've got bets on one of you two having this nineties baby,' said the midwife pushing Connie's bed.

'There's no one else in this hospital even close,' said the midwife pushing Tara.

As Connie was wheeled into the delivery room, she saw Bill sitting in a chair waiting for her. He stood up and folded the newspaper he had been reading.

'You took your time, woman, I been waiting ages,' he said.

'I'm not doing this around your convenience, Bill,' Connie snarled. 'I'll come when I'm good and ready.'

Bill sat down again, smacking his lips shut.

Connie pushed for half an hour. It took every ounce of energy she had left and she was past the point of talking. At one point Bill stood, checked his watch, grimaced and said, 'If you could just hold it in another couple of minutes love, it's only two minutes to go till midnight.'

Connie let out an ear-splitting, guttural scream, like a pterodactyl defending her young from a predator. The two midwives both jumped and Bill promptly returned to his chair, where he sat with his shoulders hunched, fingers intertwined and two thumbs rapidly circling around each other.

'I can see the head,' said one of the midwives.

The pressure became unbearable. Just as Connie thought she might burst at the seams, release.

'Here it comes,' said the midwife, 'oh, a precious baby girl.'

Everyone else in the room was silent, listening for the new arrival to make a noise, to take its first breath. A cry, an angry wail, there it was, and then through the thin hospital walls the sound of another baby wailing in unison.

'Is she OK?' Connie said, urgently searching the midwives' faces for reassurance.

'She's perfect,' said one, wrapping the baby in a towel and laying her carefully on Connie's chest.

'We was first,' said Bill firmly, 'It definitely sounded like ours was first. You made it past midnight love, you absolute trooper, Connie Cooper.'

But Connie wasn't listening; she was too busy staring at the wonderful little creature cooing in her arms.

The next morning, Connie was singing quietly to the baby when Bill returned to the hospital with William.

'Look who's here?' he said, putting William down on the ground. The boy immediately toddled over to the bed saying, 'Mama', arms outstretched to Connie.

'Do you want to meet your sister, William?' Connie said, patting the bed beside her. William clambered up, so she had a child in each arm. 'This is baby Quinn.'

She held William's hand so he could gently pat his new sister.

'You can't call her Quinn now,' said Bill.

'Why not?' said Connie, her eyes darting up to look at him.

''Cause that's what that other lady called hers, the one that won the money.'

'What?' Connie said, her voice a whisper. She carefully placed the baby back in the crib next to her bed. 'What you on about, Bill?'

'It's all over the radio. That baby what won all the money just for being born a minute before ours, he's called Quinn. I still say we were first. I reckon those midwives cooked up between them the times they logged, based on who was going to look prettier in the paper,' he said gruffly, rubbing two large palms over his bald scalp.

'Quinn? She called her baby Quinn?' Connie couldn't believe it.

'Yeah, so we can't call ours that too, we'd look daft. Their Quinn's all over the news, he's famous, plus everyone thinks it's a lad's name now.' Connie sat quietly, stunned. 'I've always liked Minnie for a girl,' Bill went on. 'What do you think, Will? Baby Minnie. She might not be rich, but she sure is beautiful.' He leant in to kiss his wife on the forehead, stroking the baby's cheek with his calloused plasterer's hands.

Connie was too tired to think. She needed to sleep. She needed to feed the baby. And she needed to work out how she was going to take care of a toddler and a newborn at the same time. She could argue with Bill about the name later.

But by the time they got home and Connie had got some sleep, baby Quinn Hamilton, the first nineties baby, was all over the national news. 'The Luckiest Baby in the Land,' read one headline. 'A win for Quinn!' said the reporter on the breakfast show. The name felt spoilt now for Connie, the newspapers taunting her with the money she might have won. Besides, Bill had already started calling the baby Minnie. Connie sat on the sofa feeding her child, watching Tara being interviewed by the television presenter.

'Someone told me Quinn was a name for luck and he's definitely been lucky so far,' Tara smiled. Her blonde hair looked blow-dried for the occasion, her face dewy and radiant. She didn't look like someone who'd recently given birth. Connie looked down at her daughter.

'I can't believe she stole your name,' Connie said softly. She felt a hot wall of tears building behind her eyes. Her milk was coming in and it was making her emotional; if she let the tears come they might never stop. She closed her eyes to quell the rising tide and whispered to the baby, 'Just a minute too late, hey.'

'So hang on,' Quinn said, holding up a finger to interrupt. 'You're called Minnie Cooper?'

Minnie and Quinn were sitting on the floor, the sun now streaming through the window. She leant back on her hands and stretched her neck from side to side.

'Would you believe neither of my parents even made that connection for a good couple of weeks? I got a lot of "vroom vrooms" the whole way through school.'

'Well, I'm sorry that you were named after a car,' Quinn grinned, 'but I don't think that's how my mother would tell the story.'

'I'm sure she wouldn't,' Minnie said. 'She's not going to admit stealing someone else's name.'

Quinn swivelled his body around to face her.

'Can you believe we were born in the same hospital on the same day, minutes apart?' said Quinn, his face animated. 'What are the chances of that? And then meeting like this, on our birthday of all days. Don't you think that's weird?'

Minnie looked back at him, returning his gaze. She'd thought about this man a lot over the course of her life. She knew it was strange to resent someone she'd never met, someone she knew nothing about, but she did. The way her mother told the story, this was the boy who'd stolen her name

34

and with it her good fortune. When bad things happened to Minnie, her mother would say, 'You were born unlucky, girl.' It was the refrain of Minnie's childhood. Memories of missteps sprung to mind.

On her seventh birthday Minnie fell down an uncovered manhole in the street and broke her foot.

'The workman swears he only turned his back for a few seconds,' the paramedic said, as he tried to pull Minnie out.

'Born unlucky this one,' said Connie, leaning into the manhole. 'This would never happen to a Quinn Cooper!'

The night before her thirteenth birthday, Minnie's parents let her host a New Year's Eve party for some friends. Minnie invited twelve people from her class, including the boy she liked – Callum Peterson. Ten of her guests went down with flu that week so the only people who turned up were Callum and Mary Stephens. Minnie spent the whole night watching Callum and Mary make out on her sofa. The kissathon only paused for oxygen when Minnie's mum came in from the kitchen to offer them baked snacks. As Connie leant over to remove a plate of uneaten vol-au-vents from the coffee table, she whispered to her daughter with a wink, 'This would never happen to a—'

'I know, I know,' Minnie hissed back, 'to a Quinn Cooper.'

The story of Minnie's stolen name had become a Cooper family legend. Her mother regaled people with the story of the injustice of it all whenever she had the opportunity.

'Not that she's bitter,' Minnie's dad would chip in with a smirk.

'Oh, shut it. That prissy woman wouldn't have had her baby for hours if it weren't for me,' Connie would say.

Bill and William made fun of Connie whenever the topic came up, but Minnie noticed that though her mother pretended to make light of it, her eyes had this pained expression. There was a grey folder full of clippings and childhood mementos, which her mother sometimes pulled out at birthdays or Christmas. It had all the old timetables from Minnie's swim-meets, Will's Mathlete certificates, and then there was the clipping from *The London News* the day she was born, with the headline about Quinn plastered across the front page. Whenever her mother reached that page, her face took on a look of solemn reverence.

Minnie never imagined she would ever meet this man. Sometimes she even wondered if the fable was real. When she was a teenager, she'd looked for him online once. She'd found no Quinn Hamilton the same age as her on social media. And yet here he was, all six-foot-something of him, sitting next to her on the floor, his warm, handsome face smiling at her as though they were old friends.

'If it makes you feel any better, I don't know how lucky the name has been for me,' said Quinn.

'You look as if you're doing all right,' said Minnie. 'That party last night probably cost more than I earn in a year.'

'Money isn't everything,' Quinn shrugged.

Minnie made a face. 'Money isn't everything' was something only people with money said.

'Listen, do you want to grab breakfast? I want to hear about my birthday twin. I'll pay, it's the least I can do after stealing your name.' He stood and held out a hand to help Minnie up from the floor.

Minnie hesitated. She was tempted, but something about his cocky demeanour made her want to say no. Besides, it was New Year's Day. In her experience it was never a good idea to say yes to anything on her birthday.

'I'm sorry, I can't,' said Minnie briskly. 'I need to get home and have a shower, and I need to find out what happened to my boyfriend. He'll be worried about me.'

'Sure,' Quinn said, dropping his eyes to the ground and ruffling a hand through his thick hair. 'Maybe another time?'

'Maybe,' said Minnie, picking up her bag to go.

'You're not seriously annoyed about the name thing, are you?' Quinn asked. 'It's only a name.'

'Maybe to you,' said Minnie, shaking her hair out so that it covered more of her face.

They walked down to the main door of the club and Quinn opened the door to the street for her.

'Listen, if you can't do breakfast, can I at least get your number?' he said. 'If nothing else I need to get that membership card from you.'

'Membership card?'

'The First of January Club.'

'Right. Well, you can find me pretty easily. There aren't many Minnie Coopers on Facebook who don't have cars as their profile picture.'

Minnie looked up at him. He was standing right next to her in the doorway, propping open the door for her to go through. She felt her arms prickle with goosebumps and she hugged them closer to her chest.

'You don't have a coat?' he said.

'I lost it on the way here.'

'Let me lend you mine, you'll freeze.'

'No, I'm fine.'

Minnie tilted her head to one side; he hadn't moved from the doorway. She felt light-headed, unnerved by his physical proximity. She was so close to him she could feel the heat radiating from his torso. She found herself breathing him in, the smell of hot skin and pressed cotton. She unconsciously wet her lips. It was a momentary gesture but he saw it and smiled. Minnie frowned then quickly ducked beneath his arm and skipped out onto the street. This man was clearly used to women wilting beneath his gaze. She doubted he'd ever been turned down for anything, least of all breakfast.

'Well Happy Birthday, Name Stealer,' she said as she turned to go.

'You too, Birthday Twin,' said Quinn, leaning against the door frame, his cheek dimpled in amusement.

Minnie darted across the street and up the small side road away from the club. She fought the urge to look back, to see if he was still watching her. As she crossed out onto the main road, the previously bright sky suddenly clouded over and giant raindrops began to fall.

1 January 2020

Minnie got off the fifty-six bus halfway up the Essex Road, just outside Sainsbury's. A few lost-looking souls were waiting outside for it to open. Plastic glasses littered the kerb by the pub opposite, and the rain had not yet washed away the fag ends and half-eaten takeaways that lay on the pavement by overflowing bins. It was still pouring with rain as she ran down the side street to her flat, her arms cradled over her head for protection. At her door she fumbled in her bag, looking for her keys – they weren't there. She stood, soaking wet and shivering, then emptied the bag onto the doorstep, clinging to the hope they might be hiding among old receipts and loose make-up. Looking down at the sodden pile of handbag clutter, she closed her eyes and exhaled slowly; her keys were in her coat pocket, the coat she'd lost on the bus earlier that night. Of course they were. It was her birthday – nothing would go right today.

Minnie looked up at the window of her flat. She could see her cat's little grey face pressed up against the window.

'Oh Lucky – poor Lucky!' she cried. 'I need to feed you, darling.'

Minnie stuffed everything back into her bag and rang the buzzers for the other two flats in the building. Maybe someone would take pity on her. She could at least charge her phone, get dry and ring her landlord to let her in. Nobody answered.

*

'You're early,' said Leila as she opened her front door to Minnie half an hour later. 'I thought I was taking you out for lunch?'

Leila lived in Stoke Newington in northeast London, half an hour by bus from Minnie's place. She lived with her boyfriend on the top floor of an ex-council building. Their block was an unremarkable concrete stack with graffiti all over the hallways, but inside the place felt light and homely. Leila stood in the doorway wearing a pink dressing gown covered in unicorns. 'Do I make you unicorny?' was written across the front in sparkling pink lettering. Leila's rainbow-streaked hair was pulled to the top of her head in a messy topknot; the stripes of bold colour had grown out to reveal several inches of mousy-brown roots beneath. When describing Leila, Minnie often said she was a 1950s film star with crazy hair; she had a curvy figure and these deep, hooded eyes that somehow always seemed to look sultry. This morning's dressing gown ensemble wasn't necessarily highlighting her film-star qualities.

'I lost my house keys and got trapped in a nightclub toilet all night,' said Minnie, walking through the front door and waving Leila away as she tried to hug her. 'Don't, you'll get soaked.'

'Nightclub toilet?' Leila dropped her face into her hands. 'Poor jinxsy girl.' She reached out to pat Minnie's head and stroke her cheek as though she were a pet. 'Happy Birthday, Min.'

'Thanks,' said Minnie, pinching the bridge of her nose then taking a loud inhalation of breath.

'Look at you, you're soaking – come in, come in. I'm impressed you braved a club, you must really like Greg.'

Minnie followed her friend down the narrow corridor through to the bathroom. Leila pulled a greyish-pink towel from the rail and handed it to her. It was stiff like cardboard, as though it had been washed at a million degrees five hundred times too many.

'Have a hot shower then borrow some dry clothes,' Leila suggested.

'Happy Birthday, Minnie,' came Ian's voice from the other room.

Minnie poked her head around the living-room door. Ian was sitting on the low beige sofa in his boxer shorts playing the Xbox. He had his feet resting on the upturned orange crate that served as their coffee table. His short shaven hair was hidden under a red baseball cap and he had a new, angry-looking tattoo on his upper arm that read 'Player One'.

'Thanks, Ian. New tattoo?'

'Christmas present from Leils,' Ian said.

'I didn't wrap it,' Leila called from the bathroom, 'and I didn't choose it, or approve it.'

'Wanna play two player? You can break my losing streak,' said Ian.

'Maybe when my fingertips have regained some sensation,' said Minnie.

Leila came back out of the bathroom and pressed a small white bottle into Minnie's hands. It had coconuts and pink flowers on the label.

'You can use my good shower gel,' Leila said in a whisper. 'I hide it from Ian or his balls smell of coconuts for weeks.'

Minnie stepped into the shower and let the warm water stream down her face. She scrubbed at her skin, trying to wash the day-old make-up and smell of the club from her pores. Her neck still felt stiff from sleeping on the toilet floor, and she rubbed it from side to side between her palms. Leila's hand reached around the bathroom door.

'Just leaving you some clothes for when you're ready,' she said.

Minnie looked over at the door where Leila had hung a red and white polka-dot dress. Leila was not a conservative dresser; most of her outfits were even more colourful than her kaleidoscopic hair. She was like the child who insisted on using every colour in the Crayola box.

Twenty minutes later, Minnie presented herself in the living room.

'I cannot wear this,' she said.

Ian burst out laughing. 'It's Minnie Mouse!'

'Don't be rude. You look lovely,' said Leila, scowling at Ian.

'You're not taking me to Disneyland, are you?' Minnie asked, hands on her hips.

'Nothing that exciting,' said Leila. 'I'm taking you to lunch. I'm tired of you saying you never want to do anything for your birthday. It's your thirtieth, it's a big deal – we have to mark the occasion somehow.'

'Oh man, you're old,' said Ian, taking his eyes from the screen to make a face at Minnie. His bottom lip trembled and his eyes grew wide in mock horror.

'Ha-ha,' said Minnie, pointing at the TV screen where 'GAME OVER' was flashing in aggressive capital letters. Ian made a 'fahhh' noise and threw the controller down onto the sofa next to him. He pulled off his cap and briskly ran his hands back and forth over his head.

'I'm not sure we should let Minnie in the flat if she's got this curse hanging over her. I don't need the ceiling falling in when I'm sitting in my pants.'

Minnie gave an exaggerated eye roll. Ian had been Leila's boyfriend for three years and he and Minnie had quickly fallen into the roles of bickering siblings. They liked to play-fight for Leila's attention.

'If the ceiling started falling in, would you move from that sofa?' Leila asked, waving a finger at the scene in front of her. 'I bet Greg doesn't sit around all day playing video games in his pants, does he Minnie?'

'Don't knock the pants,' said Ian. 'Me and these pants have been through some good times. You and these pants have been through some good times.'

Ian raised his eyebrows. Leila tried to stifle a smile.

'Shit, I must call Greg. Can I plug in my phone?' said Minnie.

Minnie moved an array of multicoloured nail varnishes from Leila's dressing table and plugged her phone into the bedside charger. She sat on the bed while Leila riffled through her wardrobe for something to wear.

'So, you'll never guess who I met last night,' Minnie said, tapping her toes on the floor.

'The Pope?'

'No.'

'Jon Bon Jovi?'

'No.'

'Hot priest from *Fleabag*.'

'You're just saying random people?'

'Yes.'

'OK, I'll tell you.' Minnie paused until she had Leila's full attention. 'Quinn Hamilton.'

Leila paused, 'Who?'

'Quinn, Quinn Hamilton.' Minnie stared at her friend in disbelief. 'Name Stealer Quinn.'

'Quinn! *The* Quinn?' Leila took a quick step towards Minnie, her eyes wide, one hand clutching a hanger to her chest. Minnie nodded slowly. 'Childhood nemesis Quinn?'

'Yes, that Quinn,' Minnie said, nodding slowly.

Leila abandoned her quest to get dressed and bounced her bottom onto the bed next to Minnie.

'What, how, w ... ?' She shook her head in disbelief. 'How did you know it was him?'

'It was his birthday party. Greg's friend from the paper, Lucy Donohue, goes out with him. I was only introduced when he let me out of the bathroom at seven o'clock this morning. I knew who he was straight away. How many Quinns born on the first of January can there be?'

'Why are you saying Lucy Donohue like that?' asked Leila, squinting her eyes at Minnie.

'Like what?'

'In a funny nasally voice with your nose all scrunched up?'

'Was I? I'm not sure – I think she was annoying. Anyway, back to Quinn. Quinn! Can you believe it?'

The screen on Minnie's phone lit up and pinged into life. Greg's name flashed up on the phone as a stream of messages came through. Minnie groaned.

'All OK?' asked Leila.

'Greg abandoned me in the club last night and now he's sending me arsy texts because he thinks *I* left without *him*.'

'I would never, ever leave without you,' Leila said solemnly.

'I know you wouldn't. I would never leave without you either.' Minnie reached out to squeeze her friend's hand. 'He does sound pretty pissed off, though. I should probably call him.'

'Tell me the story first, Bathroom Abandoner can wait.'

'OK, give me one minute, I'm just going to text my landlord to see if he can let me into my flat today. I've got to get in somehow to feed poor Lucky.'

Minnie tapped away on her phone and Leila made a tick-tock clicking sound with her tongue, nodding her head from side to side like a metronome.

'So, did you tell Quinn he stole your name?' Leila asked once Minnie had finished typing. 'What's he like? Is he hot? Quinn Hamilton sounds like a hot name to me.'

'Yes, I told him he stole my name – he laughed like it was a joke. And I don't know where you get the idea that there are hot names and not-hot names,' Minnie said irritably. She started fiddling with the dress she was wearing, swishing the skirt back and forth in her lap. She was so unused to wearing skirts that she felt as though she was looking down at someone else's body. 'You're not seriously going to make me go out in public like this, are you?'

'So he is hot?' said Leila, narrowing her eyes even further.

'I guess, but only in that textbook, arrogant, rich-boy way. He was probably born with a silver spoon in every orifice,' said Minnie grimacing.

'OK, well I need to hear every single detail. I have to get my love-life kicks through you now I'm so bloody normcore. And yes, you need to wear the dress, it will be fun, I promise.' Leila went back to her wardrobe and held up a bright yellow 1950s-style tea dress. 'Too much?'

'You can pull this look off, I can't,' said Minnie, shaking her head. Leila dropped her pyjama bottoms on the floor and stepped into the yellow skirt. 'Hang on, what do you mean "love life"? This isn't anything to do with my love life, this is just me meeting the man my mum's been comparing me to my whole life. Right, I'm going to call Greg now.'

Minnie dialled his number. Greg didn't like speaking on the phone, he preferred text, but this didn't feel like a text conversation. It went straight to answerphone. 'Hi Greg, it's Minnie. Just ringing to say, I didn't go home without you last night, you were the one who went home without me, and anyway ... wait, someone else is calling me ... maybe it's you, no, it's an unknown number. Hang on, I'll call you back, I was just calling to say I'm alive – bye.'

Minnie quickly switched callers to take the incoming call. It was her landlord, Mr Buchanan, saying he could meet her at the flat to give her a spare key.

'You're going now?' Leila asked, once Minnie put the phone down. 'What about lunch?'

'I have to go and feed Lucky. I'll go now then come and meet you out.' Minnie stood up and pulled her friend in for a hug, 'Thank you for rescuing me.'

Leila's lips twitched as she watched her friend leave, 'This better not just be a ploy to change out of that dress,' she called after her.

*

Mr Buchanan was waiting for Minnie on the street. He was busy inspecting her wheelie bin when she arrived. He was in his mid-sixties with bright white hair and he spoke with a lisp. When he saw Minnie in her polka-dot dress he did a double take.

'Thank you so much for meeting me,' Minnie said breathlessly, running up the street to meet him. 'I couldn't afford a locksmith call-out, especially on New Year's Day.'

Mr Buchanan started inspecting some of the peeling paintwork on the front door frame, picking at it with a fingernail to see how easily it came away.

'Yes, about your finances Miss Cooper,' he said, flaring his huge hairy nostrils at her. 'I see you're behind on your utility bills again.'

'Yes, I know, cash flow, but I'm on it, don't worry,' said Minnie, making two firm hand gestures with her fists to hammer home how on it she was.

'They tell me when a tenant falls into bad credit you know,' he said, turning back to face her with a squint. 'And we spoke about this before, I believe?'

'Oh yes, I know, but ...'

Minnie looked up and saw Lucky pawing the glass at her. She gave him a little wave.

'What are you waving at?' Mr Buchanan asked.

'My cat ... my catalogue.' Minnie suddenly remembered she wasn't allowed pets under the terms of her lease. 'My catalogue will have arrived. I'm just excited – do you ever get like that about catalogues? January sales, whoop-whoop ...'

Mr Buchanan turned and looked up at the window. She didn't know if he'd seen the swish of grey tail before Lucky ducked out of view.

'I see,' said Mr Buchanan, cutting her off. 'It doesn't sound like you are in a position to be shopping, Miss Cooper.' He blinked his small eyes at her. 'You're due to renew your lease on the first, that's today.' He paused, 'I don't feel—'

Minnie could see where this was going and held up a finger to stop him.

'*Wait!* Mr Buchanan, please wait, whatever you might be about to say, please can we not have this conversation now? I know this sounds crazy, but bad things happen to me on the first of January, so if there are any major decisions to be made about me continuing to live here, I wonder if I could call you tomorrow when it's not the first and, um, well, just don't make your mind up today. I know I've been a bit of a crap tenant, but just give me one more day.'

Mr Buchanan's head was making very small movements from side to side. His lips were moving as though Minnie were a book he was trying to read and she was scrolling through the pages too fast for him.

'You want me to ask you to move out tomorrow?' he asked, peering at her in bemusement.

'No, no, I don't want you to ask me to move out at all. Just sleep on it, Mr Buchanan, decide tomorrow. I might not look like such a bad tenant tomorrow.' Minnie gave him the most charming smile she could muster.

'You have a month's notice, Miss Cooper,' he said, handing her the spare key. 'But since you asked nicely, I'll wait until tomorrow to formalise it in writing.'

Minnie got inside, dropped her bag on the floor and pulled Lucky into her arms.

'Oh Lucky, it's so cold in here.'

Lucky kicked out of her arms and sprang through to the kitchen. 'OK, fine, I'll get you food.'

Minnie pulled out half a tin of cat food from the fridge door and decanted it into a saucer. Lucky devoured most of it, then he jumped up onto the counter and up again to the top of the fridge. 'Oh, you found the only warm patch in the place, hey? You won't come keep me warm next door?' Lucky tucked his head into his body – a definitive 'no'.

Minnie walked into the next room and lay down on her bed. The only noise was the 'plip-plip' of the dripping tap in the bathroom and the gentle hum of traffic from the adjoining road. She shivered, jumped up from the bed, pulled off Leila's stupid dress and riffled through her chest of drawers for something warmer to wear. She pulled on tracksuit bottoms, two thermal tops, her thickest jumper and some bed socks, then she climbed back into bed.

She looked at her phone; she should try Greg again. She should call Leila too and cancel their lunch – she couldn't face going out again today. A wave of exhaustion crashed over her. Now she was lying down, the adrenaline that had been fuelling the last twenty-four hours finally stopped pumping. As well as being shattered, she was also fearful of interacting with anyone else today. Knowing her luck, if she spoke to Greg they would argue. If she went out with Leila, who knows – they were close, but no friendship was impregnable.

She sent Greg, Leila and both her parents a text to say she was fine, not to worry about her, but she had a terrible migraine and needed to take to her bed for the rest of the day. Then she turned off her phone. Minnie didn't get migraines, she never had, but no one questioned a migraine, no one expected you to soldier through; people just accepted it and left you alone to recover. She didn't get these migraines often, only a couple of times a year, but they did tend to come on with remarkable regularity around her birthday.

Minnie reached into her bedside drawer for a small brown bottle. It was almost empty, only three little white pills left. They were powerful sleeping tablets she'd been prescribed during a bout of insomnia last year. She had been saving them. She generally slept better now, but it was reassuring to know they were there. Otherwise she would get anxious about the 3 a.m. wake-up, her mind churning and no access to an off switch. She popped one of the remaining pills in her mouth and swallowed it dry. It was only 11 a.m., but if there was ever a day she wanted to sleep through, it was her thirtieth birthday.

New Year's Eve 2015

Minnie's hammock was almost perfect. It was exactly the right angle, hung between two palm trees with the head end raised slightly higher than her feet. She could lie back and look out to sea while sipping her coconut through a straw. Her curly brown hair was damp and crunchy from her morning sea swim; her face lightly tanned and freckled from two weeks in the sun – the picture of contentment. And yet, there was something about the rough cotton fabric against her skin that irritated her and stopped her from truly enjoying this last moment in paradise.

'I don't want to fly this afternoon,' she said wistfully to Leila, who was lying in the hammock next to her.

'It's the only flight that gets us back to Delhi in time to make our connection home. Plus it was cheap because, guess what, you're not the only one who doesn't like to travel on New Year's Eve,' said Leila.

Minnie let out a weary sigh. 'Can't we just stay here, live in hammocks and drink coconuts for ever?'

'I don't think Islington Council would let me work remotely. I doubt the vulnerable members of the community I look after would appreciate chatting to their case worker over Skype, from a beach. It doesn't send the right message.'

Minnie laughed, twiddling a crunchy curl of hair between her finger and thumb.

'You never know. I just have this real Sunday-night back-to-school feeling, don't you? In seventy-two hours we'll both be back at work, you with Admin Pain Elaine and me with Pervy Pete and his stinky feet.'

'Seriously though,' said Leila, 'how did these people get to be in charge? I see so many people desperate to work who just can't get a break, but we live in a world where Pervy Pete and Admin Pain Elaine are the gatekeepers.'

'Well, when you're running the show I'll expect to see it staffed by a wonderful array of waifs and strays – a chaotic, shambolic utopia.'

Leila laughed. 'That's the manifesto I'll be running with.'

Minnie looked out to sea. Three local men in a blue fishing boat were bobbing up and down on the turquoise waves. One pulled the choke on the engine, and with an unhealthy-sounding roar it spluttered into life, emitting a cloud of black smoke as the boat chugged off towards the horizon.

Coming to India for Christmas had been Leila's idea. She'd convinced Minnie there was nothing like a holiday to help you get over a bad break-up. Minnie had only left the UK once before, to Alicante on a package tour; the one year her parents had felt they could afford a family holiday. India was another world compared to Spain, and certainly compared to the cold, grey winter of home. Stepping off the aeroplane was a sensory awakening, like seeing the world in Technicolor for the first time.

There was something magical about being away with your best friend in a foreign land. She and Leila had discovered their new favourite food together (spicy samosas), laughed so hard they could hardly breathe as they careered around corners in speeding tuk-tuks, and had lain on the beach side by side, tearing husks from coconuts and telling their dreams to the stars.

Though it had been an unforgettable ten days, it was the first time either of them had been away from their families for Christmas, and they'd both found it strange not having turkey or a tree. They had brought a few tokens of festive familiarity with them. They'd packed miniature stockings for each other and opened them on the beach on Christmas morning with their bare feet buried in the sand. They wore cheap Christmas hats on their heads and ate melted Terry's Chocolate Oranges for breakfast. Leila gave Minnie some beautiful emerald earrings and a chef's hat with the words 'Minnie's Pies' embroidered on the front.

'For when you have your own pie business,' she said, nudging Minnie with an elbow.

A lump formed in Minnie's throat. Running her own catering business was something she'd often daydream about. She'd only ever mentioned the idea to Leila once, when she was drunk – she was amazed Leila even remembered the conversation.

Minnie scratched her leg irritably. Little red welts had erupted all over her skin.

'I think I'm allergic to that suncream you lent me, Leils.'

Leila's head popped up over the side of Minnie's hammock; her bright green hair had gone wild in the humidity and the fake tan on her face had come out a little too orange – she looked like an unhinged Oompa-Loompa. Minnie jolted in surprise, sloshing coconut water down her front.

'Don't creep up on me like that,' she cried, brushing water off her kaftan.

'Your little friend is back,' said Leila, raising her eyes skyward while pointing an accusatory finger down at the dog standing next to her in the sand.

'Fleabag dog!' cried Minnie, leaping down from the hammock to greet him.

The dog launched himself at Minnie and started licking her face. Fleabag dog was a mangy-looking grey and white stray with a stumpy tail and a limp. He had been following the girls around all week. Minnie had become fond of his friendly little face and given him a few fish scraps on their first night in the beach hut. As a result of her kindness, he'd been following them around like a little dog-shaped shadow.

'Don't let him lick you,' said Leila, grimacing.

'Poor thing,' said Minnie, giving him an affectionate rub on the head. 'It's like he knows we're leaving and he's come to say goodbye.'

'You're only going to make life harder for him when we leave. Where is he going to get food from now?' said Leila.

'He'll be OK, look at him – who could resist that face?' Minnie nuzzled her face against the dog's nose.

'Minnie, I don't think that rash is a suncream allergy, I think it's flea bites,' Leila said, holding up both hands in disgust.

'Do you think?'

'Well, if you will insist on having a holiday romance with Fleabag dog.'

'That's only a silly nickname – you don't think he really has fleas, do you?' Minnie asked in alarm.

'Yes. I think you both do. Bags not sitting next to you on the plane.'

At the airport Minnie began to sweat as soon as they got out of the taxi. She repeatedly kept checking she had her passport, her wallet and her luggage, convinced one or all of them would be stolen at any moment.

'Relax, Miss Paranoia. You're only going to draw attention to where your wallet is if you keep checking it like that,' said Leila.

The air in the terminal building was cool compared to the humidity outside. In the sprawling modern concourse, there were queues everywhere: queues to check in luggage, queues to have your bags wrapped in cellophane, queues snaking around the building going – apparently – nowhere.

'Ooh there's a Cafechino! Do you want a coffee or one of those yummy spicy samosas?' asked Leila, nodding her head towards a café near the entrance.

'I'm not eating anything until I get home, I'm not tempting fate,' said Minnie, shaking her head and pinching her lips tight shut.

At baggage security, Minnie was still sweating and scratching her arms furiously.

Leila handed her a tissue. 'Don't look so guilty, Minnie, or they'll take you for a full cavity search,' she hissed.

As Minnie's bag went through the security scanner, the man sitting behind the screen eyed Minnie suspiciously. He had a neat brown moustache and dark hair combed into an arrow-straight side parting. His blue uniform was crisp and starched; his eyes darted between Minnie and the screen in front of him. He motioned to a colleague, pointed at the screen and then at Minnie.

'Miss, is this your bag?' said a tall, thinner man with old-fashioned spectacles and a more wrinkled uniform. He beckoned Minnie through to the other side of the conveyor belt.

'Yes,' Minnie said with a resigned little nod.

Of course someone had hidden drugs in her bag and now she was going to rot in an Indian prison for the next twenty years. It was all too predictable.

'Please come, miss,' said the taller man, beckoning her.

She followed him through to a small room, while the shorter man carried her black suitcase behind them. Minnie looked around for Leila who shook her head and held up her hands in an overblown shrug.

'Can I search the bag?' said the shorter man politely.

'Sure,' said Minnie, 'be my guest.'

The taller man said something in Konkani. The shorter man neatly piled all of Minnie's clothes on the bench and then pulled out an oblong box. It was Leila's birthday present to Minnie, neatly wrapped for tomorrow. Leila had thrown it in Minnie's bag at the last minute because her own was too stuffed full of pastel-coloured fisherman's trousers, crochet tops, and all the scented wooden ornaments she kept buying from the beach vendors.

'What is in here?' asked the shorter man, thrusting it towards her. The taller man frowned and picked up a clipboard. He started flicking through some sheets of paper.

'I don't know. It's a present for my birthday.'

Minnie felt her stomach drop. Would Leila have bought her drugs? Surely not.

The two men exchanged a look. The taller man said something in Konkani and tapped his clipboard.

'May I open it?' said the shorter man.

'Sure,' said Minnie, shaking her head. Maybe it was some kind of bath-bomb that set the sensors off because it looked like explosives?

The shorter man carefully began to unwrap the parcel to reveal a long purple plastic box with 'Rampant Rabbit' written along the side in excitable lettering. A large phallic pink wand was visible through the plastic window. Minnie blushed puce; bloody Leila – this was mortifying.

'What is this?' asked the shorter man, his head cocked to one side.

'Oh, er, it's a joke, it's a present from my friend.'

Both men looked at her blankly. Minnie rolled her hands into fists to stop herself from scratching. The taller man pointed to a Post-it note stuck onto the box. The shorter man started to read, 'Hey babes, have an orgasmic birthday and a dickalicious New Year. Who needs men, hey?' He pronounced the word orgasmic, 'org-gas-mick'.

'What is dickal ishus?' asked the taller man.

'Oh well, it's hard to explain,' said Minnie, covering her face with clammy hot hands. She was beginning to wish it had been drugs in her bag. Oh god, why couldn't it have been lovely, simple, less embarrassing drugs?

'This is a morally corrupting object,' said the shorter man sternly. 'You sell this in our country?'

'Oh no, no, I'm not selling it. Why would I want to sell it?'

'It is not OK to sell obscene objects in India,' said the taller man, shaking his head and tapping his clipboard.

'Really?' Minnie said, genuinely surprised. 'I didn't know that, and as I said, it's a present. I didn't even know it was in there.'

'You will have to wait here. Fill in this form,' said the shorter man.

'Very long form,' said the taller man, nodding gravely, handing her a clipboard thick with paper.

'But my flight, I'll miss my flight!' Minnie cried.

The two men chatted while Minnie furiously scratched her arms. Eventually they turned back to her and her hands froze, mid-scratch.

'If you pay a fine instead of form, you might make your flight.'

Minnie scrabbled for her wallet. She took out her last fifty rupees.

'How much is the fine?'

The men looked at her pitiful fistful of cash.

'Expensive,' said the shorter man, 'you have more?'

Minnie shook her head mournfully. The shorter man handed her the clipboard and tapped the form with his finger.

'Not your lucky day, miss.'

*

The girls spent the night on the airport floor. Minnie was one part furious with Leila for giving her an illegal sex toy to carry, three parts grateful that she had waited for her and not taken the flight to Delhi alone. Leila laughed so hard when she found out the reason Minnie had been detained that she ever-so-slightly wet herself and needed to go and change into her last pair of clean trousers. Minnie explained it might take her a little longer to see the funny side.

They struggled to get comfortable on the airport floor, propped against their backpacks beneath the strip lighting of an airport that never sleeps. At 3 a.m. Leila nudged Minnie with her foot.

'Hey Min, you awake?'

'Yes,' Minnie sighed.

'I didn't ask you last night – where do you want to be this time next year?'

It was Leila's New Year ritual. She liked to ask herself, and anyone she was with, where they wanted to be this time next year.

'Not camping in an airport covered in flea bites?' said Minnie.

'I'm serious. Where you would be? What do you have to have achieved by your twenty-seventh birthday?'

Minnie sighed, indulging her friend.

'I guess I want to not be sad about Tarek dumping me any more.'

'Oh Minnie, don't waste your "this time next year" on waste-of-space Tarek. What else?'

'I guess I'd be doing a job I vaguely enjoy. I'd like to be able to buy Tesco's Finest occasionally, not just the value range – you know me, the girl with enormous ambitions,' Minnie let out a sigh.

'Minnie, I've had the best idea,' said Leila, shuffling across the floor on her bottom until she was sitting next to her. 'You and I should go into business together.'

'Doing what? Smuggling sex toys into India?'

'No, we should set up a business making pies for the needy: you bring the pies and I'll bring the needy.' Minnie looked over at her friend to see if she was serious. 'Your pies are bloody amazing, you are Queen of Pies in my mind, you just need someone to team up with to give you the confidence to do it!'

'Queen of Pies sounds like someone really fat,' Minnie said, but she felt her heart start to race.

'You bake them and we use my contacts in community care to get them to people in need – like Meals on Wheels or some shit. I'm sure I could get us funding, there's this new initiative to support small charities. Oh, oh – ' Leila shook her fists up and down, getting carried away – 'and we can employ all the people who just need someone to give them a break – my hopeful utopia!'

'You want us to do Meals on Wheels?' Minnie said, looking at her friend as though she'd suggested they set up a business selling badger-themed underwear at car-boot sales.

'Think about it, it's not such a mad idea. I think you've lost your passion for cooking by catering to the rich and ungrateful for too long. Imagine making the food you love, for people who would actually appreciate it? And how fun would it be to work together every day? We'll just do one thing really well, and take them to people who can't get to the shops, or to people living independently who can't cook any more. "Pies by Post" or "Pie in the Sky", maybe "Hello, Good-Pie"?'

Minnie paused. 'OK.'

'OK?' asked Leila. She sounded surprised that Minnie had agreed.

'Yes, let's do it, but none of those names,' said Minnie, 'I've already thought of the perfect name.'

2 January 2020

The No Hard Fillings kitchen was on an unremarkable side street in Dalston in east London. It was in the part of town that gentrification had not yet reached, sandwiched between a funeral director's and a derelict old record store. There was a sign out front that said 'Tandoori Palace', crossed out with green spray paint. The building used to house an Indian restaurant and Minnie and Leila didn't yet have the funds to properly change the signage. The girls felt it was somehow fortuitous, coming back from India with the plan and then finding a failing Indian restaurant offering them the chance to take over their lease.

'I hope you girls have more luck with the place than we did,' Mrs Mohan had said sombrely as she helped clear out the drawers and cupboards. 'Better you have it than another KFC or Piri-Piri Chicken.'

Four years later there was still a picture of the Mohan family pinned to the steel fridge door. The girls had found it after the move and they didn't have the heart to take down the last vestige of the family's hard work.

On her way to work, Minnie bought fresh coffees for the whole team. She could ill afford it, but she thought everyone might need a morale boost. She'd woken at 2 a.m. feeling groggy and confused, then celebrated the end of her birthday by making an enormous Spanish omelette out of a suspect array of ingredients she'd found in her fridge. The early hours of the morning had been spent listening to music and cleaning, while Lucky eyed her suspiciously from his warm perch on top of the fridge.

Now it was the second of January – her favourite day of the year; the day furthest from her birthday. So, despite everything that had happened yesterday, she couldn't help walking into work with a bounce in her step. Greg had tried to call her already this morning. She hadn't answered; she'd been on the bus and couldn't bring herself to let an argument ruin her buoyant mood. Greg could be pretty uncommunicative when it suited him. If he was mid-flow with an article, she might not hear from him for days. Perhaps it would be good for him to get a taste of her being less available.

'I got coffees,' she called, as she swung through the door and the old-fashioned bell above chimed.

'Oh, you beauty,' said Alan, taking one out of her hands.

'Alan, thank you for hosting us on New Year's Eve, we both had a lovely time.'

'Endlessly welcome,' Alan said with a bow.

Alan was their delivery driver. He was a tall, wiry man in his fifties, with a mouth that constantly twitched. He had pale sallow skin and wide feline eyes with large heavy lids. He made Minnie think of an eighteenth-century poet battling a tortured soul. Alan used to captain boats for a living, but an accident with an anchor had turned him into a self-proclaimed 'land lubber'. No one knew what the accident had entailed, or what exactly he had injured – he didn't like to talk about it.

'Did you get any non-dairy?' asked Fleur, turning her head sharply.

'No, sorry, only cow cappuccinos,' Minnie grimaced.

Fleur sighed, but reached out a hand for one nonetheless. Fleur manned the phone. She was twenty-two and prone to food fads. Today was day two of Veganuary. Fleur had an elegant long neck and white-blonde hair. Like a beautiful, haughty swan, you got the feeling she might hiss at you if you got too close.

Fleur had come to work for them two years ago. It had just been Leila and Minnie back then, and when the business first got busy they needed help taking orders. Fleur had come to the interview with a proposal. She'd explained she was learning to code but couldn't do it at home because her mother believed the internet gave people asthma – she wouldn't allow a Wi-Fi router in the house. She said she would work four days a week, but they'd only need to pay her for three, as long as she could do her coding course during the downtime.

They gave her the job as it had sounded like a good deal. In retrospect, Minnie wondered whether any of the stuff about Fleur's mother or the coding course had been true. Fleur never mentioned her parents, never appeared to go home, and still seemed to be doing this six-month coding course two years later. Leila had a theory that Fleur was actually London's most glamorous tramp, who simply wanted somewhere warm to sit and scroll through social media.

'Is Leila here yet?' Minnie asked.

'No,' said Fleur, taking the lid off her cappuccino and peering into it as though hoping to find it might be soy milk after all. 'Oh, and there's been a dis-arse-terrrr.'

'What?' Minnie spun around to look at her. 'What disaster?'

'Beverley burnt the pies.' Fleur gave a slow, swan-like shrug.

'She didn't!'

Minnie rushed past the reception desk into the kitchen beyond. Beverley was standing red-faced in her white chef's coat, leaning over a countertop full of pies. They were lined up in a colour spectrum ranging from lightly charcoaled through to deeply incinerated. Minnie's jaw fell as she plonked the cardboard tray of coffees down on the countertop and took in the scene of devastation before her.

'What happened?' she asked softly.

'I think these ones are salvageable,' said Beverley, pointing at the left-hand side of the counter. Beverley was fifty-nine but looked older, with her ruddy skin and soft, jowly face.

'How ... how did you burn so many?' Minnie asked, shaking her head in disbelief. At least thirty of the forty pies in front of her were too burnt to sell.

'I came in early to get a bump on things,' said Beverley, eyes wide with remorse. Her wiry black hair was escaping in tufts from beneath her hairnet, lending her a mad-professor vibe. 'Me and the oven have not been getting along.'

'Are these the pies Leila spent the whole of New Year's Eve making?' Minnie asked, pulling the iron bar stool up to the large steel countertop. She picked at one of the burnt crusts and the black pastry crumbled beneath her touch. 'What happened to the timer we bought you? The pies always take exactly forty-two minutes.'

'Me and the timer have not been getting along,' Beverley sighed, brushing some of the errant hair away from her eyes.

Minnie sat with her head in her hands. This was not how the second of January was supposed to go.

'I'm sorry, Minnie,' said Beverley, her face forlorn. 'I don't know what's going on with me lately. One minute I'm here working, and the next my mind's gone somewhere else and twenty minutes have flashed by as though they were seconds.'

'She's having an existential crisis,' said Alan, hopping from foot to foot in agitation. 'What's it all about? Why am I here? Is pastry the meaning of life? Oh whoops, the kitchen's on fire.'

Beverley whacked Alan with a tea towel.

'Someone called for you, Minnie,' Fleur said, craning her long neck around the corner from the reception desk. 'Something about a drop-off?'

'Was it a change to today's orders?' Minnie asked.

'I don't remember the exact details.'

'Fleur, we've talked about this, you have to write down messages – otherwise there really is no point in you being here.'

Fleur rolled her eyes and went back to scrolling through her phone and sipping her inadequate bovine cappuccino.

'I'll start again,' said Beverley with a sniff. 'You can take the ingredients out of my pay. I'm so sorry, Minnie.'

Minnie checked her watch. They had to get forty-five pies baked, packaged and delivered all across London before the end of the afternoon. It would be tight.

'No, don't be silly, Bev. Come on, no point crying about it now,' Minnie said, patting a distraught Beverley on the back. 'Let's get to it.'

Minnie rolled up her sleeves, put on her apron and hairnet and set to work. She loved to bake; it was when she felt most calm. People talked about 'being in flow' and, for her, baking a pie was the perfect kind of flow. It took just enough concentration to focus her mind, but gave her brain a break from the usual clamour of concerns and anxieties vying for her attention. Clearly Beverley was not finding her flow through baking at the moment. Minnie wondered if she should encourage Beverley to see someone about this absent-mindedness. It had started a few weeks ago and they'd all noticed. It wasn't so much that Beverley was forgetful, more that her mind zoned out for a while and her attention wasn't in the room.

Leila arrived just as Minnie and Beverley were pulling ingredients together into a giant ball of pastry on the central steel countertop.

'What's happening? Why are you baking?' Leila said, turning her head sharply between Alan, Beverley and Minnie.

'Beverley burnt the pies,' said Alan, hopping up and down on one foot.

'For fuck's sake, Beverley!' Leila said, slamming her palm down onto the countertop. Alan jumped in alarm. Beverley let out a quivering sob and closed her eyes.

'Hey, hey, it's OK, she's having a bad day,' said Minnie, rubbing Beverley on the back with a floury hand. 'We're making more, it's fine,' Minnie said, giving Leila a wide-eyed stare.

'It's not fine,' Leila sighed, 'I spent all New Year's Eve prepping those pies. And you,' Leila jabbed a finger at Minnie, 'what happened to you yesterday? I was ringing on your doorbell for ages, Little Miss Migraine bullshit.'

'I don't like Leila when she's angry,' said Alan, hunching his shoulders and settling his features into a childlike scowl.

'Rainbow Bright's got attitude today,' said Fleur, appearing at the kitchen door.

'What happened yesterday?' asked Alan.

'Happy Birthday by the way, Minnie,' said Beverley, sniffing back tears. 'Did you get to do anything nice?'

'She did not do anything nice,' said Leila, leaning both hands on the countertop. 'She hid in her flat pretending to have a migraine, standing up her best friend.'

'I wasn't pretending, I did have a migraine,' Minnie said, pounding her other fist into the dough with a satisfying 'thunk'.

'Ooh, I love it when my work mums fight!' Fleur sang from the doorway, pumping both hands in the air like a cheerleader.

'It's not very mature, is it Minnie?' said Leila, ignoring Fleur. 'This fear of the first of January is getting ridiculous.'

'It's not ridiculous, and I *did* have a migraine, OK?' Minnie said, picking up the pile of dough and smashing it down onto the countertop. No one spoke. The thwack of the pastry against stainless steel reverberated around the room.

'Intermission! I'll put some music on,' said Fleur, turning back to the reception area in a swish of white hair.

Leila pulled on an apron and gazed mournfully at the line of burnt pies, which Beverley had moved to the sideboards at the far end of the kitchen.

'I suppose we can't even salvage the fillings?' she sighed, 'Come on then, Bev, help me put these out of their misery.'

Ten minutes later, with the spoilt pies in the bin and the smell of burnt pastry still lingering in the air, everyone was in a more relaxed mood. They had a good production line going, with Alan and Minnie shaping pastry into new tins, while Beverley and Leila decapitated the burnt ones and disposed of their charred remains. Fleur had curated an uplifting nineties playlist and they were all, bar Alan, singing along to 'Lady Marmalade' as they worked. If Fleur was good at something, it was finding the right soundtrack to improve the collective mood.

'So has Name Stealer been in touch yet?' Leila asked as she and Minnie crossed paths at the sink. Leila was thawing, but Minnie knew she wasn't yet forgiven for standing her up.

'Who's Name Stealer?' asked Bev.

'On New Year's Eve, Minnie met this guy who was born in the same hospital as her at exactly the same time,' Leila explained. 'Isn't that freaky?'

'Well one minute earlier than me, if we're being precise,' said Minnie.

'Minnie's mum wanted to call her Quinn, but this dude's mum stole her idea, so Minnie ended up Minnie instead,' Leila explained.

'Quinn Cooper,' Fleur sounded the words out loud, 'great name; Minnie Cooper is terrible. No offence.'

Minnie had run out of ingredients to pound so started rolling with a vengeance instead. Fleur turned the music down and placed a final pin into her hair. While the others had been working, Fleur had been crafting herself an elaborate hairstyle with neat fish plaits wrapping around each side of her head. She looked like a character from *Game of Thrones*.

'It's very romantic,' said Leila, 'Minnie and her name nemesis, reunited after thirty years – love twins separated at birth, destined to find each other again despite the odds.'

She clutched a hand to her chest for dramatic effect. Everyone laughed, except Minnie.

'What the hell's a love twin? That's not a thing,' Minnie said, shaking her head. Behind her frown she was pleased; Leila teasing her meant she was forgiven.

'That could so be a thing, like two Geminis getting together,' said Fleur. 'Did you give him your number?'

Dating was one of Fleur's favourite topics of conversation. She was a connoisseur of every dating app out there. She said she was learning to code so she could set up her own horoscope-themed dating app.

'I said he could find me online if he wanted to,' Minnie said with an air of cultivated ambivalence. 'I'm sure he won't, why would he, he's got a girlfriend ... ' Then after a pause she added, 'And I've got a boyfriend. What are you doing with my phone?' Minnie looked over to see Leila scrolling through her phone.

'You changed your Facebook profile picture,' said Leila, giving Minnie a sly grin. 'Why would you do that? You never even go on Facebook.'

'Well new year, new photo. I'm allowed to change my photo if I want to.' Minnie blushed and turned her back to the room, hiding her face in the fridge as she pretended to look for something.

'This isn't a new photo, this is four years old. She's changed it to one of her in India looking tanned and sexy,' said Leila, showing the phone to Fleur.

'Give that to me,' said Minnie, turning around and striding across the kitchen with her hand outstretched.

'You do look good in that photo,' said Fleur, nodding approvingly. 'If you want me to set you up an online dating profile, you should use that one. You look young, thin and a little bit stupid – guys like that.'

'Thanks Fleur, but I am very happy with Greg,' Minnie said huffily. She took the phone, purposely didn't check it for messages, and placed it firmly into her apron pocket. Then she went back to busying herself lining tins. The others all stood watching her. 'Come on guys, stop dicking around, we've got serious time pressure here if no one noticed. There are forty orders to be made, baked and delivered today, and if we don't get them out, we don't get paid, and if we don't get paid, none of us will have jobs tomorrow, OK, so can we just …'

Everyone was quiet. Beverley dropped a tin and it clanged to the floor, rattling around and around on the hard cream tiles. Minnie's phone pinged loudly in her pocket. She caught Leila's eye and then turned her back on the room as she checked it. She had a notification on Messenger from Quinn Hamilton. She clicked it open.

'Minnie, I'm hoping this is you – the first of January girl. Can you call me? There's something I'd like to discuss. Quinn.' Then he'd linked his number in the message.

Minnie felt her cheeks flush with heat; he'd tracked her down. She felt relieved, as though the growing bubble of anticipation over whether or not he would be in touch had finally been burst.

'Who's that message from?' Leila asked, her eyes locking onto Minnie like heat-seeking missiles, trained to identify the suspicious glow of embarrassment.

'No one,' Minnie said, thrusting her phone back into her apron pocket. 'Come on, let's get this batch in.'

Minnie clapped her hands together, creating a cloud of flour in the air and closing down Leila's interrogation on the subject. Leila put the first tray of pies in the oven, Beverley sweated over the timer, and Alan went to pull the van around front in preparation for loading up the day's deliveries. Fleur looked at her phone and took selfies of her new hairstyle with various filters.

'Hey, Minnie, I forgot to say, I need next Tuesday off,' said Fleur, still snapping away on her phone. 'My cousin's mates with Tarantino and he's in London researching ghost stories on the Underground for some new movie idea. It's what I did my dissertation on, so I said I'd help him out, show him some of the spookiest sites. Mega-bore, I know.' Fleur rolled her eyes skyward.

'Fine,' Minnie muttered. She didn't have time to delve into one of Fleur's fantasies today. Fleur had a habit of telling the most ridiculous tales about why she needed a day off. It was never simply, 'I've got a dentist appointment.'

A few minutes later, Alan bounced back into the kitchen wringing his hands, his mouth twitching furiously.

'We have another problem,' he said, mouth opening and closing like a goldfish.

'What now?' shouted Leila.

'Van's been clamped,' Alan said, his feet skipping from side to side.

'You are kidding me?' Minnie said wearily. 'Where did you park it?'

'On the double yellow,' he said with a frown, 'but double yellows don't count on a bank holiday, it's a parking amnesty.'

'A – they do count. And B – it's not a bank holiday today,' said Minnie, closing her eyes in despair.

'Oh,' said Alan, his mouth stretching into a long, slow grimace.

How could all this be happening on the second of January? Maybe the jinx knew she'd tried to cheat it by sleeping through her birthday? Maybe the bad luck had been paid forward? Minnie thought for a minute. There was only one person she knew who had a car they could borrow at such short notice. She walked out onto the street for some privacy and made the call.

'Greg?' she said, as he picked up.

'Finally.' His voice was quiet on the phone. 'How's the migraine that's so bad you can't answer the phone?'

'Much better, thank you.' Minnie paused. 'How was the party I missed because I was trapped in a bathroom and no one came to find me?'

'How was I to know you were stuck somewhere? Some waiter said he saw you leave. I walked up and down the street looking for you for at least half an hour; it totally ruined my night.'

'Why would I have left without telling you?'

'Some kind of jinx-related paranoia, I don't know why you do half the things you do, Minnie.' Greg paused, 'I mean, if you only kept your phone charged ...'

'Well I didn't leave, I was stuck in the loo, all night.' Minnie took a deep breath, tempering her irritation and reminding herself that she was calling Greg for a favour. 'Listen, I'm sorry the night was such a disaster. Are you at home? I'm having a nightmare at work. Please can I borrow your car?'

'No Minnie, you can't borrow my car ...'

Greg sounded annoyed. The phone made a noise like screws in a blender and then the line went dead. Had he hung up on her, or had she just lost the connection? Minnie pawed at the keypad, trying to call him back. Greg had a thing about people hanging up on him. Maybe he had tried looking for her – whatever the truth, right now she needed to swallow her pride and get him back on side for the sake of today's pies. Her phone screen looked as if it was resetting some temporary glitch. Minnie started to sweat as she desperately thumbed the keypad again, and finally it started to ring.

'Hello?' he said.

'Look, I'm sorry if you are pissed off about the other night,' Minnie blurted out, 'I didn't mean to get stuck in the toilet, did I? I tried calling you as soon as I could, and I really did have a migraine yesterday. Now I've got forty pies to deliver all over London and Alan got our van clamped and if we don't get them out today, we're going to be in serious trouble, and you're the only person I know with a car, so please, please can I borrow it and I'll make things up to you later?' she paused, weighing up how much ground she needed to recover. 'Maybe I'll even dress up as a dental nurse again, I know how much you liked that. I could pick up some new toothbrushes and appointment cards on the way home?' Minnie closed her eyes, willing Greg to soften.

'Minnie?' he said, but he didn't sound like Greg any more.

Minnie looked down at her screen. The caller ID was displaying some random number she didn't recognise.

'Greg?' she said.

'No. It's Quinn. Quinn Hamilton.'

Minnie froze, not knowing whether to hang up the phone or throw it across the street like a burning lump of coal that had scorched her hand. How in the name of dentistry had she managed to call Quinn Hamilton?

'Oh god, sorry,' she said, clutching the phone to her ear and closing her eyes. 'I don't know how I managed to call you, I was trying to call someone else.'

She must have somehow clicked on the Facebook message when the call dropped.

'Clearly,' said Quinn. He sounded amused. 'You got my message then?'

'Uh-huh.' Minnie still had her eyes closed. So much for her plan to play it cool and leave it a few days before replying.

'And you need a car?' said Quinn.

'No,' said Minnie, shaking her head. 'Well yes. Sorry, I honestly don't know how I ended up calling you, my phone must have a mind of its own.'

'I have a car you can borrow,' said Quinn.

'No honestly, I don't need your car, I can borrow my boyfriend's car ... ' She paused. 'Thank you, though, it's kind of you to offer.'

'Well if you borrow Greg's car, you'll have to go and buy new toothbrushes and that sounds – ' his deep voice cracked slightly – 'like hard work.'

Minnie flexed out the fingers on her other hand, every fibre of her body cringing.

'Honestly, Minnie, I'd be happy to help you out. Let me know where you are and I'll come drop off the car. Consider it restitution for stealing your name.'

Minnie walked back into the kitchen with a dazed look on her face.

'Is Greg bringing his car?' Leila asked, as she folded flat-packed cardboard into pie boxes.

'No,' said Minnie staring off into space, still shell-shocked. 'Quinn Hamilton is bringing his.'

New Year's Eve 2015

Quinn had booked a private dinner on the beach. He'd been deliberating between the hotel's 'Romance at Sunset' package and the 'Anniversary Package'. Optional extras included a serenading violinist, your own personal butler, or an upgrade to the waterfront gazebo complete with 'waterside entertainment', whatever that involved. When had eating food become so complicated? He'd opted for the basic 'Romance at Sunset' with none of the optional extras – good to keep this simple.

Throughout the afternoon, hotel staff had been back and forth to the beach outside their villa setting everything up. Jaya had spent the day at the spa and, when she returned, Quinn shut the villa blinds while she got changed so that their dinner plans would be a surprise. As he led Jaya outside, he saw how much effort the staff had gone to. A trail of paper lanterns made a path across the beach to a solitary white-linen-covered table. Tiki lights were positioned in a circle around it, demarking an island in the sand, and garlands of opulent white flowers hung between the flaming tiki lights.

Jaya gasped, 'Oh Quinn, how romantic!'

'The hotel set it up,' said Quinn, anxious not to get too much credit for this ostentatious display.

They walked through the screen doors onto the sand and Jaya paused, bending down to take off her heels. Quinn wore a dark blue linen suit and Jaya was dressed in the green silk evening gown that Quinn had bought her during their stopover in Munich. She looked beautiful; the dress hugged her body in all the right places and she'd spent hours at the hotel salon, getting a blow-dry and various other treatments Quinn had soon lost interest in hearing about.

Quinn put one hand against the small of her back, guiding her forwards; with the other he pulled out the white cotton-covered chair for her. He noticed there was a pink bow tied to the back of it. It looked slightly frayed on one side and he wondered how many 'Romance at Sunset' packages this ribbon had been witness to.

It had been Jaya's idea to come to India for the holidays. She wanted to see her family in Mumbai and she'd persuaded him to come too, promising him a week on the beach in Goa at the end of their trip. On one level the trip had been a success; Jaya's family had all greeted Quinn like some celebrity, parading out cousins and aunts to meet the 'man from Cambridge University'. Now they were at the most luxurious resort Quinn had ever stayed in, or paid for. Jaya had been an obliging companion, as insatiable as ever. He wouldn't admit this to anyone, but last night he'd wondered if, just once, they couldn't simply watch a DVD and not have sex four times.

On the plus side, Jaya had been so busy using all the hotel facilities that Quinn had had plenty of time to himself. It was such a relief to be away from home, not to be needed by someone at a moment's notice, not to be called in the middle of the night. It was only being away that made him see how draining it was being in permanent standby mode.

He felt bad being away for so long, especially over Christmas. His mother had reassured him she'd be fine. She had her sister over from America; Aunt Patricia – one of the lucky, trusted few.

'Oh look, how precious,' Jaya said, wrinkling her nose into a smile, 'they made the napkins into hearts, isn't that cute?'

'Nice,' Quinn said, shaking his heart out with a sharp flick of the wrist.

'The perfect setting for a special evening,' Jaya said, leaning over to touch his arm, her deep brown eyes gazing into his. Looking across the table at her, he noticed that each of her eyebrow hairs had been perfectly combed into conformity.

On a cold, snowy November day in Cambridge, when Jaya had suggested sundowners on the beach for New Year, Quinn had not been hard to convince. Especially knowing his aunt was coming over, and it might be one of his few opportunities to get away. But as the trip went on, and Quinn was presented to more and more of Jaya's relations, he started to worry that 'meeting the family' might have more significance to Jaya than he realised. He and Jaya had only been dating a few months – he wouldn't want her to get the wrong idea.

Jaya smiled at Quinn across the table. He could see she was wearing the make-up she reserved for 'big nights out'; the gold dust that made her cheekbones glow. She was wearing it on her cleavage too, and some of the make-up had smudged onto the dress by her breast. Quinn had a sudden urge to pick her up in a fireman's lift and run with her into the sea, plunging both their heads beneath the waves. Jaya didn't like to get her hair wet. It made Quinn smile, just thinking about how cross she would be.

'Can you?' Jaya asked, pulling out her camera phone and handing it to Quinn. He obliged, snapping four photos of her at a flattering angle. She was never happy with any less than four.

'Thanks, hun, I'll get the guy to take one of both of us when he comes,' she said, placing her phone face down on the table next to her fork.

Jaya had numerous social media followers, who she updated regularly about her life. Quinn noticed she posted a lot more on days when she'd taken time to add the golden glow to her face. Quinn didn't have a social media account before going to Cambridge to do his Masters. It was Jaya who'd convinced him he needed to have one. She liked to tag him in photos of them together with comments like, 'I want to let my beau know he means the world to me!' Jaya was very worried he might miss these messages if she couldn't tag him, so he had created an account to please her.

'This holiday has been so magical, Quinny,' Jaya said, looking out to sea where the sun was beginning to dip below the clouds. 'Would it sound selfish if I said it's been wonderful to have you all to myself for so long?'

'I've enjoyed it too,' said Quinn picking up the menu. 'Hey, they have those curried clams you like, should we get a ton?'

'Because sometimes in Cambridge, well, don't take this the wrong way, but you can seem a little distracted,' Jaya said, picking up her knife and checking her reflection in the blade.

'Hmm,' Quinn made a nondescript noise as he looked out to sea.

He wanted to see the sunrise tomorrow, and he was working out where the best place from which to view it would be. He'd get up early and say he was going for a run. He liked to be alone for the first sunrise of the year.

A waiter approached from the hotel. He was short and dressed in an impeccable white shirt, black trousers and a purple waistcoat imprinted with the hotel's insignia. He placed a basket of naan bread wrapped in linen and a delicate pot of yoghurt dip onto the table, then he presented Quinn with a wine list. Jaya asked the man if he would take a photo of them together. The waiter nodded politely and took the phone from Jaya's hand. He took one photo and made to hand it back. Quinn quickly shook his head, trying to warn the man, but he just grinned at Quinn and soon Jaya was lecturing him about composition and lighting positions. She wouldn't let him leave until she had checked the photos and then directed him to try again at a higher, more flattering angle.

'Too short,' Jaya whispered to Quinn once she'd finally dismissed the poor man. 'You never get a good photo when you ask a short person. Maybe the wine waiter will be taller?'

Quinn wondered how many hours of his life he'd have to spend posing for photographs if he and Jaya stayed together.

'So, will I finally get to meet your mother when we get back to England?' Jaya asked, stroking one of her hands with the other, drawing attention to her new manicure. 'Mothers love me, you know, I'm great with moms.'

'Oh, I don't know, I doubt there'll be time, especially if you want to go shopping on Oxford Street – the sales will be on, remember,' Quinn said.

Jaya paused, her eyes drifting off into space. He'd thrown her by mentioning the sales, but she gave her head a brisk shake, exorcising the distraction.

'Isn't she curious about me?' she asked, tilting her head and smoothing a hand through her hair. 'I'd want to meet the girl monopolising my son's time and attention.' When Quinn didn't respond, Jaya pouted, 'Don't you want her to meet me? All those times you scurry up to London at a moment's notice, and you never take me with you.'

Quinn hadn't mentioned Jaya to his mother. He'd told her he was going to India with a group of friends. Quinn buried his head in the wine list and the wine waiter appeared at just the right moment.

'Oh, much better,' said Jaya, raising her eyebrows at Quinn and looking the waiter up and down to convey how happy she was with his height. She leant in and touched Quinn's wrist. 'You will give them plenty of notice, won't you?' He looked up to see she was staring intently at him. 'If there is any particular moment we'd like him to come back and capture. It's just too perfect a setting not to have it recorded.'

She narrowed her eyes as though trying to convey some secret code. Quinn's dark eyebrows furrowed in confusion, then he went ahead and ordered an eye-wateringly expensive bottle of Meursault. The import prices here were criminal, but it was their last meal out. As Quinn closed the wine list, he glanced down and saw Jaya stroking her clove and orange scented hands and it hit him.

No.

Why would she think that? Surely she couldn't think that? They'd been dating a matter of months, *why the hell would she think that?* Maybe he was wrong. He had to be wrong. Of course he was wrong. As he looked back into her smiling eyes, he knew it – he wasn't wrong. She thought he was about to propose.

The wine waiter nodded and left. Quinn started to feel hot and pulled at his collar uncomfortably. He should have ended things earlier; this was never supposed to be long-term. How had he let it get to this point? His usual relationship cap was six months; no one got hurt if you kept it below six months. Now he had to endure a treacly romance-by-numbers evening, with a pink polyester bow attached to his chair, knowing she was waiting for a small box that was definitely not on the menu.

His eyes darted down the beach and he saw a scrawny-looking dog trotting up the shoreline towards them. It was a scruffy white and grey mutt with a stump for a tail and a slight limp in its hind leg.

'Oh, look at that cute dog,' he said, his voice coming out higher than he'd ever heard it before. Jaya turned to look.

'Quinn, no! It's a filthy stray. Don't pay it any attention or it won't leave us alone,' she scowled.

'Poor thing looks hungry,' said Quinn, clicking his fingers to get the dog's attention.

'Quinn,' Jaya was kicking his shin under the table. 'Don't!'

Quinn held out some naan bread for the dog. It bounded towards them, gently taking the bread, then licking Quinn's palm with gratitude.

'Poor little fella,' said Quinn, giving the dog an affectionate rub behind the ear. 'When did you last have a meal, buddy?'

'The hotel won't be able to get rid of it now,' Jaya said sharply. 'You aren't helping it in the long run.'

Spurred on by Jaya's anger and grateful to the dog for appearing, Quinn fed him another piece of bread. Though the dog was scruffy and underfed, he had a friendly face and he nuzzled affectionately into Quinn's arm.

'He must belong to someone – he's so tame,' said Quinn.

'He just knows a sucker when he sees one. Honestly, Quinn I'm serious, I don't want that dog anywhere near our dinner or me. Call the waiter to get rid of it,' Jaya pouted, folding her arms in front of her gold-dusted cleavage.

'OK, I'll take him back the way he came,' said Quinn, jumping up and tossing his napkin onto the chair. 'He probably lives down by those beach shacks beyond the palm trees. You relax, take in the view, I'll be back soon.'

Before Jaya could respond, Quinn scooped the dog up into his arms and strode off down the beach with him. He took a deep breath of sea air – the smell of freedom. A pang of guilt told him that the dog only offered a temporary reprieve. He'd have to go back, set the jilted record in its place and face whatever music was coming his way. But not now, not this minute. Once he was far enough away, he nuzzled his face into the dog's head and whispered, 'I owe you one buddy. Come on, let's find you a proper meal.'

2 January 2020

Quinn had said he would be in Dalston in thirty minutes. He hadn't given Minnie a chance to object, and before she knew it, she was desperately trying to get all the pies finished whilst surreptitiously making herself look less like a dowdy dinner lady in a hairnet.

'You don't happen to have a make-up bag here, do you?' she asked Fleur as casually as possible.

'Always,' said Fleur with a wink, pulling out a hefty tote from beneath the front desk.

Minnie rationalised that she wasn't going to any particular effort; she just wanted to look normal. She would have put on a dab of mascara if she'd planned to meet anyone other than her colleagues today. She didn't want Leila to see her putting on make-up, though; Leila would read something into it. Unfortunately, this whole covert borrowing and putting on of make-up caused such a distraction that another batch of pies came out of the oven overbaked.

'See, easily done,' said Bev triumphantly, as Minnie pulled a tray of dark brown pies from the shelf.

'They're fine, I like them like this,' said Minnie, though she knew these pies wouldn't pass her usually stringent quality control. Alan had already taken one box of deliveries off on the bike and trailer, and soon Quinn would be here. They didn't have the manpower or the time to be fussy today.

Leila walked through from the store cupboard with more flat-packed cardboard boxes and a stack of aluminium pie cases.

'Look at all this packaging,' Bev sighed, 'how much of it do you think gets recycled?'

'Bev, give me a break, we're feeding the elderly and isolated, we can't be expected to save the planet too,' said Leila, dumping all the packaging on the central steel countertop.

'You know my granddaughter Betty, she's four, she said to me last week, "Gran, what are you doing to save the planet from snowball warming?"'

Minnie and Leila laughed.

'I couldn't think of anything, isn't that terrible?' Bev chewed her bottom lip as she carefully transferred pies from the cooling rack into cases.

'Bev, I think you've got enough to worry about with your forgetfulness, I wouldn't be getting stressed about global warming too,' said Leila.

'She's got eco-anxiety, it's all the rage right now, all the celebs have got it,' said Fleur, poking her head around the doorway from reception. 'My friend had it so badly she stopped showering and shopping for like a month, and just lived in the dark with no TV; well, she had the basic channels, no Netflix or Amazon. Then she invented this new biodegradable packaging that's made of seaweed or mushrooms or some hemp shit, and now she's like a millionaire and has a private jet, but she's almost totally carbon-neutral so it's fine.'

'Is this the same friend who invented armbands?' Minnie asked, sceptically.

'No,' said Fleur pointedly, 'armbands were invented like ages ago, Minnie.' Fleur made a huffing sound and flounced back through to reception.

'I can't keep up with all her famous movie director and inventor friends,' Minnie whispered, and Leila giggled.

'He's here!' Fleur called in a singsong voice from reception.

Minnie handed the box she was folding to Bev, pulled off her grease-stained apron and hairnet, and hurried out to meet him. Standing in their pokey reception, Quinn looked even taller than she remembered. He was dressed in jeans and a soft camel-coloured jumper with a blue Barbour jacket slung over one shoulder. He stood with his weight backwards, one leg bent, surveying the space around him like a king surveying a newly conquered land. Minnie could see Fleur was desperately trying to catch her eye, so she purposely avoided looking in her direction.

'Hi,' said Minnie.

'Hi,' said Quinn with a slow grin.

'You really didn't need to do this. I don't expect people I hardly know to loan me their car at a moment's notice just because I phone them by accident,' Minnie said, fluffing her flattened hair out from behind her ears.

'Was it an accident though?' Quinn asked, slowly leaning forwards, one eyebrow raised. Minnie opened her mouth to speak but no words came out. 'I'm joking. Besides, I wasn't doing anything,' Quinn broke the silence, 'nor was my car.'

Fleur giggled, a stupid schoolgirlish giggle. Quinn gave her an indulgent smile, his eyes sparkling with approval. So predictable – she was probably just his type.

'This is Fleur, by the way.'

Minnie gave a half-hearted wave in Fleur's direction. Fleur jumped up to sit on the reception desk, swinging her legs childishly in front of her.

'Have you ever had your aura read, Quinn? You know you have a really strong energy around you,' said Fleur.

'I haven't,' he said.

'Maybe I should and come see where you've parked?' Minnie suggested, before Fleur could monopolise the man with her wanton quackery.

'So how was the rest of your birthday?' Quinn asked as they walked down the street away from the kitchen.

'Oh, um, great,' Minnie said, giving him a tight smile.

He was looking at her with cool amusement, as though he somehow knew what a pathetic, depressing day she'd had yesterday. She was pretty sure Quinn Hamilton would not have spent his birthday drugging himself to sleep in an attempt to blot out the big 3–0. He'd probably spent it having sex with Lucy Donohue on a speedboat, or doing some luxurious couples spa day where you got matching dressing gowns and a salt body scrub, followed by a nut-based salad on a scenic veranda. 'You?'

'I spent most of it asleep in the end,' said Quinn. 'Tuesday was a big night.' His eyes flashed her a conspiratorial look. Minnie cleared her throat and swallowed – was he teasing her or was he telepathic?

As they turned the corner of the street, Minnie saw an enormous black Bentley taking up most of the side road behind their building. It let out two high-toned beeps as Quinn unlocked it with a key fob.

'This is your car?' Minnie asked. 'You're kidding me, I can't drive that.'

'Why not?' Quinn asked, throwing her the keys. She caught them in one hand, savouring her unlikely catch with an internal high-five.

'It's the size of a tank. A very expensive tank.'

Who drove a Bentley, and in this part of London? Minnie stood staring at the car, unsure what to do or say next.

'It's insured for anyone to drive. I'll swing by and pick it up tomorrow.' Quinn gave a staccato salute with his hand, then turned and started walking away.

'Hey wait, you're not serious?' Minnie said, her voice squeaky with panic. 'I honestly can't drive this. I don't drive in London much and when I do it's only Greg's Mini.'

'Your boyfriend drives a Mini?'

Quinn turned back to face her, his eyes dancing with amusement.

'Don't start with the Mini Cooper jokes,' Minnie said, her eyes narrowing.

Quinn took a large stride towards her. Minnie's body tensed, the confidence of his gait slightly intimidating. He reached out a hand, sweeping the keys from her grasp, his fingers grazing her palm.

'I'll drive you then.'

'What?'

'You don't want to drive the car, I don't have plans, I'll take you where you need to go.'

Minnie started making shapes with her mouth to object, but she couldn't think of anything to say. She also lacked any other options for how she was going to get everything delivered today.

Quinn followed her back into the kitchen to help her collect the pies for delivery. Leila and Bev hadn't quite finished packing pies into cases, and Quinn cheerfully rolled up his sleeves to help with the last bits of labelling and packing.

'These smell amazing,' he said, taking a long slow inhale as he held one of the boxes in his hands. 'What's in here?'

'That there is steak and Guinness,' said Leila, handing him a label, 'and these are chicken and vegetable, our two most popular flavours.'

'I thought we were calling them Steak Gyllenhaal and Chick Jagger?' said Minnie.

'No,' Leila said, shaking her head. 'None of our customers liked those names.'

Quinn laughed as he held a box up to his nose. 'I don't think I've ever smelt a pie this good.'

'Don't suck all the smell out, that's the best bit,' said Leila, taking the box from his hands.

'It's the buttery pastry that makes them smell like that,' Bev explained, 'Minnie's secret recipe.'

'It's not a secret, Bev, it's just butter,' Minnie laughed. 'Butter makes everything great.'

'Yeah, everything,' said Fleur, gently tugging her lower lip down with the pad of her middle finger. Minnie glared at her. Leila steered Fleur out of the way, with a hand on each shoulder, then started ushering Minnie and Quinn out of the door.

'Anyway, you guys should head off. I'm sure you have lots to catch up on, you know, first of January stuff.'

She and Bev followed them out to the car to help load the last of the boxes into the boot.

'Blimey, people are going to think they're paying us too much,' said Bev.

'Or that these are some seriously classy pies,' said Leila, opening the passenger door for Minnie. As she shut the door she bent down and silently mouthed 'love twins' through the window, and made a little heart shape between her thumbs and forefingers.

Quinn tapped the first delivery address into his satnav. Minnie sat awkwardly on her hands, trying not to touch any of the beautiful cream leather.

'How come you drive a Bentley then?' she asked. 'Compensating for something?' Quinn burst out laughing. Minnie felt herself blush.

'Sorry, I don't know why I said that.'

Minnie glanced up to look at Quinn as he started the ignition and pulled away from the kerb. When he smiled, a fan of lines radiated out from his eyes. When he stopped smiling, some lines stubbornly remained, as though they knew they'd be used again soon, so there was no point in going away. There was something so warm and familiar about his face, though she couldn't explain what.

'It was my mother's. It's not something I would have chosen, but she doesn't like to drive any more so she gave it to me,' Quinn said.

He tilted his head to one side and briskly scratched his neck.

'My mum gave me a meat thermometer for my birthday,' said Minnie.

'My dad got me a card saying "Happy thirty-third",' said Quinn.

'I'd take the car and the card with the wrong age any day.'

Minnie gently bounced up and down on her hands; she felt fizzy with an unexplained energy, as though she'd downed eight coffees.

'So what do you do when you're not driving Miss Daisy around?' she asked.

'M'lady,' Quinn doffed an imaginary cap, 'nothing as interesting as owning my own pie business.'

'Are you sure you're not a drug dealer? This feels like a drug dealer's car.'

Quinn laughed. 'Bit conspicuous for a drug dealer. No, I'm a management consultant.'

'I feel like that's what a drug dealer would say.'

Minnie gave him a slow wink. He let out a deep rusty sort of laugh that caught in his throat. It was the kind of laugh that lulled people into an unearned familiarity. Hearing it made Minnie feel as though she was drinking hot wine by a log fire wrapped in Nordic furs. Not that she'd ever done this, but she imagined it would be a very enjoyable thing to do.

*

Their first delivery was to a social centre for the elderly near London Fields. Minnie said she would run in, Quinn could wait in the car, but he wanted to come too. Mrs Mentis, one of the regular volunteers at the centre, opened the door for them. She was a sweet lady in her late sixties. She wore purple varifocals and a chunky green cardigan trimmed with large buttons shaped like hedgehogs.

'Oh, hello Minnie, we haven't seen you for a while,' she said in a soft Yorkshire accent. 'It's usually your man Alan who comes. He's not poorly, I hope?'

Mrs Mentis looked up at Quinn and then moved her glasses down her nose to inspect him more closely. She pulled a grey handkerchief out of her pocket to wipe her nose.

'Oh he's fine,' Minnie said, 'just a mix-up with his van. This is Quinn, he's helping me out today.'

Minnie nodded a head towards Quinn and then made a 'these pies are quite heavy, can we just get to the kitchen please' face. Mrs Mentis took the hint and moved aside.

'Just down to your left, Quint,' she said, pointing the way with a wavering arm. Minnie and Quinn walked past her and Mrs Mentis hobbled after them. She was plagued by bunion trouble; Minnie had heard about it at great length over the last few years. She had named her bunions Billy and Boo and talked about them as though they were her grandchildren.

'How are the feet, Mrs Mentis?' Minnie asked.

'Oh Billy's not so bad, Minnie, but Boo's playing up no end she is – doesn't like this weather.'

The kitchen was small and beige. It smelt of cleaning fluid and marmalade. There were a few old coffee cups and an abandoned game of checkers on the beige Formica table.

'Everyone loves pie day,' said Mrs Mentis, opening one of the lids to see inside. 'I hope steak and Guinness is on the menu?'

'Always,' said Minnie. 'Do you have someone to help you warm them up? They're fresh this morning but could do with thirty minutes in the oven.'

'Yes, everyone likes to volunteer on pie day,' said Mrs Mentis, licking her lips. Then she turned her attention back to Quinn, who was stacking boxes straight into the fridge. 'Oh isn't he helpful? Is this the boyfriend Alan mentioned?'

Mrs Mentis waggled a finger at Quinn.

'Afraid not, I'm just the driver,' Quinn explained.

'You haven't taken Alan's job I hope?' Mrs Mentis frowned. 'The ladies upstairs would be most aggrieved. They like having a cuppa with Alan, they do – bit of a dish, they say. Not that Quint here isn't, but not such a one for the over-sixties perhaps.'

'Don't write me off too quickly, Mrs Mentis, you haven't seen me play bridge.'

Mrs Mentis let out a slow, throaty chuckle. 'I can see why he's your type, dear – nice to have a bit of girth to hold onto, isn't it?'

Minnie's eyes widened; Mrs Mentis was prone to getting words slightly wrong. Minnie doubted she meant to use the word 'girth'.

'No, he's not my type, Mrs Mentis, Quinn's just a friend helping me out today.'

Quinn silently mouthed 'not your type?' at Minnie, then made a mock wounded face, his dark eyebrows knitting together in overblown consternation. Minnie couldn't help smiling.

'You aren't this funny journalist then?' asked Mrs Mentis, counting the pies off on her fingers. Minnie was beginning to see why Alan took so long doing the deliveries.

'That's Greg, he's *ever* so funny,' said Quinn, leaning conspiratorially towards Mrs Mentis. 'Not quite as gifted as me in the girth department though.'

Minnie let out an involuntary high-pitched noise. She clutched a hand over her mouth, turning the sound into a strangled sort of sneeze.

'Bless you dear,' said Mrs Mentis, turning her attention back to Quinn. 'I used to be lithe and bonny-faced like Minnie here, you know. Had the pick of them in my day, I did.'

'I can certainly believe that, Mrs Mentis,' said Quinn.

'Now Quint, while we have you here, you wouldn't mind having a peek at the air vent in the social room, would you? It rattles no end on a windy night, and we're hard pressed to reach. Someone of your size won't have any problems giving it a little sort out.'

The next dozen deliveries were equally time-consuming. Quinn found himself fixing a dodgy aerial at Mrs McKenzie's flat, volunteering to hold Mrs Terry's wool with his 'nice big spool hands', then wrangling a broken flea collar back onto one of Mr Marchbanks's cats.

Quinn was obliging and charming with all her customers and Minnie felt herself softening towards him – he was impossible not to like. Yet beneath the surface there remained some ingrained mistrust, some Pavlovian conditioning that bristled at the name Quinn Hamilton and everything he stood for. When she saw him being kind and funny with her customers, her resolve to dislike him would melt. Then they'd get back to his Bentley and she'd remember – it's easy to be charming when you've led a charmed life.

'You have a way with the old folks,' Minnie said, looking across the bonnet at him as they stood outside Mr Marchbanks's house.

'I definitely don't have a way with cats,' Quinn said, holding up his scratched forearm to show her. Minnie opened the passenger door laughing.

'Poor diddums, did little puss-puss scratch you with his tiny claws?'

'I didn't see you volunteering.'

Quinn's cheek puckered into a dimple.

'The look on your face when he told you that you had the wrong cat,' Minnie said, letting out a little snort.

'That man didn't know which cat was which,' said Quinn, shaking his head. 'I could have collared next door's dog for all he knew.'

'Just because he's blind doesn't mean he can't tell his cats apart, Quinn. He says they all have very distinct smells,' Minnie said primly.

'His flat certainly has a very distinct smell.'

'Don't be mean, he's had a hard life that man.'

Quinn paused, the jokey expression falling from his face. 'I know. It's amazing what you do for these people, Minnie.'

'Oh yeah, pastry for pensioners – it's Nobel Prize-winning stuff.'

Minnie opened the car door and climbed in. Quinn got in next to her, his face still serious as he stared ahead out of the windscreen.

'You're clearly a lifeline to these people. It's so much more than just food delivery, it's ... ' Quinn trailed off, turning back to the windscreen. 'People need that connection in their day, someone dropping in just to see if they're OK.'

Minnie watched a small muscle in his jaw start to pulse. He turned back to Minnie and forced a smile. 'Not that I need to tell you, it's your brilliant business.'

'Not that brilliant,' Minnie sighed. 'Not financially anyway.'

'Well you need to start charging for cat collaring,' said Quinn, holding up his forearm again and pointing to the scratch marks.

'Aw, you need me to kiss it better?'

It was the kind of sarcasm she might have used with Ian or her brother, but Quinn responded with this piercing look. It felt as though someone had pressed pause between them and then Minnie realised she was holding her breath. He looked away and someone pressed play.

'Maybe we'll save the kissing for next time.'

Minnie knew he was joking, but him saying it sent a flurrying sensation through the depths of her belly. It felt like a nest of baby owls living dormant in her stomach had all woken up at once and started flapping their wings, ravenous to be fed. She clenched her teeth together, annoyed with herself for being so predictable, getting all Fleur-ish when someone like Quinn said anything vaguely flirtatious.

'Ha-ha,' she said, shaking her head slowly from side to side, trying to quell the feeling in her stomach. 'Right, enough of the chit-chat, chauffeur, we've got a lot more old folks to feed,' said Minnie, clapping her hands together.

*

By the time they came to the end of the delivery round, it was five o'clock. Quinn pulled over in a bus stop as there was nowhere to park. Minnie handed him the last pie box from the back seat.

'And this one is for you. It's hardly a fair trade for a whole day's driving, but if we factor in you stealing my name and taking a lifetime of good luck meant for me, I'd say we are near on quits.'

She should jump out, let him go before a bus came, but Minnie didn't move. She just sat there looking at him, her mouth stretching into an unconscious smile. His smile mirrored hers, then he rubbed a palm across his mouth and his eyes fell to his lap.

'Listen ...' said Quinn. The word hung in the air. 'If you have time, maybe ...' He looked down at his hand, flexed his fingers and then screwed them into a fist.

'Yes,' she nodded encouragingly.

'Well, I ... I know someone else who would love this pie.'

'Who's that?'

'My um, my mother.'

Quinn explained that he'd mentioned the story of her name to his mother and she wanted to meet Minnie. Minnie had a sinking feeling that she'd been set up. Had this whole offer of a ride been planned to make her feel obligated to go and meet the woman her mother reviled? Quinn had saved the day and she was sitting in the woman's car. She could hardly say no.

2 January 2020

Tara Hamilton lived in Primrose Hill in north London. As Quinn drove down the Camden Road, Minnie looked out of the window at all the street signs that were so familiar to her. She had grown up close to here. Seeing these streets through the window of a Bentley, she felt like Alice through the looking glass, peering at an alternate version of reality. After being born at the hospital in Hampstead, Minnie had lived with her parents and her brother in a two-bedroom ex-council flat in Chalk Farm, which was just over the railway bridge from Primrose Hill. They'd stayed there until Minnie was fifteen, when her parents had moved further north to get a house. Every memory from her childhood was tied up in this square mile of the city.

As Quinn turned onto Regent's Park Road, the city changed. The busy, dirty streets of Camden made way for the green gentility of Primrose Hill. Beautiful town houses with well-kept front gardens and perfectly painted shutters overlooked the park. Runners in designer Lycra with swishing ponytails bounced past. There were well-heeled people walking well-heeled dogs and distinguished-looking gentlemen in long camel coats, walking purposefully along the pavement with newspapers tucked beneath their arms.

'This is only about a mile from where I grew up, but it feels a world away,' said Minnie, watching the people and the houses that they passed. 'I haven't been back here for years. Isn't it funny how a place can revive such vivid memories from your childhood? There was a youth club we used to go to up in Kentish Town – if you didn't get off the night bus at the right place, you ended up on the bridge right there,' Minnie pointed down the street.

If you lived in a city for long enough, Minnie thought, the streets and the places where life happens fold inwards like paper, making space for new memories. Yet visiting old haunts and a long forgotten road was like stretching the concertina out again – the memories leap out, fresh as the day you folded them away.

'Bambers,' Minnie muttered to herself.

Quinn laughed, 'I remember Bambers.'

'I think Bambers has the honour of being the first place I threw up in after being introduced to Hooch,' said Minnie grimacing.

Quinn turned to look at her; a strange flash of something crossed his face. He squinted his eyes, a twitch of confusion. His reaction made Minnie feel as though she must have said something wrong. She turned to look out of the window. No doubt girls in Quinn's world didn't talk about times they got drunk and threw up.

When she was ten or eleven, Minnie and her best friend Lacey sometimes used to walk down to Primrose Hill Park after school. They'd make up stories about who lived in these colourful houses and what they'd done to make their money.

'Inventing cheese graters,' Lacey would say, pointing to a yellow mansion with frosted windows.

'Bouncy castles,' Minnie would laugh, pointing to the cream-coloured house on the corner. Every time they walked to the park, the stories would become more elaborate. Lacey concocted a whole back-story for the Cheese Grater Family – apparently there had been a family rift about the optimal size of the grating holes.

As Quinn pulled up beside the largest detached house on the street, Minnie's mouth fell open in disbelief; this was one of the houses she and Lacey used to make up stories about. A light blue, five-storey mansion that resembled a giant dolls' house, the kind of house a child might draw if they were drawing the perfect London home. There were neatly pruned box trees either side of the front door, and the blue frontage looked freshly painted. Black railings lined the property, with a hedge growing just behind them, shielding the ground floor from street view. It was an oasis of pristine calm in the centre of a bustling city.

The house sat in a line of other detached houses, all painted in different colours. Minnie and Lacey used to call them the Ice-Cream Houses. She wanted to tell Quinn he lived in the blueberry ice-cream house, but then she thought he might think she was some kind of weird house stalker so she didn't.

'This is where your mum lives?'

Quinn nodded.

'I grew up here. Now I have a flat up the road, but Mum's still here, rattling around.'

He got out of the driver's seat and came around the car to open her door. Minnie picked up the last pie and followed Quinn up the steps to the enormous front door. The light was starting to fade and she didn't have a coat. She shivered slightly. Quinn reached out to put his arm around her, rubbing the top of her arm. It was an instinctive, familiar gesture, as though he'd forgotten for a moment he was standing on the doorstep with a relative stranger, rather than his girlfriend. Minnie's skin tingled where he'd touched her. He dropped his arm as quickly as he'd offered it, thrusting hands into his pockets, searching for his keys in the half-light.

'Mum,' he called out as they went inside. 'I've brought a friend to see you.'

In the living room, they found Quinn's mother, sitting in an armchair, reading. She must have been in her early sixties, but she looked like a woman in her late forties. She had neatly combed blonde hair pinned up in a bun and her skin was dewy and unblemished. She wore a loose lilac housecoat tied at the waist, her feet girlishly curled beneath her in the chair. To Minnie, she looked like a film star.

'Quinn,' she said, closing her book and placing it carefully on the side table, 'I wasn't expecting you.'

She blinked a few times when she saw Minnie, as though checking to see if there was really another person there. Then she got to her feet, smoothing down her hair and her housecoat with the palms of her hands.

'Look at the state of me. I'm not dressed for house guests.'

Her forehead wrinkled into a soft frown, but she smiled at Minnie as she reached up to kiss her son on the cheek. Her voice was calm and gentle. Minnie felt a pang of envy for a mother like this, a mother who greeted you with a kiss and talked in hushed, honeyed tones.

'This is Minnie,' said Quinn, 'I told you about her; the girl who would have been Quinn.' Quinn took both his mother's hands in his and gently moved them up and down, as though physically channelling information to her. 'Minnie, this is my mother Tara.'

Tara turned to look at her, reaching out a hand to touch Minnie as though wanting to test her physicality. Tara's eyes grew wide as she took Minnie in, and Minnie squirmed under her gaze, embarrassed by such focused attention.

'Hi,' she said, with a brisk wave of her hand. 'I brought you a pie.'

She thrust the pie box towards Tara.

'Minnie? Minnie ...' Tara was still staring at her.

She didn't look as though she was going to take the pie box, so Minnie put it down on a side table.

'I don't know if you like pies, Quinn said you would.'

'Minnie, goodness, aren't you pretty? I always longed for curly hair,' said Tara. Minnie self-consciously pulled one of her curls straight. 'I'm so pleased you've come. When Quinn told me he'd met you, what you'd said about your birth ... I haven't been able to stop thinking about it. I've thought of your mother so often. I tried to find her after we left hospital, she helped me so much.'

'I know,' said Minnie, 'she told me. She also said you stole her name idea.' Minnie laughed awkwardly and gave a little shrug. She didn't want Tara to think she was angry about it. Who could be angry with a woman like this? It would be like being angry at a kitten.

'No, no,' Tara's face fell, 'that's not what happened. Quinn, didn't you tell her how it was?'

105

Tara looked distressed all of a sudden. She felt behind her for the arm of the sofa, sinking down into it. Quinn sat down beside her and held one of her hands between the palms of his.

'Don't get upset, Mum,' he said softly. 'I did explain, but I thought you could tell her yourself.'

Quinn went to make a pot of Earl Grey tea and Minnie took a seat on the sofa next to Tara. She looked so frail and small against the giant white cushions, as though she might sink into the sofa's folds and never be able to get out again. Minnie sat quietly, letting Tara talk.

The times Minnie had imagined meeting this woman, this villain from her childhood, the person who'd upset her own mother so much, she'd imagined all the things she would say. Now she was here, she didn't want to say anything, she just wanted to listen.

Tara explained how much Connie's help had meant to her, how alone she'd felt during labour, how close to breaking point she had been.

'Connie told me the story of the name Quinn, and it was as if this light went on in the darkness. My body was being pulled in two and this name, Connie's face – it was the only part of reality I could hold on to.' Tara looked up at the ceiling, temporarily lost in thought. 'When the baby was born, I couldn't think of any other name that would do. I wanted to have a Quinn too – a tribute to your mother and the help she gave me. I didn't even think about the stupid newspaper competition; it didn't cross my mind she wouldn't call you Quinn too.'

Now Tara was looking at her, waiting for some response.

'You were all over the papers. Quinn's not a common name. My dad thought they'd look silly if they chose the same name as the baby in the news.'

'I tried to find Connie afterwards, I couldn't remember her surname. I even looked at the birth announcements for another Quinn. The hospital wouldn't give me her details. I thought maybe she'd get in touch with me.'

Quinn came back into the room and put a tray of tea things down on the large ottoman-style coffee table.

'Don't get too worked up,' he said, pressing a hand gently onto his mother's shoulder. She reached up to squeeze it and Minnie felt another pang for this closeness between them. She didn't have that kind of relationship with her mother.

'And now I hear all these years later that she despises me, that I'd stolen your name and you've been seething with resentment all these years. I can't bear it,' Tara let out a sniff and pressed the back of her hand to her nose, her eyes welling with tears.

'Well, I wouldn't say seething exactly.' Minnie felt her cheeks go pink. She started biting the nail on her left thumb, then yanked it away from her mouth and sat on her hands.

'I would love to see Connie again, to tell her how sorry I am. When I think what she must have thought of me.'

'It's only a name, I shouldn't worry about it,' Minnie said, reaching out to pat Tara's hand.

Over Tara's shoulder she saw Quinn mouthing 'only a name?' at her. Minnie narrowed her eyes at him; he was relishing this.

107

'And then to be called Minnie Cooper instead,' Tara shook her head, her lip puckering in distaste. 'You poor thing.'

'It's not that bad,' Minnie said, retracting her hand.

'No, it could have been worse, Ford Fiesta or Vauxhall Corsa,' said Quinn. Minnie felt a strong urge to throw the teapot at him.

She took Tara's number and said she would get her mother to call her. She warned her that her mother could be a little prickly, but she was sure she would listen. Tara clutched her thin hands around Minnie's and shook them gently. Then she excused herself to go to the bathroom.

'Thank you,' Quinn said quietly from across the room.

'What for?' Minnie asked.

'For being kind to her.'

When Tara returned, she insisted Minnie stay for dinner. She said she never had visitors and wanted to hear all about Minnie's life. Minnie felt as though she was having some kind of *Sliding Doors* moment. She was Gwyneth Paltrow with the short blonde hair, living in an alternate reality where her mother's nemesis invited her to dinner at the blueberry ice-cream house. Perhaps another version of Minnie was currently finishing the deliveries with Alan in the van. Minnie made a mental note to suggest *Sliding Doors* for her next movie night with Leila.

As they moved through to the kitchen, Quinn told his mother all about No Hard Fillings, about the people he'd met that day and how great Minnie's pies were.

'You haven't tried one yet,' said Minnie.

It made her feel a little giddy hearing him talk about her business in such glowing terms.

'Finally, I get to sample one,' Quinn said, turning on the oven. 'I only had to give up my day, chauffeur you around London, get mauled by a cat, fix a dodgy aerial and try to put right a decades-old wrong.'

Minnie smiled, wrinkling her nose at him. Quinn smiled back at her, their eyes connecting for a moment, and Minnie felt the room close in around her. Tara looked back and forth between them as though observing something for the first time. Minnie's phone started to ring and it took her a moment to realise it was hers.

'I, um, I'd better get this,' she said, seeing from the screen it was Leila.

She stepped back into the living room, leaving Quinn and his mother talking in the kitchen.

'How did it go?' said Leila. 'Did you get everything done?'

Leila's tone was more perfunctory than Minnie expected; she thought Leila would be calling to get the low-down on her day out with her love twin.

'Yes, pies all delivered, customers happy. I'm just at Quinn's mother's house, Leils, she wanted to tell me all about—' said Minnie, but Leila cut her off.

'Listen, we've had a bit of a shocker this end. I just got off the phone with the bank and they won't extend our loan.'

'I thought we had until next month to pay?' Minnie said.

'So did I,' sighed Leila. 'I thought if we could just get the subsidy funding through from the council and then push our deliveries this month, we'd be able to scrape by, but we won't find out about the funding until February and we just don't have enough orders this month to make what we owe.

Everyone's broke after Christmas. I can't see a way around it, Minnie.'

Minnie sat down on the plush white sofa and hung her head in her hands. She and Leila had put four years of their life into this. They'd sweated, they'd worked seventy-hour weeks, they'd put in all their savings, and now what? They'd just close up shop, let their staff go, hand the kitchen's lease over to the next naïve young fool who wanted to watch their dream slowly wither?

'There's nothing we can do to hold them off?' Minnie asked, squeezing her eyes tight shut. Was she really going to lose her flat and her business in the same week?

'Minnie, I just can't see a way through this,' Leila said quietly. 'Every month feels like the Pamplona bull run, just madly dashing to stay alive and not to get gored by some raging bank bull. I've tried not to stress you out with the funding side of things, but I just can't hold up the dam any more.'

Minnie could hear the stress in her friend's voice. Leila took on most of the company's financial responsibilities. Minnie hated that it was her dream to run a baking business that had brought her best friend this low. 'Listen, let's just meet at the office on Monday and go through how we're going to manage this. I can't do anything more this week, I've got Ian's sister's wedding tomorrow.'

'Should I call the others?' asked Minnie. They only employed Bev, Alan and Fleur part-time, so no one would be in until Monday now.

'No, I'd rather tell them the bad news together, once we know what's happening. We've got pre-paid orders we need to deliver, so we need them to come in.'

Once Minnie had put the phone down, she looked around at the enormous living room she was sitting in; the luxuriously thick cream rug, the plush linen cushions in perfectly coordinated duck egg fabrics, the enormous ottoman coffee table with a shelf beneath full of exquisite, hardbacked coffee-table books. She heard Tara laughing in the kitchen.

'Everything OK?' Quinn said from the doorway to the living room.

'I need to go home, I'm afraid,' Minnie said, taking a slow breath in through her nose.

'Really? I've just put the pie in,' Quinn's face fell.

'I have to go,' she said, 'I can get the Tube.'

Minnie suddenly needed to be far away from Quinn. What was she even doing here? She knew it wasn't his fault, that it was ridiculous to compare her life with his, but something about the fact that they'd started life on the same day, in the same place, just made her current situation feel all the more pathetic.

'I'll drive you,' he said.

She shook her head, she could feel a flush creeping up her neck, the telltale sign that she was about to cry.

'Has something happened? Is there anything I can do?'

'Well, my business is bust and now I have to go to work on Monday and work out how to close it down, so no, there's nothing you can do.'

111

Minnie dropped her eyes to the floor; she couldn't look at him. Why had she told him that? She sensed him taking a step towards her, she felt he might be about to hug her. For a moment her body tingled in anticipation, hoping for him to put his arms around her. Then her body tensed, angry with herself for feeling this primal urge to be hugged. Besides, Quinn wasn't even her boyfriend; if she wanted to sink into anyone's arms (which she didn't, there would be no pathetic arm-sinking), it should be Greg's. Shit, she really needed to call Greg.

'But your pies are great? People love them, surely there's a way—' Quinn started to talk but Minnie cut him off.

'Yeah, but in the real world we have to take loans to start a business, loans with massive interest on them, and if we have a month with fewer orders or we have to buy a new door for the oven, then we don't have much margin for error,' Minnie said through gritted teeth. 'It's not like in your world where you just get money from your family to set up whatever business you like and probably never even deal with a bank. I mean, look at this place!'

Minnie flung out her arm to illustrate the point. In doing so she knocked over one of the china lamp-stands and it flew off the side table, smashing onto the floor. The room was silent. Minnie stared at the broken shards. The light bulb blinked, made a quiet fizzing sound, and then died.

'Oh shit,' Minnie said under her breath.

She looked up to see Quinn's face had turned ghostly. Tara came running into the room. When she saw the lamp, she started hyperventilating.

'Don't touch it, don't touch it, you'll cut yourself!' She started shaking her hands, her eyes bulging in panic. 'Quinn, there's broken china everywhere.'

In two swift strides Quinn was at her side, 'It's OK, I'm not going to touch it.' He was talking to her in a strange tone, as though he was talking to a child. Tara was shaking, she covered her head in her hands and let out a strange panicked burst of cries. Quinn turned back to Minnie.

'I think you'd better go,' he said.

'Don't let her touch it!' cried Tara. 'Don't touch it!'

'She's not going to touch it, Mum,' said Quinn as he led the hunched figure of his mother out of the room. 'Come on, I'll take you upstairs.'

Minnie was left alone in the living room, frozen to the spot. What just happened? She'd shouted at Quinn, broken a really expensive-looking lamp and then Tara had totally lost it. Should she stay and clear up the mess? Offer to pay for it? Not that she had any money anyway. Why had she taken her anger out on Quinn like that? They'd been having such a great afternoon and she'd ruined it. She picked up her bag from the floor and quietly let herself out of the enormous front door.

Minnie paused at the grey, paint-chipped front door of her parents' house. She hugged the mustard-yellow woollen cape she was wearing around herself. The cape had been an ill-advised purchase from a charity shop last year; something Leila had persuaded her was a 'must-have' fashion item. Minnie had quickly concluded the cape made her look like a walking banana, which is why she'd only worn it two times (and one of those was to a fruit-themed fancy-dress party.) Now, since she'd lost her only coat and it was two degrees outside, the cape had, by necessity, been resurrected from the depths of her wardrobe.

She could hear the hum of noise inside the house, the ticking audible even from the doorstep. She took a moment to savour the quiet of the street. Since her brother Will had moved to Australia with his girlfriend, Minnie had tried to come home most Sundays to have a meal with her parents. She knew they missed having Will around, he had a way of being with them that felt easy. She couldn't fill the hole his absence had created in the family dynamic, but she felt she was doing her bit by showing up every week.

'Minnie's here,' shouted her dad from above. Minnie looked up to see him leaning out of the bedroom window. 'Just dealing with a blocked toilet up here; your Ma had too much quiche past its "best before" again.'

Her dad was wearing his work T-shirt, covered in paint and sweat stains, his round face looked ruddy and dishevelled, as though he'd been doing jobs all morning and hadn't got around to taking a shower. He winked at Minnie and she shook her head. Minnie heard her mother shouting up the stairs inside, something about it not being funny to make crude jokes to the whole goddamn street.

'What you hanging around outside for, Minnie Moo? In you hop,' said her dad, waving her in.

The house was part of a 1930s terrace. It looked the same as most other houses on this particular suburban street of Brent Cross, north London. Theirs had slightly rotten wood on the downstairs window frames and an unruly front yard swamped by brambles and wild roses, but otherwise, there wasn't much to distinguish it from the neighbours. From the back garden you could see lots of the other houses on the street had added kitchen extensions, or done loft conversions, but the Coopers' house looked pretty much as it had nearly a hundred years ago. When Minnie mentioned Brent Cross to people, they thought of the huge out-of-town shopping centre, or the busy motorway flyover. For Minnie, Brent Cross would always mean this house, this street, this tiny spot of London she called home.

Inside, number thirteen looked like a pretty normal house; well, normal if you didn't look at the walls. Every inch of wall space was covered in clocks, a testament to her father's interest in horology. He had spent the last thirty years collecting and repairing antique clocks. He had a workshop in the garden full of boxes and tools, and spent his evenings scouring the internet for broken clocks or half-repaired clocks that everyone else had given up on.

Sometimes her Dad spent years on one clock, waiting for the right piece to come online or trying to fashion a missing cog himself. The time and effort that went into each piece meant he never wanted to part with one. So the clock army grew, ticking, tocking, some tick-tick-tocking; it was an overwhelming sound when you first walked through the door. Neither of her parents noticed the sound any more. 'It's the heartbeat of the house,' her dad once explained, 'you don't spend all day being annoyed by the sound of your own heartbeat, do you?'

Minnie didn't think that was a good analogy, but there was no point arguing with Dad about the clocks. The orchestra of ticks and tocks had been the soundtrack to her childhood. She and Will used to play a game where they took turns to blindfold each other, and then they'd take a clock from the wall and try to identify it by sound alone. Will called the game 'Name That Clock' – not an especially inventive title. The game had come to an unpleasant conclusion when Will had dropped a clock and broken one of the hands off. Minnie had never seen her dad so mad before or since.

Minnie's mother met her in the hallway, and her eyes instantly fell to Minnie's hair.

'You've cut your hair. I thought you were growing it out?' she said, reaching up to gently tug one of Minnie's curls.

'Well, I felt like a change,' Minnie shrugged. 'Don't you like it?'

'If you want to grow it, it takes time, you have to persevere.' Connie gave an exasperated sigh. 'Your generation never stick anything out.'

'Mum, I don't think me getting a haircut is symptomatic of my being in the snowflake generation.'

Minnie took off her cape and hung it on one of the coat pegs in the corridor.

'It's like your swimming lessons all over again.'

'Mum, you can't still be mad at me for giving up Saturday morning swimming – I'm thirty!'

Her mother gave a little shake of the head, like a duck shaking off rainwater.

'I spent an arm and a leg on those lessons, and you had such a talent for it, Minnie. Now, did you at least bring a pie?'

'Was I supposed to?'

Her mother groaned.

'Well, it'd be nice not to cook once in a while, when we've got a "chef" in the family.' She said 'chef' the way she always said it, in a posh accent with a regal hand flourish. 'Your dad's just got back, been no help to anyone, and I didn't sit down all shift. We were a nurse short on the ward, and not enough beds as usual.' Minnie followed her mother through to the kitchen and watched her sit down on one of the kitchen chairs with a resigned sigh. 'My poor Mr Cunningham got sent home, and he was in no fit state to go.'

'I'm sorry you've had a hard day, Mum,' said Minnie.

'I don't know what the world's coming to sometimes,' her mother said, closing her eyes. 'How can some people have so much, and then our hospital doesn't even have a bed for a man who just wants to pass on with a little dignity?'

Minnie reached out to touch her mother's hand, but her mother didn't see, and moved hers from the table before she could reach it. Minnie picked up a button instead. There was a collection of broken objects in front of her, waiting to be mended: a saucepan without a handle, a small button with 'hot' written on it, and the decapitated head of a ceramic dog.

'You don't need to go to any trouble, Mum. I'm honestly happy with beans on toast. I've just come to see you both.'

'Well, that's what you'll be getting at this rate. Now, would you help me find this dog's body, Minnie? It must be in that lounge somewhere.'

Her mother waved a hand towards the front room and Minnie did as she was asked. In the lounge the tick-tock of the clocks was marginally quieter. Her dad had designed it that way so as not to disrupt his programmes.

Of all the clocks in the house, there was only one that Minnie was genuinely fond of. It hung in pride of place above the TV – Coggie. She'd bought it for Dad from a car-boot sale up at Pick's Cottage when she was sixteen. When she found it, it didn't work; the bell on top had rusted and the seven and the four on the face had been scratched away. It had clearly been uncared for and unloved for many years, yet there remained some understated regal quality in that clock's face, as if – even though it couldn't tell you the time – it might tell you something else important, if only it could speak.

Minnie liked the hole in the face that let you watch the cogs whirring behind. The bell on the top was struck by a small pin every hour, and in amongst the clamour of clocks, it was the one bell she didn't mind the sound of. Such a gentle proclamation of another hour gone, not a grandiose gong like some of the more entitled clocks.

Minnie bent down on her hands and knees and reached beneath the sofa searching for the lost piece of dog her mother was looking for. She heard her father's footsteps heavy on the stairs.

'Let's have no more talk about beans on toast – we'll just get a takeaway, shall we, love?' Minnie's dad bellowed in the direction of the kitchen, then he stomped into the lounge. Minnie saw his big workman's boots stop next to her head. 'What you doing down there?'

'Looking for half a dog,' she said.

He frowned. 'Don't be putting her to work, Connie. Get the girl a drink and let's get a Chinese in, hey?'

He sat down in his worn brown cord armchair. The chair made a slow wheezing sound as though it had been winded. He reached for the remote control on the side table.

'Notice anything different in here, Minnie Moo?' he asked. Minnie stood up and straightened the blue woollen jumper she was wearing. She looked around for a new clock.

'Up there,' she said, pointing above the bookcase to the left of the TV. There was a small wooden Vienna regulator wall clock, with a pendulum as large as its face.

'Finally found that missing piece, didn't I. Bloke in Hamburg sold it to me for a pretty penny, I've been haggling with him for months.'

'Very impressive, Dad – looks good as new.'

Her father grinned, his broad ruddy cheeks balled to the size of apples. To look at him you wouldn't imagine Bill Cooper had the sleight of hand or the patience to repair minute pieces of machinery. He had arms like tree trunks and shoulders like an ox, perfect for hauling heavy loads. Yet his real strength lay in the fine-motor coordination of his fingertips and an unlikely interest in antique clockwork.

'Anyway, *Bake Off* time. Have you been watching, Minnie Moo?'

'What series is this?'

'It's a repeat – never gets old. I reckon you'd get a handshake off Paul Hollywood for your pies.' He raised his voice. 'Con, it's pastry week!' Then he turned back to Minnie. 'Grab me a beer, love, would you?'

Minnie stopped searching for the dog and went back through to the kitchen. The sound of the television accompanied by a cacophony of ticking, coupled with her instant reappointment as resident barmaid, made Minnie feel as though she'd never left; life felt exactly as it had nine years ago. Technically, she'd only moved out three years ago – she'd had to move home briefly when they were setting up the business. Then there were those few months back in 2011 when she'd suddenly found herself unemployed. Minnie felt queasy thinking about that period of her life. Was this the pattern she was condemned to: move out, try and make a go of a new job, fail, move home and start all over again? The Brent Cross house toying with her as if she were a yo-yo, spitting her out into the real world only to reel her back in again as soon as she overstretched herself.

Now, here she was about to ask her parents if she could move back in again. Minnie's palms felt cold and clammy at the thought of living here again. She'd considered looking for a flat share, but with all the scratch marks Lucky had made in her current flat, she wasn't holding out much hope of getting her deposit back. She didn't have the funds to put down another one, and most people weren't keen on living with an extra four-legged furry flatmate anyway. She opened the fridge door to get two beers, one for herself and one for her dad.

'So, what happened to you on your birthday?' asked her mum, hand on hip. 'There's usually a tale to tell.'

Minnie didn't want to lend fuel to her mother's narrative about her birthday bad luck. She shrugged.

'Not much – went to Alan's for dinner, then on to a party.' Minnie nipped through to give her father his beer, then came back to the kitchen and opened her own. 'Oh, but guess who I met, Mum?' Her mother had started chopping onions. 'Well? Who do you think I ran into?' Minnie asked again.

'If it's a celebrity, I won't have heard of them. Unless it's Paul Hollywood because his is the only voice I hear around here,' she said loudly. 'Your father is obsessed with that show. You know he watches them all on repeat?'

Minnie didn't know which it was better to reveal first – her meeting with Tara and Quinn, or the news about her business failing and needing to move home. Part of her would relish seeing the look on her mum's face when she mentioned Tara's name; no part of her would relish admitting that No Hard Fillings was broke. She decided to go with the more relishing option.

'Have you spoken to Will recently?' asked her mother, veering off on to a new topic.

'No.' Minnie rolled her eyes to the ceiling.

'Says he's put an offer in on a house out there, somewhere in Bondi. So impressive at his age – we didn't manage to buy till we were past forty.'

'Well, it's probably cheaper out there,' Minnie said, feeling her jaw tense.

'I don't know how you're ever going to get on the property ladder, Minnie. We were saving for eighteen years to get our deposit together.'

'Well, I don't think my generation are going to be able to buy, are we,' said Minnie, pulling the metal tab from her beer can and squeezing it into her palm.

'You're brother's buying.'

'*Quinn Hamilton! I met Quinn Hamilton,*' said Minnie loudly.

Connie dropped the knife on the chopping board and Minnie savoured the moment – finally her mother was listening.

'And I met his mother, Tara. She lives in a mansion in Primrose Hill. She's ever so elegant, she looks like a film star,' Minnie pinched her lips together.

'Tara Hamilton? You went to Tara Hamilton's house?' her mother asked, her voice lacking any of its usual resonance.

'Yup,' said Minnie, taking another swig of beer and leaning back against the fridge, one foot up against its door.

Her mother frowned at her, then went back to aggressively chopping onions.

'Well, I'm sure it's easy to look like a film star when you're a millionaire, living the bleeding life of Riley.'

'I ran into Quinn by chance at a party and I told him what you said about Tara taking my name. It's not what she meant to do at all, Mum; she meant to call him Quinn as a tribute to you for all the help you gave her. She never imagined you wouldn't call me Quinn too.'

'What are you bringing all this up for, Minnie?' her mum said, turning around and frowning at Minnie. 'Why are you going around town talking about me to people?'

'It's not people, Mum, it's Tara Hamilton – can you believe it, after all this time?'

'I don't need you rewriting history, Minnie. No one wants this all raked up.'

Her mother turned back to her chopping board. She picked up a saucepan from the counter and briskly swiped the onions into it, turning her back to Minnie as she moved the pan to the hob. They stood in silence. The *Bake Off* theme tune blared out from the next-door room; a hundred clock hands ticked.

'You going to find that dog for me or what?' said her mother.

'Look, I got her number, I said you'd call her. Here, I'm writing it down and putting it on the fridge.'

Minnie couldn't see her mother's face but she saw her back go rigid before she reached up to the cupboard above the stove for a can of tomatoes. This wasn't the reaction Minnie had expected.

'Right, ad break, what are we ordering? I got a hankering for a vanilla and pistachio mille-foy with crème anglaisey,' said Minnie's dad, chuckling to himself as he came through to the kitchen. 'It doesn't half whet your appetite, that show! Oh, you're cooking are you, Con?'

He pulled out a kitchen chair and sank his weight down onto it. He looked back and forth between his wife and daughter, then started tapping the broken pan-handle against the wooden kitchen table. 'What you both looking so gloomy about?'

'Nothing, stuff and nonsense,' said her mother briskly. 'Right, someone get the cheese out of the fridge. Can't have pasta without cheese, can we?'

Over dinner, Minnie broke the news about the business. She asked if she could move home for a while. Her dad kicked back in his chair, balancing it precariously on two legs.

'That's a real shame, love, I always loved your cooking, thought you were onto a real winner there.'

He reached out and patted Minnie's back. When her dad said something nice to her, it made Minnie want to curl up on his lap like she had as a girl. They used to watch endless *Star Wars* films together, and her dad would do all the characters' voices. Minnie turned to look at her mother, who was methodically chewing a mouthful of pasta. She swallowed loudly, then without looking at Minnie started twirling another forkful of pasta.

'You're not going to say anything, Mum?'

'I think I'm getting déjà vu,' she said, reaching for a glass of water.

'Come on, love, that's not fair,' said her dad. 'She's not had a business fail before. There might have been other things gone wrong, but it's not the same.'

Minnie's mother stared wordlessly at her husband.

'I think she means you, Dad, your business,' Minnie said quietly.

'Oh.' Once he'd said the word, Dad held his lips locked in an awkward 'O' shape, and he lowered the chair slowly back onto all four legs.

'I said it was a mistake,' her mum went on, 'I said it was a disaster waiting to happen. You didn't even go to college, Minnie, how you supposed to know about money and bookkeeping?'

'Leila did the books, Mum, and just because I didn't go to university doesn't mean I haven't got a brain for business. It's all been going fine for the last few years, we've worked our arses off, we just hit a ... a rough patch.'

'I said all this to your father. Why will no one ever listen to me?' her mother said, shaking her head.

'Look, I know you're disappointed,' said Minnie, feeling her voice catch in her throat. 'I'm disappointed too. You think at thirty I wanted to be broke, unemployed and moving home? You think this is how I planned my life to pan out. Mum?' She paused. 'At least I gave it a go.'

'Your dad gave it a go too. Gambled all our savings on that property he was doing up. Cooper Development Company might have sounded grand, but a fancy name's not much use to you when the bottom falls out of the market.'

'Bad luck, wasn't it. I would have done a great job on that house,' said her dad wistfully.

'Some things aren't worth the risk. You risk, you lose, that's what I've learnt. Best to keep your head down and play the hand you're dealt.'

Minnie pressed her fingernails into the underside of her chair. She felt the familiar grooves in the wood from where she'd done this before.

'Well, if you're coming home, there's not much room upstairs,' said her mother flatly. 'The loft room's full of all your dad's clock bits now.'

'I can clear that out in half a jiffy,' said her dad, 'or she could stay in Will's room?'

'And what is Will supposed to do when he comes to visit?' said her mum.

'He hasn't been home in two years, Mum,' said Minnie.

'Give her a break, Connie. You can stay as long as you need, Minnie Moo. I'll clear out space in your old room this afternoon,' said her dad, reaching out to squeeze Minnie's shoulder.

Her mother took another mouthful of food. The crushing feeling of inadequacy broke over Minnie like a wave. How could her parents spend so much of their lives fixing things and fail to see what was broken right in front of them?

New Year's Eve 2010

'Don't touch that plate before it's garnished,' Rob the pastry chef screamed across the kitchen.

Minnie whipped her hand back from the service counter as though she'd been scalded. She hadn't even planned on picking it up, she had just been straightening the plate. In any other environment she would have talked back, defended herself, but in this kitchen she'd quickly learnt you said, 'Yes chef', and took whatever criticism was dished out.

Minnie had been working in Le Lieu de Rencontre for six months. It was a Michelin-star restaurant in Mayfair and a very different experience to the place she'd worked before. Victor's, where she'd got a job straight out of school, had been a family-run restaurant in Kentish Town. There had only been three chefs in a cramped kitchen, whereas here there were usually over twenty people cooking at any one time. The clientele at Victor's had been families and young foodies, whereas Rencontre was stuffed with city suits with expense accounts who liked to be seen in expensive places. At Victor's she'd been allowed to cook. Here she was barely allowed to turn on the oven.

Minnie had left school with no clear career plan or vocation. It had been Leila who'd suggested she learn to cook.

'You've got a natural taste for food, you always know what's going to work well together,' Leila said.

'What bangers and mash, spag and Bol, Weetabix and milk?' Minnie laughed.

'I'm serious, Min, you've got a natural flair. If you got trained up in a proper kitchen, you could be really good.'

She'd been amazed when they'd offered her the job at Victor's; she had no experience and barely a CV. Paul, the head chef, had asked her to cook him a Spanish omelette and hired her on the spot as he watched her make it. She'd loved working with Paul, the atmosphere of the cosy family-run restaurant, the regulars who came in, learning about food, improving her skills week on week. It was Victor himself, the elderly French owner, who had told her to leave.

'Minnie, you have a gift, but you can't learn everything from Paul. You need to work in more kitchens, see how other chefs work. Only then will you grow.'

'But I love it here, I've still got so much to learn,' Minnie protested.

'We have a saying in France, "À chaque oiseau son nid est beau" – the bird loves his own nest. You don't know any other nest, Minnie. You must spread your wings and learn to fly.'

As Victor spoke, a slow smile spread across his leathery lined face. It was the face of a man who'd lived well, who'd spent a lot of time in the sun and drunk red wine every day of his adult life.

So she'd spread her wings and landed at Rencontre. She'd been there six months and she hated it. It was a huge team and every commis chef around her had sharp elbows and even sharper tongues. She was on rotation working beneath various specialist chefs. This month she was assigned to the pastry chef, and he was the worst yet. Rob had taken against Minnie from her very first day. There was a dish on the menu served with a saffron butter sauce. Minnie had mentioned how at Victor's they'd made a similar sauce but with a squeeze of lime rather than lemon. Rob humiliated her in front of everyone, asking if she wanted to rewrite the whole menu that had been designed by a Michelin-star chef. She'd quickly learnt to keep her thoughts on the food to herself.

She wanted to stick it out for a year, try and move up from second commis to first. This place would look great on her CV if she could leave with a good reference. But the hours were gruelling, the pace exhausting, and she didn't even feel she was learning much.

Tonight was New Year's Eve and the place was packed. She didn't want to work tonight, but she'd been rota'd on all week without a break. She'd missed Christmas with her family and worked fifteen-hour days; her whole body ached with fatigue. All week she'd been charged with the monotonous job of piping brandy crème patissière into miniature Christmas puddings. They were to be served as *mignardises* – or petits fours – after the dessert course. The puddings were the size of walnuts and they had to be delicately holed out then filled in such a way that not a drop of filling was visible.

'No.'

'Again.'

'Not right.'

'Sloppy!'

'Minnie, you're a fucking disgrace of a pastry chef. Where did you learn to bake again? Greggs?'

Rob had been screaming at her all afternoon. Her piping was good and she knew it; he was just making her do it again and again because he could. She'd just finished a perfect sheet of twenty when he'd loomed over her, inspected one, then tossed the whole batch on the floor.

'The crème pat is warm, you've overworked it.'

Rob's face darted forward, inches from hers. His grey skin and stinking breath made her want to gag. He had eye bags that stretched down to his cheeks, giving the impression that his face was melting. 'Do you even taste your food, or are you trying to watch your figure?'

Minnie composed a blank expression, trying not to react. A few of the other commis chefs looked on sympathetically; they knew Rob went too far with Minnie. The first week she'd worked there, a few of them had gone for a drink after their shift. Rob had made a pass at Minnie after a few too many beers. She'd pushed him away as politely as possible, but Rob wasn't the kind of guy who could brush off a perceived slight. He acted as though any woman working in his kitchen was another ingredient in his pantry, to be used as he saw fit.

'If you're packing on a few extra pounds, it's not my problem, Minnie,' Rob hissed. 'If you're going to overwork the crème like an amateur, you'd better taste every batch before it leaves this station.'

Minnie had tasted it; it wasn't overworked. She cleared up the mess and picked up a new piping bag. If she could endure one more week she'd move out from Rob's rotation, maybe then life at the restaurant would get easier.

'Don't let him get to you,' hissed Danna, giving Minnie's elbow a squeeze as she walked past. Danna worked in the fish section and hardly ever spoke to Minnie. She was Norwegian, aloof and as ambitious as the rest of them. If she was being sympathetic then it must have looked bad.

At ten to midnight, Minnie had just plated up two miniature puddings for table fifteen. Rob breathed down her neck as she added the final garnish, a delicate holly leaf and a sprinkle of edible gold glitter. He glared at them and made a low growling noise. Even he couldn't find anything to fault and they were now too busy for him to be inventing problems.

'Service!' Rob called to the serving staff on the other side of the line.

Minnie was almost done, her shift ended at one o'clock. She needed a shower, she needed to sleep, she needed to not see another miniature crème-patissière-filled Christmas pudding for a very long time.

She started cleaning up her station, wiping down the surfaces and collecting utensils for cleaning when she heard Rob's voice screaming across the kitchen.

'Minnie, did you send a pudding to table fifteen?' Rob strode across the room towards her, holding his hand – balled into a fist – out in front of him.

'Yes ...' she said, nervously.

He opened his hand, pointing at the remains of a pudding in his palm. Inside, was a tiny, chewed piece of clear plastic.

'Just been sent back. Plastic in your piped filling.' He spoke slowly, relishing every syllable.

Minnie looked down at his hand and her face went pale. It looked like a piece of the plastic from the piping bag she'd been using. How could that even have come off, let alone got in the filling? Then she remembered she'd started a new one, cutting the end off to let the crème run out. Had she definitely cut off the end properly?

A grin spread across Rob's face as he waved the tiny piece of plastic in her face.

'I've just been waiting for a reason to fire you,' he said quietly, his crooked front tooth snagging on his bottom lip.

Minnie felt numb for a second. If she got fired she wouldn't get a reference, it would all have been for nothing. Every mean thing Rob had ever said flashed through her mind and she didn't feel numb any more, she felt angry.

In her mind, she visualised picking up the piping bag from the counter next to her, aiming it at Rob's face and squeezing it as hard as she could. The crème pat would spray out in a perfect consistency, covering his face and hair. He would freeze in shock, or rage, rooted to the spot. The kitchen staff would all turn to see what was happening; a few brave people would whoop and cheer.

'Go, Minnie!' Danna would yell from the back.

Minnie's heart raced. She would reach out for a handful of holly leaves and add them to Rob's head as a garnish.

'And don't forget the glitter,' she would say, picking up a handful of gold and adding it with a flourish to his crème-covered face. 'Service!' Minnie would shout.

She would hear laughter all around her, people with hands clasped over their mouths – she would be a hero! Rob would wipe the crème from his eyes, his grey skin now puce, his mouth hanging open in shock. Minnie would pull off her hairnet, turn and walk out of the kitchen with her head held high, a soundtrack belting out Aretha Franklin's 'Respect' at full volume as she danced from the room and everyone watched her go.

In reality, there was no soundtrack, no spraying of crème pat, Minnie would not dare. She simply picked up her apron and left with her hat in her hand. No one watched her go and the sea of the kitchen closed around her, like water filling the space where a small fish used to swim.

'It sounds like Leila's fucked this up royally,' said Greg.

Greg and Minnie were having breakfast in Greg's Islington flat. After dinner with her parents, Minnie had gone back to Greg's for the night. He'd been busy most of the weekend with a deadline for an article on offshore fishing titled, 'Mussel-ing in on Salmon Else's Water; This Whaley Needs to Stop'. Sometimes Minnie wondered whether Greg didn't just think up titles first and then decide what news needed writing. She didn't know if he was still sulking about New Year's Eve, but when she'd turned up on his doorstep he'd given her a much-needed hug.

Greg asked her not to go into the details of why she was upset last night, he found it hard to sleep after 'emotional downloads' from other people. So they'd gone straight to bed and now, over breakfast, she was explaining the bleak situation the business was in.

'Leila hasn't done anything wrong,' Minnie said. She was perched on the bar stool at Greg's narrow kitchen counter brushing her wet hair after a shower. 'We've probably only survived as long as we have because of her.'

'I don't agree. You were in charge of cooking – you delivered. She was in charge of funding and finance – she's the one who failed.' Greg reached out and took the brush from her hand. 'Please don't do that in the kitchen. I find your hair everywhere.'

Minnie shook her head. She felt a vertical line crease between her eyebrows.

'You're not being very helpful, Greg. It's not Leila's fault. We were doing fine, we're just being suffocated by loan repayments.'

'Not that well if you're calling around to borrow cars at the last minute.'

'And it's so nice to know I can rely on you in an emergency.'

'Everything's an emergency, Min. Life's an emergency. Do you know how many fish there are left in the sea? That's a fucking emergency. We're going to have to stop using the expression "plenty more fish in the sea", because it's factually inaccurate.'

Greg took his glasses off and pulled a lens wipe from the kitchen drawer. Minnie sat watching him. It had been comforting to see him last night, to cushion herself in his familiar bed, his familiar body and his familiar smell. This morning, nothing about Greg felt comforting or familiar; he felt alien and unknowable. As he cleaned his lenses she realised he'd hardly looked at her, barely made eye contact over breakfast, yet he was examining his lens with such fastidious attention. She stared straight at him, willing him to look up and really see her.

'Anyway, all you need is a rich benefactor, or go back to working in restaurants like most chefs.'

He turned to his coffee machine and started sifting through the different-coloured capsules in the metal basket next to it.

'Fucking Clive never replaces these, I mean hello, this isn't a Travelodge, the coffee doesn't come free with the room.'

Clive was Greg's flatmate. He was forty-two and married. He split his time between London three nights a week, and his family home in Kent the rest of the time. From Minnie's perspective it looked like an ideal situation for Greg – he got half his rent paid, yet Clive was hardly there.

'If you break down the cost per pod and the number of pods he uses a month, do you know how much that works out as?' Greg jabbed a finger against the kitchen counter.

Minnie nodded sympathetically, then realised he was waiting for an answer.

'A tenner?'

'Seven pounds twenty. I swear he wouldn't even know where to buy replacements. You think they have coffee capsule shops in Kent? They do not.'

Greg picked up two green pods and shook them at Minnie. He slammed them both down on the counter and started scratching his short beard. 'There's only Fortissio Lungo left. I hate Fortissio Lungo – Clive *knows* that. If you're going to drink a man's coffee, at least have the decency to drink the ones you know he doesn't like. Right?'

Minnie nodded. Greg glanced at his Apple watch and made an impatient clicking sound with his tongue against his teeth.

'Right, I've got to go, I'll get a decent coffee on the way. Let yourself out?'

Minnie got the bus to work, buzzing with irritation. Was she expecting too much from Greg? She knew he had his own pressures and concerns to deal with, but surely being with someone you loved should make both your life loads feel lighter. She was leaving his flat feeling heavier than ever. To be fair to him, she didn't know if anyone would have been able to make her feel better about the day she had ahead – telling the others they were losing their jobs was never going to be easy.

As she walked through the door of No Hard Fillings, heard the familiar bell chime and breathed in the smell of pastry that clung to the air, she felt a stab of sadness. This might be one of the last times she heard that bell and smelt that comforting smell.

'Minnie.' Leila jumped out of the kitchen and started doing star jumps on the spot. She was wearing a bright pink boiler suit and neon-yellow-framed glasses. 'Jump with me, Minnie!'

'Is this some kind of money rain dance?' said Minnie, shaking her head from side to side.

'Do it, jump with me,' Leila cried, reaching out to take Minnie's hands and lifting them over her head.

'OK, we're jumping,' said Minnie, shaking off Leila's hands and joining in with the star jumps. 'Is this a new fad – jump meetings? The endorphins make you feel better about the crap news you've got to deliver?'

'The opposite,' Leila grinned, 'I've got great news: star-jump-worthy news!'

The bell chimed behind them and Bev pushed open the door to come in.

'What the ...' said Bev, the jowls on her neck wobbling in confusion.

'Jump in Bev – join the jump,' said Leila, clapping her hands in Bev's direction and letting out a 'whoop'. She was acting like some kind of deranged Jane Fonda.

'No,' said Bev, looking at them as though she'd discovered them dancing naked with a corpse dressed in a ra-ra skirt. 'I … I'll go and warm up the ovens.'

Bev sidestepped past without taking her eyes off them, as though if she turned her back, they might somehow involve her in their weird ritual. Leila and Minnie both giggled.

'I'm not fit enough for this, you'd better get to it quick,' said Minnie with a smile. That was the thing about Leila – even in the worst situations she could make Minnie smile.

'We just had an order this morning,' said Leila, stepping up the pace of the star jumps. 'An enormous order, delivering pies to fifteen different offices this month.'

Minnie stopped dead in her tracks.

'What?'

'No, don't stop, there's more.'

The bell tinged again as Alan came through the door. He surveyed the scene for a minute, then without saying a word joined in and started jumping with them. It was a lopsided star jump on account of his bad leg, but he had a good pace.

'And they paid up front in full. Can you believe it? It's enough to keep us afloat and then some.' Leila started punching the air. 'A stay of execution – a death row pardon!'

Minnie burst into song, with the lyrics from Alanis Morissette's 'Ironic'. And then they were both laughing and jumping and singing the words at the top of their lungs. Well, Minnie and Leila were singing the words, Alan was humming a strange beat-box-style accompaniment, and it didn't sound as if he knew the song they were singing at all. At this point Fleur arrived, gave them a withering look and informed them that their generation were all intensely weird.

When the dizzying excitement of the jump meeting had worn off, Minnie kissed the silver four-leaf clover necklace she wore around her neck. She couldn't believe their luck getting an order like this, just when they needed it. Then she paused. The timing of an order like this couldn't be luck.

She asked Leila to see the details of the order. A woman had called, paid over the phone with a credit card and given her the names and addresses of fifteen companies to deliver to on different dates this month. No Hard Fillings didn't cater for corporate clients; they made pies for people who could no longer cook for themselves, for the vulnerable and socially isolated. Why would businesses like these want pies delivered from a company like theirs? How would they even have found out about them?

'Oh, and they asked if we could bring them ready to eat, so we'll need to buy more insulated packaging,' said Leila.

Minnie looked down at the list of addresses Leila had given her. She only recognised one of them – the newspaper where Greg worked.

'This has got to be someone helping us out,' said Minnie.

'I thought the same,' said Leila.

Minnie knew Greg didn't have that kind of cash. Maybe these were all business affiliates connected to his newspaper somehow? Maybe he'd been able to do her a favour through work. She suddenly had a rush of affection for Greg. Maybe he was trying to lighten her life load after all.

'Hmmm,' said Minnie, poring over the list of addresses again, 'it's just not what we're set up for though, is it? We're not corporate caterers; we're supposed to be making pies for the needy – our ability to fundraise and receive subsidies relies on that.'

'Minnie, we're not in a position to be picky, and we charged them a higher rate so they're not being subsidised.' Leila shot Minnie a wide-eyed, exasperated look. 'Frankly, I don't care if Attila the Hun is ordering pies to feed a marauding tribe of murderers, or a clown school is ordering pies for face-splatting practice – they've paid, we'll make them, end of.' Leila narrowed her eyes at Minnie and gave a brisk shake of her head. 'I'm going to go call the bank.'

Leila turned and stomped off to the narrow wooden desk at the back of the kitchen where her laptop was set up. Minnie pulled out her phone and typed a text to Greg, 'Did you order thousands of pounds' worth of pies from us this morning by any chance?! Xxx.'

'Has Greg saved the day?' asked Fleur.

'I don't know,' Minnie said.

'So predictable for a man to think he needs to rescue the situation,' Fleur made a pretend yawn. 'More importantly, tell us what happened with that hot Quinn guy last week? And if you're not dumping Greg for him, can I have him?'

Leila glanced up from her screen. Minnie had given her the full Quinn debrief over the phone on Saturday. Well, perhaps not the *full* debrief. She'd told her about meeting Tara and breaking the lamp. She'd said Quinn was good company, but the type of guy who was friendly with everyone. She hadn't mentioned the 'owls waking up in her stomach' feeling or that thoughts of him kept popping up unannounced in her head.

'He was very helpful,' said Minnie. 'But no one's dumping anyone. Besides, he has a very pretty and successful girlfriend.'

'Probably not as pretty as me, though, let's be honest,' said Fleur, framing her face with her hands and fluttering her eyelashes at Minnie.

The phone started ringing in reception.

'Fleur, can you answer that?' Leila shouted.

Fleur sighed and gave a little pirouette as she flounced back to the tedious task of doing her only job.

The kitchen soon returned to its normal routine. A smell of pastry and positivity filled the air. Alan de-clamped the van and headed out with deliveries. Fleur made phone calls to customers, confirming orders for the next few weeks.

'So, no news from the love twin?' Leila asked quietly, once the others were out of earshot. Her curiosity about Quinn clearly trumped her annoyance about Minnie's response to the pie order.

'I wish you wouldn't call him that. It's not a thing.'

'Oh, it's a thing, trust me.'

'Look, he's a nice guy, he helped us out with the car, that's it.'

Was that it? It had ended so awkwardly between them. She'd sent Quinn a text on Saturday, thanking him again for his help and apologising for breaking his mother's lamp. He'd replied a few hours later saying, 'No problem'. Two words. No problem. What did that mean? No problem about the lamp? No problem about helping? No problem about her having a go at him for something that clearly wasn't his fault? Minnie thought she'd got beyond the stage of dissecting the meaning of texts from men. Clearly she had not.

'You haven't spent all weekend working out how you're going to see him again, then?' Leila said with a knowing look.

'Leila, don't you have some Excel spreadsheet you need to create?' said Minnie, crossing her eyes at her.

'I do. I'm going,' Leila said, picking up her laptop and snapping it shut. 'I'm going to work in the coffee shop around the corner; too many delightful distractions here.'

Once Leila had gone, Minnie went to help Bev start unpacking a box of ingredients on the workbench. Minnie had been so distracted by everything else going on, she hadn't properly registered Bev's appearance – she looked terrible. She had dark purple circles beneath her eyes and her body hunched in a stoop. She looked as though she was carrying the weight of the world on her shoulders.

'Bev, are you OK?'

Minnie stopped what she was doing and put a hand on Bev's arm. Bev blinked at her through tired, heavy eyes. 'Is this related to your forgetfulness, or the eco-anxiety? I'm worried about you Bev,' Minnie said softly. 'I'm here if you want to talk.'

'You'll think I'm nuts if I try to explain,' said Bev quietly, her head bowed over the kitchen counter.

'Try me.'

Bev let out a long, slow exhale.

'It all started a couple of weeks ago, when I was watching one of these Brian Cox shows on the BBC.'

Minnie nodded encouragingly. Whatever she'd imagined Bev was about to say, she had not imagined it starting with Brian Cox.

'He was talking about how, if the universe was a day, then our planet's only been around for a blink of an eye, and if that blink of an eye was another day, humans have only been around for a blink in that blink. Then I got to thinking, if humans have only been around for a blink, then my lifetime is probably only a blink of that blink.'

Minnie was listening attentively but she was already lost. She moved her eyes from side to side trying to keep up.

'Right,' she said slowly.

'And if my life is just a blink in a blink in a blink, then what's the point in any of it? Nothing I do, nothing I say is ever going to matter in the grand scheme of things. Even if I fixed global warming or invented some spaceship that could get us all to Mars, it wouldn't mean anything in the long run, would it? And I'm not doing any of those things, am I? I'm just fixing the house and feeding my family and making pies.' Bev's face fell when she saw Minnie's expression of bewilderment. 'I told you you'd think I'm crazy.'

'I definitely don't think you're crazy Bev, I just, wow ... those are pretty heavy thoughts to be having on a Monday morning.'

Alan came back in with a plastic pallet to load up and overheard the tail end of their conversation.

'Are you telling her about your existential midlife crisis, Bev?' he asked.

Bev nodded.

'She's got it bad, Minnie. She zoomed out way too far on Google Maps and now she can't get back.' Alan shook his head. 'She needs to watch a bit more *X Factor* or something. Anything on ITV will sort you out, Bev. Cut down on the BBC4 for a bit.'

'Look, I don't think any of us should be thinking too much about our place in the grand scheme of things,' said Minnie. 'I'm sure Brian Cox didn't mean to make you question the validity of your existence. Even if you don't invent a spaceship to Mars, that's not to say you aren't leading a rich and fulfilling life, Bev. Your husband loves you, your family love you, we all love you. What more can you hope to achieve in life?'

'Wise words,' nodded Alan, loading pie boxes into his pallet. 'All you can hope for is to do more good than harm in this life, that's my motto. I've already sunk three boats in my lifetime, so I figure I've got at least four boats to float till I'm up.'

'You're floating quite a lot of boats at the London Fields Social Club from what I hear, Alan,' said Minnie, giving him an exaggerated wink.

'What are you all gossiping about?' asked Fleur.

Fleur was incapable of staying at her desk if she thought something interesting was being said in the kitchen.

'Bev's existential crisis,' said Alan.

'Alan's elderly admirers,' said Minnie.

'Alan's a Scorpio; Scorpios always get loads of attention,' said Fleur, twiddling her hair and pulling a stool up to the worktop.

'I don't want to think like this,' Bev said mournfully, unpacking more packets of flour and lining them up on the counter. 'But now I've thought it, I can't turn it off. Like, I was in the shower the other day and I was looking at this shampoo bottle my daughter bought me. It was made of real nice-feeling matte plastic, like someone had taken a lot of time over it. This bottle that was only made to hold shampoo for a month or two and it will probably be around on this planet longer than me. I'll be dead in thirty years, and my kids might remember me, maybe even my grandkids, but then what? There will be no record I was ever here. But this shampoo bottle will still be existing somewhere with its list of ingredients and its lovely matte finish.'

Fleur, Alan and Minnie all stared silently at Bev.

'You got to stop having such long showers, Bev,' said Alan, lifting up his pallet of pies and heading for the door.

'Wow, and I thought we were supposed to be the anxious generation,' said Fleur. 'We're the ones consumed by social media pressures and the fear of robots taking our jobs. We're the ones with nowhere to live because your generation won't recycle and eats way too much ham.'

'Ham?' Minnie asked.

'Only old people eat ham,' Fleur said, as though it was the most obvious point in the world.

Minnie looked back at Bev. She felt as though some sage words were required, but she couldn't think of anything wise to say.

'What about going on a protest march? You could take Betty, show her you care?' she said. 'There's nothing like waving a placard in the air to make you feel like you're doing something.'

Bev looked up at her curiously. 'What kind of march would I go on?'

'I don't know, something you feel strongly about,' said Minnie.

'I'll tell you what's coming up,' said Fleur, scrolling through a website on her phone. 'Right, you've got Climate Action on the twelfth, Action on Climate on the fifteenth – bit basic; Save the Badgers, blah blah blah, Rage Against Palm Oil, politics, politics, blah blah politics, Save the Bees ... Oh, here we go, Ban Single Use Plastics on the thirtieth: that sounds like your cup of tea, Bev.'

'There you go,' said Minnie cheerfully, 'there's something for everyone to get angry about, isn't there.'

'You really think that might help?' said Bev, looking up at Minnie with hopeful eyes.

'No one's too small to make a difference; just ask Greta Thunberg,' said Minnie.

'Make sure you take a compact; there's never anywhere to check your make-up on a protest march. Also, throat lozenges and water, you get hoarse from all the chanting, "WE WANT THIS! WE WANT THAT!"' said Fleur.

'Do I need to buy a ticket in advance?' asked Bev.

'No Bev, you don't need to buy a ticket,' said Minnie.

'Such a classic Pisces,' Fleur nodded. 'All this anxiety about helping everyone.'

'I'm not a Pisces,' said Bev.

'Really? You definitely should be,' said Fleur, squinting her eyes. 'While we're on the topic of star signs, Minnie, I've been looking up Capricorn compatibility and it's not good news. Don't dump Greg for your hot love twin, the stars say it will never work.'

Minnie frowned at Fleur. Why was she spending time googling Minnie's compatibility with people? She also felt an inexplicable stab of irritation that Fleur had decreed her and Quinn incompatible, which was ridiculous – Minnie didn't even believe in astrology.

Minnie's phone pinged, a reply from Greg. 'No, did not order pies. Do you want to watch *Life of Pi* tonight, though?' Then another text pinged through, 'Or The Pie Who Loved Me? With Nail and Pie? Pieture Perfect? (Jennifer Aniston!)'

Greg had a bit of a thing about Jennifer Aniston. Minnie frowned.

'What star sign is Greg if his birthday is twenty-fifth of April?' she asked Fleur.

'Taurus,' said Fleur. 'Perfect for you, Minnie.'

Alan pulled the van into the next address on their delivery list, a private car park just off Old Street.

'Private car park, *très* fancy,' said Alan, buzzing the intercom through the driver side window.

Minnie looked out of the window at the silver plaque which listed the businesses in the building. They were delivering to Tantive Consulting on Level Four.

'Huh,' Minnie made a nondescript noise.

'What's that?' asked Alan.

'Nothing,' Minnie shook her head, 'it's just the name of this company. I think it's a *Star Wars* reference. It's the name of one of the ships.'

'Minnie, I do believe behind that pretty face of yours you are hiding an inner geek.'

They both carried a pallet of pies into the lift and headed up to the fourth floor. A striking redhead welcomed them at reception as if they were valuable clients rather than caterers delivering lunch.

'If you could just lay them out in the boardroom, there's a table set up all ready,' said the receptionist with quick, blinking eyes and a Julia Roberts smile.

Tantive Consulting's office space was smart and modern. The place was tastefully furnished and, by the looks of things, expensively. There were Chesterfield armchairs made from soft, worn-looking leather, and plush thick pile carpet throughout. The vibe was professional and minimalist, yet homely and welcoming. On the walls hung framed photographs of strange landscapes and interesting faces; art that drew your attention, not the generic abstracts you'd normally see in an office such as this.

Minnie and Alan unpacked the pies in the boardroom. It was a large room, partitioned down the middle with a temporary room divider. A white linen tablecloth had been laid out with cutlery and plates at one end. As they unpacked the pies, they could hear people talking on the other side of the partition.

'Do you smell that? Something insanely good,' said a man's voice.

Alan and Minnie glanced at each other and smiled.

'Top man ordered pies for lunch,' said another voice.

'Nice,' said the first voice, 'I'll work from the office more often.'

'Free pies – probably some perk of the job for shagging that food bird,' said a third voice. 'He's been eating like a king since dating her.'

'Who?'

'Lucy Donohue, that food writer, and you know she's …' the man made a groaning noise and his companions laughed.

Minnie froze. She didn't want to eavesdrop, but it was impossible not to with a partition that thin. She felt a hard knot form in her stomach as she processed what she'd just heard. This was Quinn's office, Quinn's company; he was the one responsible for the huge order that had bailed them out.

Alan looked at her with bulging eyes – he'd joined the dots too.

Minnie started unloading the pallet faster. She didn't want to be here, she didn't want to listen to this conversation; she just wanted to get the pies unloaded and get out. Why would Quinn do this? Their day together had ended so strangely and he hadn't been in touch since. Why would he be doing her a favour? This didn't sit well with Minnie; she didn't want to be a charity case and she didn't want to be making pies for arseholes like the men in that room. She was supposed to be making her pies for people who needed them.

She and Alan laid out the last of the food and Minnie scurried back to the front desk to tell the receptionist they were done. Behind them, office workers were gravitating towards the boardroom, drawn from their desks by the aroma of warm pastry.

'Mr Hamilton would like to see you before you go,' said the receptionist, cocking her head to one side and showing Minnie her enormous teeth. She really did look uncannily like Julia Roberts. 'Can I take you up to his office? He's stuck on a call.'

'We're in a bit of a rush,' said Minnie weakly.

'You don't need me, I'll wait here,' said Alan, taking a seat in the reception area and picking up a yachting magazine. 'Ooh, boaty boats.'

The receptionist led Minnie through the open-plan workspace to a glass-panelled office at the far end. Minnie couldn't believe Quinn ran such a large company; there had to be thirty people working here. Through the glass she could see Quinn, who was wearing a well-tailored blue suit with a white shirt. He was talking on the phone, but when he saw her hovering with the receptionist he smiled and beckoned her to come in.

The receptionist opened the door for her. Minnie picked at her thumbnail. Why did she feel like a schoolgirl being called in to see the headmaster? Quinn mouthed 'sorry', and patted the top of a large brown leather armchair. Minnie gave him an awkward smile and sat down on the sofa opposite. His office was huge. He had a giant glass desk with a large black swivel chair, a meeting room table with four chairs around it, a sofa, armchair and a walnut coffee table. His office was bigger than her entire flat. Oh god, maybe this was some kind of *Fifty Shades of Grey* scenario and the pies had just been a ruse to get her up here and show off his big fancy office and secret sex dungeon.

Minnie looked around the room, wondering where the entrance to a secret sex dungeon might be. There was a bookcase at the far end of the room – maybe you pulled out a book and the whole wall swivelled around. Maybe the sofa had a lever and dropped you down into a hidden vault below. Perhaps that would be more James Bond than Christian Grey. Minnie found her mind wandering – contemplating whether there were architects who specialised in designing secret office sex dungeons.

'Yes, I know,' Quinn said into the phone, 'but that's what my recommendations are. If you don't want to implement them, that's your business. You paid me to find the holes in your growth strategy – those are the holes.'

There was a pause while the person on the other end spoke. Quinn rolled his eyes at Minnie, conveying that he was trying to get off the call.

'Listen, Donald, can we pick this up in person tomorrow? I've just had someone walk into my office and I ... yes, someone more important than you ... Did you get those pies I sent over today? Well, it's the chef who made them.'

Quinn sat down in the armchair opposite Minnie. He crossed one leg over the other, leaning back in the chair. Minnie couldn't help looking at Quinn's legs, they were so muscular and firm, his trousers cut perfectly around his sculpted thighs.

'Yes I know they are good ... Well, yes she is, but that's irrelevant ... I will give you her details, I have to go.' Quinn smiled at her as he hung up, the dimple on his left cheek creasing into life, 'Sorry about that.'

Minnie clutched her hands together.

'You didn't need to order all those pies,' she said, shifting her gaze to the floor. 'When I mentioned about my business issues, I didn't mean for you to ... If anything, I owe *you* money for the lamp.'

'Please don't worry about the lamp, Minnie. I should have explained about my mother,' Quinn exhaled slowly, pausing to find the right words. 'She has health issues. She finds some things difficult to deal with.'

Minnie looked up at him. His playful tone was gone; the sparkling blue of his eyes clouded over by a film of grey.

'You don't need to explain, and you didn't need to bail me out either,' she said.

The dynamic between them felt so different. Doing deliveries together they'd been equals, they'd joked around. Now he was a client and a very generous one at that. Sitting opposite him in this apartment-sized office, she didn't feel like an equal any more, she felt like the hired help.

'I know,' said Quinn, a slight frown creasing between his dark brows. Just looking across at him, with his dimpled smile and his strong long legs in those tailor-made trousers, Minnie felt the owls in her stomach waking up, ruffling their wings.

'And I don't need you pimping me out to your friends,' she said haughtily. 'I didn't set up my business to cook for rich city boys.'

She got to her feet and started pacing back and forth behind the sofa.

'Wow,' said Quinn, putting his hands behind his head and stretching his legs out in front of him. 'You know it makes you walk slightly off centre?'

'What?'

'The massive chip you carry around on your shoulder.'

Minnie's mouth dropped open. Ingrained resentments bubbled up inside her, her mother's voice in her head like a dripping tap she couldn't turn off.

'I don't have a chip on my shoulder. I'm just saying this kind of gig isn't what I set out to do. If I'd wanted to cook for entitled men in suits, I'd have stayed in the restaurant business.'

Quinn laughed, brushing a hand through his sandy-brown hair.

'I can see why your business isn't thriving if this is the rapport you have with clients.'

'Excuse me?' Minnie said, her fists on her hips. Quinn stood up and walked around behind the back of the sofa towards her.

'Look, your pies are good. You clearly have a market, yet you're not making money – evidently you're doing something wrong.'

'Thank you, but I don't need you to management-consultancy me.'

'Why not?' Quinn spread out his arms in an exaggerated shrug. 'I charge five hundred pounds an hour and I'm offering you free advice. It's sheer petulance not to take it.'

Minnie felt her face grow red, her chin jutting forward.

'Is that the way you speak to all *your* clients?'

Quinn took a step towards her. Minnie stepped backwards towards the wall. She had that strange feeling again, except this time more intensely. Almost as though he was moving in to kiss her. Of course her brain knew he wasn't, but her body felt as though he was and it sent a heady mixture of indignation and anticipation pumping through her veins.

'You're not a client,' Quinn said softly, standing a foot away from her. He looked down into her eyes, the hint of a smile still playing at his lips. Minnie narrowed her eyes and looked right back up at him. She wasn't going to be physically intimidated by him.

'You don't know enough about my business to have an opinion.'

'Maybe not, but I can see you're an idealist. You don't want to compromise your mission statement, even if it means losing your business.' Minnie felt a little rush of pride, before realising he didn't mean it as a compliment. 'Why not deliver to a few corporates if it means staying afloat for your community gigs? Plus, you clearly aren't employing the right people – the driver who loses the car, the chef who burns the pies. If you want to run a company effectively, you've got to pick the right people to work for you.'

Quinn turned and started pacing the office again. The irrational feeling that he was going to kiss her passed, along with any thought he might be about to show her his office sex dungeon with a secret access panel through the bookcase. Quinn picked up a pen from his desk and started clicking the end of it.

'No doubt you would just cull anyone who had a bad day,' Minnie said, folding her arms in front of her chest. 'My team are like family. They've all had problems in life, that's why we hired them. We want to give a chance to people who need one.'

'Even if it means destroying your business?'

Minnie narrowed her eyes at him. Between Greg, her mother, and now Quinn, she was sick of people telling her how bad she was at running a business.

'They aren't the problem. Look, if it's not going to work how I want it to work, maybe it's not meant to be.'

'Spoken like a true fatalist. You need to start taking responsibility for your life, Minnie. You lose your coat on New Year's Eve because you're careless, not jinxed. Your business is failing because you're a bad manager who won't take free advice.' Quinn shook his head and thrust his hands into his pockets. Minnie felt the red prickling back up her neck, flushing her cheeks.

'Well, maybe I don't need life advice or handouts from some rich kid, mummy's boy who has no idea what the real world looks like.'

Minnie felt a falling sensation in her stomach as soon as she'd said it. She didn't know why she'd gone that far; it was too harsh. She felt like a cat being cornered, darting out a sharp claw in a pre-emptive strike. Quinn's face changed, the glint in his eye disappeared and his jaw clenched, a muscle pulsing above the sharp line of his chin.

'You don't know anything about my life, Minnie, and this whole hard-done-by working-class routine is deeply unattractive.'

'I don't need you to find me attractive,' said Minnie.

'I think you'd better go,' Quinn told her for the second time in their short acquaintance. 'Try not to smash anything on your way out.'

Quinn sat on the bottom stair picking at the chipped varnish covering the crack in the banister. In the blue house, the banisters snaked up from the bottom floor four and a half whole turns. If Quinn lay on the floor in the hall and looked up, he couldn't see where the banister ended; he liked to imagine the curling wood went on and on, winding upwards like Jack's beanstalk to the castle in the clouds, or – in this case – to the attic. When he was little he used to try climbing to the top without touching the stairs – the carpet was lava and the banisters were safe. He had to get to the top to rescue his sister from the evil tribe who lived in the attic, threatening to throw her into the fearsome volcano.

He'd made it as far as the second floor, balancing his feet on the thin rail of wood, holding on to the railing above before he'd slipped and fallen down arm first onto the banister below. He'd broken his arm and taken this chunk out of the wood. It had only been a small chunk, but his father had gone ballistic.

'That banister is irreplaceable! It's carved from a single piece of oak!'

'What were you thinking? What were you doing?' cried his mother, crouching down to Quinn's level, blue eyes blinking wildly, her blonde hair rolled in curlers and black streaks running down her cheeks. The spiders that lived on her eyelids looked as though they were melting.

'Rescuing my sister from the attic,' Quinn said, through breathy sobs.

His mother's face turned white; she covered her mouth with a hand, pushed him away and fled back upstairs, taking them two at a time.

It was Daddy who had taken him to hospital. Quinn remembered because it was the first time he'd been allowed to sit in the front seat of his father's convertible. Daddy couldn't work out the car-seat straps in Mummy's Volvo, so they went in his car, which didn't have a car seat or a roof. 'Don't scuff the leather with your feet,' his father instructed. Quinn didn't have any shoes on because his father hadn't known where they were kept and Quinn was crying too much to tell him. That was years ago. Daddy didn't live with them in the blue house any more.

Today, Quinn was waiting on the stairs for his mother to come down and give him his birthday presents. He'd been awake for hours, but he could be patient – eleven year olds were supposed to be patient. He'd got dressed and made himself breakfast – a bagel with peanut butter. At least it was the Christmas holidays, so he wasn't in any rush to get to school. Quinn looked up at the clock in the hall, ten to ten. Would she be cross if he went to check whether she was awake? He crept up to the third-floor landing.

Her door stood slightly ajar. The curtains were open and light was streaming in. Maybe she was having a bad morning? Sometimes, when she had a bad morning, Quinn had to get a lift to school with William Greenford from four doors up. Sometimes, when she was having a bad day, he had to stay at

William Greenford's house after school, and he didn't even like William Greenford.

His mother was lying on the bed in her pink silk dressing gown. It lay open with the cord undone. Quinn blushed to see his mother wasn't wearing nightclothes underneath, just cream-coloured pants. It didn't look like a sleeping position; her body sprawled like that with her arms up around her head and her face buried between two pillows. Quinn crept backwards out of the room – he didn't want her to know he'd seen her without clothes on.

Maybe this afternoon she would get up. She would get dressed and come downstairs. She would make herself coffee and then he could unwrap his presents and she could pretend this wasn't one of her bad days, just a bad morning. Maybe she'd even take him to Primrose Hill with his bike, if she worked up to it this afternoon.

Quinn had asked for the Lego Millennium Falcon for his birthday. If she could just give him his present now, he wouldn't even mind so much about her having a bad day. She didn't need to take him anywhere; it wasn't like he expected a party. If he could just start building the Falcon, he would be happy for hours.

Ten minutes later and there was still no sound from her room.

'Mummy?' he said, quietly. 'Mummy, are you awake?' he tried again.

'Not now, Quinn,' her voice sounded like a dying bird. 'Today's not a good day.'

Quinn carefully pulled the door to; it didn't lie straight on its hinges any more and you had to lift it to make it close. The door had been slammed so many times – maybe the hinges had grown tired, like Mummy.

Quinn looked across the landing at his mother's bathroom. He didn't like going in there. The white tiled floor had never been white again; that much blood seeping into the floor had turned the grouting grey. Daddy got them to take out the whole floor. Then he redid the guest bathroom too, so that the new tiles would match.

Quinn didn't remember all the details – he'd been six. His memories of that day felt like a trailer for a film, flashed images and sounds branded onto his young brain. He remembered being woken by the screaming downstairs. First he thought it must be the television, but then it went on and on. He saw the blood before he saw his mother. She was on the floor in a pool of it, sitting against the toilet, clutching her balloon stomach. The screaming had stopped; she was so white, she could hardly speak. She told him to find her phone. Quinn didn't remember getting the phone or calling for an ambulance.

He remembered thinking the bath must have overflowed, but he didn't know why the water was red. He remembered thinking he'd never seen his mother look so scared. He remembered waiting outside a hospital room the next day with his father. Daddy kept clicking the strap on his Rolex watch open and shut. He smelt of smoke and dirty washing. Then Daddy went in to see her and Quinn was told to wait outside. Mummy cried and screamed at him for not being at home.

He remembered his father moving Quinn's old cot back up to the attic, along with all the other boxes that had been brought down and stacked up in the spare room. He remembered walking into that room and seeing his father on the floor with his hands over his eyes, his body moving up and down making the strangest sound. When his father saw him in the doorway, he took off his shoe and threw it at the door and it slammed in Quinn's face.

Quinn thought about that night in the bathroom a lot. If it hadn't happened, would his mother be more like a normal mother? Would it have happened if his father had been home? Would it have happened if he had gone downstairs sooner? Mrs Jacobs the counsellor at school said he couldn't think like that. Mrs Jacobs said the bathroom incident wasn't the only reason his mother was like she was. She said some people were just anxious, but things could happen that made them more anxious, that made it harder for them to leave the house. Then Mrs Jacobs had mentioned him going to live with his father in New York and Quinn had stopped telling her these things about his mother.

Quinn stood up and closed the bathroom door – he didn't like to think about all that. He padded quietly downstairs and went to the laundry room in the basement. He took the stool from the corner and opened the cupboard where all the cleaning things were kept. He pulled out a bottle of bleach and behind it he saw a paper bag. It was where she always hid things she didn't want him to find. He wouldn't open it – he just wanted to know if it was a Falcon.

He pulled out the bag and there was one large Falcon-shaped box and three smaller presents all wrapped in matching blue wrapping paper. He peeled away a corner of the largest box. He knew straight away it wasn't Lego. He knew the texture of a Lego box, he knew the colours – this was too bright, too neon. He pulled away a little more paper; walkie-talkies. Who was he going to talk to on a walkie-talkie? He carefully pressed back the edge of the paper and returned the bag to the shelf.

Upstairs Quinn poured himself a lemon squash and turned on the computer in the kitchen. He picked up the postcard from his father that had arrived last week. It had a picture of the Empire State Building on the front. He turned it over and re-read his father's words,

> Quinn,
> The Empire State Building is 102 storeys high. It was completed in 1931. The building has a roof height of 1,250 ft and stands a total of 1,454 ft tall. Impressive isn't it!
> Maeve and I can see it from our apartment.
> Dad.

This was a standard postcard from him – a picture with some facts. Quinn saw him sometimes when he came to London for work, but the talk of Quinn visiting New York had stopped, he didn't know why. There was no birthday card from his father today. He usually sent one about a week late. Last year he'd sent Quinn twenty dollars in the envelope. Quinn still had it, because his mother couldn't get to the bank to change it into something he could spend.

The computer dial tone finally connected and Quinn logged onto his favourite website – a site that hosted chat forums for *Star Wars* fans. This is where Quinn went when he felt lonely. Talking to other people about the world of Obi-Wan and Princess Leia distracted him from the silence of his own.

He clicked on the chat forum tab and a little black box popped up on the screen:

<LukeQ has entered the chat room>

Jedi454:   LukeQ, welcome back you are. How U?

Jedi454 was a regular forum user who Quinn had chatted to before.

LukeQ: Feeling Lego Falconless, Quinn typed back. He didn't know who Jedi454 was, but he knew he would understand.

Jedi454:   FanGirl90 is building one now. Wait, I'll intro.

A new chat screen opened and Jedi454 started typing.

Jedi454:   FanGirl90, meet LukeQ. He's Falconless. She's just landed one.

<Jedi454 has left the chat room>

LukeQ: Hi FanGirl90, why r you online if you have a Falcon to build?

FanGirl90:   Had to log on here for instructions – mine is second-hand, doesn't have all the pages!

LukeQ: How far you got?

FanGirl90:   Page 11. Rest missing.

LukeQ: Send me pic.

FanGirl90:   <photo attached>

LukeQ: Wow, pretty good going for a girl – assume girl you are?

FanGirl90:   GirlsLikeStarWarsToo

LukeQ: None I've ever met.

FanGirl90:   Because they are at home trying to build Millennium Falcons without instructions.

LukeQ: Do or do not, there is no try.

FanGirl90:   Nice! My dad bought it second-hand for my birthday. Said 'how hard can it be?' Answer, very.

LukeQ: Your dad sounds cool. I wanted one for my birthday but ... walkie-talkies.

FanGirl90:   Ugh.

LukeQ: Ugh.

FanGirl90:   Luckily lots of Star Warriors on here helping me out with photos of instructions.

LukeQ: Resourceful you are.

FanGirl90:   Wish me luck LukeQ?

LukeQ: In my experience there is no such thing as luck.

FanGirl90:   I think Yoda is wrong on that one.

LukeQ: Yoda is never wrong.

FanGirl90:   Got to go, Mum shouting up the stairs. Maybe see you in another galaxy, LukeQ. Until then, may the force be with you.

<FanGirl90 has left the chat room> blinked on the screen.

Quinn was disappointed she had gone. He smiled to himself – who tried to build something that complicated without instructions?

'So let me get this straight, the guy spent a day driving you around London to help you out, introduced you to his mother, spent thousands of pounds bailing out our business – and you shouted at him and called him a spoilt brat?' Leila asked.

'Kind of,' said Minnie, burying her face in one of Leila's scatter cushions.

They were in Leila's front room going through paperwork.

'Minnie, with all this self-sabotaging behaviour, you're ruining the fun of living vicariously through you. I really thought you might have slept with the love twin by now, or at least had a cheeky snog.'

'Leila! I have a boyfriend? What do you take me for?'

'Boyfriend schmoyfriend. Bathroom Abandoner doesn't deserve you, and he clearly fancies you. No one buys a thousand pies from someone they don't want to sleep with.'

Minnie slumped back against the sofa arm.

'I don't know what is wrong with me. He was just being so arrogant and annoying, trying to give me all this advice, telling me I should be grateful to get his opinion because "he earns five hundred pounds an hour",' Minnie said, imitating Quinn's voice.

'Maybe you *should* be grateful for his opinion,' said Leila, closing the pink ring binder of accounts and rubbing her eyes with her palms. Her hair was scraped back in a messy bun, her eyes looked sunken and tired. 'One month of good orders doesn't put us in the clear, you know. It's going to be an uphill slog to build any kind of financial buffer.'

Minnie stretched out on the sofa and looked up at the ceiling.

'I could hear myself sounding all bitter and bitchy, I don't know where it came from. Do you think I walk around with a chip on my shoulder?'

Leila scrunched up her nose and stuck her teeth over her front lip like a rabbit.

'What?' said Minnie, leaning up on her elbows. 'What's that face?'

'I wouldn't say a whole chip, not a thick-cut chip-shop chip anyway, maybe a skinny fry,' said Leila. 'A McDonald's chip.'

Minnie picked up the sofa cushion and threw it at Leila. They both laughed.

'Working hard?' asked Ian, coming through to the living room holding a burrito in one hand. He was wearing a black T-shirt that said, 'Don't grow up – it's a trap', in a messy white font.

Leila looked at the clock on her phone.

'Right,' she said, jumping to her feet, 'I've got to go. I've got a meeting with Monsieur bank manager.'

'You sure you don't want me to come?' asked Minnie.

'No, our bank manager is quite hot – I don't want you smashing his lamps or starting some sort of sexy slagging match.'

Leila winked and jumped out of the room before Minnie could land another blow with a cushion.

'Who's hot?' mumbled Ian through a mouthful of burrito. He sat down next to Minnie on the sofa. 'Want to play two-player mode, Minnie?'

Minnie picked up the two controllers from the floor and passed one to him.

'If we can play *Star Wars* Battlefront, but only one game then I have to go bake.'

Ian leant forward, put his leaking burrito on the coffee table and started riffling through the games drawer beneath the TV.

'Something I wanted to talk to you about, Minnie,' said Ian, loading the game into his Xbox.

'If this is a coming-out speech, you're telling the wrong person,' she said, tilting her chin and looking down at him with wide, serious eyes. Ian leant back and gently punched her on the shin.

'No, dickhead.'

The game clicked through to split screen and they both started selecting their weapons. 'You always choose the wrong weapons; you need better rate of fire on your blasters,' said Ian, shaking his head.

'Not if you've got an accurate aim, you don't.'

'I know you're going to die first,' said Ian, scooting backwards onto the sofa next to her.

The game jumped into life. Ian and Minnie both leant forward, hands clasped on their controllers, blasting at storm troopers.

'I'm going to ask Leila to marry me,' said Ian, eyes still locked on the screen.

'What?' squealed Minnie, turning to face him.

There was a huge explosion on the screen as her avatar was hit by a grenade and blown into a thousand pieces.

'Didn't I say you'd die first?' said Ian with a smirk.

'This is not a game-play conversation!' cried Minnie, reaching out to take Ian's controller from him. 'You're going to ask her to marry you? When, how? Have you bought a ring? This is so exciting!'

Ian shifted uncomfortably next to her.

'Yes. Don't know. Maybe. I don't know how to do it, that's what I wanted to ask you. You know what Leila's like, she won't be happy with a bent knee in the bathroom.'

'No, she definitely would not be happy if you proposed in the bathroom,' said Minnie. She clasped her hands together, shuffling forward to rest her elbows on her knees.

'She likes a bit of pizzazz. She'd want something original, I know that, but I've got no idea what kind of pizzazz, what kind of original,' Ian scratched his head.

Minnie jumped up off the sofa and clapped her hands together.

'I know *exactly* what you need to do. Oh Ian, I am so glad you asked me, this is going to be amazing. We're going to plan the most brilliant proposal anyone has ever seen, she's going to love it!'

Ian smiled and then frowned.

'I don't want to do anything involving nudity.'

'Why would it involve nudity?'

'And no singing, I won't do singing.'

'How many proposals have you heard of that involve singing and nudity? Look, I've got it sorted, I will mastermind everything,' said Minnie. 'What about a ring, you said "maybe"?'

'I've got a ring,' said Ian, shaking his head from side to side slowly. 'I dunno if it's right though.'

'Show me,' Minnie said, holding out a palm.

Ian skulked off to the bedroom and she heard drawers being opened and rummaging sounds. Minnie tapped two fists together in excitement. Over the course of their friendship, she and Leila had talked a lot about meeting 'the one', the person you'd just know you wanted to share the rest of your life with. Here was Leila's 'the one' saying he felt the same.

Minnie felt her sixteen-year-old self squeal with delight. That wide-eyed naïve romantic, unjaded by disappointment. Ian came back with a blue velvet ring box and opened it carefully in front of her.

'It's my gran's,' he said with a lopsided shrug. 'My mum gave it to me when Gran died, dunno why.'

The ring was a delicate vintage gold band with five small diamonds in a line across the top. Minnie felt a warm rush of excitement when she saw it – it was so Leila: quirky but classic. She would love the fact that it was vintage, that there was a story behind it.

'It is perfect, Ian. This is the ring, this is definitely the ring!'

Minnie squealed, punched the air and started doing a little jig on the spot.

'It's got a mark on the back 'cause it had to be sawed off my gran when she died on account of her fingers all swelling up from the diabetes.' Ian turned the ring over in his palm to show her. 'My ma said they almost didn't know it was there when she was at her fattest, 'cause the finger just grew around it like a bird's neck stuck in a plastic beer-can loop. It started cutting off the oxygen and her finger went all rank and blue.'

'Don't tell Leila that story when you propose,' said Minnie firmly, reaching out to grab Ian's wrists. 'Promise me you won't tell that story when you give her the ring.'

Ian tapped his nose, as though making a mental note.

'There's something else,' said Ian, sitting down on the coffee table.

'If you want to adopt me, the answer is yes,' said Minnie.

Ian stared down at his shoes in silence. He clicked shut the ring box and started passing it between his hands like a baseball player warming up to pitch. He fumbled it, finally clasped a fist around it, and thrust it back into the pocket of his grey tracksuit bottoms.

'I want you to think about giving up the business,' he said, closing his eyes.

Minnie looked to see if he was serious.

'What? Why?'

'Because it's killing her,' said Ian, opening his eyes again. 'She's so stressed, Minnie. She can't sleep; she's up half the night worrying. She's put all her own money in just to prop it up. We want to buy a house, Min, maybe have kids; we're never gonna get a mortgage as things stand.'

Minnie let out a loud exhale. She had never heard Ian sound serious before.

'She should have said something.'

'She wouldn't,' said Ian, shaking his head. 'She's your best mate, she wants you to have your dream. She'd run herself ragged for you.'

'Our dream,' Minnie corrected him. 'This business is our dream.'

'Is it?' Ian looked up, his eyes finally meeting hers. 'Is it Leila's dream? Or is it the dream you told her about, that she wanted to make a reality.'

Minnie shook her head.

'You know what she's like, she's like a dog shaking a rat. She won't let it go, she won't stop attacking with everything she's got, until you say it's dead. You should put it out of its misery and let her move on.'

'The business isn't dying,' Minnie started biting her thumbnail, 'and it's not a rat. We've just had a few cash-flow issues.'

'That's what she tells you,' Ian said, staring at her with piercing, unblinking eyes.

Minnie stood up, shaking her head.

'She loves it as much as I do.'

'She loves you,' said Ian.

They stayed in silence for a moment. Ian rubbed both hands across his scalp. 'You know she got offered a job at a fashion start-up last week. Did she tell you?'

'No,' said Minnie. She suddenly felt unsteady on her feet, as though Ian had pulled a rug out from under her. Why wouldn't Leila tell her something like that? They told each other everything.

'You know she'd love doing something like that. She won't even consider it as long as you need her.' Ian hung his head. 'I'm not saying this to be a shit-stirrer, Min, it's just I love her and ... it's like, you know when Sonic the Hedgehog is in Invincibility Mode and he's in this bubble running super-fast, and the music goes all uptempo and there's nothing he can't do, he's just bashing everything straight out the park?'

'Yes,' Minnie said slowly, unsure where this analogy was going.

'Leila's born to live in Invincibility Mode, that's what she's like, it's where she thrives – dashing about in a little bubble with the music racing, totally nailing everything. Right now, it's like she's been hit by a Badnik and lost all her rings – all her energy's gone.' Ian sighed then spoke more slowly, 'I want to be her Invincibility bubble. I want to shield her, let her live in that mode for the rest of her life if I can.' Minnie felt a tear roll down her cheek. 'That probably sounds like total bollocks,' said Ian, thrusting his hands deep into his pockets.

'No,' said Minnie, sniffing back a tear, 'I think that's one of the most romantic things I've ever heard. You should say that about the Invincibility Mode when you propose.'

Minnie hung her head; she felt a heady mix of emotions hit her all at once: fondness for Ian and how much he loved her friend, and sorrow for the fact that he might be right. If he was right, that meant the end of No Hard Fillings, the end of seeing Leila most days, four years of hard work wasted. Ian reached out to put both hands on her shoulders.

'Minnie – I think it's time for you to play one-player mode.'

That evening, as Minnie walked along Upper Street towards Greg's flat, she couldn't get Ian's words out of her head. She hadn't even considered she might be holding Leila back. She'd been so busy worrying about her own career, she hadn't stopped to consider if this was the right path for her friend.

Greg opened his front door and grimaced.

'Clive is here,' he hissed.

Minnie nodded. She had nothing against Clive, but Greg always acted indignant about his flatmate's occasional presence in the flat. He never expressed an interest in coming to hers, even though it would mean they had the place to themselves.

'Question for you, headline for my latest piece – I need an Africa pun. Kenya help me out?'

Minnie groaned and pushed him backwards into the flat.

'I'm serious,' said Greg, slapping the back of a hand into his other palm, 'are you Ghana help me or not?'

They walked through to the kitchen, where Clive was making himself a coffee with Greg's coffee machine. Clive had red hair, freckly skin and a warm, paunchy face. He made Minnie think of a young Fat Controller from *Thomas the Tank Engine*.

'Bit late for coffee, hey Clive?' said Greg, turning to face Minnie and giving her an overblown horrified face. 'You're

174

going to be bouncing off the walls, my friend, and the walls here are none too substantial.'

'I've got a presentation to write for tomorrow, I won't be in the way of your romantic evening,' said Clive. 'PowerPoint and I will be reacquainting ourselves in my bedroom.'

Clive took his coffee mug and plodded back to his room with a backwards wave.

'Space leech,' Greg groaned under his breath. 'Hey, did you read the paper today?'

'I read your column on immigrant mice – very thought-provoking. I didn't get the chance to read much else, I—'

Greg cut her off.

'You didn't see Lucy Donohue's column then?' said Greg, slapping a copy of the paper down on the kitchen table in front of her. His lips pulled into a Cheshire cat grin. 'Hell hath no fury like a food writer scorned.'

Minnie picked up the paper and looked at the page Greg was pointing to. She clutched the paper with both hands, quickly scanning the words in front of her.

Dining with Lucy Donohue

This week I am supposed to be reviewing La Côte in Windsor, a restaurant The Times *called 'out of this world', 'the perfect place for a romantic meal' and 'love in edible form'. I was due to go with my boyfriend for a tasting menu that takes over three hours to consume. Reader, I dined alone. My boyfriend of over a year decided that his New Year's resolution was to cancel his regular booking at the table of Lucy Donohue. I feel it only fair to La Côte to disclose this, as a seven-course tasting menu was not designed to be eaten alone, and it is a truth universally acknowledged that a broken heart doth dampen the taste buds.*

So, rather than giving La Côte an unfairly miserable review, I thought this week I would review my ex – Q, in restaurant form, for any unwitting girl out there who might be considering making him her next meal.

***Ambience:** While the décor at Q is beautifully proportioned and the place appears brimming with character, don't be fooled by this veneer of charm. This is a restaurant where you will never relax or feel at home because all diners are seated in the entrance hall rather than in the heart of the restaurant.*

***Food:** The food at Q first appears beautifully seasoned with a delightful sharpness. In fact, it proves tough to get your teeth into and unevenly cooked, with patches of hot and cold throughout. (As an aside, all the dishes at Q are served with a little more spice than a well brought-up girl might be accustomed to.)*

The dessert looked to possess the perfect sweet finesse to round off a meal, but in fact left a sour taste in my mouth. I fear Q was being overly ambitious in tackling this sophisticated dessert, and should perhaps stick to little tarts and light, airy sponges in future.

***Service:** The maître d' might welcome you with open arms, but he knows full well he will be taking you off the guest list before long. They don't value loyal customers at Q, they aim for a fast turnover – people too awed by the façade to notice that this restaurant has no heart at all.*

'Wow,' said Minnie, once she'd finished reading. She instantly felt bad for Quinn, to be so publicly attacked like this. Then she wondered if there was any truth to the article, was he really such a heartless boyfriend? He and Lucy had looked like the perfect couple from the outside.

'I'm surprised the paper ran with it,' said Greg with a snort. 'Pretty brutal.'

Minnie neatly folded the paper and pressed it down on the counter with both hands. She didn't want to talk to Greg about Lucy or Quinn.

'Listen, I have to start moving out of my flat at the weekend. Could you help me? I don't have much, maybe one car-load.'

Greg tilted his face to a disapproving angle.

'Just go online and hire a man with a van, they'll be better at lifting stuff than me.'

'I don't want to hire a man with a van, and I can't afford to. I'm asking you, as my boyfriend, to help me.'

'Jeez, Minderella, I'll pay for it then,' Greg sighed. 'I don't want to spend my weekend moving boxes around.'

Minnie heard the inner voice of her sixteen-year-old self let out a silent wail and start beating her fists against the inside of Minnie's chest. When had Greg ever done something that he didn't want to do for her sake?

Minnie stared at him as he peered down at Lucy Donohue's byline on the counter. 'You're never going to champion my Invincibility Mode, are you?' she said quietly.

Greg didn't move, he was still looking at Lucy's article. Minnie had ignored Greg's unchivalrous behaviour for the last time. It she was Minderella, he was definitely not Prince Charming.

'I think we should break up,' said Minnie.

'Huh?' said Greg, glancing up at her.

'I don't think this is going to work between us.'

'Jeez, I'll lend you the car, Minnie! You don't need to be a baby about it.'

'It's not about the car, I don't think we're right for each other.'

'And you this second decided that, did you? Five minutes ago we were right for each other, and now we're not?' Greg made a 'pfff' noise and waved the newspaper at her. 'Women are so bloody tempestuous.'

'No, I should have seen it earlier, I've been—'

'It's not like you're perfect you know, Minnie,' Greg said, interrupting her. 'You think if someone asked me who my ideal woman was, I would paint a picture of you? No, I would paint a picture of Jennifer Aniston circa 2010. No one gets perfection! Reality is someone you fancy despite their shortcomings; reality is accepting that seventy per cent is pretty good going.' Greg's voice softened, his mouth twitched into a smile. 'Look, I might not be perfect, but you have to admit we're pretty good together? We have the same politics, the same sense of humour – we work, you and me.'

'I never realised I was settling for seventy per cent, Greg, I guess that's the difference between us.'

At that point Clive wandered back into the kitchen.

'I forgot my toast,' he said, plodding over to the toaster, oblivious to what he'd walked into. 'I didn't even pop it down,' he said, raising his eyes to the ceiling, exasperated at his own forgetfulness. Clive busied himself pulling out plates and cutlery. Minnie watched Greg's face growing redder by the minute as his eyes followed Clive around the kitchen, willing him to leave.

'So how's life, Minnie?' asked Clive amiably. 'Business going well, is it?'

'No, not really,' said Minnie with a smile. 'Terribly, in fact.'

'Oh dear, well at least you've got Greg here to cheer you up.' Clive gave her a double thumbs up. 'Problem shared is a problem halved and all that.'

'Actually we just broke up,' said Minnie.

'We didn't break up,' Greg spat, 'you were talking about the possibility of breaking up. You haven't broken up until you've both agreed.' Greg's hands curled into fists at his sides.

'I've walked into the middle of something,' said Clive, briskly buttering his toast. Then after a pause he added, 'Though I'm not sure that's true, Greg. If Minnie says you've broken up, you've broken up, I don't think it needs to be by mutual agreement.'

Minnie nodded.

'Nobody asked for your legal opinion, Clive!' Greg shouted. 'Just take your toast and fuck off.'

Clive drew his lips closed and gave Minnie a wide-eyed sympathetic shrug.

'Don't talk to him like that, Greg. I'll go; there's nothing more to say anyway.'

Minnie stood up and lifted her handbag from the chair.

'You really think you're going to do better than me?' Greg snarled. 'Unemployed, thirty, and living at home – you aren't exactly catch of the century you know, Minnie.'

'Now that was uncalled for,' said Clive, putting down his plate of toast and laying a reassuring hand on Minnie's arm.

'It's OK, Clive,' said Minnie, combing a shaking hand through her hair.

'No, I won't have you end it like this. You're both good people – people break up, they move on; it doesn't mean you can't stay friends and it doesn't mean you have to leave things on a bad note. Come on, sit down.'

Clive pointed to two chairs at the kitchen table. Minnie looked at Greg, who crossed his arms in front of his chest and looked firmly up at the ceiling. She glanced out of the window. It was pouring with rain outside. Part of her just wanted to leave, to call an end to this horrible scene, but another part of her didn't want to end things like this. This side to Greg – she knew it wasn't who he was.

'Sit down,' Clive said firmly, pulling both chairs out from the table. They slunk into the chairs like chastised children. 'Right,' said Clive, taking the third seat between them. 'How long have you been together? Six months? Now, you've decided you don't want to be together any more.'

'She's decided,' said Greg, nostrils flaring.

'Whoever initiated it, it's happening. But you saw something in each other once, so before anyone goes anywhere, I want you both to say three positive things about the other person, and then share a favourite memory of your time together.' Greg let out an irritated 'humpff' sound.

'It will save you months of bitterness, trust me,' said Clive.

Minnie looked across at Clive's hopeful round face, then she looked back at Greg. She knew this spiteful petulance was simply Greg's way of masking a hurt. She still cared for him enough to feel that if she could temper that hurt, she should.

'Well,' said Minnie softly, 'I can go first.'

Greg glared at her, arms still folded tightly across his chest, nostrils wide as caves, mouth pinched into a thin pout.

'I always admired your passion for your work. You're a really good writer,' said Minnie.

'Excellent!' said Clive clapping his hands together. 'Greg, you go.'

Greg paused. He looked at Minnie and his eyes softened slightly.

'Go on Greg,' Clive said gently.

'You're a pretty good cook, I guess,' said Greg, rolling his eyes to the ceiling.

'Great. Minnie?' said Clive.

'You used to make me laugh with your silly jokes. You're good company, you know how to tell a story and make everyone listen.'

Greg jutted out his chin and gave the smallest nod of acknowledgement.

'Greg? What else?'

'Well I suppose we always had good bedroom ... stuff. You're very imaginative in the—'

'OK, we don't need any more details there. As mentioned previously, the walls in this flat are not that substantial,' Clive blushed.

'You always appreciated my opinion on your writing and I liked that. It made me feel valued,' said Minnie, speaking more assertively now.

She watched Greg's defensive veneer melt. He turned to face her and reached a hand across the table.

'You make me want to be funny,' he said gently. 'You have the most beautiful laugh. It's so satisfying to be the one to unleash it.'

Clive was looking back and forth between then. He took a loud bite of his toast and munched away noisily.

'OK, favourite memory now – Minnie,' Clive said spraying crumbs across the table.

'I'll always remember the time we went to Brighton for that column you were writing and we swam in the sea and went skinny-dipping and you said you loved my feet, even though I hate my feet.'

Minnie reached out and squeezed Greg's hand. He squeezed back and she glimpsed sight of the man she had loved, his petulant mask discarded.

'I'll always remember the first night we kissed. I felt like a teenager, I couldn't sleep for thinking about the girl from the street rally with the "mousing" sign.'

Minnie and Greg were looking directly into each other's eyes now. Reminding each other of these good memories felt like playing a favourite song on a worn-out record player before closing the lid.

'Now you say goodbye without regret and without bitterness. Perhaps in time you can be friends,' Clive said, wiping the crumbs from his mouth with both hands. 'Anyone for more toast? This Waitrose granary loaf is delightfully nutty.'

'Goodbye Greg,' said Minnie.

'Goodbye Minnie,' said Greg. ' I can still help you move if you need me to?'

'It's OK, I'll get my dad to help.'

Minnie stood up, hugged Greg, hugged Clive and then left. It had stopped raining outside. On the doorstep she paused, confused by what had just happened. She hadn't gone there tonight to break up with Greg, but she'd felt this shift inside her. It was as though Ian's speech had awoken her inner romantic, a voice she'd been silencing for years. She wanted to be with someone who spoke about her the way Ian spoke about Leila, and she definitely didn't want to be anyone's 70 per cent.

Lucy Donohue's column flashed into her mind. Dumping Greg had nothing to do with that column. The fact that Quinn was now single was irrelevant; this was about Greg not being her Sonic the Hedgehog, or whatever Ian's analogy was.

As she neared home she got a text from Greg.

'Did we just consciously uncouple?'

She smiled. 'I think so,' she replied.

'Am I living with male ginger Oprah?'

Minnie laughed out loud. Though she knew it was the right decision, she might miss his jokes. Greg was a jigsaw piece she'd been trying to make fit and the effort of forcing it felt like wearing a corset, pressuring her to conform to its shape. Now she had no Greg and soon she might have no Leila.

'Player one,' she whispered to herself as she unlocked her front door.

New Year's Eve 2003

There was going to be a party at the youth club on Castlehaven Road up in Camden; some of Quinn's mates from school were going. It would probably be lame, but it was the first New Year's Eve party not hosted by someone's parents.

Matt Dingle said he was bringing vodka, Deepak Patel said some of the grammar school girls who played netball were going; his mate Shiv went out with one of them and he said they were definitely, a hundred per cent going to be there. Quinn wanted to go, not necessarily to meet girls but just to get out of the house, to hear noise and hang out with his friends.

His mother was watching TV in the living room. She was curled up under one of the soft pink blankets that used to live in the spare room. Her hair was lank and she was wearing one of Dad's old T-shirts. She'd been watching the news and then some programme about fishing had come on. She hadn't bothered to change the channel.

'I'm going out now, Mum,' Quinn said, coming around the side of the sofa and sitting down next to her. 'OK?'

'Where are you going?' she said, slowly lifting her gaze to his face.

'To the youth club in Kentish Town; Bambers. There's a party, remember?' he said softly. He'd put on a clean white shirt. He'd washed and ironed it himself. 'Do you want me to ask Mrs Penny to look in on you while I'm out?'

Mrs Penny was a nice northern lady in her fifties who lived on one of the high-rise estates near the park. Once a week she cleaned the house, laundered the bedclothes and did a weekly food shop for them.

'You look so grown-up, Quinn, so handsome,' she said, stroking his face. 'You'll need to start shaving soon.'

'I'm fourteen tomorrow, Mum, I already shave,' he said, letting her leave her hand on his face.

On the sofa next to her, he noticed she'd got the russet-coloured wedding album out again. This was never a good sign.

'Mum, you're not making yourself upset again are you?' he said softly, nodding towards the album.

She covered the album with a sofa cushion.

'Just thinking about happier times,' she said flatly, her eyes pensive and still.

Quinn walked around her, picked up the album and went to put it back on the highest bookshelf he could reach. 'Never give your heart away, Quinn, because you don't get it back, you know,' she said, staring up at the ceiling.

She often said things like this to him. Quinn had already decided that if this was what it did to people, he didn't want anything to do with love.

'OK, Mum, I'm going now.'

'You'll keep your phone on?' she asked, a note of anxiety creeping into her voice. 'And you'll take the spare, just in case?'

'Yes and yes,' said Quinn, tapping both sides of his jeans. He hated how they bulked out his pockets.

'And you won't put your drink down; you know how easily people spike drinks these days?'

He needed to leave before she talked herself out of letting him go.

On the street, Quinn felt the stifling atmosphere of the house dissipate into the cool night air. He felt free for a moment, though he knew he was not. Sometimes it felt as though he was under house arrest. His phones were like those electronic tags – he could go outside the prison walls but he was still permanently connected.

School was release. It was always harder over the holidays when there were fewer reasons to go out. His friends had packed holidays full of skiing and 'getting out of London'. For those left in town, most of the mothers planned endless entertainment. Pete Thompson's mum had organised Laser Quest for eight of them last Thursday and it wasn't even anyone's birthday. At least this year he'd been allowed to start travelling on public transport alone – that was a game changer.

Quinn liked the street where he lived. He liked the multicoloured houses and the symmetrical trees along the road. He liked the bakery on the corner and the bookshop that smelt of toasted cinnamon. He liked the old lady with the funny felt hat who sat on the wall with her cats and said, 'All right young lad?' whenever he passed.

When his parents split up there had been talk of selling the blue house and his mum moving out of London to somewhere quieter. Maybe she would have been better off in a small village, somewhere where people were nosy and wanted to know your business. In London, if you wanted to keep yourself to yourself there was no one to stop you.

Quinn crossed the railway bridge and London changed in an instant, like crossing through curtains from front stage to back. The scene transformed from boutique shops, flower stalls and cafés that sold four types of milk, to a road full of buses, noise, graffiti, and street vendors thrusting newspapers at you. Most of his friends lived on this side of the tracks. Often Quinn felt more at home here – people didn't look at you so closely here, it was easier to get lost in the crowd. Up in the sky a single firework exploded. Quinn looked up to see tendrils of light cutting a slash through the grey sky, a loner firework breaking free.

*

Bambers was packed by the time Quinn arrived; he couldn't get over how popular it was. Clusters of teenagers were crammed into the room, swaying self-consciously to the music. In the middle of the dance floor the older, drunker kids were taking up all the space, swinging each other around, screaming the words to 'Around the World' by ATC. The air smelt of cheap Superdrug body spray with 'going out' names like Twilight Seduction or Midnight Mist. Sweat hung in the air like in a hot locker room after games. Disco lights were set up at the far end, strobing circles of red, blue and green that jumped across the ceiling of the dimly lit hall. A DJ was on decks in front of the kitchen kiosk, a purple banner covered in musical notes that read 'Music Melvin' was draped over the kiosk. There was a trestle table bar selling soft drinks, crisps, and those glow sticks you snapped in half to make them work. The table was being manned by the usual selection of mums – the kind of mums who baked cupcakes with 2004 written on in gold icing, the mums who came early to help hang paper bunting and label Coke bottles with stickers saying one pound.

'Quinno!' called a voice across the hall. Quinn looked up to see Matt strutting towards him. 'Quick, have some of this.'

Matt handed him a bottle of warm Coke that smelt like it was 80 per cent vodka. Quinn took a sip and tried not to gag.

'Painter's already pulled,' said Matt, elbowing Quinn in the ribs.

Matt was short with pointed features and deep-pitted acne across his chin and the lower half of his cheeks. He was friendly, funny and brilliant at football, but he didn't get much attention from girls even though, recently, girls were all he talked about. 'Fucking Painter, look at him!' Matt pointed out Paul Painter, a well-built blond rugby player in their year. He had his arm around a girl in a black velvet minidress over by the vending machine that only sold out-of-date crisps.

Quinn felt one of the phones in his pocket buzz. His mother was texting him already. He slapped his friend on the back and handed him back the bottle of Coke.

'You won't make it to midnight if you drink this.' Quinn looked around the room to see who else he knew. 'Is Jonesy here? Patel?'

'Jonesy's smoking. Patel said it was all lame twelve year olds and went to try the pub; says he knows the doorman, such bollocks. Have this, I've got plenty.' Matt handed him back the Coke.

Quinn felt his shoulders begin to relax as he took another sip of alcohol.

He replied to his Mum; he'd arrived – he was fine. She'd messaged telling him to get a cab home on the account; she said she'd ordered him one for twelve fifteen. It was only a short night bus back to the railway bridge and then a five-minute walk home, but there was no point arguing with her.

'Your mental mum let you out then?' came a voice behind him, and Quinn felt a friendly punch land in the side of his ribs. He turned to give Jonesy a thump on the arm. 'It's yer birthday, it's yer birthday,' Jonesy sang, grinding his hips into Quinn and waving his arms in a dance.

Duncan Jones was one of Quinn's best friends and one of the only people who could get away with making jokes like that about his mother.

'You got Dr Quincey here drinking?' Jonesy asked Matt, taking the Coke out of Quinn's hands and sniffing it. 'The mentalist isn't going to like that.'

'He's got to have the odd night off,' said Matt.

'Let's not talk about my mum tonight, dickheads,' Quinn said.

'Let's talk about Matt's mum then. Mrs Dingle is looking proper MILF these days,' Jonesy said, making a kissing, clicking sound with his tongue and giving Matt a wink.

'Don't you ...' Matt took a lunge at Jonesy. Quinn stepped between them and held out a palm to intercept Matt's flailing fist.

'Boys!' came a warning voice from one of the trestle-table mums. 'We'll have none of that, please.'

The night rolled on. Deepak Patel reappeared, having failed to get into the pub, DJ Music Melvin turned out to be half decent, and Quinn danced and drank and laughed with his friends. At one point a few girls came shuffling over to dance next to them but Matt scared them away with his version of breakdancing.

'If you want to pull, you'll have to ditch pizza-face,' Deepak said, pointing at Matt, who by this point was staggering around the dance floor, sloshing his drink down his T-shirt, shouting out lyrics to 'Bootylicious' by Destiny's Child. 'Those girls clearly want to get to you, but Matt keeps leching on anyone who gets close.'

Quinn hadn't thought about trying to kiss anyone tonight. He never tried to kiss girls, it just happened sometimes without him doing very much. His school was all boys, but whenever he and his friends hung out with girls, it was usually his louder, more outgoing friends who did all the talking, while Quinn, without trying to, came off as the quiet, interesting one.

A group of girls wearing crop tops and faded denim were watching him from a line of plastic chairs at the side of the room. They all clasped disposable red cups between both hands. One wearing too-red lipstick smiled at him. She was pretty but, even with the vodka, he wouldn't know what to say if he went over there alone.

At ten to midnight, Quinn slipped off the dance floor and hid in the corridor by the loos. He didn't want to be exposed at midnight. Music Melvin would start playing 'Lady in Red' or some other saddo slow dance. There'd be the awkward shuffle as people tried to line themselves up with someone to kiss, his mates nudging each other, merciless in their mocking of both success and failure. He couldn't deal with that kind of pressure. He replied to another text from his mum, the fourth of the evening, 'Happy New Year, Mum. Honestly, go to bed, I'm fine.'

When he looked up from his phone there was a girl standing in the corridor opposite him. She had straight blonde hair, soft freckled skin, and a bright, cheerful face.

'Don't mind me,' she gave a little shrug and leant back against the wall, resting one foot up behind her. 'I'm just hiding from lemming o'clock on the dance floor.'

Quinn gave a nonchalant nod.

'Don't you hate how everyone just gets off with whoever they're standing next to at midnight? It's such a meat market. I bet most people don't even know the name of the person they're kissing. So gross,' said the girl, shaking her head and making a disapproving little scowl.

Her checks were flushed and she rubbed her neck with the heel of a palm. Music Melvin was playing 'Two Minutes to Midnight' by Iron Maiden – not so predictable after all.

'Yeah, gross,' Quinn said quietly, then after a pause. 'Did you say lemming o'clock?'

'Lemmings all copy each other, don't they? They don't think for themselves.'

She gave him a coy smile. Then she looked off down the corridor and pushed her foot away from the wall. Quinn felt as though she was about to leave. He didn't want her to go. He tried to think of something else to say.

'Apparently there are like, thirty different species of lemming.'

Of all the things to say, why had he gone with that? How did he even know that? He must have picked it up from one of the nature documentaries his mother watched. This is exactly why he didn't talk to girls. He glanced up at her face, convinced she was going to laugh at him.

'Good knowledge,' she said, leaning back against the wall again, 'I love a lemming fact.'

Quinn felt his shoulders relax.

'What species do you think is out there on the dance floor then?' she asked, fiddling with a strand of blonde hair.

'Probably the lesser-known urban species – Teenagius Drunkerus,' he said.

She let out a laugh like a garden sprinkler, firing out little bursts of joy. The sound sent a fizz of energy through Quinn.

Voices back in the hall started shouting in unison, 'Ten, nine, eight ...'

Quinn was suddenly filled with an overwhelming compulsion to kiss this girl. His mates wouldn't have noticed someone like her, with her DM boots, roll-neck top and high-waisted jeans, but something in her face stood out to Quinn. She was luminously pretty, but clearly had no idea that she was. Her whole way of being felt magnetic to him.

'Six, five, four ...'

He tried to catch her eye. He'd overheard Toby Sampson in the locker room once saying that was the key to it, just look at them long enough without blinking and they'll know you want it. She looked back. He looked away. He was no good at the looking game. He took a step towards her, pretending to be intensely interested in something on the wall behind her shoulder. He put a hand up against the wall by her head, then he just stared at his hand, unsure of what to do next. God this was awkward. She was going to laugh at him, ask him what he was doing. She'd tell all her friends about this weird lemming-fact guy who'd tried to kiss her by the loos.

'Three, two, one – Happy New Year!'

He dared another sideways look at her. She was looking up at him, her pupils flushed wide. Then her eyes darted nervously from side-to-side.

'Um, hi,' she said.

'Hello,' he mumbled, dropping his gaze to the floor. 'Can I … Would it be OK if I …' Oh god, what if she said no? He wasn't sure any kiss was worth this level of stress.

'Yes,' she said, her voice breathy and nervous, her cheeks flushed pink.

She shut her eyes, and tilted her head up towards him, as he closed the space between them. Quinn felt his stomach flip as her soft full lips pressed gently against his.

Quinn had kissed girls before but not like this. The kisses before had been wet and mechanical, pleasurable, but consciously so, and somehow a bit ridiculous. Like the girl from the hockey club who just stuck her tongue out and moved it back and forth into his mouth like a lizard. This was something entirely new; every part of his body was invested in this, her mouth entirely in sync with his own. He felt an instant firm reaction beneath his jeans and pulled away, embarrassed that she might notice.

'Wow,' she said softly, her face flushed. 'Um, Happy New Year.'

'H...'

Quinn couldn't even repeat the sentence back to her, his mind was so full of questions; was this what kissing was supposed to be like? What was her name? Could he see her again? Could he kiss her again now without pressing his offensively hard jeans against her?

Before he could answer any of these questions, his phone started to ring, then his other phone started ringing too. The girl glanced down, perplexed.

'Sorry.' Quinn took a step back, pulling both phones out of his pocket. His mother was calling on one, the taxi company on the other. It was one minute past midnight. Quinn turned his back on the girl, not wanting her to look down at his jeans. 'I'm ... I need to take this, but wait here, please. I'll be one minute.' He gave her an apologetic, pleading look and backed out of the side door into the courtyard beyond.

'Yes,' he said, answering the phone to his mother. 'Mum I'm kind of bu—'

'Quinn.' She was crying, 'I need you to come home right now.'

'Mum I'll be back in half an hour, I said—'

'You need to come back now, Quinn, I think there's someone in the garden, trying to get into the house.' She sounded breathless, panicked.

Quinn sighed a slow, resigned sigh. He called back the cab; he'd be five minutes, just long enough to get the girl's name and number. But when he went back inside to the corridor, she had gone.

1 February 2020

Minnie woke up in a panic. She couldn't breathe. Something was suffocating her. She sat bolt upright, gulping for air, her arms flailing frantically. A grey ball of fur flew across her bed with a screeeeoooow sound. Since moving home last week, Lucky had taken to sleeping on her face. Whether he had separation anxiety, or he simply missed having a warm spot to sleep on at the top of the fridge, Minnie didn't know, but it was turning into a life-threatening situation.

Looking around the room, Minnie had that momentary feeling of not knowing where she was. The ceiling was too close, the windows weren't where they should be and there was the ominous sound of ticking, like a hundred bombs about to go off. Then she remembered she was at her parents' house on a mattress on the floor in her old attic bedroom. There were no bombs, just the combined sound of a hundred clocks.

The small, eight-by-ten-foot space was packed with boxes and old suitcases. Her father's workbench was set up in the middle of the room, covered with the remaining tools and magnifying lenses he hadn't got around to moving. The wooden frame of her deconstructed bed leant against one wall, stacked away to make more room for boxes.

The last few weeks felt like an unravelling to Minnie, wool being pulled from her body, stripping her of comfort and leaving her naked. All the ways in which she defined her current life had been removed. Minnie was a chef, she ran a pie company, she lived off the Essex Road, and she dated Greg. Breaking up with Greg felt like stripping off that last piece of identifying clothing.

Handing back the key to her flat had been painful.

'It's only temporary,' Leila had reassured her as she helped move boxes into the hall. 'You won't be at your parents' for ever.'

But Minnie couldn't see how she was ever going to manage to rent a place on her own again. What with moving house, breaking up with Greg, and the flurry of orders to fill at work, she hadn't had a chance to plan what she was going to say to Leila about the business. She'd been waiting for inspiration to strike, but it hadn't struck.

She glanced up at one of the clocks on the wall to see what time it was, but each clock showed a different time. She checked her phone, 11 a.m. She'd been awake half the night, her brain too full; she must have finally dozed off around six. The jostle of thoughts now began again in earnest and she knew she would have no peace until she plucked them out one by one and confined them to a list. She typed a note on her phone.

TO DO:

1) Apologise to Quinn Hamilton for being horrible cow.

2) Tell Leila I want to close the business.

3) Think of excuse – why do I want to close the business?

4) Help Bev, Alan and Fleur find new jobs.
5) Secretly plan Leila's perfect engagement.
6) Get new job for self.
7) Find somewhere to live.
8) Stop being so shit at life.
9) Buy cat food.
10) Help Bev resolve existential crisis.
11) Build bed/Sort out room.

Then she moved number eleven to the top of the list. It was best to start the day with achievable tasks. She picked up a box which had 'Minnie's stuff' scrawled on the side. Inside was an old karaoke tape player with a broken pink microphone, a half-built Lego Millennium Falcon and an old owl money-box she'd painted herself. She shook it hopefully but it didn't rattle. At the bottom of the box was a pink photo album decorated in blue glitter glue. In round cursive twirls she had written, 'Summer Camp 2005'. Minnie flicked reverently through the pages. The book was full of pictures of her with Leila the summer they'd first met. Every year, she'd begged her parents to let her go to that summer camp and every year they'd said they couldn't afford it. They usually just asked Will to watch her in the holidays, but then Will got a summer job, so Dad relented and she was allowed to go.

On that first day at camp she'd seen Leila walking towards her wearing a pink leotard and green hot pants. She was the coolest person Minnie had ever seen in real life. Minnie had cowered as she'd approached, convinced someone like Leila would only be coming over to say something cruel to her

– but she'd just smiled and asked Minnie if she wanted to join them for a water-balloon fight. For Minnie, it had been platonic love at first sight.

It took Minnie most of the day to sort out her bedroom; there was so much nostalgia imbued in each object from her childhood. Eventually, she was satisfied that the room felt habitable. She'd rebuilt the bed, stacked all her dad's boxes neatly against a wall and categorised all her things into: 'Old To Keep', 'Old To Bin', and 'Things For Now'. She didn't want to unpack the 'Things For Now' boxes; it would be conceding that her stay at home was more than temporary.

As a final gesture to brighten the space, she propped the only piece of art she owned against a pile of boxes at the foot of her bed. It was a print of a painting called *Automat*. Leila had given it to her for her twenty-first birthday and Minnie had treasured it ever since. It depicted a woman in hat and coat sitting alone in an American diner, gazing thoughtfully into a cup of coffee. She looked alone, but not lonely, there was something self-contained and contemplative about the woman. You wanted to know what she was thinking, where she had come from, where she might be going. On the back, Leila had scribbled a note – 'Be a good companion to yourself and you will never be lonely.' It was one of Leila's highest aspirations: self-sufficiency.

Minnie surveyed the room and nodded to herself. The simple task of sorting through the chaos had calmed her anxious mind, and putting *Automat* up made the room feel like home. She climbed onto her freshly built bed, sat cross-legged against the wall and opened her laptop. She typed

Lucy Donohue's name into Google – she wanted to see whether people were still commenting on her article. There were a few tweets about it on Twitter, lots of people asking if they could be Lucy's next dinner date. Minnie groaned – of all the things she had to do, why was she spending time googling Lucy Donohue? She needed to get some fresh air. Downstairs, the house was empty; both her parents worked on Saturdays. She scrolled through the new list on her phone and moved number nine and ten to the top – achievable goals.

Minnie got the Tube down to a shop near Old Street station. She remembered seeing it when they'd driven past on the delivery round. It was a printing shop and in the window hung a sign saying, 'We personalise anything'. She handed the man behind the counter a USB stick and a plain matte-plastic bottle she had saved. It was an unusual request. She wanted to put a picture of Bev and a few words about her on a shampoo bottle. It was a silly gesture but maybe it would ease Bev's existential fears about being outlasted by a shampoo bottle. The man said it could be ready in an hour if she didn't mind waiting. Minnie had nothing to rush home for, so she decided to spend the time meandering the streets watching other, more interesting people going about their lives.

Minnie enjoyed speculating about strangers in the street; where they might be going, and who they were going to meet. She passed a tall woman in tiny shorts and silver tights with huge Afro hair and bright blue eye shadow. She wore a T-shirt that said 'Queen' in gold glitter. Minnie watched heads turn in the street as the woman sashayed past.

Minnie had never been someone to turn heads in the street; she just didn't have that head-turning quality. She knew if people talked to her, took time to acclimatise to her features, then she might be deemed ordinarily pretty, but it wasn't the kind of beauty that would stop a stranger in their tracks. When she was with Leila, people turned to look, though usually that had more to do with Leila's outlandish hair and outfit than anything else. Minnie wondered if people who dressed unconventionally were after the kind of attention usually reserved for the strikingly beautiful people. Leila would say it was a case of not caring, of wanting her exterior to match the way she felt inside. Minnie had no idea what a reflection of her inner self would look like. Maybe that was her problem – she didn't know who she was.

Minnie had always yearned to blend in, to not draw attention to herself. Attention meant criticism, attention meant being teased. She had read an article about how beautiful women, especially models, find growing older particularly hard. They are so used to turning heads in the street that as the gazes from strangers fall away, they lose their sense of identity. Maybe it was better to be invisible in the first place and never know what you were missing. Minnie's thoughts turned to Tara. She must have been someone who turned heads when she was younger. Would aging have been harder for her than for Minnie's mum, who had always been a little bit stocky and plain? Was it her receding beauty that caused Tara's frailty, that air of vulnerability Minnie had sensed? Then she remembered the fear in Tara's face at the smashed lamp, the panic in her eyes.

She couldn't imagine that kind of pain had anything to do with the outside world – there had to be something more going on.

She walked aimlessly on, not looking where she was going. When she looked up from the pavement, she realised she was outside Tantive Consulting. Had she walked here accidentally, or had her subconscious led her here? It was five in the afternoon on a Saturday, but the lights on the fourth floor were on. Apologising to Quinn Hamilton was the next point on her list.

Minnie pressed the buzzer. She didn't expect anyone to be there at the weekend. It was probably the kind of office where lights were left on twenty-four seven, ruining the planet one light bulb at a time. Then again, Quinn was probably the kind of workaholic who couldn't switch off at the weekends. She thought it with a mental sneer and then chastised herself for her hypocrisy – she was that person too.

A sound came over the intercom.

'Hello?' she said.

There was a noise and the door clicked open; she'd been buzzed in. Minnie stepped tentatively into the lift and pressed the button for the fourth floor, her heart pounding in her chest. She hadn't meant to come here, she'd meant to call him and apologise over the phone. He was going to think it was weird, her showing up at his office unannounced.

The lift doors opened and Quinn was standing in front of her with a beaming smile, arms held wide in greeting. She'd forgotten how tall he was.

'Hi!' he said, then his neck retracted and his arms dropped to his sides. 'Oh, it's you.'

'Sorry,' Minnie blinked her eyes closed and shook her head. 'I was just passing and the lights were on and I just … I wanted to apologise about the other day. I don't want to intrude if you're expecting someone else. I can go …'

'No, it's fine.' Minnie looked up from the floor and Quinn gave her a perplexed smile, 'Come in.'

He led her over to the reception area, and waved an arm towards one of the low brown leather chairs. 'Sit, sit.'

In the glass-walled meeting room beyond, Minnie could see an open laptop and a sprawl of papers fanning out across the table. Minnie sat on her hands to stop herself from biting her nails. She couldn't get comfortable so decided to stand instead. This felt awkward, so she settled on splitting the difference and perching on the arm of the chair instead. Quinn watched this self-conscious dance of hers with amusement.

'Look, I'm just going to say what I wanted to say, then I'll leave you in peace to get on with your work. I was rude the other day. I don't know why I was so angry with you when you've been nothing but nice to me and, well, I'm sorry. Maybe you are right, I do have a bit of a chip on my shoulder.'

'You don't need to apologise,' he said, tidying the papers on the coffee table between them.

'I really do.'

'OK, maybe you do.'

'I probably am doing a crap job with the business – I guess you hit a nerve.'

'Well, I've had calls from clients asking how they can order from "the pie lady". You're clearly doing something right.'

She acknowledged the compliment with a nod. He sat watching her for a moment. His blue eyes looked soft, unfocused. 'Anyway, it's nice to see you … not shouting at me,' he grinned.

Minnie's lips twitched, she didn't want to laugh.

'I'm not usually a big shouter. You bring out the worst in me.'

'It's not all bad,' he said, picking up a pen from the coffee table and twiddling it between his fingers. 'You have a very sexy indignant face.'

'A what face?' Minnie felt herself scowl.

'That face there, sexy indignant – it's your signature look.' Quinn looked up at her, pointing the pen in her direction. She noticed his hair was ruffled and disordered.

'Wh … wha … ' Minnie floundered. This was not the same Quinn she'd met the other day.

'Anyway, apology accepted, I'd-forgotten-about-all-it.' Quinn slurred the last few words, merging them into one. 'I guess I'm sorry you think I'm obnoxious and patronising,' he said in an odd, deep voice.

'Why are you being strange?' Minnie frowned. Then it dawned on her – his glassy eyes, his languid body movement. 'Are you drunk?'

'Am I drunk? Am I drunk?' Quinn screwed up his face, leant forwards and then flung his body back in the chair. His eyes darted over to the sideboard. Minnie followed his gaze and saw an open bottle of whisky sitting there.

'Look, it's none of my business,' said Minnie. 'You're free to drink alone in your office on a Saturday afternoon if you want to. It just explains a lot.'

'Do you want a drink, Minnie Cooper?' Quinn asked, leaping to his feet and doing a little dance around the reception chairs before landing next to the sideboard where the whisky stood. 'Non whisky-based beverages are also available.'

Minnie shrugged. 'Sure, why not?'

She had nowhere else to be and she was intrigued to hear more from drunk Quinn. He poured her a whisky over ice. He had a drinks cabinet hidden behind a black lacquered bureau, complete with vintage silver ice bucket and tongs. He poured himself another at the same time. Minnie sat back down in the armchair properly. She felt more relaxed now she knew Quinn had been drinking – the drunk version of Quinn was less intimidating, less virtuous. She felt her mental guard slacken.

'So why the office? Secret drinker not a social drinker?' Minnie asked.

'You drove me to drink, Minnie Cooper – your elusive enigmatic quality.' He said it with a wry smile, toasting her with his glass in mid-air.

'Ha-ha.'

He locked his gaze on hers, unblinking. For a moment he looked entirely serious and sober. Minnie felt as though she was in an elevator plummeting several floors. She put a hand to her stomach, recalibrating her balance by studying the cracks in her ice cube.

'Are you drowning your sorrows about Lucy Donohue's article?' she ventured.

'Not especially,' said Quinn, 'but I'm still dealing with damage limitation.'

'It was pretty harsh,' said Minnie.

Quinn shrugged. 'Better to be hated for what you are, than loved for what you're not.'

'Profound,' said Minnie. 'Where did you read that – the back of a cereal packet?'

'I thought it was incredibly lucid and poetic for four whiskies in,' Quinn grinned, inhaling the rest of his drink in one mouthful. 'So, tell me about you, Minnie Cooper – what's happening in your life? Funny Greg still making you chuckle in all the right places? Still too principled to cook for obnoxious arseholes like me?' Quinn sniffed and the dimple on his cheek creased into life.

'Greg and I broke up.'

She watched Quinn's face for a reaction. He slowly raised one eyebrow. 'Stopped being funny, did he?'

'No. Maybe I just need more than jokes right now.'

'Ouch. Poor Greg,' Quinn said, wincing theatrically.

'So what did Lucy do to get binned? All the posh meals got a bit rich for you? Found yourself getting paunchy?'

Quinn rubbed his washboard stomach and frowned. 'There's no paunch here, and recently I've been eating more of your pies than anything else.'

They sat in silence for a minute. Minnie regretted asking him about Lucy. He clearly wasn't going to elaborate and now she felt foolish for prying. Then again, he'd asked about Greg and she hadn't volunteered many details. Maybe they didn't know each other well enough to be honest about such things, or maybe the answers were too loaded with meaning.

It had been the conversation with Ian that made Minnie realise things with Greg weren't right, but if Minnie was honest with herself, the fluttering owl feeling she had around Quinn was also a factor. Logically, she knew the owl effect was simply a chemical reaction based on pheromones; some ancient animal instinct. It did not mean he was viable boyfriend material, or that the feeling was mutual. No, the owl effect simply served to remind her of what she no longer had with Greg.

All of it faded eventually. In every relationship, that initial fluttering feeling would simmer down and then disappear. She imagined the young excitable owls inside her aging into wise old birds; they'd wear spectacles and have less energy for flapping about. The ephemeral nature of it meant you had to think with your head. You had to choose a partner based on logic; someone with similar life experience who would share your point of view and your interests. Quinn did not fulfil any of these criteria.

'You know the truth is, I don't find it easy to commit to anyone,' Quinn said, looking up at her with glassy eyes. He swallowed, pinching his lower lip back with his top teeth. 'Apparently I have "commitment issues." '

He whispered the last words, as though confiding a secret. Then he blinked, collecting himself.

'We can talk about it if you want?' Minnie prompted, softly.

'I wouldn't know where to begin, Minnie.'

'Try me,' she said, leaning forward in her chair.

Quinn looked pensive, his features halting as though stealing themselves to take a plunge from a high board. Then he leant back in his chair, pulling away from the brink, the opportunity to jump missed.

'Then you'd know things about me, Minnie Cooper, and I know next to nothing about you. You need to trade some emotional currency first.'

'OK,' Minnie tilted her head to one side and took a slow sip of her drink. She felt the warming whisky loosen her tongue. 'My best friend's boyfriend just told me he's going to propose. He also told me the stress of work is killing Leila, and he wants me to fold the business. He wants her to be free to thrive and he doesn't think she'll thrive while she's having sleepless nights over No Hard Fillings.'

Quinn was watching her intently as she spoke. She plunged on, 'I might have been cross that he was interfering, or sad that he might be right. Mainly, I just felt happy that my friend has someone who thinks about her that way.' Minnie paused. 'I guess I was cross and sad but also happy and a bit jealous. I think I decided if I can't have a relationship like that, then maybe I'd rather be on my own.' Minnie paused and then added, 'Greg didn't like me to call him unannounced. He liked me to text first, can you believe that? When you love someone, you want to be able to call them without having to make an appointment.'

Quinn looked incredibly sad for a moment; she saw it flash across his face. His eyes, usually flickering on the brink of amusement, took on this rheumy, lifeless quality, a distillation of misery. Minnie had said too much. She shuffled back in her chair, putting the glass in her hand down on the side table with a bang. 'Come on then, I got all serious on you. Spill your guts, Hamilton; what's your emotional constipation about? Not a misguided romantic like me?'

He brushed a shaking hand through his hair and then the look was gone. A shrill, buzzing noise pierced the air and Quinn and Minnie both jumped in surprise.

'It's the intercom,' said Quinn.

'Expecting someone?' asked Minnie.

Quinn looked confused, then his eyes bulged and he slapped a hand to his mouth.

'Shit,' he said. 'I arranged a Tinder date.'

Minnie laughed awkwardly. She felt her cheeks prickle.

'I'll cancel, I'll tell her to go.'

'No, no you can't do that. Poor girl!' said Minnie, standing up and brushing down her creased jeans. 'I'll leave.'

'This is awkward.' Quinn grimaced.

'It's fine, it's none of my business how you spend your afternoons – whisky and Tinder is an excellent combination.'

Minnie brushed her hair out from behind her ears in an attempt to cover her burning cheeks. Quinn stood up and followed her to the lift, where he answered the intercom with a shaking hand.

'Hello, Quinn?' came a woman's voice.

'Yeah, I'll be right down,' he drawled.

Minnie called the lift, the doors opened and they both stepped in. She fiddled with her hands and fixed her stare on the silver reflective doors as they closed.

'Do I smell of whisky?' Quinn whispered out of the corner of his mouth.

Minnie turned to look at him and then leant over to sniff him.

'Only like you bathed in it.'

He did smell of whisky, but he also had this manly, hot sort-of Christmassy smell that made Minnie inexplicably want to nuzzle into his neck. No, she mustn't think like that; Quinn was a player with commitment issues, and she had just broken up with someone – neck nuzzling was not an option.

The lift opened onto the street and a girl was waiting there. She was tall with long blonde hair, impossibly bee-stung lips and large breasts on display. Clearly Quinn had a type – this woman was a bustier, younger version of Lucy Donohue. The girl's eyes lit up when she saw Quinn, then she saw Minnie and her delicate features tensed in confusion.

'Hi, Amanda?' Quinn greeted her politely with a kiss on the cheek.

'And this is ... ?' Amanda asked in an airy voice, pointing a taut, unblinking smile at Minnie.

'This is Minnie, she's ...' Quinn faltered.

'I'm nobody, I'm the caterer.'

Quinn winced. Minnie stood between them and they both turned towards her. She was the third wheel, she needed to leave, but her feet were glued to the ground; she physically couldn't make herself walk away.

'Well, what would you like to do then?' said Amanda, in a squeaky, youthful voice. She tilted her body away from Minnie, closer to Quinn. 'There's an Edward Hopper exhibition on around the corner that I thought we might go to?'

Minnie did a double take. Edward Hopper was the artist who painted *Automat* – he was Minnie's favourite artist. She was impressed Amanda was a fan. That would teach her not to judge a book by its busty cover.

'You like Edward Hopper?' Quinn asked, in exactly the tone Minnie had been thinking it.

Amanda blushed, 'Oh no, I don't know who he is, but I saw in your profile he was on your list of interests. I thought maybe you could educate me?' Amanda gave Quinn a flirtatious little smile.

'I love Edward Hopper,' Minnie chipped in without thinking. Amanda and Quinn both turned to look at her with what-are-you-still-doing-here expressions. 'Sorry, I should go. Enjoy yourselves, kids, play safe, ha-ha.'

Minnie backed away with a little wave. That was excruciating. Why had she stayed standing there like that? Now all she wanted to do was go to that Edward Hopper exhibition herself to see if the original *Automat* was there. Clearly she could not do that because it would be weird and stalkerish to follow Quinn around on his Tinder date. Instead, she went back to the printing shop to pick up the present for Bev, back to her attic room full of boxes and a solitary print, back to her list of horrible jobs.

*

'How was Hopper?'

Minnie lay in bed the next morning looking at the words she had typed out on her phone. Her thumb hovered over the send button. What was she doing? Why was she thinking about texting him? She was just curious to know what had happened with Amanda. Yesterday felt like watching the first half of a movie and then not having the chance to see how it ended. Was it that? No – there were plenty of movies she hadn't seen the ending to, and it didn't keep her awake at night.

It was the owls egging her on to text him. The predictable, undiscerning fluttery owls, which would have her embarrass herself in front of a totally unsuitable City boy like Quinn. Minnie pulled the duvet over her head and made a noise like a dying animal. What did she think he was going to say if she sent him a text asking about his date? 'Oh, Amanda was awful, total bimbo, I wish I had gone with you instead – and you know when you poured your heart out to me about not wanting to compromise in love any more, about wanting someone to fuel the best version of yourself? Well, I want that guy to be me, how about it?'

Why was she even thinking about this? Minnie deleted the text. She wouldn't text him. She'd just broken up with someone because she was finally starting to place more value on her self-worth. The last thing she needed right now was to fuel some self-esteem-crushing crush on a man like Quinn Hamilton.

'So what's this about?' asked Will. 'A guy with a fish fetish?'

'No!' cried Leila, reaching out to bash his shin with her forearm. She was sitting on the floor of the Coopers' lounge, while Will sat, legs stretched out, in the cord brown arm-chair. '*Splash*! It's an epic love story about star-crossed lovers who want to be together despite their differences – it's very romantic.'

'They're different species, how's that gonna work? If the mermaid's got a tail surely she doesn't have a ... you know,' said Will, grimacing.

'Ignore him,' said Minnie, 'he's seen it before. He's just trying to show off 'cause you're here.' Minnie was perched on the edge of the sofa braiding Leila's newly blue hair as she sat on the floor between her legs. Both girls were dressed in pyjama bottoms and scruffy T-shirts. 'I saw you welling up over it last time.'

'I haven't seen it – it's a chick flick,' said Will, reaching out to flick Minnie behind her ear.

'Ow!' she squealed, batting away his hand.

'Are you three going to sit there all night?' asked Minnie's dad, coming down the stairs and walking through to the living room. 'It's New Year's Eve – you not got parties to go to?'

'I'm going out now,' said Will, jumping up, 'there's a gig in Kilburn.'

When Will stood up, Minnie noticed her brother was now taller than their father. Though he had a very different build, with his long, lanky legs, angular face and foppish brown hair.

'Take the girls too, why don't you?' said their dad, elbowing Will in the ribs.

'I'm not her babysitter any more. And they're underage, they might not get in,' said Will, walking into the hall to put on his coat.

'We don't want to go to your lame party anyway,' Minnie called after him.

'OK, well enjoy your fishy fanny film, losers!' Will called as he shut the front door behind him.

'Two seventeen-year-old girls with no New Year's Eve parties to go to. What dimension have I walked into?' said her dad, shaking his head.

'The jinx is less likely to get me if I'm home doing nothing,' Minnie explained. 'Leila's keeping me company.'

'Pfff,' laughed her dad. 'So you're never going to leave the house at New Year again, are you?'

'Not if I can help it.'

'Parties are overrated,' said Leila. 'Movie marathons and Ben & Jerry's are where the cool kids are at these days, Mr C.'

'Well, I'm going down the pub. Big year to celebrate,' said her dad, leaning over to search the folds of the brown armchair. 'The year 2008 is going to be the one we Coopers make our fortune.'

'Dad's building a property empire,' Minnie explained. 'Thinks he's going to be the next Donald Trump.'

Her dad grinned as he pulled his house keys out from the depths of the armchair.

'You watch this space girls – we Coopers are going up in the world.'

'Ooh, let me ask you before you go, Mr C – where do you want to be this time next year?' Leila asked, clapping her hands together.

'This time next year?' Minnie's dad said, rubbing his chin between his thumb and forefinger thoughtfully. 'Well, I'd have a new home office for my property business, one for my clocks, and another one for miscellaneous odds and sods.'

'It's supposed to be realistic, Dad,' said Minnie.

'OK, then I'd settle for losing two stone so I can see my toes again in the shower,' he said, letting out a cackling belly laugh.

'Dad! Gross!' squealed Minnie. 'I don't need that image in my mind!'

'I'm going, I'm going,' he marched back through to the hall, still chuckling to himself. 'Now, I've told your ma to come and join us when she gets in. You sure you girls can't be persuaded? Drinks are on me tonight. Only after midnight for Minnie, mind. I can't be seen supplying alcohol to a minor,' he said with a wink as he pulled on his coat.

'We're good, thanks Mr C,' said Leila.

Once her dad had gone, Minnie pulled the wine bottle out from beneath the sofa. Her parents didn't really mind her drinking alcohol; they only minded her drinking *their* alcohol.

'I'm sorry, but now your dad and brother have gone, can I just say, what the fuck is with the clocks?' Leila asked, hands flying outwards as though she were about to break into a dance routine.

'I know.'

'The noise is *so* annoying.'

'You get used to it.'

'Are your parents like obsessed with knowing the time or something?'

'My dad likes fixing old clocks.'

'I feel like I'm on a game show and the time is ticking down and someone's about to ask me what the Countdown Conundrum is and I've got nothing, *nothing* I tell you.' Leila lolled her head back into Minnie's lap and looked up at her face.

'Half the clocks don't even tell the right time. Dad can't keep up with winding them all.'

'Don't ever bring a guy back here, Min, they'd freak out.'

Minnie secured the end of the braid she'd been working on with a tiny elastic band.

'I'm hardly likely to bring a guy back here, am I?' Minnie paused. 'You sure you don't mind staying in with me, Leils? I don't want you to miss out on Steve's party because of me. We know Dan Deaton's going to be there.'

Minnie picked up another piece of blue hair from the front of Leila's scalp. She was beginning to regret how small she was doing these plaits. She'd started half an hour ago and was only a quarter of the way up one side of Leila's head.

'Nah, if Dan Deaton liked me last week he'll like me next week too. No New Year's Eve party's going to change that,' Leila shrugged. 'Plus, my hair's only half done and we've got

all these films to watch: *Pretty Woman, The Princess Bride* ...
what a line-up.'

'But I'll feel bad if Dan Deaton gets off with Hester at that
party. You know she's into him, and with all the magic of
fireworks at midnight he might forget how much hotter you
are than her?'

Leila pulled her head around to face her friend, making
Minnie drop the braid she was working on. 'Do you want me
to stay in and watch movies with you or not?'

Minnie shifted her eyes from side to side as though
considering her answer. 'Yes.'

'Then stop winding me up about Dan! Honestly, if his
head gets turned by a few fireworks, a couple of beers and
Hester Finley in a short skirt, then he wasn't worth having in
the first place, was he?'

Leila shook her head, exhaled loudly and turned back to
the TV.

'Are you sure you want these braids like cornrows? You
can see a lot of your scalp this way,' Minnie asked, biting her
lip in concentration as she tried to pick up the pieces of the
plait she had dropped.

'My head's a good shape, I can pull it off.'

When Minnie's mother came in they were still watching
Splash. They had just reached the part where Tom Hanks
realises something fishy is going on with Daryl Hannah's
legs.

'A little help, please!' her mum shouted from the front
door.

Leila and Minnie jumped up. Minnie's mother was carrying bags full of shopping balanced in both arms and had a fistful of post she'd scooped up from the mat.

'What's all this, Mum?' Minnie asked, peering into a carrier bag.

'Your birthday lunch, isn't it. All the shops are going to be closed tomorrow so I need something to feed everyone.' Minnie's mother dropped the bags onto the floor and started flicking through the pile of letters in her hand. She made a nervous clicking noise with her tongue.

'What's wrong?' Minnie asked.

'Nothing, just with your dad's new ventures I can hardly keep track of these bills.'

'We'll take these for you, Mrs C,' said Leila, picking up the bags and carrying them through to the kitchen.

'I said I didn't need any fuss for my birthday,' Minnie said quietly, picking up the last two bags from the doorstep. 'You've got enough on your plate, Mum.'

'Your brother's bringing this new girlfriend over tomorrow. I'm not presenting her with Christmas leftovers. We want to make a good impression.'

Her mother followed Leila through to the kitchen and sank into a chair. She pressed the pile of bills onto the table, closed her eyes and squeezed the top of her nose between her thumb and forefinger.

'Have you got one of your headaches again? You need to take it easy, Mum.'

'I'm fine, don't make a fuss, Minnie.'

Minnie began to pull quiches and pre-packaged sausage rolls out of the shopping bags, while Leila started opening cupboards to see where things might go.

'And what have you gone and done to your lovely hair, Leila? You look like Christin Aquila Area.'

'Christina Aguilera, Mum,' said Minnie.

'Well, you won't get lost in a crowd, will you? Come on now, back to your own plans, whatever party you're out to.'

'We're staying in,' said Minnie.

'Hiding from the jinx,' said Leila, putting an empty shopping bag over her head. Minnie laughed and pulled the bag off her friend's head. Leila squealed. 'It got me! It got me!'

'Don't joke girl,' said Minnie's mother, 'you haven't known this one long enough to know the truth of it. Do you know that song by Albert King, 'Born Under a Bad Sign'? I always think of that as the soundtrack to Minnie's birthday.'

Minnie's mother started moving seamlessly around the kitchen, putting food away in cupboards, humming the song to herself.

'Oh, well that reminds me, I got you something,' said Leila, running back through to the living room. She returned with a small square package of gold tissue paper, which she handed to Minnie. Minnie opened it with a puzzled look.

'It's not my birthday just yet.'

'I thought you might need it now,' said Leila. Minnie unwrapped the paper to find a delicate silver necklace with a four-leaf-clover pendant. 'To counteract any bad luck,' Leila explained.

'I love it, Leila, thank you!' Minnie cried, flinging her arms around her friend.

'It's a nice idea, but it might take more than jewellery, Leila,' said Minnie's mother.

'Oh, Mrs C, since you're here, I've got to ask you now – where do you want to be this time next year?' said Leila.

'Excuse me?'

'She asks everyone at New Year,' Minnie shrugged.

Minnie's mum shook her head, then looked pensive. 'If I'm no worse off than I am now, I'll be happy,' she said.

'Oh Mrs C, you've got to dream a little bigger!' said Leila, spinning around on the spot.

'Dreams are for sleep, Leila,' she said, tapping Leila on the head with a bag of spaghetti.

Minnie and Leila settled back down to watch the end of their film. Once Minnie's mother had finished in the kitchen, she came through to the lounge. Minnie and Leila were both in tears at the ending.

'What are you two blubbing about?' she asked.

'Oh, it's so romantic, Mrs C. He gives up life on land to be with the love of his life underwater,' said Leila, her face streaming with tears. She reached out to take a tissue from the side table.

'Honestly, you lot and your romantic notions,' tutted her mother. She picked up the pile of DVDs they'd lined up and started shaking her head as she looked through the titles. 'Fairy tales and mermaids and prostitutes made good; I tell you, all these films are filling your heads with rot. You're only going to be disappointed when you see what's out there in the real world.'

'Not a romantic then, Mrs C?' said Leila. 'Come on, why don't you watch *The Princess Bride* with us? You might like it.'

'I'd rather gnaw off my own feet, Leila.' Minnie's mother started clearing up around the girls as she talked, plumping cushions and picking up empty popcorn packets. 'I tell you, what matters is a man who'll work hard and who'll stick around, a man who'll never lay a hand on you in anger, and a man who won't drink away his wages.' She leant over and pulled the bottle of wine from the folds of the couch. 'Buy your own bleeding wine, Minnie! Right, I'm going to find your father before he starts buying rounds for the whole pub again.'

She paused, hovering over Minnie. Her face softened. She reached out to touch Minnie's hair, pushing it back behind Minnie's ears in an uncharacteristic tactile gesture.

'I guess you'll be a grown-up when I see you next.'

'Have fun, Mum,' said Minnie, reaching up to squeeze her mother's hands.

She moved Minnie's hand back to the sofa and made a noncommittal 'hmmm' sound, before heading for the door.

Leila snuggled up next to Minnie on the couch.

'Your mum's funny,' Leila said through a yawn, dropping her head onto Minnie's shoulder. 'You think she really feels like that about love and stuff?'

'I dunno,' said Minnie, 'she's married to my dad, he's hardly your typical romantic hero, is he?'

They both giggled.

As they were weighing up what to watch next, Minnie's phone began to ring. It was an unknown number.

'Hello?' she said cautiously.

'Is that Minnie?'

'Yes.'

'It's Tony. From school.'

Tony Grinton, she recognised his voice. He was one of the popular boys in their year.

'Tony Grinton', she mouthed to Leila.

Why would Tony Grinton be calling her? Minnie sat behind him in maths. She'd come to know his neck better than she knew her own. He had this beautiful chestnut hair that fell just below his ears, the lowest part of his neck was shaved and there was this line where the stubble turned to thicker hair. She had spent a lot of maths classes wondering what it would feel like to run her hand across that stubble, up into his hair. Once, she'd picked up his phone for him when he'd dropped it on the floor. He'd said 'thanks'.

'Hi Tony!' Minnie said in a high-pitched voice and then covered her mouth.

'Leanne gave me your number. You're in my maths class, right?'

Minnie could feel her eyes getting wider and wider as she tried to communicate her excitement to Leila. Leila was bouncing up and down on the sofa, silently clapping her hands together. Then she waved a hand at Minnie to hold the phone between them so she could hear too.

'Well, I've got this maths problem I hoped you could help me with. You're good at maths, right? Leanne said you wouldn't mind.' It was noisy in the background; it sounded like a party.

'Sure,' Minnie said, confused.

'How many men can you fit in a Mini Cooper?'

She heard laughter on the line, other people listening in.

'Twenty-eight is the record,' shouted another male voice.

'You want to be a record-breaker?' Tony sang through grunting laughter.

'Fuck off Tony!' shouted Leila, grabbing the phone from Minnie and hanging up the call.

Minnie's face fell. She should be used to being the butt of that joke by now, but it still hurt, especially when it came from someone like Tony.

'Don't let them get to you, Min, they're such babies.'

Leila shook her head. Then her own phone pinged and she frowned as she looked at the message.

'What is it?' asked Minnie.

Leila turned the phone around. It was a picture of Dan Deaton, kissing Laura Crosby from the year below.

'Who sent you that?' Minnie asked.

She felt terrible. Leila would be at that party if it weren't for her. Leila and Dan weren't exclusive, but they'd kissed a few times and Minnie knew she liked him.

'Fuck him, fuck all of them,' Leila said, rubbing her eyes with her hands.

'You know when I meet the right guy, and I mean a real man, not one of these dick nicks we're at school with. When I meet the *right* man, he will believe in romance; he will get that it's important. Life can't just be about coupling up like yoghurts in a multi-pack. There's got to be more to it, right?'

Leila looked at Minnie with wounded, puppy-dog eyes.

'Sure,' said Minnie, 'don't listen to my mum, she's just old and bitter.'

'And when the right man asks me to marry him, I expect him to deliver the fairy tale. I want unicorns, I want doves, I want the whole fucking Disney fest.'

'Is your future husband gay?' Minnie laughed.

'Possibly,' she said, the wounded look leaving her eyes.

Leila stood up and started prancing around the room, caught up in her vision for this future proposal. 'He'll ride into a field on a unicorn, dressed as a knight in shining armour, and there will be doves and mer-people and baby rabbits that sing like they do in *Enchanted*. There'll be a massive picnic of all my favourite food, specifically Nutella pancakes, and there will be a giant blue princess dress for me to wear and I will put it on and reclaim the princess narrative and I will look visionary and he will say, "Leila, I love you, and if you want the fairy tale, I will give it to you." And I will eat those Nutella pancakes in my fuck-off princess dress and I will say, "Fuck yeah!"'

Minnie laughed. 'You know, it's funny, that's exactly how my dad proposed to my mum.'

3 February 2020

'Mer-people?' said Alan.

'Rabbits that sing?' said Bev.

'You know neither of those things exist, right?' said Fleur slowly, looking at Minnie as though she had grown an extra nostril.

'Look, I know it sounds weird, but she told me this vision she had for the perfect engagement when we were seventeen. It's symbolic, trust me she will love it.'

Minnie, Fleur, Bev and Alan were sitting around the No Hard Fillings kitchen table. Minnie had called a secret meeting to commission their help planning Leila's perfect engagement. She also thought it might provide a positive distraction from the potential 'shutting down the business' conversation that might be coming next.

'The mission needs a secret code name,' said Alan. 'How about Operation I Do, or Operation Unicorn, something we could mention in passing that Leila won't suspect?'

'I think Leila would be suspicious if we start mentioning weird operation names,' said Fleur, as she picked raisins out of a *pain aux raisins* that Bev had baked for them that morning. 'My great-great uncle was like a spy in Russia and apparently he so nearly assassinated Stalin, but then he had this really bad wheat allergy so it didn't happen. I think his code name was like Baguette or something, which was supposed to be ironic, because bread was the only thing he couldn't handle.'

'What if we called it Operation Uncle? I could say, "My uncle needs an operation", or something. It might sound more normal bringing that up in conversation?' suggested Alan, spinning around and around on his bar stool.

'Or I could just set up a WhatsApp group between the four of us and then we wouldn't need to discuss it out loud at all,' said Minnie.

She was beginning to regret asking this lot to help her – so far no one had offered any practical suggestions as to how they were going to pull off her plan.

'My old Zumba instructor works in the costume department at the Royal Shakespeare Company – he might be able to loan us some outfits,' suggested Fleur. 'Oh, and my astrologer owns a horse down in Richmond, so we could probably borrow it and fashion a strap-on horn if you really want a unicorn.'

'Brilliant!' said Minnie, starting a list and putting giant question marks next to anything Fleur suggested.

'I can do the picnic,' Bev said with a half-hearted shrug.

'There have to be Nutella pancakes,' said Minnie, tapping her list.

'I can dress as a merman,' said Alan, 'a fellow man of the sea, like me.'

'My old lecturer slash boyfriend slash driving instructor now runs an animatronics studio. I bet he could find us some weird-talking animals. He owes me a favour and a thousand pounds bail money,' said Fleur.

The others looked at her to elaborate; there was a lot to unpack in that sentence. Minnie had come to the conclusion that either Fleur was a compulsive liar or she led an intensely interesting life outside of work. Fleur ignored their enquiring eyes, focusing her attention on the de-raisining of the *pain aux raisins*.

'That all sounds great, Fleur,' said Minnie, writing another giant question mark next to 'animatronic animals'.

'You really think Leila is going to find this romantic?' Fleur asked, making the face of someone who'd just caught a whiff of old cabbage left fermenting in old shoes for a week. 'Sounds kind of creepy to me.'

'She will love it, trust me Fleur,' said Minnie.

'We'll all just decay into nothing in the end,' Bev muttered bleakly.

'Oh Bev, are you still feeling down? Maybe you should go and talk to your GP if you feel this low? Did you try going to one of those environmental marches we talked about?' Minnie asked.

'I don't think it will help.' Bev shifted on her stool and looked down at her hands. 'I was going to go with Betty but she got chickenpox that week, so it didn't work out.'

'OK, well, I will go with you to the next one if Betty can't, I think it would be good for you just to see how many other people out there care, Bev. And that reminds me, I bought you something,' said Minnie, running over to her bag.

She pulled out the bottle wrapped in silver paper and a gold ribbon and presented it to Bev. Minnie rubbed her hands together and pressed them against her lips in anticipation; she couldn't wait to see Bev's face when she opened the gift. Bev gave her a quizzical look as she peeled off the paper. Once she'd unwrapped it, she stood stock still staring at the bottle. Alan peered over her shoulder and read out the words that had been printed onto the front.

'Bev McConnaty, 59,

Wife, mother, fun lover,

Baker of pies and ever so wise,

Loves M&S socks and Brian Cox,

A friend so fantastic,

Now she'll last as long as plastic.'

Then he looked up at Minnie and shook his head. 'Why have you given her a tombstone on a bottle?'

Bev started to cry. 'Is this to remind me I'm going to die?' she sobbed.

'No! No!' Minnie grabbed the bottle from her and pointed to the poem. 'Look, it's all the amazing things about you, branded onto plastic so you'll outlast us all and you'll never be forgotten!'

'That's what a tombstone does,' said Alan, shaking his head.

'No, it's because you said you were upset in the shower, about the shampoo bottle lasting longer than you!' Minnie looked back and forth between her friends.

Fleur's mouth contorted into a wide grimace, her eyes silently asking, 'What the hell were you thinking?'

'Socks and Brian Cox, is that all anyone's ever going to remember me for? And look how old I look in this photo? Do

I really have that many chins?' Bev rested her head on the countertop, sniffing back tears.

This wasn't how that was supposed to go. Minnie had meant to cheer Bev up. How did she manage to get things so wrong sometimes? The bell above the door chimed in reception and then Leila appeared at the kitchen door.

'What's going on?' she asked as she saw Bev crying and Fleur and Alan looking pained and pensive. 'Oh great, you told them already. Minnie, I thought we said we wouldn't say anything until we'd worked out a plan together?'

'Told us what?' asked Fleur.

'Is this about the cheese graters?' asked Alan. Everyone turned to look at him. 'OK, it's not about the cheese graters.'

'I didn't say anything,' said Minnie. 'Bev's upset about something else.'

'Bev's always upset,' Fleur said.

They all stood in silence for a moment. Alan slowly removed the list that was sitting on the countertop in front of them. Leila gave him a questioning look.

'My uncle needs an operation,' Alan said with a wink.

'Well, I'm sorry to hear that, and I'm sorry you are all so upset about it. Minnie, can we talk in private?' Leila said, beckoning her through to the reception area and then shutting the door behind them.

'You OK?' Minnie asked. 'What's wrong?'

Leila looked stressed and thin, her hair scraped back in a nondescript bun. She wasn't wearing any of her usual colour – just grey sweatpants and a mauve hoodie.

'The bank won't extend our loan. I can't bridge the gap until our funding comes through.' Leila hugged her arms around herself. 'I'm sorry, Minnie, I thought I could fix it.'

Minnie watched her friend. She gave a slow sigh.

'Maybe we could go back to that list of Quinn's clients we delivered to. He seemed to think they'd all order from us again. It might tide us over,' said Minnie, scratching her nose between thumb and forefinger.

'OK,' said Leila nodding. 'So we cater corporates for a few months until the charity funding comes through and regular orders pick up.'

Minnie watched her friend try to paste on a smile, to look enthusiastic about this new plan. Minnie knew this was her opportunity to give Leila a get-out.

'I don't think we want to do that though, do we?' Minnie watched her friend closely for a reaction. 'It was supposed to be fun running a business together, and it's not much fun any more, is it? If we can only survive by baking for city boys, I might as well go back to working in restaurants and earn more. As for you, if you're going to have this level of stress, it might as well be for something you're genuinely passionate about.' She paused. 'Ian mentioned the fashion job.'

Leila looked up, surprised. 'I wasn't planning to take it!' Leila threw her head back and closed her eyes.

'I didn't think you would. I'm just saying, maybe we've come to the end of the road here. Maybe fate is trying to tell us something.'

Leila sat down on the little bench by the front door and hung her head in her hands. Did she look relieved? Minnie hoped she looked relieved. Then Leila looked up at Minnie with a scowl – it wasn't a relieved kind of scowl.

'So that's it then?' Leila shook her head. 'Fate doesn't want it to work so we're done? I've poured four years of my life into this place, into building this business. There's a way to save it and you don't want to try?'

'No, no, I just don't think it's what we want!' cried Minnie.

'You've decided it's not what *you* want. You haven't even asked *me*! You think I'm not passionate about this? This whole business was my idea, in case you've forgotten.'

'Where's all this coming from?' said Minnie, her brow knitting in consternation.

'I do all the shit stuff,' said Leila, throwing her hands in the air. 'I deal with the banks, I fill out all the funding applications. You've never offered to help with any of that side of it.'

'I have! I didn't think you wanted my help. You just took control of it.' She was shaking her head, confused by Leila's reaction.

'So I'm controlling now, am I?'

Minnie reached out to touch her friend's arm; she didn't know how this had escalated so quickly into an argument. She softened her voice.

'Leila, listen to yourself. You need to start sleeping again, to … I'm sorry but you look terrible. This isn't good for either of us, this level of stress, and I don't want you to be here just because of me.'

Leila got to her feet. 'Don't tell me what I need. I've been slogging my guts out to make this work and now you're all "oh well, if it's not meant to be I'll just sack it off and go back to waiting tables."'

~Not waiting tables, I was a chef,' said Minnie defensively, watching Leila through narrowed eyes.

'You want to throw everything we've worked for away.'

'No, I just think we should cut our losses while we're still standing. What we wanted to do doesn't work, we were naïve to think it would.'

Leila stood up and walked closer to Minnie, pointing a finger at her chest, her eyes fierce with anger.

'I remember the day we met. You were hugging your knees to your chest on this bench at camp trying to make yourself as small as possible so the world wouldn't notice you. You were so self-conscious and afraid and I felt sorry for you. All these years we've been friends, I desperately wanted to give you back whatever confidence someone had stamped out of you. I thought if you just had someone to believe in you, then you'd come out of your scared little shell and this butterfly would emerge.' Leila's face was growing red with rage. Minnie had never seen her angry before, not like this. 'Maybe I was wrong; you're not scared, there's just no butterfly in there.'

Minnie flinched. Leila had never said anything so cruel in the sixteen years they'd known each other.

'Well, nice to know all this time I was just your pity project! I don't need you to butterfly me, Leila, you're enough bloody butterfly for the both of us – it's exhausting.'

They stared at each other, bulls in a ring ready to charge or run. Minnie made a move towards the door.

'No, I'm going to leave,' said Leila. 'You want to give up on this place, you deal with it.' And then she left, the door rocking back and forth against the bell in her wake.

4 February 2020

Minnie sat on the garden step watching the cigarette between her fingers burn down. She hadn't smoked for years, not since she worked at the restaurant, but there was something about her life tumbling down around her ears that had made her reach for the comforting feel of a packet of cigarettes in her hand. The nostalgia was more potent than the reality – the tobacco felt stale in her mouth and she stubbed it out after a few drags. That was another tenner she couldn't afford.

She heard keys in the lock and groaned – she'd planned to be safely hidden upstairs before either of her parents got home. Now her mother would smell it on her and there would be more cross words. She rummaged around in the cupboard under the sink for an air freshener. She found an old can of Oust and pressed the sticky nozzle. It sprayed up rather than out and went straight up her nose. She coughed and spluttered, rubbing her nose with her hands, trying to shake out the sensation of a nasal enema.

'Minnie, that you?' called her mother.

'Uh-huh,' Minnie called out, quickly hiding the packet of cigarettes in the bread bin.

'Why're you looking so suspicious?' asked her mother.

'I'm not.' Minnie clasped her hands behind her back.

Her mother wore black leggings and a top with beige and red patterns across it. It looked like the kind of fabric you found on bus seats. The top was stretching at the seams; her mother had put on weight recently and the eczema on her arms had spread up her neck and around her hairline in angry red patches.

'You never stay at Greg's any more,' her mother remarked as she picked up the kettle and started filling it from the tap.

'Greg and I broke up,' Minnie said flatly.

Her mother looked over at her, dropping the kettle down in its cradle.

'I'm sorry to hear that, you never said.'

Minnie shrugged. Her mother stuck out her bottom lip, her eyes creasing into slits.

'What's that face for?' Minnie asked.

'Greg seemed like a sensible boy – steady job, rents his own place.'

Minnie exhaled loudly. Her mother watched her closely, cogs whirring. 'He ditched you?'

'Not exactly,' said Minnie.

'Oh Minnie, you're not twenty-one any more. When are you going to learn to stick something out?'

Minnie shook her head. She felt a tide of tears build instantly behind her eyes. Her mother's words had knocked a barely healed scab and the skin beneath was paper-thin.

She watched her mother go through the ritual of making tea, pouring the water from a height, pressing the teabag against the side of the cup with the back of a spoon. There was something strangely comforting about the way her mother made tea.

'I fell out with Leila too, so now I'm totally mate-less.'

Minnie felt her shoulders start to heave and suddenly she was sobbing uncontrollably. Her mother was not usually good with tears, yet to Minnie's surprise she put an arm around her, led Minnie through to the lounge and sat her down with the cup of tea she'd made for herself. Through sniffing sobs she extracted the whole sorry tale from Minnie; about the fight with Leila, the conversation with Ian, Quinn trying to help them out by ordering pies for his clients but none of it being enough to rescue the business.

Her mother listened patiently, only making the occasional 'tssking' sound as Minnie spoke. She stood by the window titivating the net curtains to ensure they were evenly spaced along the rail. Once Minnie had finished, she came and sat next to her on the sofa.

'It sounds to me like you're better off out of it,' she said with a sigh.

Minnie closed her eyes. Why had she been expecting sympathy from her mother?

'Can I tell you something, Minnie? I always used to think that if you worked hard and you did right by people, life would come out OK. I had this sense the world was fair somehow.'

Minnie opened her eyes and met her mother's gaze reflected in the blank television screen. 'When you were born, if I hadn't helped that woman, we might have won that money, life might have been easier. But it went to her – someone with more money than she could know what to do with. The injustice of it got to me.' Minnie listened quietly, turning to watch her mother's profile. 'Still, your father and I got on, tried to save, to give you and your brother the best lives we could. Then we lost it all – bad luck, wrong timing, or your father took too big a risk. I don't know.'

'It wasn't Dad's fault. You can't blame him, Mum,' said Minnie.

'Maybe, maybe not.' Her mother finally turned to look at Minnie. 'Never put your chips on someone's gamble, that's all I ever wanted you to learn, Minnie. I don't think this business was ever likely to end well, Minnie, not with your luck.' She patted Minnie's leg. 'You can't change the wind, it's always gonna blow. All you can do is plant your feet firmer on the ground,' she sighed.

'I always feel like you're so disappointed in me, Mum,' said Minnie, hanging her head.

'You're too sensitive, love,' said her mother, reaching out to push a curl behind Minnie's ear. 'You always have been. It's hard for a parent to see her child struggle, and you seem to struggle more than most. I won't always be here to pick up the pieces.' Minnie closed her eyes and dropped her head onto her mother's shoulder. 'Maybe just avoid taking any more big risks for a while, love.'

'OK, Mum.' Minnie let out a sigh. 'I'm going to go to bed.'

As she got up and headed for the stairs, Minnie suddenly felt calmer than she had done in weeks.

'Minnie,' her mother called softly after her. 'This Quinn Hamilton's got nothing to do with you ending things with Greg, has he?'

'No, why? What makes you say that?' Minnie was taken aback; it was strange to hear her mother mention Quinn's name.

'I just wouldn't trust someone like that, you'll only end up disappointed. You need someone cut from the same cloth as you, someone who knows what life's about.'

'I thought you'd be all for me marrying him then divorcing him and getting that fifty grand back?' Minnie said with a smile.

Her mother's mouth twitched in amusement. 'You don't need someone else's money love, you'll be all right.'

Twenty-nine pounds for sea bream on a bed of samphire and wild rice; twenty-nine pounds! Quinn did some quick mental arithmetic; if they had three courses and the cheapest wine on the menu, this was still going to set him back a hundred and fifty quid. The restaurant was on the top floor of a hotel. Outside he could see the huge expanse of Hyde Park, beautifully illuminated by moonlight and round pools of light from the street lamps, which lined its long wide avenues. The Serpentine looked like a black mirror, still and glassy. The whole park glowed with a pink aura bleeding from the city lights, cocooning it in dark tranquillity. At midnight they'd be able to see firework displays all over London.

When Quinn had reserved the table one month in advance, he'd been on hold for an hour. Now he saw the prices on the menu he knew he'd overstretched himself trying to impress Polly. He closed the menu sharply. There was no point worrying about the bill now; she would love it, that was all that mattered.

'Quinn, the bathroom is bigger than my flat,' said Polly in hushed excitement as she returned to the table. 'We could set up a dance floor in there later.' She giggled, picking up the napkin from her chair and slipping into the seat opposite.

Polly had short blonde hair and a delicate angular face. She had prominent cheekbones that gave her face a beautiful elfin quality, yet her deep blue eyes transmitted a steely intelligence.

'Are you sure you can afford this?' she whispered, lifting a hand to cover her mouth.

'It's a special occasion,' he said. 'I did promise we'd celebrate your university scholarship properly.'

'Well, I feel very spoilt. I have been fantasising about this meal all month. It all looks so delicious, Quinn.'

Behind Polly, Quinn watched an older man with grey hair lean forward in his chair and squeeze the hand of the woman he was with. It was a confident, intimate gesture and he saw the woman gaze back at her partner with doe-eyed admiration. Quinn reached out to take Polly's hand.

'Don't worry about it. I want you to enjoy yourself,' he said, giving her hand a squeeze.

Quinn had borrowed one of his father's old jackets for the occasion. It was a beautifully cut blue woollen blazer, hand-made on Savile Row. His father was a slighter build and it was too tight for Quinn across the shoulders. Extending his arm caused him to hunch uncomfortably.

Quinn had met Polly six months ago. He'd spent the summer backpacking around Brazil with his university friend, Mike. It had been a rare opportunity to escape London, afforded by his aunt coming over from the US to hold the fort at home. Quinn and Mike had run into Polly and her friend Gina in a bar in Salvador. The girls were in Brazil on their gap year, planting trees for a charity. The four of them had spent the evening comparing travel tales and drinking caipirinhas so full of lime they made their eyes water. Quinn had been besotted with this beautiful, funny, generous soul, from that first caipirinha.

'So what shall we make our toast to?' Polly asked, picking up her glass.

'Your academic brilliance,' said Quinn.

'What about your birthday tomorrow?' suggested Polly.

'How about finally being in the same place?' said Quinn.

Polly had only returned from South America in August, and then she'd started university in Reading that September. Quinn would go and visit her for a day at weekends, but found it hard to stay away overnight. He sent her train tickets so she could come up to London, but Quinn was still living at home and Polly often felt awkward staying with his mother.

The waiter arrived and presented their main courses. Hers, delicate slices of duck balanced on a tower of red cabbage and gratin potato, a perfect obelisk of food in the middle of a large white plate. His, the pan-fried sea bream he estimated at about ten pounds a mouthful.

'Wow, this looks spectacular,' said Polly, her eyes dancing with delight. 'I don't want this evening to end – maybe we should go clubbing later? Imagine if we could stay out until four and then spend all of tomorrow in bed,' said Polly wistfully as she rubbed his leg with her foot beneath the table. 'But I'm not sure that would be allowed at your mother's house.'

Quinn glanced down at his lap. Living at home did mean there were some restrictions on his nocturnal activity – his bedroom was right above his mother's room. A couple of times he had splashed out and hired a hotel room for an evening, just so they could be free of any inhibitions, but he felt seedy taking Polly to a hotel where they checked in at seven and out at eleven.

As if she knew they were talking about her, Quinn's phone began to vibrate.

'Right on cue,' Polly said quietly. 'Go on then.'

'I'm sorry,' he said, leaving the table to take the call out in the corridor.

New Year's Eve was always hard for his mother. It was the anniversary of the day his father left. Quinn had learnt it was better to answer quickly, talk her down from whatever trigger had upset her. If he ignored her calls, it only made it more likely she'd have a full-blown panic attack.

Over the phone he managed to calm her. She was anxious about the locks on the French windows again. He was patient, he listened, he spoke in soothing tones, but inside he felt himself growing tense at the sound of her voice. He willed her to rally. He didn't want to go home; he didn't want to cut this evening short.

Back at the table, Polly had finished her main course.

'Is everything OK?' she asked. 'Do you need to go?'

'No, it's fine. I'm sorry.' How many times had they had this conversation in the last six months? How many times had he apologised?

Polly rearranged the wine glasses on the table, setting them into a symmetrical pattern.

'She knows we're celebrating tonight,' Polly said with a sigh.

'She doesn't do it on purpose, Pol. It's been a tough few months, with Dad getting married again.'

Polly watched him across the table as he tried to paste on a smile.

'And it was a tough month in September when your aunt went home.'

'Yeah, there are a lot of tough months … what do you want me to do?' he said, more sharply than he meant to.

'It just doesn't seem fair on you,' Polly said, reaching out to squeeze his hand.

Quinn wordlessly shook his head. 'Please, let's not talk about it tonight,' he said, shuffling forward on his chair. 'I want this evening to be about us, about you.'

He looked up and caught her blinking away the concerned look in her eyes.

'My favourite topic,' she said. 'No, I lie, my favourite topic is cheese, as you know.'

'Look Pol, I know it's not been easy to see each other, but everything in my life changed when I met you. I meant what I said the other night – I love you. You're the first girl I've ever said it to and I've never felt so sure about anything.'

'I love you too, Q,' Polly said, holding his gaze.

Quinn felt a warm pulse of energy pump through his whole body. To be loved by the one you love – was there any greater feeling?

After dessert, an extra course arrived from the kitchen.

'The chef has prepared a miniature Christmas pudding, filled with brandy-infused crème patissière, compliments of the season,' said the waiter with a bow.

'This is such a treat! Thank you so much – the food has been superb!' Polly gave the waiter a beaming smile. Her effusive energy caught him off guard and he gave her an awkward nod.

Just as Quinn picked up a spoon, just as the evening felt it was back on track, he felt the phone vibrate in his pocket again. As the same moment, Polly started making a gagging sound and he turned to see her spit out the pudding, which she'd popped whole into her mouth. Quinn reached into his jacket pocket as he asked, 'Are you OK?'

Polly's whole face creased in a grimace. Quinn glanced at his phone. He didn't need to look, he knew who was calling.

'There's something in it,' Polly said, 'something grisly.' Polly started poking the tiny pudding with her fork. 'I think it's plastic.'

Quinn shifted uncomfortably in his chair, moving the pulsing phone to his lap, every muscle in his body tensed, the air in the room suddenly feeling dense and suffocating. Polly shook her head and cleared her throat again.

'Quinn, I just choked and you're looking at your phone.'

'You didn't choke,' he said weakly. 'You spat it out.'

'Just answer it,' she said, closing her eyes.

Quinn hung up the call, switching his phone from vibrate to silent. He topped up Polly's water glass with a shaking hand.

Polly called a waiter over and told him about the plastic in her dessert. She said she didn't like to complain, but she was worried someone else's pudding might be affected. He was profusely apologetic and brought over a complimentary bottle of champagne. Quinn tried to relax, but he couldn't stop thinking about what might be going on at home. This feeling, of being made to be a bad boyfriend or a bad son, he hated it; it made him feel physically nauseous.

There was no crass countdown at Le Lieu de Rencontre. New Year was announced by the sound of glasses clinking and murmurs of 'Happy New Year' echoing around the room. Outside, the dark horizon erupted into shards of light tearing through the darkness. The distant boom and crackle of explosions audible even through the thick glass. Directly across the park, the fireworks appeared to converge in a fountain of light, and stardust rained from the sky.

They both sat in silence watching the spectacle outside. Then Polly slowly raised her glass to his, a pensive look in her eyes.

'To us, to the next chapter,' Quinn said with forced jollity. He could feel his forehead beading with sweat.

'Just call her back,' Polly said quietly, 'I know you won't relax until you do.'

Quinn walked out to the landing by the toilets. It would be rude to take a call at the table in a restaurant like this. He slumped to the floor at the top of the stairs and stared at his phone, his portable prison. To his left were double doors through to the kitchen, where he could hear clanking pans and curt voices. It was a room full of fiercely paddling feet that made the restaurant on the other side of the wall appear like an effortless gliding swan.

As he was about to call, a girl in chef's whites with curly brown hair, came running through the doors. She was crying, and their eyes met for a second. She looked how Quinn felt – consumed by misery. He wanted to ask if she was OK, but she carried on down the stairs before he had a chance to speak. As she disappeared around the corner, he saw that the girl had dropped her chef's hat on the stairs. A thought of Cinderella and a glass slipper flashed into his mind. In an alternate universe, he might run after that girl and return her hat. In this one he did not have the headspace for gallantry. He would hand her hat in to the kitchen.

His mother didn't answer his call. He would have to go home. He walked slowly back into the restaurant to see a spectacle of fireworks still lighting up the horizon over the park. As he took his seat, Polly didn't turn her head away from the window.

'I'm sorry, Polly. I have to go,' he said.

'She'll always come first, won't she?' Polly said.

'No, not always. It's New Year, it's a bad time for her, Polly …'

'I don't think I'm an especially needy person, Quinn, but you make me feel so needy and I hate it.'

'You're not needy, Polly. You are the only good thing in my life — '

She cut him off.

'Quinn, go home, let's not do this now, just go and do what you need to do. I'm going to go and meet some friends at a club in Hoxton. Thank you for a lovely meal.'

She kissed him on the cheek, a lingering kiss. Something about it felt more final than simply a goodbye. And as she left, Quinn found the nauseous feeling began to recede and the tightness across his chest finally started to ease.

Minnie stood on the grass bank, starring down into the murky brown water. Minnie first swam in Hampstead Ponds as a teenager, but the look of the water and the unnerving feeling of swimming when you couldn't see your hands or feet had put her off. Plus, she'd been conditioned to swim fast in those days, and the ponds weren't the best place for speed. Swimming was the one thing Minnie had been good at as a child, a sport she could do alone, with no one jeering at her. Or if they were jeering, she couldn't hear them with her head underwater. She wasn't sure why she'd given it up in her twenties – life and work had got in the way. Over the last few months, she had found herself drawn back to the water.

Hampstead Ponds were old reservoirs, now open to the public to swim in. They were dotted around the edge of Hampstead Heath – a beautiful, wild parkland which sprawled across nearly eight hundred acres of north London between Hampstead and Highgate. From the highest point you could see most of London, a Legoland of buildings and skyscrapers receding towards the horizon.

Minnie had always loved the heath. It was an idyllic, unspoilt oasis of nature in an otherwise tamed landscape. It served to remind the homogenised city dweller what wild grass and tumbling, tangled tree roots looked and smelt like. It wasn't just the wild landscape Minnie loved, but the familiar characters she saw there. While all of London migrated to the heath in the summer, during the rest of the year you saw the same faces again and again. The regular pond swimmers were a tight-knit community in themselves, with some diehards going in all year round, cracking ice in the winter to get in.

Last autumn, Jean Finney, one of Minnie's No Hard Fillings clients, had encouraged Minnie to give the ponds another chance. Jean swam regularly there herself, and spoke about the experience of wild swimming with almost religious reverence. Minnie hadn't got around to it last year. Now, she had time on her hands and a newfound motivation – maybe bracing cold water would toughen her up, body and soul. She'd come for the first time a month ago. Today, the water still looked uninviting, but this time, once she was in, she soon forgot about the murk below, losing herself in the exhilarating sting of the cold and the simple pleasure of wild swimming.

Minnie thought Jean must be doing something right if she at the age of eighty-six was still swimming most days. Jean had a calm demeanour that belied a life well lived. 'Don't cry about something you wouldn't cry about in five years' time,' she once told Minnie. 'And swim – swim when you can.' Those were her two pieces of life advice.

This morning Jean's familiar white ruffled head was nowhere to be seen. Launching herself into the water, Minnie felt needles stab into every part of her skin. She struggled to control her breathing as her body fought against the cold. She blocked out the pain and started to swim rapid breaststroke.

She counted her breaths; it took twenty for the pain to subside, then her body mellowed, the needles softening to warm tingles, and every part of her felt infused with energy, her brain burning off its early morning fog.

Swimming had become part of Minnie's new routine. Now she was working for the catering company she had mornings to herself and felt healthier than she had in years. She had time to cook herself good food, do exercise, and she'd even started reading again. She worked six nights a week, and was trying to live frugally. She was saving up a rental deposit to move out of her parents' house, and in another month or two she'd have enough. Life was simpler, easier, less stressful. Of course she missed the No Hard Fillings kitchen, she missed working with her friends, she missed Leila, but she was trying to be more optimistic, to see the positives.

Since their argument three months ago, she and Leila had patched up a practical peace. They'd had to communicate to wind down the business, but it was a sticking plaster on something that ran much deeper and they both felt it. The administrative hassle of dismantling the company had been easier than either of them imagined. By selling off the kitchen equipment and the delivery van, they'd had just enough to pay remaining salaries and settle the majority of their debt. Everything was made easier by the fact that a chicken-themed fast-food chain wanted to take the lease off their hands and agreed to buy their equipment at a fair price. In a matter of weeks, the deals had been done; it was like watching a giant, painstakingly crafted sandcastle being swept away by one giant wave.

The catering company Minnie now worked for was a production line of salmon *en croûte* and goat's cheese tarts with a balsamic glaze. She worked in a rotation of venues, creating meals for weddings, parties, lunches and functions. She didn't have much to do with the people who ate her food, or even the people who served it. She cooked, cleaned up, got paid and went home. She liked the impersonal nature of it. She didn't have to think about the business model, about other people's livelihoods depending on her. She didn't have to think at all.

She'd stayed in touch with Alan and Bev. Letting them down had been the worst part of the whole thing.

'We'll be fine, don't be thinking about us,' Bev said, once she'd told them the news.

'Ah, we'll find another ship to rig in no time,' said Alan.

As it turned out they had; the chicken shop had taken them both on, wanting staff who knew the premises. Alan was on deliveries, Bev worked the deep-fat fryer.

Fleur had disappeared, Minnie wasn't sure where to. Perhaps she was living offline at home in her parents' Wi-Fi-free zone, or maybe she'd finally set up that horoscope-themed dating app she'd always talked about. Minnie was surprised how much she found herself missing Fleur, of all people.

Giving up the business had been a seismic shift. Like tectonic plates grinding against each other, this small earthquake had released the pressure, preventing more cataclysmic consequences. It had been the right thing to do, she was sure of it. Yet she missed her colleagues, she missed her customers; she missed hearing about Mr Marchbanks's cats and Mrs Mentis's bunions. Most of all she missed Leila, and she missed her with a yearning she could only describe as heartache.

They still communicated, sent texts, occasionally exchanged news over the phone. But something had changed between them since their argument. Leila worked days, Minnie worked evenings. They'd met up for Saturday morning coffee a few times, but a polite distance had settled between them. Minnie felt she was catching up with an old acquaintance, exchanging information. She found herself commenting on the coffee, which was never a good sign. Patching together pieces of their friendship in a semblance of repair had not healed the underlying wound.

So Minnie worked and she swam and she saved and she swam, and she kept her head down and she held her breath. Swimming and breathing, living and working, waiting for the next seismic shift to move the ground beneath her feet and right everything again. Or perhaps to suck her under and drown her.

Minnie took four long strokes beneath the dark, cold water, then another, then another. As she ran out of air she felt the fight in her lungs push her to the surface. Survival took over and she broke the surface with a gasp of relief. As she climbed out of the pond onto the jetty, she saw that her towel was not on the bank where she'd left it. She shivered, looking for who might have taken it – a cruel trick at this time of year. A few yards away stood a man, rubbing his face with her blue swimming towel.

'Excuse me,' she said, striding over to him, 'I think that's my towel.'

The man pulled the towel down from his face. Quinn.

Minnie's eyes fell unconsciously on to his sculpted torso and she quickly forced her gaze back to his face.

'Minnie? Hi,' he grinned. 'What are you doing here?'

'Freezing,' she shivered. 'That's my towel.'

She pulled it away from him and quickly wrapped it around herself. Quinn looked around and then picked up another blue towel from the bank a few yards away.

'Not this one?' he offered.

Minnie looked at the towel. It did look pretty similar to the one she'd just seized. Now she came to think about it, this one was a little fluffier than she remembered hers being.

'Oh,' she said with a frown. 'Here you go,' she tried to swap back.

Quinn laughed. 'Um, you made mine all wet now. I'll use your dry one, thanks.'

They looked at each other, amused smiles on both their faces. It was strange running into Quinn again now. Though they'd only met a handful of times, something in his demeanour and body language felt so familiar to Minnie, like sinking into a favourite armchair.

'So is this a normal Sunday morning activity for you – stealing people's towels from Hampstead Ponds?' Quinn asked.

Minnie started towel-drying her hair. 'No, I just come here to get my fix of hot naked men.' She nodded towards a man in his seventies with a large belly just emerging from the water in tight brown Speedos. 'Phwoar.'

Quinn laughed. He opened his mouth to speak and then paused. Finally he spoke.

'Have you got plans now? I know you've turned me down for breakfast in the past.' Quinn started towel-drying his own hair with Minnie's towel, and Minnie couldn't help glancing again at his bare chest and his skintight black swim shorts. She wrapped his towel back around her own body self-consciously.

'I could do breakfast. Or at least coffee until your next Tinder date turns up.' Minnie raised her eyebrows at him, brushing a hand through her wet hair. Quinn pushed a tongue into his cheek, his pupils flushed wide. Minnie wondered whether it was the thrill of an early morning swim, or if he enjoyed being teased by her.

'My mum used to bring me up here when I was little,' Quinn said, as they walked side by side back through the park after retrieving their clothes. 'I would sit on the bank reading while she swam.'

'I find places like this so packed with memories. Visiting them can be like opening a memory jar. You take off the lid and the smells and sounds of a place hit you, unlocking things folded away deep in your brain,' Minnie said, swinging her towel as she walked. Quinn didn't respond and she looked over at him. 'Sorry, that sounded pretentious,' she said, shaking her head.

'No,' Quinn was watching her with an unblinking gaze, 'that's exactly how I feel coming here – it's a memory jar.'

255

They walked a little further in silence, their footsteps falling into rhythm.

'You know, for someone so uncompromising in their business vision, you have a lot of self-doubt,' Quinn said.

Minnie looked at him sideways without turning her head.

'You said something beautifully evocative, then undercut yourself saying it was pretentious. I've noticed you do that.'

'Don't try to analyse me, Dr Hamilton.'

Minnie gave him a friendly frown and flicked her wet towel in his direction. She only meant to tap him, but her wrist got it exactly right and the towel landed a resounding smack on Quinn's behind. He let out a yelp, clutching his bottom.

'Oh god, sorry, I didn't mean to do that so hard!' Minnie laughed, covering her mouth with her hand and clutching her stomach with the other.

'My god, woman, remind me to never really piss you off,' said Quinn, putting on an exaggerated limp as he clutched his wounded buttock.

Minnie got the giggles and had to stop walking.

'Seriously, I've never done a successful towel whip in my life. I don't know how that landed so hard.'

'Let's hope you didn't leave a permanent mark,' he said wryly, peering down the back of his trousers. 'Or my days of bottom modelling are over.'

They walked down towards Hampstead Heath railway station. A mobile food van was parked next to the car park, selling breakfast baps and instant coffee in small polystyrene cups.

'Oh, shall we just get something from here?' Minnie suggested. 'Then we can sit on the heath.'

Quinn looked at the van then turned to look down at the row of smart coffee shops by the station. 'Unless you wanted something a bit fancier?' Minnie asked, following his gaze.

'This is perfect,' said Quinn.

'Hi Barney,' said Minnie to the burley bearded man who ran the van. 'How are things?'

'I'm good, Minnie – how was your swim?'

'Bracing,' said Minnie. 'We'd like two bacon rolls and your best cup of something hot please.'

They walked back up to the top of the heath with their breakfast.

'So, how's business going?' asked Quinn.

'Well, we closed,' said Minnie. Quinn frowned.

'That's a shame.'

'It got too hard walking a financial tightrope all the time. Let's not talk about work, you'll probably start trying to charge me by the hour for your insights again.'

Quinn laughed.

'How was your date at the art gallery?' Minnie asked. 'What was her name? Amanda?' She said it as though struggling to remember.

'I'm embarrassed you had to witness that,' Quinn said, holding a hand to his forehead.

'Which part, the office drinking or the dial-a-date?'

'Both.'

He gave her an embarrassed grimace. She waited for him to elaborate, but he didn't, he just took a large bite of his bacon roll.

'How's your mother doing?' Minnie asked.

Quinn paused as he finished his mouthful. 'OK.'

'You don't like talking about her.'

'It's been a while since anyone asked me about my mother.'

'I'd like to hear more about her,' said Minnie softly, looking over the rim of her coffee cup at him. 'You mentioned she struggles with some things.'

Quinn puffed out his cheeks, exhaling. He put his cup down on the grass and started massaging one wrist with his palm.

'OK, well, the potted version – she suffers from anxiety; sometimes she struggles with leaving the house. She wasn't so bad when I was a child, but when my father left it got ten times worse.' Quinn stared down at his hands.

'I'm sorry, that sounds tough. Does she see someone? Do you have anyone to help look after her?' Minnie asked gently.

'She sees a therapist, a doctor. I've paid for carers in the past but she takes against them all in the end. She's up and down. And when she's down she'll only see me.'

'That must be hard,' said Minnie, 'to be that relied upon.'

Quinn brushed a hand through his hair; he sat up and pulled his knees to his chest.

'Enough about me.' He picked up his coffee again. 'I'm sure it's very boring. People have bigger problems.'

Minnie watched him, waiting for him to look over at her again.

'I don't think the scale of other people's problems make your own any easier to live with.'

Quinn paused, dropping his gaze to the grass between them.

'I think what I find hardest is that I often feel I'm enabling her to be a prisoner. I do errands for her, order her shopping, I come running when she needs something. She has this ongoing anxiety about house security, the locks not working, or paranoia that someone's in the garden. Every time I'll come over to check, just to ease her mind.' Quinn's brow puckered as he stared down at his empty cup. 'Once I didn't go when she called. I just said, "No, walk out of the front door and go to the pharmacy yourself, it's a three-minute walk."' Quinn paused. 'I'd had enough.'

'That's understandable,' said Minnie.

'She had this terrible anxiety attack, fell down the stairs, twisted her ankle. The cleaning lady found her the next morning, still lying there. God, why am I telling you all this?'

'Because I asked.' Minnie put an arm on his shoulder.

'What kind of monster leaves an agoraphobic alone in the house without her medication?' he said, turning to look at her, his eyes burning with emotion.

'Someone who tried everything else and didn't know what else to try.'

This confident, sure-footed man suddenly just looked like someone in desperate need of a hug, but Minnie didn't dare initiate one.

'The worst thing is, I can't sympathise any more. I know she can't help it, but part of me thinks, "Come on, just try, do the steps!" There's this treatment strategy for agoraphobics; they take small steps to face their fear, open the door, on to the street, walk one block. Baby steps every day and gradually you see progress. She did it before – there were a few years when she wasn't so bad. Now, it's like she doesn't even want to try. She's given up, and I let her.'

Minnie paused, looking over at him. She didn't know what to say so they sat in silence. It wasn't an awkward silence; it was one of those companionable silences when you don't need to speak in order to communicate.

They finished their breakfast, walked up Parliament Hill to see the view of London, and then back down towards the train station. Minnie looked sideways at Quinn as they passed the cafés and shops near Hampstead Heath train station. His mother's health issues were clearly a lot worse than she'd imagined. How had her first impressions of Quinn been so wrong? This man who she'd assumed must've had such an easy life; clearly it had not been easy at all. Minnie always thought about her own upbringing with a sense of regret. She regretted not having a better relationship with her mother. She regretted that everything felt like a battle with her family – battling to get away, battling to stay, battling to be heard. Then again, maybe everyone had something to complain about when it came to family – at least her mother was able to leave the house.

As they got to the train station, Minnie turned to Quinn with a hopeful look. She didn't want the morning to end.

'So what are you up to now?' she said, brushing away a chunk of tangled hair.

'I was going to go to my office. I need to sign some paperwork,' Quinn said. 'I know, Fun Time Quinn, aren't I?' He rubbed the stubble on his chin with a palm.

'OK,' said Minnie, biting her lip and looking away.

'I'm sorry about all that back there, I didn't mean to get so heavy on you. I don't tend to talk about her with my friends any more; I've bored them all to death over the years.'

'I'm glad you did,' she said.

Neither of them made a move to go. Quinn swayed his weight slightly from side to side.

'There is this other thing I need to do. Maybe you could help?'

Minnie's head sprung up to look at him. She couldn't temper her smile. 'Oh?'

'I need to adopt a penguin from the zoo.'

Minnie burst out laughing. Of all the things she'd expected him to say, it wasn't that. Quinn explained that every year his mother struggled with what to get him for his birthday. She'd set upon adopting a different animal each year. He now supported a snow leopard, an orang-utan and a rare breed of Chilean bat. This year, she'd suggested a penguin. Quinn liked to do his research, so he'd been meaning to check out the ones at London Zoo.

'You know you don't actually get to take a penguin home from the zoo, right?' Minnie said as they went through the station ticket barrier together.

'Really?' Quinn's eyes darted back and forth in alarm. 'I've got a bath full of fish at home, and I downloaded *Happy Feet* – in HD.'

'Oh High Definition, in that case ... You know, it's lucky you asked for my help, I am amazing at picking out penguins.'

'You know, that was one of the first things I thought when we met – I bet she knows a good penguin when she sees one.'

Quinn placed his hand on the base of her back as he steered her out of the way of a family running for the train. Minnie felt a tingle down her spine and curled in towards him as they stood inches apart on the busy platform. The fluttering owls had woken up, but instead of making her dizzy and anxious, she now felt these nesting birds like a warm comfort blanket, as though some dwindling hearth inside her had been rekindled with a gentle puff of oxygen.

She was going to the zoo with Quinn Hamilton. She felt like an excited child, full of bubbling anticipation and expectation. There was nothing she would rather be doing right now, no one she would rather be with; and it felt liberating to admit that to herself.

Quinn bought them tickets and they meandered along the little zoo streets looking at animals.

'I have never been to the zoo before,' Minnie confessed.

Quinn did a double take. 'You poor deprived child. Do you even know what a giraffe looks like?' Quinn pointed at an enclosure of warthogs. 'You know they're not giraffes right?'

'Ha-ha,' Minnie elbowed him in the ribs. 'No doubt you're an expert after all those childhood holidays on African safaris. Both my parents worked at the weekend, they never had time to take me to the zoo.'

Quinn made a face of mock sympathy. 'Poor little Olivia Twist – such a deprived, Dickensian upbringing.'

Minnie stuck her tongue out and gave him a friendly glower.

When they reached the penguin enclosure, Minnie let out a cry of delight. 'Oh look at them, they're so sweet! Look at their waddly little legs. Oh, and look at that one with the silly hair sprouting out of his head!' she cried, pointing out one of the penguins. Quinn didn't say anything. She turned to check he was still there and found him gazing down at her with a look of charmed amusement.

'What?' she said.

'You're very sweet,' he said softly, his eyes locking on to hers.

Minnie's stomach flipped.

'I don't think I want to be sweet,' she said, turning away and looking back at the penguins. She rested her hands against the glass to anchor herself.

'Oh look, what's that one doing?' Minnie said, pointing to a penguin shuffling something between his feet.

'He's bringing a stone to his mate as a gift,' said a deep, gravelly voice beside her. Minnie turned to see an elderly man with white hair and a large nose speckled with liver spots. He had a hunched back and a cane in his hand. He pointed a wavering finger at the penguin. 'They give gifts to each other like humans do. That one there is trying to win her affections. She's a tough cookie, though, she is,' the old man laughed. 'There aren't enough rocks in the enclosure to please her.'

'You know a lot about penguins,' Minnie said to the man.

'Come here most days. My wife and I used to come together,' said the man, tapping his cane twice against the floor. They stood quietly beside each other, watching the penguins until the old man spoke again. 'They mate for life, you know.'

'Maybe our lives would be easier if we were more penguin-y,' said Minnie.

'Not easy for all of them,' said the old man, shaking his head. 'There was a Humboldt penguin like this in Tokyo Zoo; Grape-kun was his name. They put a cardboard cut-out of a little anime girl in his enclosure – advert for something, I think. Anyway, Grape-kun fell in love with that cardboard girl. Stood staring at her every day, wouldn't move to get food, just stared mournfully. Unrequited love.'

'What happened to him?' Quinn asked from behind Minnie.

'He died,' sighed the man, 'some say of a broken heart. He'd spent years of his life staring at that cardboard girl, willing her to love him, but she could not love him back. I always think of that story when I see penguins. I think it was cruel for the zoo to keep the cardboard girl there. Brought in the tourists, though, didn't it? Everyone wanted to see the love-struck penguin.'

'That's a sad story,' said Minnie with a sigh, turning her attention back to the enclosure. 'Quinn, I think you should adopt that one,' she said, pointing at the penguin shuffling around with the pebble between his flippers.

'He's called Coco,' said the old man.

'Maybe he'll get an extra ration of fish or something – might make his poor little love-struck day.'

Quinn and Minnie spent hours strolling around the rest of the zoo. Minnie was intent on reading all the information about every animal. She bought them ice creams as they walked. Quinn bought a headband with giraffe ears on for her and a hat with elephant ears on for himself. They chatted so easily about everything and nothing, veering effortlessly between silly and serious in the space of a sentence. Minnie liked this version of Quinn; she liked his manner, his humour, the ease he had with his own body. Minnie liked this version of herself, too; she liked the person she was around him. Now she didn't have her defences up, she felt fun, optimistic, interesting. She hardly recognised herself and yet, somehow, this person felt like the truest reflection of who she really was.

When they'd finally seen all the animals, they stood near the exit and turned to face each other.

'Well, thank you for that,' Minnie said, biting her lip. 'I've had a lovely time. Plus, now I finally know what a giraffe looks like.'

'You're welcome,' said Quinn with a little bow. 'Thank you for helping me choose a penguin.'

'I can't take you seriously with those elephant ears on,' Minnie laughed.

Quinn pulled the hat from his head and looked back at her.

'That's better,' said Minnie, reaching up to tap his nose with a forefinger. 'You don't have a big enough nose to pull off the elephant look.'

Quinn reached up to intercept her hand, to stop her from tapping his nose, but he held on a beat too long before letting her go.

'I don't know if you really get to adopt a specific penguin,' Quinn said, his gaze following the hand he had let go.

'That's why I smuggled Coco out under my coat,' Minnie whispered as she leant in towards him.

He reached out for her coat collar, gently pulling her towards him, pretending to look beneath her coat for the stowaway.

'You're full of surprises, Minnie Cooper,' he said in a deep, soft drawl.

She looked up into his eyes, her face so close to his. He was going to kiss her; Minnie felt her heart in her throat, every part of her alive with anticipation. Then something flashed across his face. Doubt? Fear? He pinched his lips shut and turned their physical proximity into an awkward hug. He patted her back then extracted himself and turned briskly towards the exit.

What the hell was that? Minnie blanched. She hugged her arms around herself, wounded by the indignity of being patted like a dog. She'd been sure he was about to kiss her. Was she so deluded that she'd entirely misread this chemistry between them?

'OK, well, this is where I ... ' he said as they stood next to each other in Regent's Park. 'I really should get to the office.' He nodded his head to the right.

'And I'm getting the bus up there,' Minnie said, nodding to the left. 'See you, I guess.'

She couldn't conceal the hurt in her voice. She felt as though she'd just had the most perfect date of her life, and then had a door slammed in her face.

She dared to look up at him again, trying to see what that look had been a few moments ago, where the hesitation had come from. As soon as their eyes met again, he closed his.

'Don't look at me like that, Minnie.'

'Like what?'

'Like you want me to kiss you,' he said, unable to look at her.

'Why not?' Minnie felt her voice catch in her throat.

'I thought we could just hang out. I didn't plan ... ' Quinn squeezed his forehead between finger and thumb. Finally, he looked at her, then dropped his gaze again. 'I'm kind of seeing someone. I don't want to be a dick here.'

Minnie felt the words like a punch in the stomach. 'Oh right,' she said quietly. 'Amanda?'

'No.' Quinn shook his head. 'Someone else. It's not like, a relationship but ...'

'I see. Busy man.'

Quinn took a step towards her. He blinked slowly. 'I wouldn't be good for you, Minnie, not like that, trust me.'

Quinn's phone started to ring. He took it out of his pocket, looking at the display, momentarily distracted. Minnie set her jaw firm, trying to stop herself from crumbling where she stood. She watched him torn between saying more and taking the call – no doubt from her, whoever she was.

'You can take it, I need to go anyway. And for the record, I wasn't looking at you like I wanted to be kissed. I was just looking at you, Quinn.'

Minnie marched past him and kept walking. Hot tears instantly sprang from her eyes. She started to run. He called after her but she didn't turn around, determined he should not see he had made her cry. What was wrong with her? She'd been so stupid to get caught up in today, feeling as though she was on some kind of magical first date when clearly he thought it was nothing of the sort. How could she read people so badly?

As she blinked away the blur of tears, there was only one person she wanted to speak to right now, one person she needed to see. She pulled out her phone.

It rang twice.

'Leila?'

'Yes.' It was a civil yes, a polite yes – the new tone of their friendship.

'Can I come over?'

Leila heard the tears and her tone instantly changed.

'Where are you, Min? I'll come and get you.'

17 May 2020

Despite Leila's offer to fetch her, Minnie said she would rather come to hers. By the time she arrived on Leila's doorstep she had stopped crying. She now felt nervous about being here. Though they'd met for a few coffees in town, she hadn't been to Leila's flat since their fight. She also hadn't seen Ian in three months but, as far as Minnie knew, he hadn't proposed yet. Surely she would still be the first person to hear if he'd asked the question?

Ian had sent her a text after the fight, saying he felt responsible for her and Leila falling out. He said he'd told Leila about their conversation, tried to broker a peace. Yet strangely their argument had felt like it was about more than just the business. Years of being so close, rubbing against each other's hard edges, finally causing a friction fire that needed to burn itself out. Perhaps, like in the aftermath of a wildfire, there would now be room for new shoots.

As Leila opened the door, Minnie's eye went instantly to her hand just to check there wasn't something there she hadn't been told about. No ring. She felt her chest decompress. If there had been a ring, if Ian had proposed and Leila hadn't told her – it might have felt like the death knell for their friendship.

'Min, what's happened?'

Leila wrapped her arms around her and Minnie sank into her with a heaving sob. It wasn't even about Quinn bloody Hamilton any more, it was about her friend hugging her in a way she hadn't been hugged for months and only now, this second, realising how deeply she had missed her.

'Quinn Hamilton,' Minnie sniffed.

'Whaaat?' Leila clenched her hands around Minnie's shoulders and dragged her into the flat. 'I knew it, I knew that was on the cards! How, when, where? Tell me everything.'

'Nothing happened. I ran into him this morning at Hampstead Ponds.'

'Since when do you go to Hampstead Ponds?' Leila drew her head back into a 'do I know you at all?' expression.

'I always used to swim, remember, before life got busy. I thought I'd finally listen to Jean and try outside. Anyway, I ran into Quinn and we went for breakfast and ... ' Minnie let out a loud exhale, blinking her eyes closed. 'Leila, we got on so well. I don't know, he was just being so normal and funny and strangely vulnerable, not arrogant and obnoxious like before. We ended up going to the zoo and—'

'The zoo?'

'He wanted to adopt a penguin.'

'Classic day date.'

'What do you mean day date?'

'Zoo is a classic day date. Looking at all those animals humping each other – starts you thinking about sex. He suggested it? You only take someone to the zoo if you want to hump them too.'

Sophie Cousens

'I don't think it's romantic watching animals hump each other, but yes, he suggested it.'

'Then what? You snogged by the snow leopards, locked lips by the lemurs, canoodled by the canoe frogs?'

'What are canoe frogs?'

'I couldn't think of anything that went with canoodle. There might be canoe frogs.'

Minnie shook her head, distracted from her story.

'Anyway, Quinn and I had this amazing morning just hanging out, and it felt … I felt there was this amazing connection between us. We were about to leave and we had this moment …'

'A moment?'

'Yeah, like we were looking into each other's eyes and he was about to kiss me, and …'

'And?'

'And then he said, "Don't look at me like you want me to kiss you – I'm seeing someone and it would never work between us."'

'Ugh.'

'Ugh, I know.'

'I was expecting a little more steam in this story though, Min. This is barely U-rated. I was guessing he'd have at least shagged you and then ghosted you.'

'I know, I'm overreacting. I just felt this real connection, and then to think I'd imagined the whole thing. It made me feel so stupid.'

Minnie shrugged. She felt a strange layering of emotions. On one level she still felt rejected and embarrassed; on another she felt so pleased to be back with Leila, talking like they used to, that the rejection and the embarrassment didn't seem so bad. She reached out to hug her friend again.

'I've missed you, Leils. I'm sorry if you think I'm not a butterfly, and I'm sorry I berated you for being a butterfly. I love your butterflyiness, I can't handle being a boring wingless caterpillar on my own.'

Leila laughed. 'You're not a boring wingless caterpillar, I shouldn't have said that. You're wonderful just as you are. I don't think I realised how stressed I was back then. I took it out on you and I'm sorry.'

Minnie still held tight to the hug.

'Clearly Quinn thinks I'm a wingless caterpillar too.'

'Don't take it so personally. You don't know what's going on with him.' Leila paused, blinking owlishly. 'Don't take this the wrong way, Minnie, but you let other people screw with your sense of self-worth too much.'

Minnie tapped a fist to her lips and swallowed. She would usually respond defensively to this kind of comment, but she was so glad to be back on good terms with Leila that she bit her tongue and simply said, 'What do you mean?'

Leila took a deep breath, appraising Minnie's reaction as she spoke.

'Well, if a guy rejected me, I might be disappointed short-term but then I'd figure he wasn't cut out to be the beneficiary of my excellent Leila energy.' Minnie gave a reluctant lopsided smile. 'Whereas you, Minnie Cooper, would take it to mean you're worthless and hideous and doing something wrong.'

Minnie's phone started ringing from her bag. She picked it up and showed Leila the screen – Quinn was calling her.

'Do you want to answer it?' Leila asked.

'No.' Minnie shook her head, 'I'm going to try to be more Leila,' she said, hanging up the call.

They chatted all afternoon, catching up on all they had missed in each other's lives. Leila loved her new job at the fashion start-up, but had a new nemesis – a colleague who kept trying to outdo her in the fashion stakes. Minnie told Leila all about working at the catering firm, about living back at home with the endless soundtrack of clocks, and how Lucky kept trying to murder her in her sleep.

The afternoon evaporated and when Ian came home, they were still on the sofa eating Pringles with salsa, cradling large glasses of Pinot Grigio.

'Ah,' he said in a deep drawling voice, 'the prodigal Player One returns. How you getting on out there, Han Solo?'

'It's lonely,' Minnie sighed, getting up to give Ian a hug, 'but I'm learning all sorts of things about myself.' She turned to Leila with bulging eyes and a taut grin.

'Right, I have to pee, bladder the size of a harvest mouse,' said Leila, jumping up and walking in a comedy cross-legged waddle towards the bathroom.

Minnie took the opportunity to quiz Ian.

'You haven't asked her yet?' she hissed.

'I was waiting for you. I need you to sort out all the weird shit you said she wanted,' Ian mumbled, hands plunged into his tracksuit bottom pockets.

'I'm on it, I promise. I'm sorry, things have been—'

'I get it, you were off doing a bonus level.'

'Is she going to know it's me?' said Ian from beneath a heavy domed metal helmet. Fleur's prop contact had come up trumps.

'Who else would it be, you goon,' said Minnie, as she made the final adjustments to his body armour. The plates were specially layered so the wearer could ride a horse. The prop guy said it had been used in *Game of Thrones* by the Lannister army.

The sky over Hyde Park was cornflower blue. Buttercups and daisies peppered the lawn and regal swans preened themselves around the edge of the reservoir. It looked like an idyllic children's book illustration – the perfect place for a proposal. The whole No Hard Fillings gang had come back together to put Minnie's plan into action. Minnie was dressed as a mermaid with a long sparkling green tail and a huge wig of tumbling red curls weaved through with glittery silver seaweed. She wore a sheer body suit on her top half with a coconut bra that clonked when she moved. She hadn't planned on being a mermaid, but when she'd seen the choice of costumes, she'd decided this was her best bet. At least Leila would recognise her in this outfit.

Surprisingly, Fleur had come good on all her contacts. An animatronics specialist had brought them an array of singing animals from the last movie he had worked on, *The Singing Sheep of Pontyre Creek*. It was a bit sheep heavy for Minnie's liking; Leila had not specifically mentioned sheep in her fantasy. She'd imagined singing woodland animals like they had in Disney cartoons, but no doubt Disney had sheep in there somewhere and Minnie wasn't going to complain, especially when she saw the generator that had been brought down especially to power the singing sheep.

The costume contact of Fleur's at the RSC had roped in half a dozen actors who loved the sound of the plan and the promise of a free picnic. A further thirty people had been rounded up through a crowd-sourcing campaign Fleur had set up online. Minnie wasn't sure Fleur had been specific enough with the crowd-sourcing brief, because people were dressed as leprechauns, a pineapple and there was even a Tinky Winky and a Po lurking somewhere near the back.

Bev and Minnie had spent all of yesterday preparing the picnic to end all picnics. It had taken longer than Minnie planned because Bev wouldn't let them buy any food that came in plastic packaging. She'd finally gone along to some rallies and was now evangelical in her quest for a plastic-free world.

Today, Bev was dressed in a fancy-dress costume she had made herself. The outfit comprised of a strange, short green dress that had been ripped around the bottom, some kind of pillow tied around her shoulders, a very unflattering wig that looked to be made from the fur of an old teddy bear (there was a suspiciously bear-like nose above one ear) and make-up that had been done in the dark with too much eyebrow pencil. Minnie couldn't bring herself to ask which

Disney character Bev was supposed to be, but she was assuming it was some kind of Hungry Caterpillar.

'Great outfit by the way,' she said, giving Bev a nod as she arrived with another hamper of food.

'Thanks, I made it myself. I figure the world has enough fancy dress going straight to landfill. Oh Minnie, did I show you a picture of the T-shirt my daughter made Betty for the march next week?' Bev said, pulling out her phone. Minnie leant in to see a photo of a toothy three year old with long brown plaits wearing a green T-Shirt that said: 'MY GRAN'S FANTASTIC, SHE SAYS NO TO SINGLE-USE PLASTIC'.

'Oh Bev, look how cute she is. I'm so glad you're getting into all this campaigning.'

Minnie put an arm around Bev to give her a hug, but found herself hugging the pillow Bev had secured around her shoulders.

'Oh, you're the hunchback of Notre-Dame!' she said, finally clicking.

'Who else would I be?' said Bev.

Bev set about adding the final hamper to the scene. They had laid out a giant red and white checked picnic blanket with hampers full of pork pies, ham, cheese boards and fruit. It looked like a feast fit for Henry the Eighth (if Henry the Eighth had been friends with a mermaid, the cast of the RSC, Quasimodo, some freaky animatronic sheep and half the Teletubbies).

'Wow,' said Bev as they stood next to each other surveying the scene. 'Not bad, hey?'

Fleur had taken on the role of event coordinator and was ushering people into position, while a sweaty Ian was being manhandled onto a horse dressed as a unicorn by the sturdy horse handler. There were actors dressed as merpeople, elves, a snowman and a dancing hedgehog in a tutu. Minnie frowned: where had the dancing hedgehog come from?

'You do think this reads Disney fantasy, don't you, Bev, not weird trippy Christmas panto?' said Minnie.

'I haven't watched much Disney so I've got no idea what this is all about,' Bev said, shaking her head.

Minnie's eyes darted around for someone else to ask as Bev wasn't filling her with confidence. She hopped over to Fleur, holding up her tail with both hands – it wasn't easy to manoeuvre with your legs tied together.

'Fleur, this does look like a Disney fantasy scene, like *Enchanted*, doesn't it?' Minnie said. 'It's just, the dancing hedgehog and the Teletubbies—'

Fleur had a headset on and touched a finger to her ear, holding out her other hand to silence Minnie.

'Leila is out of the Tube so ETA five minutes people – *five minutes!*' Then she turned to Minnie with an eye roll. 'I know Bev is really letting the side down with her weird dead-bear-head outfit, but I'll hide her at the back. Don't worry, Leila loves all this weird crazy shit.'

Minnie hardly recognised this efficient and organised version of Fleur – she had never been like this when she had been working at No Hard Fillings. It was too late to worry whether the scene was Disney enough. Leila would know what it was supposed to be the second she laid eyes on it – that was what mattered.

Everyone took their positions around the picnic rug, shielding Ian and the horse from view. The plan was for Leila's new colleague Iggy to bring her here under the pretence of going to a mutual friend's birthday picnic. The set-up was perfectly positioned behind some trees, so you would only see the full spectacle when you turned the corner.

Tourists stopped to take photos of them, asking if they were shooting a movie, and a group of small children started hugging one of the Teletubbies. Fleur yelled at them all to get out of the way. A crowd of onlookers had now gathered, and people had their phones out, filming, waiting to see what was going to happen. Minnie felt a surge of adrenaline as she looked around her. Even though they no longer worked together, everyone had come to help her create this fantasy for her best friend. Leila was going to be so impressed that Minnie had remembered every detail all these years later.

Finally, Leila and Iggy arrived. Minnie saw them coming around the line of trees, and she felt her chest buzz with anticipation. Leila stopped in her tracks when she saw the scene. Iggy, a willowy brunette in her twenties, pulled Leila's hand and guided her over to the front of the picnic rug.

'What the actual blazing fuck-nuts is going on here?' Leila asked through nervous laughter. 'Am I hallucinating? Is it *This Is Your Life*?' Leila's eyes darted around, and she pointed as she started recognising faces in the crowd.

'Minnie? Is that you?' she said, squinting at the mermaid.

'Put this on,' Iggy instructed, picking up the voluminous sparkling blue Cinderella dress folded neatly in a picnic basket.

This had been another excellent find from Fleur. One of her contacts ran a Cosplay site with replica dresses from all the movies. It turned out Fleur wasn't a compulsive liar after all – she had delivered on everything she had promised. Her millionaire friend who'd invented seaweed packaging was here dressed as a fairy, and the location producer for Tarantino's new ghost film was somewhere in the crowd too, recording everything for Fleur's YouTube channel. Minnie felt bad for ever doubting her.

Leila shook her head in bewilderment, looking around as though expecting some TV presenter to jump out of the bushes. Then the crowd parted and the horse trainer guided Ian and the 'unicorn' forward. Ian tried to open his helmet but the eye flaps kept clanking shut. Leila started laughing as soon as she saw him; bent-double belly laughter. Ian huffed and clanked, then decided to dispense with the helmet altogether, taking it off and letting it drop down onto the grass.

'Leila, I love you with all my heart, you crazy, sexy woman. If you want the fairy tale, even this incredibly weird fairy tale, I promise I will try every day to give it to you. Leila Swain, will you marry me?'

Then he pointed to the fake sparkly gold unicorn horn where his grandmother's ring was glinting in the sunshine and the singing sheep on the front row started bleating out a sinister rendition of 'The Lion Sleeps Tonight'.

Leila was crying and laughing, clutching her sides and gazing up adoringly at Ian, while everyone in the crowd started clapping and cheering.

'Get down here, you mug,' she called up to him.

The horse handler and the hedgehog in a tutu helped lift Ian down in his clanking armour. He lumbered over to Leila, crushing a tray of pork pies as he went, causing Bev to let out an involuntary yelp.

'Well then?' Ian said. 'Will you?'

'Of course I will, you absolute mentalist,' Leila squealed, grabbing him with two hands and kissing him. 'But first explain to me what, in the name of the weirdest trip imaginable, is going on here? Why are there mermaids and singing sheep and a hedgehog doing ballet?'

Minnie stepped forward with a Nutella pancake carefully folded on a pink paper plate.

'This was your dream proposal, remember?' she said, beaming from ear to ear. Leila looked blank. 'Remember!' Minnie said, nudging Leila, 'We were seventeen, we were at my house watching romcoms and you said that when the perfect guy proposed to you it would be exactly like this. Well, not exactly like this, but you get the idea – it's the romantic Disney fantasy you always dreamed of!' Minnie spread her arms in a 'ta-da' gesture, waiting for Leila to click.

'I have absolutely no memory of that conversation,' said Leila, her mouth locked in a confused smirk, her eyes wide and unblinking. She turned back to Ian. 'Tell me you didn't organise all this based on some random conversation Minnie and I had thirteen years ago?'

Ian turned to look at Minnie and covered his face with his hands.

'I thought it was a seminal conversation!' cried Minnie.

'It definitely wasn't a seminal conversation,' said Leila, laughing.

'What's going on?' said Fleur, striding over to join the discussion.

'Leila doesn't remember the engagement fantasy,' said Ian, shaking his head.

'It was a seminal conversation!' cried Minnie, jumping up and down. How could Leila not remember? She'd been so impassioned about it.

'You are kidding me?' said Fleur, glaring at Minnie with her hands on her hips.

Then there were whoops of delight from the crowd as Leila jumped into Ian's arms and they both collapsed into a heap on the picnic blanket. As they started rolling around kissing, everyone cheered. Minnie smiled – even if Leila didn't remember, she looked happy. Her friend was engaged to the man she loved, and now even Fleur had a tear in her eye.

Minnie's tail started to vibrate. She turned around, patting herself down; she'd tucked her phone into one of the scales. She backed away from the group, using the phone as an excuse to get away from any more interrogation by Fleur.

'Mum?'

'Minnie,' her mother was panting, breathless on the other end. 'Something's happened, I don't know what to do.'

'Is Dad OK? Where are you?' said Minnie, holding a finger to her ear and walking away from the group so she could hear what her mother was saying.

'I'm with Tara Hamilton at her house in Primrose Hill.' Why would she be with Tara? 'She had this turn, said she was having a heart attack and started hyperventilating – I think she's having a panic attack. I thought I should call an ambulance just in case, but she screamed at me not to. She's asking for Quinn, but I can't find her phone. Do you have his number?'

Minnie couldn't understand why her mother would be at Tara's house. After all these months had she finally decided to meet her and hear Tara's side of the story?

'She suffers from severe anxiety – it probably is a panic attack. I'll come, I'm not far, I'll call Quinn on the way.'

Minnie turned to shout, 'I've got to go!' to the others, then hitched up her tail and started running towards the nearest road. She flagged down a cab on Bayswater Road and told the driver to hurry. In the car she called Quinn. He picked up straight away.

'Minnie.' He said it in a way that sounded almost affectionate, which was strange given how they had left things and that they hadn't spoken in a month.

'I think your mum's had a panic attack,' Minnie said briskly. 'My mum's at her house, she called me, said she was hyperventilating. She thought she might be having a heart attack.'

Quinn was silent on the other end of the line. Minnie listened to the sound of her own laboured breathing, the result of running through the park.

'I'll head over there now. Thanks for letting me know, Minnie.' Quinn's voice sounded hoarse.

'I'm in a cab, I'm going to be there in a minute.'

Minnie's cab pulled up to the blue house and she slithered out of the side door. Slithered because she was still wearing a constricting mermaid tail skirt that limited her leg movement to five inches in any direction. She rolled onto her front and flapped her legs backwards out of the taxi door, so she could push herself to standing, like a totem pole being winched upwards. Dashing through the park, she'd unzipped the side of the tail but the zip only stayed in two positions, all the way up or all the way down, so she'd been flashing bright pink pants to everyone in the park as she ran. In her haste to leave, she hadn't picked up the bag with her change of clothes in, only her handbag and purse. She shuffled to the front window to pay the cab driver.

The driver was an elderly Liverpudlian with long greying sideburns and a beige flat cap.

'Thought you'd be wanting Finsbury Park,' he said, flashing her a mouth full of cigarette-stained teeth. Minnie shook her head, confused. 'Fish,' he said, nodding to her tail, 'like Fins-bury Park.' He gave her a slow wink, cocking his head at her.

'Oh I see, ha-ha, very funny,' she said.

Minnie hopped up the front steps and rang the doorbell. Her mother answered the door. She did a double take and then looked Minnie up and down. Her lips started to move, as though trying to find words that refused to form. Finally she said, 'What you come as?'

'Long story. Is Tara OK? What are you even doing here?'

Her mother beckoned her in with a brisk flap of the hand, her eyes darting from left to right as though she were worried about the neighbours seeing a mermaid on the porch.

'We were just talking,' said her mother in a whisper, leading Minnie through to the sitting room. 'I don't know what set her off but she had some kind of panic attack, clutching her chest. She was trembling all over, gasping like she couldn't breathe.'

In the sitting room, Tara was lying on the sofa propped up against some cushions. She looked paper white. Her hands were pressed over her eyes and she was gently rocking her head back and forth.

'I would have called an ambulance but she begged me not to. She shouted for her pills. I turned her bathroom upside down to find the ones she wanted. I figure they've kicked in because she's been like this for the last ten minutes.'

Minnie pulled off the wig she was wearing so she wouldn't scare Tara. She crouched down next to the sofa and placed a hand on her arm.

'Tara, it's Minnie. I don't know if you remember me.' Tara glanced at her sideways from beneath her hands. 'What do you need, what can I do?'

'Quinn,' murmured Tara.

'Quinn's on his way, he'll be here soon.' Minnie gently squeezed her arm. Tara took a rapid panting intake of air, juddering like a breathy machine gun. 'OK, just breathe, Tara.

Look at me now.' Tara uncovered her eyes, blinking at Minnie. She squeezed her eyes shut. 'Just breathe with me.'

'I've done all this,' muttered Minnie's mother.

Minnie exhaled slowly and then inhaled loudly through her nose. Gradually Tara started to focus on Minnie, to replicate her breathing pattern.

'There you go, perfect, just in and out,' said Minnie's mother, then in a different tone of voice, 'hello.'

Minnie turned to see Quinn standing in the doorway, watching her. He was stock-still, a strange look in his eyes. Minnie smiled up at him – it was a reflex, like a sunflower opening towards the sun. Then she remembered the zoo, the rejection, the fact he hadn't called her since that day, and she reined it in, turning it into a more perfunctory greeting – a small nod of the head.

Quinn watched her face change and the look in his eyes disappeared. He stepped forward and bent down to his mother, Minnie stood up and shuffled backwards out of the way. Quinn looked her up and down with a quizzical 'what the hell are you wearing?' expression, then moved to take her place where she had been crouching next to Tara. He patted his mother's hand, a precise, rhythmic patting, as though communicating some code. Minnie turned to see Tara's head relax back on the pillow, her hand folding around Quinn's.

'Did she take something?' Quinn asked, turning between Minnie and her mother.

'Two of these,' said Minnie's mother, stepping forward to hand Quinn a brown pill tube. 'I wanted to call an ambulance but she was very insistent.'

Minnie's mother knitted her hands together, twirling her thumbs around each other.

'It's OK, you did the right thing,' said Quinn. 'Thank you for being here, Connie. I know how much Mum's enjoyed talking to you these last few months. It will have meant so much to her that you came.'

Minnie looked over at her mother in confusion. Her mother had been talking to Tara for months? Why hadn't she said anything? Her mother prickled uncomfortably, glancing at Minnie and then rubbing the back of her neck with a hand.

'I'm going to take Mum upstairs,' said Quinn.

Minnie nodded. She watched as Quinn gently propped one of Tara's arms over his shoulder and lifted her from the couch as though she weighed no more than a child. Watching him pick her up sent a spark of memory through Minnie's mind; that day at the pool – his dripping wet torso. She chastised herself; this wasn't the time to be mentally undressing the man!

'Don't leave. I'll come back down,' Quinn said to Minnie as he carried his mother towards the stairs.

When he had gone, Minnie shuffled towards her mother and hissed, 'So, you have been speaking. Why didn't you tell me?'

Her mother shrugged and walked off towards a side table full of silver photo frames and ornaments. She picked up a white china dog and examined it. 'Would you look at that, just like mine.'

Minnie looked at the dog. It couldn't have been more different to the tacky old ornament her mother was talking about. Tara's was probably an expensive bone-china collectors' item; her mother's had come from the Odds 'n' Ends shop off Kilburn High Road.

'Well?' Minnie hissed again, hands firmly planted on her scaly mermaid hips.

'We've just been talking. It's not your business, Minnie, that's why I didn't say.'

'Not my business? I was the one who gave you her number, I was the one who said you should hear her side of the story!'

Her mother shrugged again. She picked up a framed photo of Tara with a young Quinn on her lap – they were watching a sunrise together, somewhere tropical. She looked back at Minnie, who was watching her wide-eyed, waiting for an answer.

'I've got to do some things in my own way, Minnie. We've been talking here and there; she's had a difficult time of it, she has.'

Minnie couldn't understand why her mother wouldn't have told her. Then she paused, tempering her irritation. She was glad they had been in touch. Perhaps some closure on the 'name-stealing incident' would smooth at least one of her mother's jagged edges, redress her cynicism about human nature.

'Well, what did you say that made her ... ' Minnie paused, not sure what to label Tara's episode as. ' ... React like that?'

'I didn't say anything,' her mother said. Then, after a pause, 'She was telling me how upset she was I didn't call you Quinn, how bad she feels.' She shook her head. 'She got so worked up just thinking about back then. I said it's only a name, isn't it – it doesn't matter. But then she started hyperventilating.'

Minnie laughed in disbelief – 'only a name'. She looked at her mother as if she'd started speaking some strange Martian dialect.

'Why you laughing?' her mother frowned. 'You don't know what sets these things off. Poor woman's traumatised – postnatal anxiety, a terrible miscarriage, husband left her high and dry. No wonder she's a walking bag of nerves.'

Her mother picked up another frame from the collection of photos on the side table. This one showed a couple in their twenties, standing on the doorstep of the Primrose Hill house holding a baby in their arms. Quinn's father was making a show of holding up the key for the photographer. It must have been taken when they'd first moved in.

'You see a big house like this, Minnie, and you think people got it all. Sometimes it's like too much icing on a cake – it's covering over a crumby base that's cracked down the middle.'

Minnie put her face into her palms and inhaled deeply. She couldn't believe the words coming out of her mother's mouth; this kind of empathy didn't sound like her at all. How many times had they spoken? Minnie doubted Tara would have confided all this in a few phone calls. Clearly this dialogue with her mother had been going on a while.

'Don't you have a panic attack and all,' said her mother with a sniff, pushing out her bottom lip defiantly.

There were footsteps on the stairs. They both turned to see Quinn come back through to the living room. He looked tired, deflated. He brushed a hand through his hair and leant a shoulder against the door frame.

'Thank you for being here today,' he said to Minnie's mother. 'She doesn't have many people she'll speak to, she doesn't let anyone in. I hope today won't –' he paused, looking for the right word – 'put you off being in touch.'

Minnie's mother blushed and then jutted out her chin. Minnie had never seen her blush in her life.

'Takes a lot more than that to put me off.'

They all stood in silence for a moment until her mother said, 'Right, best be off. Can't stand around all day gassing. I'll call to see how she is in the morning.' She looked back and forth between Quinn and Minnie, gave Quinn a curt nod and then marched back towards the front door. 'You make your own way home, Minnie, you'll only slow me down with that ridiculous get-up you're wearing.' She gave Minnie a firm stare, as though trying to convey something with her eyes, though Minnie had no idea what it might be.

Once she had left, Minnie turned around to see Quinn standing next to her in the hall. He looked exhausted and forlorn.

'Well, I'd better be off too,' Minnie said, looking around for her purse and phone.

Quinn let out a deep, audible sigh. He put a hand across his chest and grasped his other shoulder.

'Can I do anything?' Minnie asked, nodding in the direction of the stairs.

'No,' he said. 'I'll just stay here until she wakes up. When she takes her medication, she comes around all groggy, forgets things. She'll need me here.'

His gaze turned to the floor. Looking at him now, Minnie couldn't be cross. Whatever awkwardness had passed between them, he was still a decent person dealing with a difficult situation.

'Do you want some company?' she asked quietly, her heart in her chest. Such an innocuous question, but she didn't know if she could take the humiliation of being rejected again.

His head shot up. 'Yes.' Then a smile played on his lips. 'But can we talk about the mermaid outfit now? And is that wig in the living room part of it because, if so, I think I need to see the whole get-up.'

Minnie gave him a playful shove as she hopped past him, but she pushed him a little too hard, lost her balance and fell into him. He caught her, clasping both hands around her shoulders. She breathed him in; he smelt like every good Christmas she'd ever had. The owls went into overdrive, pulling crackers and chirping owlish Christmas songs.

'Maybe you have something I could change into,' she said, righting herself and stumbling backwards.

Quinn found her some of his gym shorts and a T-shirt to wear. She went to change in the downstairs bathroom. She didn't have another bra with her, so she just put the T-shirt on over the coconut bra. Once she was back in the living room, she realised how ridiculously big and solid this made her boobs look. While Quinn was in the kitchen, rather than go back to the bathroom again, she decided to subtly perform the magic trick that all girls know – the one that involves taking your bra off beneath your T-shirt and pulling it out of an armhole. Unfortunately, this was not a smooth operation when the bra in question was made of two giant coconut shells.

Quinn came back in with a bottle of wine and averted his gaze when he saw what she was doing.

'Is my T-shirt attacking you?' he asked. 'Do you need some privacy?'

'All good,' said Minnie, finally pulling the coconuts out through the bottom of the T-shirt. Oh, why hadn't she thought to pick up her change of clothes?

Quinn poured them a glass of wine and she told him about Leila's engagement. She covered her face as she told him about Leila's reaction, how she hadn't remembered the conversation at all. The lines around Quinn's eyes creased into deep grooves and he let out a deep, hearty laugh.

'So she had no idea what this whole scene was in reference to?'

'Not an inkling,' Minnie gave a wincing smile.

'Oh Minnie,' Quinn leant back against the arm of the sofa, laughing. 'That's very sweet of you to plan all that for your friend.'

As he looked over at her with his warm blue eyes, she couldn't help but feel again that she'd known this man for far longer than the time they'd spent together. They sat in contented silence for a minute and then Quinn leant over to top up her glass. She shouldn't have anything else to drink; if she did she'd say something stupid. She'd mention the elephant in the room and she'd ruin things again.

'So, how are things with you?' she said, looking up at him over the rim of her wine glass. 'How's Amanda, or Amanda two, whatever her name is? Any madly romantic proposal on the cards there?'

Oh great, she'd done it – she'd mentioned it. Why had she brought up Amanda? Quinn didn't want to talk to her about his love life! Quinn shuffled forward on the sofa, then took a long sip of his wine.

'I guess we should talk about what happened at the zoo,' he said.

'It was a month ago, Quinn, you don't need to explain. It's fine, whatever, I was just making conversation. You know; how's work? How's the weather? How's your girlfriend? We don't need to talk about it at all, if you'd rather talk about the weather, this sunshine we're having is lovely, isn't it?'

She was babbling.

'Minnie,' he said, cutting her off, 'I felt like such an idiot as soon as you left.' He leant forward, putting his wine down on a side table and then propped an elbow on each knee. 'We had such a great day together and I ruined it, I'm sorry.'

'Well, they do say penguin poo is a real aphrodisiac.'

'You don't need to make a joke about everything, Minnie. I'm trying to do the decent thing here.' Quinn closed his eyes but carried on talking. 'I'm no good at relationships, I just end up hurting people. I've got my business, my mother – I don't have the capacity to look after ... for anything else.'

'Quinn, it's fine. It was a moment, I'm over it. Wow, do you have this much angst every time you almost kiss someone?' Quinn made a face of embarrassed amusement. 'Anyway, what makes you think I'd need looking after?'

'Well, I know you're now holding out for your knight on a shining unicorn.'

Minnie scrunched up her face. She knew she shouldn't have told him all that stuff when he'd been drunk at the office.

'Look, you don't have to give me the whole "tortured loner" routine.' Minnie rolled her eyes at him and his mouth twitched in the hint of a smile.

'Is that what I'm doing? I wasn't aware there was such a routine.'

'Yeah, guys do it all the time,' Minnie said, with a limp-wristed flap of her hand. 'Poor me, I can't get close to anyone because I had a tough childhood.'

She said it in a mocking voice, then flashed him a quick grin. Humour was the only way she knew to defuse an awkward conversation, the only way to salvage some sense of dignity in this dynamic.

'Wow, OK. Sorry for being so obvious,' he said, brushing his stubble with a palm and leaning back in his chair.

'It's fine, I forgive you. I'd just rather you were playing a more original character trope in this romcom. "Tortured commitment-phobe" is so nineties.'

'Is it now?' he laughed. 'And who said we were in a romcom? If I'm going to be in any kind of film, I'd want it to be a thriller or an action movie.'

'I don't think management consultants get to be action heroes,' said Minnie. She was relieved to be on safer ground. The elephant in the room had been dealt with. Now they could pack it up in a giant elephant-size box, bury it in the garden and never speak of it again. It could all just be banter and friendly conversation again.

'So what film are you playing a leading lady in?' Quinn asked.

Minnie bounced slightly in her chair. That second glass of wine had sent a buzz to her head. '*Finding Nemo*, when I had the fish tail on, but usually *Ratatouille*. Maybe my genre is kids' films.'

'Ratatouille?'

'It's about a rat who's a chef.'

'You're definitely not a rat, I see you in a superhero franchise,' Quinn said, taking another sip of wine. 'They'd call you Coco Nuts, and you'd take out all the bad guys by bashing their heads together with these enormous coconuts.'

Quinn glanced at the coconut bra lying between them on the sofa.

'I don't know if I could kill a man with those.' There was a fruit bowl on the coffee table and Minnie reached out for a banana. 'I think Coconut Girl would have some other fruit-themed weaponry up her sleeve.' She held the banana against Quinn's chest like a gun and Quinn raised his hands in surrender.

'Ah Coco Nuts, we meet again. I see you have foiled my cunning plan to steal all the fruit in Fruitopolis.' Quinn affected a deep American drawl.

'You won't get away with it this time,' said Minnie, in a theatrical voice of her own.

'Unfortunately for you, my superpowers involve telepathically forcing you to eat your own weapon,' said Quinn, still in character.

'I don't think so, Evil Baddie Man,' Minnie said.

'Is that my name?' Quinn asked in a stage whisper. 'It's not very good.'

'You didn't introduce yourself,' Minnie deadpanned, trying to compose herself. 'Very bad manners.'

Quinn reached for the banana, Minnie grabbed his elbow, and then followed what Minnie could only describe as a sort of play-fight, which ended up with Quinn pinning her to the sofa and taking the banana from her hand. Minnie suddenly felt very aware that she was not wearing a bra.

'I'm not eating it,' she said, still in character. 'You can't make me.'

'Can't I?' said Quinn, his voice an even deeper drawl. 'I have very persuasive powers.' He peeled the banana and held a piece to her mouth. Minnie pretended some supernatural force was taking over her body.

'Oh, no, not the banana!' she said breathily, putting her mouth around the chunk he was holding out for her.

She started eating it with her eyes closed, and when she opened them, their eyes met. He was looking at her wide-eyed. Oh god, how had this suddenly got so weird? She'd stayed for a glass for wine, and now they were engaged in some kind of sexy fruit-themed role play. Quinn cleared his throat, and slowly moved to his side of the sofa. Minnie swallowed the piece of banana in her mouth and stood up.

'Sorry, I got carried away,' Quinn said awkwardly.

'It's fine. I should um ... I should get home anyway.' She paused, looking down and remembering she was wearing his clothes. 'Can I borrow these to get home? My land legs only last until midnight and then I'll just be thrashing around in some Tube stop somewhere, begging someone to throw water on me. I can post them back to you tomorrow.'

'Of course,' said Quinn, 'or I can pick them up sometime.'

He found Minnie a bag for her mermaid costume and ordered her an Uber. At the front door he paused.

'I promise not to force-feed you bananas next time we see each other,' he said. The muscle in his jaw flexed and he dropped his gaze to the floor.

'Lucky for you I like bananas,' said Minnie, daring to make eye contact.

Quinn looked as though he wanted to say something else but didn't know how.

'You're great company, Minnie. I know we've had a few false starts, but I'd – I'd like us to be friends,' he said, looking at her hopefully. 'I need more laughter in my life.'

'Court jester at your service,' she said, crossing her leg in front of her and giving a bow.

'I don't mean it like that,' he said, reaching out to touch her arm. He looked worried he had offended her. 'I just can't handle anything more at the moment.'

'Of course.' She reached out to give him a reciprocal tap on the arm. 'Any time.'

He opened the door for her, the cab was waiting outside. She hovered in the doorway. Why was she hovering? He'd think she was hovering because she was waiting for him to kiss her and he had just established that she was firmly in the friend zone. So why was she still standing here? She jumped down the steps, tripped and stumbled on the bottom stair.

'Are you OK?' he called after her.

'Fine, totally fine. See you later friend,' she said with a backwards wave.

21 June 2020

The next Sunday, Minnie went back to Hampstead Ponds. She could have gone to the Ladies' Pond further into the park. It was smarter, had better changing facilities and more sun in the morning. But she found herself at the Mixed Pond, peering at each head that glided through the water, wondering if one might belong to him. Clearly he was not likely to be there. She always looked for Jean Finney too, with her distinctive white ruffled swimming cap. It was just something you did when you went to the ponds, you looked out for people you knew.

Minnie swam for longer than she planned to, pulling the water back and down as though her life depended on it. She felt strong. These last few months she'd noticed new muscles developing in her shoulders, her stomach felt flat for the first time in years and her legs and arms felt longer somehow. On the downside her hair was a wild frizz bomb. Did any swimmers have good hair? Maybe if she was really serious about swimming she should chop it all off and go full otter.

When all her energy was spent, she pulled herself out of the water and dried herself standing on the patch of grass just in front of the changing rooms. Flashes of memory from this exact spot surfaced – stealing Quinn's towel, their breakfast together, his dimpled smile as they walked side by side through the park. She needed to stop thinking about him.

'Are you leaving?' came a voice behind her.

She turned and then blinked, as though she didn't trust her eyes. Was he really there, or had she conjured him up just by thinking about him? He was standing holding a towel, fully dressed in jeans and a pale blue shirt rolled up to the elbows. His hair looked longer, dishevelled. His face was unshaven; she'd never seen him with stubble before. The stubble made her conclude he couldn't be a mirage. If her subconscious was going to create a vision of him, it would create him in the way she knew him to look, not some new, unshaven version.

'Hi,' she said, feeling her mouth launch into an unconscious smile.

'I hoped I'd run into you,' he said. 'Shame we're not in sync to go for a post-swim bacon roll. You must get up at the crack of dawn.'

'Oh, I've only done a few laps,' she lied. 'I could swim longer if you ...'

Minnie couldn't swim another stroke, she was exhausted.

'Great, shall we meet back here in thirty minutes?' he said, pulling off his shirt in one smooth movement.

Minnie's body protested as she sank back into the water behind him. She watched Quinn set off at a pace across the pond. Had he genuinely hoped to see her here? She hadn't been in touch with him since last weekend. She'd wanted to send a text asking how his mother was, but then she didn't want to be the instigator, didn't want to look too keen.

As she swam half-heartedly across the pond in his wake, she wondered what it was about Quinn that she liked. She had now admitted to herself that she did like him, even if it was not reciprocated. Maybe the very fact that he didn't want to be with her was part of the appeal. She'd always gone for men who kept her at arm's length. Greg had been far more interested in his job than her. Her previous boyfriend Tarek had been selfish at best, verbally abusive at worst. Leila used to say that you got the relationship you thought you were worth. If you thought you were only worth part of someone's attention, perhaps that was all you looked for.

And yet.

She had ended things with Greg because she wanted more; because she knew she was worth more. So why was she now swimming around like an idiot just to go for a coffee with a guy who wasn't interested in her? Did she actually want to be friends with him? Was that the consolation prize?

Minnie's skin was wrinkled and white by the time Quinn finished swimming. They dried off next to each other on the bank; retreated to the changing rooms to get dressed and then met up again outside the iron-gated entrance to the pond. They walked across the heath, down the hill towards Hampstead Heath train station. Quinn said he wanted to go back to the same breakfast van Minnie had taken him to before.

'So how's your mum doing after last week?' Minnie asked, swinging her wet towel as she walked.

'Talking to your mother a great deal,' said Quinn.

Yesterday, Minnie's mother had told her she was popping down to Primrose Hill with a homemade quiche. A quiche?

Minnie couldn't remember the last time her mother had baked a quiche from scratch.

'I know, it's strange,' Minnie said, ruffling her wet hair so that it looked less flat against her head. 'She's never really had female friends, my mum. None that I've known of in any case. She's always too busy working to socialise.'

'Nor mine,' said Quinn. 'What do they talk about?'

'What it's like to give birth on the first of January in 1990?' said Minnie with a laugh. 'That's literally all I can think of that they have in common.'

'Maybe they're both lost souls,' said Quinn thoughtfully, 'they see themselves reflected in the other.'

'That sounded very poetic, Quinn Hamilton. No one would imagine you were a boring management consultant.' Minnie sucked in her cheeks to stop herself from laughing.

He reached out his rolled-up wet towel and playfully patted her on the bottom with it. 'Watch your tongue, Cooper.'

'You call that a towel slap?' Minnie laughed. 'Pathetic.'

'Well, unlike you, I don't go around beating people with towels until they bleed, I've still got a mark where you branded me, you know.' His voice took on a husky quality.

'You do not,' Minnie said, elbowing him in the ribs.

'And now with the elbowing.' Quinn clutched his side as though deeply wounded. 'I'm going to be black and blue being friends with you.'

They got breakfast rolls from the van. Quinn suggested they walk back to the top of Parliament Hill to eat them in the sunshine. They sat in the grass looking out at the London skyline, a vast carpet of buildings rolling out in front of them, dotted with cranes and skyscrapers.

'Feels incongruous having this giant heath here, doesn't it?' said Quinn.

'I love it. It's like the last spot of wilderness in London, where nature has yet to be pressed flat beneath the concrete.'

'Now who's sounding poetic?' Quinn said, looking sideways at her.

'Oh shut up.'

'The heath has inspired many poets: Keats, Wordsworth, Coleridge, now Cooper,' Quinn said in a lofty, English-teacher voice.

'I'm certainly not a poet,' Minnie said with a sniff, biting into her bacon bap. She knew he was only joking but, when Quinn said things like that, it made her acutely aware that he had gone to university and she had not.

'"My heart aches, and a drowsy numbness pains my sense",' he said.

Minnie turned to look at him with startled eyes. She stopped chewing mid-mouthful.

'Keats. "Ode to a Nightingale". Written here, I think. I can't remember any more of it.' He blushed, perhaps realising she hadn't registered he was quoting from a poem. 'He died at twenty-five, what a waste.'

'Is this how you usually try to impress girls, quoting poetry and Wikipedia at them?' Minnie asked, turning her focus back to her coffee.

'No,' Quinn leant back in the grass, resting his weight on his elbows. 'Why, are you impressed?'

304

'I'm not supposed to be being impressed, this is just a friendly post-swim blap chap – bap chat.' Minnie stumbled over the words. 'That's hard to say – Post. Swim. Bap. Chat.'

Quinn turned on his side, resting his head on one hand as he looked up at her. 'You think that's my modus operandi, do you? Dropping in poetry where I can?'

'You just dropped in Latin. What do you want from me, Quinn, a B plus?'

Quinn lay back in the grass and laughed, a deep chesty laugh.

They talked for over an hour – about everything and nothing. Minnie felt that warm hum of contentment as she sparked into life. She felt relaxed and fun, interesting and interested – it was the version of herself she most enjoyed being. They strolled the long way back around the heath down to the Tube.

'Thanks for the post-swim bap chat,' he said, hands in his pockets as they stood outside the station.

'No problem,' she nodded, combing a hand through her tangle of curls.

'I guess I might see you next time,' he said. The train roared into the station. 'I'm going to get this one south.'

'I'm going north,' she said, indicating the other platform with her thumb. The train doors opened and Quinn got on. He turned around to look at her as the doors slid shut and he held his hand up, in a motionless wave. Their eyes connected and he gave her a little smile. She stayed on the platform watching his train pull away, their eyes locked on to each other until the tunnel pulled him out of view.

'So you just talk?' Leila asked her.

'Yes, we just swim, walk, talk and eat bacon sandwiches,' said Minnie.

'And nothing in between? No texts, no emails, not even an emoji?' Leila looked confused.

'No, no emojis. What emoji would I send? Swimming man, bacon and a wavy hand?'

'Oh, there's this cute little baker emoji, I always think of you when I see it.'

Minnie and Leila were sitting in the audience of a fashion show Leila had helped produce. Minnie was there as her 'plus one'. They sat in prime position on the front row watching outlandish outfits parade past. There were models dressed in giraffe-print hot pants, wearing huge elongated hats with giraffe's heads on the top. The fashion show was taking place in a converted church near Aldgate. The pews had been turned inwards towards the raised catwalk and the church ceiling was alive with light projections pulsing in time to the DJ's music. The whole event had a very cool east London vibe.

'Are these all animal-themed outfits?' Minnie asked. 'I'm not sure I could pull off a giraffe-head hat.'

'It's sustainable, animal-friendly fashion – one designer's been a bit literal,' Leila explained.

Leila was dressed in her usual demure style – a 1950s-style cocktail dress in silky silver fabric, with a superhero-style cape made of what looked like pink candyfloss. On her head she wore a small top hat with a placard attached to it, which read, 'It's a hat, deal with it.' Minnie felt conspicuous wearing black jeans and a simple blue cotton blouse.

'Anyway, tell me more about these swim dates. Are they as fuelled with sexual energy as the banana role-play situation?' Leila said, turning back to her friend.

'They aren't dates, that's the whole point; we're just friends,' Minnie explained. 'And no, nothing as weird as the banana scenario.'

After that first Sunday on Hampstead Heath, a new routine had evolved between Minnie and Quinn. Every Sunday they would meet at the ponds at seven thirty. They didn't arrange it, they just both started going when they knew the other would be there. They swam for half an hour, sometimes longer, they got breakfast and coffee at the van, they walked, talked, and then circled back to the train and said goodbye.

Minnie didn't want to question what they were doing. She never wanted to leave when they reached the station, but she couldn't bring herself to ask him to go on somewhere with her. Outdoor swimming was a hobby they both shared; having a coffee afterwards was casual, friendly. Anything more and it might verge into 'date' territory. If he suggested it, fine, but he never did.

She looked forward to Sunday mornings every minute of the week. She dreaded Sunday afternoons when it would be a whole week until she could see him again. She turned down invitations from other people to do anything on a Sunday morning: swimming was an immovable fixture in her calendar, just as it had been when she was a child.

When it rained she worried he wouldn't come. Who went swimming in the rain? She went anyway and he was there; they were the only ones. She didn't ask him about his love life again, and he didn't ask about hers. Minnie purposely avoided the subject. Perhaps he was still seeing whoever she was, perhaps he was still dating pneumonic blondes from Tinder – she didn't need to know. Talk of other people would taint the nature of their meet-ups. These Sunday mornings were bell jars full of precious conversation. Minnie didn't want too much of the outside world getting in; she thought that he understood and felt the same.

'And you talk about what?' Leila asked.

'Life, work, parents, books – everything. We joke around a lot, he's quite philosophical; he's so smart, such easy company. I feel like we could keep talking for hours and then the morning is suddenly over and it feels like no time at all.'

'Uh-oh,' said Leila, fanning herself with her programme.

'Uh-oh what?'

'Sounds like you in lurrve.'

'No.'

Minnie shook her head, scrunching up her face as though squinting to see. On the catwalk a group of models wearing pink and beige army fatigues came hopping onto the stage.

'What are they doing?' asked Minnie.

'They're supposed to be flamingos, in military camo gear,' said Leila, as if she was explaining the most obvious thing in the world. ''Cause we're all fighting for survival, right, it's just a different kind of war.'

Minnie nodded. She didn't understand fashion but everyone else in the front row was looking immensely impressed.

'I'm not in love with him, we just get on really well,' she said.

Leila turned to look at her friend – a piercing, interrogatory look.

'OK, I know that face,' Leila frowned. 'I'm being serious now. If you love your love twin and if he's not interested in you in that way, then it's only going to mean heartache for you, Min.'

Minnie made a 'tsk' sound and crossed her legs, bobbing her top foot rapidly up and down.

'The other weird thing is that our mothers are spending all this time together. It's like my mum's taken on Tara as this project. She wants to fix her like my dad fixes his clocks. Every time I call home, Dad says she's over there helping with the gardening or the shopping or something. It's kind of sweet, I guess; I don't think my mum's ever had many friends.'

'Right, answer these questions truthfully,' said Leila, looking down at her programme as though she was finding the questions on the page. 'Do you think about him when you go to bed at night?'

All the time – he was the first person she thought of when she woke up.

Sophie Cousens

'No, not every night. Occasionally,' said Minnie.

Leila frowned. 'Has anyone else asked you out in the last few months and you've said no because they're not Quinn?'

'No ... well.' Had she told Leila about that guy Tino from the catering firm? Shit, it was a trick question. 'There was that one guy, but I said no because he had weird sideburns, not because of Quinn.'

'Um, weird sideburns have not put you off before. OK, question three, would you be fine with it if he brought his girlfriend along to your little swim club?'

'How do you know he has a girlfriend?' Minnie bolted forward in her chair, leaning into her friend, 'Have you seen him with someone?' her voice sounded strangled and urgent.

Leila turned to her and moved her hands apart like a performer preparing to take a bow.

'I rest my case.' Then she quickly pointed a hand back at the catwalk. 'Oh look, this is one of the most exciting designers – what do you think?'

On the catwalk were seven models each dressed in a different colour of the rainbow; they wore strange ballgowns that looked both rigid and graceful at the same time. 'It's all made out of plastic reclaimed from the sea,' Leila explained.

'Wow, incredible, Bev would approve,' said Minnie. The dresses were genuinely spectacular, but she pulled her attention back to the conversation in hand. 'Seriously, though, have you seen him with someone? I don't care if you have.'

Leila turned to look closely at her friend.

'Listen to what you're saying. Look, you said yourself he's a self-confessed commitment-phobe. For whatever reason he likes disposable relationships that don't require him to give too much. Maybe he's never been friends with a cool, interesting woman before, he doesn't want to ruin things. Fuck me, this cape is hot,' Leila pulled off the candyfloss cape and stowed it under her chair. 'Does my look work without it?'

Leila might as well have been asking a camel what he thought of the political situation in Mozambique.

'Totally works,' Minnie said. 'So you think Quinn might be biding his time?'

'No, I think he's having the best of both worlds. He gets to have these lovely soul-searching chats with you – no commitment or expectation; then he gets to shag Little Miss Tinder when he likes – no commitment or expectation. Win-win situation for him, lose-lose for you.' Leila paused, reaching out to squeeze Minnie's knee. 'You're a hot, fun, incredibly awesome woman. Don't sell yourself short, Minnie, that's all I'm saying.'

Leila stood up and started clapping as the designers came out for a turn of acknowledgement on the catwalk with their models. Minnie slumped down in her chair and clapped despondently. Maybe Leila was right. She'd never thought about it that way. Was she his platonic weekend girlfriend? A companion with no expectations, no dates or obligation. He could simply not turn up one week and she would have no recourse to be cross with him for standing her up. What would happen if she didn't go tomorrow? They'd been meeting for about seven weeks now. If she didn't go, would he call her? Would he be disappointed?

Would it make him seek her out and commit to more than a post-swim bap chat?

The next morning she woke up at six, hungover from the fashion show and restless with indecision. She'd resolved the night before that she wasn't going to go to the ponds. She had too much to do here anyway. She'd finally saved up enough deposit and found a flat to rent in Willesden – she'd picked up the keys yesterday. She needed to move her things out and get the flat set up before work tomorrow.

Six fifteen. But she desperately wanted to go to the ponds. She couldn't deny herself the short-term enjoyment of seeing him. Six thirty. She had to leave now if she was going to be there on time. She got dressed. She'd head that way and then decide what to do. She could always go for coffee alone in Highgate. She didn't need to go as far as the ponds if she decided against it.

Seven thirty. Who was she kidding? Clearly she was going to go and meet him. She walked up the path to the ponds with a sinking feeling. Testing herself like that made her realise how dependent she'd become on this weekly dose of happiness. She looked around for him; he was usually here by seven thirty. What if he didn't come this week? What if he hadn't come, and she hadn't come, and he wouldn't even have known she hadn't come, so her stupid test would have been pointless.

'Hey.' She felt a hand on her elbow, a bolt of electricity.

She turned to see him looking down at her with a dimpled smile. Her blood pumped faster through her veins – an addict getting her fix.

'I thought maybe you weren't coming,' she said, locking eyes with him.

'Why wouldn't I come?' he said, staring right back.

They swam as usual, dried off and got dressed. Sometimes, when they dried off on the bank, she thought she saw him glancing at her legs beneath the towel. If she saw him looking over at her, he'd immediately turn his gaze and then she wondered if she had imagined it.

As they walked towards Barney's breakfast van together, Minnie towel-dried her hair.

'So, how's your week been?' he asked.

'Good. I got the keys to my new place in Willesden. I'm moving in this afternoon.'

'No more ticking clocks, or I could come and hang some in your new place, make it feel more like home?'

He gave her a lopsided grin.

'No thank you. I am looking forward to some blissful tick-free sleep.' She paused. 'You could help me move a few boxes in though – if you don't have plans?'

What was she doing? She was breaking the unwritten rule; she was smashing the bell jar, breaking the bubble. Their friendship only worked on Hampstead Heath, a flat move was uncharted territory. He turned his head sideways to look at her, a questioning expression in his eyes. She could tell he was thinking it too. It sounded like such an innocuous request, one friend asking another to help them move. They both knew it wasn't.

'Are you sure you'd want me to help?' he asked, his voice quiet and serious. 'I'd probably be more of a hindrance.'

He was trying to get out of it. She was stupid to ask. Why would he want to help her move house?

'Forget I asked,' she said, giving him an overly cheerful smile, crushing her cheeks into tight baby fists. 'Clearly not how anyone wants to spend their Sunday afternoon.' She skipped forward to get ahead of him; she didn't want him to see her look disappointed. 'Right, whose turn is it to buy the baps? I think it might be yours, my friend.'

They got down to Barney's and there were a couple of people queuing ahead of them. Quinn hadn't said anything in a few minutes, and Minnie found herself pinching the skin between her thumb and forefinger.

'I will help if you want me to,' he said softly. She turned to look at him as they queued for the van. She saw something behind his eyes: sadness, resignation? She couldn't read him at all. 'I have my car here today, I could drive you.'

Minnie was about to protest, to say it had been a silly idea and she could easily do it herself in an Uber, but then she stopped herself. The conversation with Leila had made her realise the extent of her feelings for Quinn. She couldn't go on like this, just living for Sunday. She wanted to open the bell jar, take this beyond the heath, whatever that meant.

'That would be mega-helpful, thank you,' she said.

'What are friends for?'

It felt strange taking Quinn to her parents' house. She had never brought a man there.

Once they were inside, she held her fingers to her ears and moved her head like a metronome.

'See, relaxing isn't it?'

'I don't know – it's quite charming. It's like the house where time lives.'

She wrinkled her nose at him. She'd taken to making this face whenever he said something poetic.

'Maybe that could be the title of my autobiography,' she said.

She led him up to her small attic bedroom and he had to hunch to get through the rabbit-hutch-style door.

'Oh, I love Hopper, I have a print of *Nighthawks* in my flat,' said Quinn, instantly honing in on *Automat*.

'No way,' she said, 'I love his paintings.' Clearly Quinn didn't remember she'd been privy to the Amanda conversation outside his office. 'This school friend of mine, Lacey, she moved away from London when I was fourteen. We stayed in touch writing postcards to each other for a while. She must have had a multipack of Hopper prints, because they were all his. His pictures have that association for me – kind word from a sorely missed friend.'

'She looks so lonely, doesn't she,' said Quinn, looking down at the picture. 'You want to know why she's sad.'

'You think she looks sad? I never thought that, I always thought she looked content in her solitude. I envy her – I'd never be brave enough to have coffee alone with my thoughts.'

Quinn looked sideways at her, still holding the print.

'That's a very optimistic outlook.'

'Leila gave it to me.' Minnie shrugged, 'Maybe that's her world view rubbing off on me.'

As he put the picture down, Lucky sprang through the door and started weaving in and out between Quinn's legs.

'Who's this?' he said, bending down to stroke the cat's head.

'This is Lucky. Lucky hates moving so we have to trick him and pretend it's some kind of cat game show and he's won a holiday. You can play the part of the glamorous assistant.'

Minnie had far more boxes than she remembered. It would have taken her at least two trips in an Uber. Willesden was only fifteen minutes' drive south of her parents' house. It wasn't quite as edgy and cool as her previous address in east London, but it had character and her flat wasn't far from the Tube station. She could afford a place to herself here, even if it was on a rundown estate next to a noisy main road. She and Quinn finally got her boxes and an unhappy cat unloaded into the hall of the new ground-floor flat.

'It's nice,' said Quinn, craning his neck to look into the various rooms of her tiny one-bedroom apartment. To the right of the front door was a small wet room, estate-agent speak for a shower with a toilet in it. 'Who doesn't like to wash while they're on the loo?'

'I'm sure it's not as palatial as you're used to in Primrose Hill, but it's all mine and it's blissfully quiet,' said Minnie. As though on cue, several lorries went roaring past on the road outside, which made them both smile.

To the right of the front door was a kitchen the size of an ant's nostril, with cupboards stacked three layers high all the way up to the ceiling. There was a small stepladder, presumably used to reach the highest level.

'You don't want to keep the booze up there,' he said, pointing to the top cupboard. 'Three gin and tonics and this kitchen's a deathtrap.' He banged a hand twice on the stepladder.

'Thanks, Dad,' she said.

'OK, I'll admit that did sound very dad-like. But can I just say, Minnie, I never had a father figure, so dad jokes are very triggering for me.'

Minnie's face fell, her eyes darted up to look at him.

'I had you for a second,' he said. 'You had a very concerned look in your eye.'

'No I did not,' she said, flicking him on the neck with a finger. 'You're an idiot.'

'Ow,' he said, laughing as he rubbed his neck. Then he reached out and squeezed her shoulder affectionately.

He walked back through to the hall and picked up another box marked 'kitchen'. There was a bottle of champagne poking out of the top of it. 'Good to see you've packed the important stuff,' he said, nodding towards the bottle.

'Leila gave it to me as a moving-in gift,' said Minnie. 'I'll put it in the fridge.' She paused, looking up at him. 'Unless you'd have a glass with me now? There's probably ice in the freezer. I can't face unpacking any more boxes today.'

He had that look again, that look by the breakfast van, as if she was tempting him to do something he shouldn't.

'I have to drive back,' he said.

'Of course, silly idea, it's warm anyway.'

'I could have one glass.'

They abandoned the rest of the boxes in the hall and moved through to her sitting room. It was supposed to be a furnished flat, but the living room only contained a small two-seater sofa and a low rectangular coffee table. Though the room was tiny, there was a large window looking out over an empty block opposite, so the light streamed in, making it feel warm and inviting compared to the dark, claustrophobic kitchen. They sat next to each other on the small green and white baize sofa. There was no ice, and no glasses, so they drank the champagne warm out of mugs.

'So I noticed one of the boxes I carried in was labelled "pie-making kit",' Quinn said, looking down into his mug of champagne. 'Do you think you'll go back to it one day?'

Minnie took a gulp of champagne.

'I can't really, can I? We sold everything.'

'You gave up your lease – you didn't get rid of whatever is in that box.'

'Well, I didn't say I was never going to bake a pie ever again, did I?'

'That would be a travesty.'

The sofa was so small their legs were touching. Minnie felt very aware of every point at which his body was in contact with hers.

'Warm champagne isn't great, is it?' Quinn said with a comical grimace.

'Sorry,' she said, taking a large swig. 'Drink faster, it doesn't taste so bad.'

He followed suit and then topped them both up. What were they doing? He had to drive home. But she didn't want to ask questions; she just wanted him to stay.

'I'll leave my car here, fetch it tomorrow,' he said, as though reading her mind. 'Can't leave you to celebrate alone, can I?' He picked up his mug and clinked it with hers.

Minnie realised she wanted to be drunk, she wanted to relax, to turn off the anxious inner narrative that kept asking what she was doing, what she was hoping would happen. The champagne would dull that questioning voice, allow her to relax and enjoy herself. She got so tired of the barrage of questions constantly knocking away at the inside of her head; alcohol was sometimes an excellent mute button.

'So, no more baking, just catering,' Quinn said, getting comfortable on the sofa, sinking down into it.

Minnie didn't want to talk about work, she just wanted to snuggle down into the nook beneath Quinn's shoulder and feel the warmth of his body against her face. She blinked. She felt drunk already. Had she said that out loud about putting her face into his nook?

'I think you loved running your own business, though. You loved helping those people.' He looked up at her, sensed in her face that the direction of this conversation might puncture the pleasant atmosphere. He changed gears. 'But then you wouldn't have time to enter the wild swimming Olympics and that would be a tragedy for Great Britain.'

She smiled and briefly patted his knee, acknowledging she appreciated him changing the subject. They sat in companionable silence for a moment. Minnie glanced over at him. She knew now she was deluding herself if she thought she could be happy just being his friend. She had lifted the bell jar by bringing him here – she might as well just smash the glass now – say what had not been said.

'So, what is this do you think?' she asked, moving a hand between them to indicate him and her. She was doing it; she was digging up the elephant in the room from the giant elephant-shaped box they'd buried in the garden months ago.

'What do you mean?' he asked. His eyes darted around the room like a prisoner looking for an escape route. She should drop it, talk about something else.

'I mean you and me. What is this? Are we really just swimming buddies?'

He gave her a smile that looked self-consciously sheepish.

'I will take all the credit for your illustrious swimming career.'

'Seriously though, Quinn.' She wouldn't let it go. 'You genuinely don't have any feelings for me other than swimming buddy feelings?'

He shifted uncomfortably on the sofa and closed his eyes. She'd done it now. There was no papering over that.

'Because I know you said you didn't want that, but when,' she exhaled loudly, 'when we're together it just feels – I've never had anything like this connection with someone. I can't,' she closed her eyes, she couldn't look at him as she said it, 'I look forward to seeing you all week. When we're together it just feels – like it's meant to be. Am I imagining this?'

She opened her eyes and looked over at him. He looked up into her eyes and she saw clearly that she hadn't imagined it. He leant in towards her, the blue of his eyes suddenly wild, like a raging sea as he reached a hand behind her head and then he pulled her towards him, his lips meeting hers – a forceful, urgent kiss that took Minnie by surprise. She knew it! She knew he felt the same! Her mind fizzed with victory. The kiss softened, his lips gently parting hers, and she felt dizzy with desire as she pulled herself closer to him, wanting to erase any molecule of space between them. He gently pushed her back onto the sofa, his body controlling hers. Being held in his arms she was suddenly very aware of the strength of him, his broad shoulders, his arms, the sheer size of his frame. A bolt of heat coursed down through her belly and between her legs; she was falling, intoxicated, with no sense of solid ground beneath her. She lifted her face to kiss him again, but the sofa was too small, restricting them from pressing their bodies against each other.

'Shall we move?' she asked, her voice breathy against his cheek.

In one deft movement, he was on his feet, picking her up and setting her gently on hers. He danced her in a circle over to the wall by the door, but she turned and pressed him against it, pulling his jumper and T-shirt up over his torso, her hands searching out the firm skin of his chest. Then he clasped his hands around her waist, gently easing her top off, and she felt every pore burn with pleasure where his hand made contact with her skin. She unclipped her bra and he looked at her body as though it was some rare marvel he had just discovered. He traced one hand gently down from her neck over her breastbone, around her waist and into the small of her back. Minnie thought she might explode with pleasure and her lips reached up again to find his mouth –

A trill noise suddenly rang out – the doorbell.

They froze. Her face whipped towards the door.

'Is that mine?' she said, breathlessly.

'I think so,' Quinn said, his voice hoarse, pained by the interruption.

'I don't know anyone here, it's probably a wrong number. Ignore it.'

Quinn put his hands up to her face, cradling her chin between his palms – he drew her face gently towards his, their eyes locked and she felt this earth shifting moment of—

BBBBBBBBRRRRRIIINNNNG, the doorbell again, then, 'Hello? Minnie? You in there?' Her mother's voice.

The earth-shifting moment between them turned to panic, and they both leapt apart, searching around for their clothes.

'What is she doing here?' Minnie hissed. There was a rap on the door. 'Maybe the bell's broken,' she heard her mother say.

'I'm coming!' Minnie yelled, 'just on the loo.'

She gave Quinn an 'oh my god, sorry' look as she quickly pulled her top back over her head. She also tried to convey an 'I'll get rid of them and we can pick this up from *right* where we left off' with her eyes, but that was a harder emotion to condense into an eye roll.

'Hi,' Minnie said, opening the door to find both her parents standing on the doorstep.

'You *are* here,' said her dad. 'We saw you'd taken all your boxes while we were out and we thought you might need a hand settling in.'

Her mother bustled past her carrying bags of shopping.

'I bought you some essentials. Can't have you moving into a bare kitch ... Oh.' She held a hand to her chest in surprise when she saw Quinn emerging from the living room, his hair dishevelled.

'Hi Mrs Cooper,' Quinn, said, clearing his throat and raising a hand in greeting.

'Quinn helped me move,' Minnie explained.

'I see,' said her mother, turning to Minnie and staring at her with wide, bulging eyes.

'We won't get in the way,' said Minnie's dad. 'We just didn't want you to be on your own in a strange flat with no food in.'

'Your father thought we should check out the neighbourhood. Not quite as nice as your last one, is it?' said her mum.

'This lock on the front door is no good; they always play up, these ones do. You got to have a double lock on a ground floor. Get your landlord to fix you a new one,' said her dad, locking and unlocking the front door to demonstrate.

'Aren't these impractical,' said her mum, eyeing up the tower of kitchen cupboards. 'Now, we won't stay, but I am gasping for a cuppa, have you got teabags unpacked yet?'

Minnie's parents took themselves off to inspect the rest of the flat, while Minnie started scrabbling around in boxes looking for teabags.

'Is this the whole of it?' called her mum from the living room, then, 'Sweet Jesus!' as she walked into the bedroom. 'Did someone die in here?'

'You sure this is better than my clock room, Minnie Moo?' called her dad.

Minnie carried a tray full of teas through to the sitting room. Her parents had made themselves comfortable on the sofa, while Quinn sat on the floor. As Minnie put the tray down on the coffee table, she noticed her black bra on the floor behind the door and tried to subtly scoot it beneath the sofa with her foot.

Minnie's mother frowned at the tea that had been placed in front of her.

'Use one bag between the four, did you? I suppose you'll be making economies now you have to buy your own.'

Minnie's father shifted uncomfortably on the sofa.

'Not much room for two on here, is there?' he said.

Minnie looked over at Quinn who shifted his gaze to the window.

'Quinn, hasn't your mother got that garden looking good lately? She's a font of knowledge, that woman. Very green fingers, you must be pleased she's out and about again?' Minnie's mother said proudly.

Minnie couldn't read Quinn's expression; he looked distant all of a sudden. His smile a polite veneer, painted over something unreadable.

'Yes, you've been a very positive influence, Connie. It's wonderful to see her out in the garden again, it genuinely calms her,' he said, getting up from the floor. 'Listen, I'm afraid I have to head off. It was nice to see you both.'

'Don't go,' Minnie said, turning to face him and shaking her head, 'you haven't had your tea?' She tried to convey with her eyes how much she definitely did not want him to leave. His eyes wouldn't meet hers.

'I don't think the tea's worth staying for, love,' said her dad with a grimace.

'I'm sorry, I have to be somewhere this afternoon. I'm glad I could help with the boxes,' Quinn said, already in the corridor.

'But your car?'

'I'll get it tomorrow,' he said, already halfway out of the door.

'Oh, I hope we didn't chase him away?' said her mother, as Minnie came back through to the living room.

Minnie felt her heart sink down through her chest and into her feet. Of all the ways that kiss could have played out, this was not high on the list of optimal outcomes.

'Minnie Moo, I brought you a moving-in present,' said her dad, picking up a carrier bag from the floor next to him. He pulled out a square box wrapped in bubble wrap and presented it to Minnie. She peeled back the plastic; it was one of his clocks, the one with the silver hands and the most annoying tock of all.

'On loan, just so you feel at home,' said her dad with a wink.

New Year's Eve 2003

The bath water was getting cold. Her skin above water level had sprouted goosebumps and the tips of her fingers had wrinkled into white, alien-like pads. She put her hands over her chest – still practically flat as a pancake. She was going to be fourteen tomorrow, surely they'd have to grow soon. She wanted to run the hot tap and stay in longer but her mum was in the bedroom – if she heard the tap she'd shout at Minnie to get out.

The school holidays felt like life in slow motion. Time could be stretched out; a bath could take an hour, preparing a meal could take two, a walk around the park could take the whole afternoon. Life in term time was faster, harsher; you couldn't pause for a second. In five days she'd be back in the fast lane, back in Hannah Albright's sights. Five days.

Last term, the girls in her class had invented a game where they sang songs whenever Minnie came into a room. They all high-fived each other when someone thought of a new one. 'Driving in My Car', 'This Car of Mine', 'Life Is a Highway'; it was amazing how many songs there were about cars and driving.

Minnie had learnt to cope with the name-calling and the singing. Let them sing, let them laugh, don't react – it stopped quicker that way. Hannah Albright was always the one that took it furthest, goading her for a reaction. In the last week of term things had notched up a gear. 'Notched up a gear,' Minnie sunk her head beneath the surface of the bath water – now she was even thinking like a car.

Part of the problem was that her best friend, Lacey, wasn't in her class any more. She didn't have anyone to stand up for her. Hannah, Pauline and a few of the other girls had taken to physically pushing her, yanking her hair. At one point someone had stabbed her with a pencil. This new violence scared Minnie. She didn't know how to deal with it; it wasn't something she could just ignore or silently endure.

She opened her eyes underneath the water, looking up at the stained, beige ceiling tiles through the shimmering lens of water. She broke the surface, filling her lungs with air, then pulled her legs towards her, hugging them against her chest. On her thigh she could still see the small purple welt from the pencil wound. It felt as though the girls at school just wanted to keep needling her, poking her until she snapped.

Was it just her stupid name that made her a target? She was studying *Romeo and Juliet* in school and one quote had stuck in her head all term; 'a rose by any other name would smell as sweet'. Would life with any other name still be as shit? There were other kids at school with strange names who didn't attract the kind of grief she did; Isla Whyte in Year Nine was too beautiful to tease and Ziggy Zee Zane in Year Ten had a dad who used to be in a band – that bought him a free pass. There must be something else about Minnie that made her so pick-on-able. Was it her brown frizzy hair, her plump hamster cheeks? She'd secretly thrown away the Quality Street chocolates Grandma C. had given her for

Christmas. Maybe her cheeks would shrink if she stopped eating chocolate.

Tonight she'd done something drastic; she'd bleached her hair blonde and spent six months' pocket money on hair straighteners. Maybe a new look was all she needed? She was scared to show her mother what she had done, that's why she'd been in the bathroom for over an hour. Tonight was going to be her first night out as a blonde – maybe her luck would change.

A knot had been growing in her stomach all afternoon, knitting itself into a painful ball. Minnie got these stomach aches whenever she was anxious. In term time she had them constantly. What if she changed how she looked and things didn't improve? What if it wasn't the hair, the cheeks, or even her name? What if it was something she wasn't able to change?

What she wouldn't give to swap lives with someone like Grace Withies. Grace who was so pretty, so good at hockey and who smiled like a celebrity. People buzzed around her like bees around a flower. No one wanted to buzz around Minnie. Life must be so easy for someone like Grace; going to bed every night, safe in the knowledge that no one was setting out to make your life a misery the next day.

'Minnie, have you drowned in there?' her mum shouted through the door.

'No, just getting out,' Minnie said, pulling herself out of the water and shivering as she grabbed a towel.

'I've got to go out,' her mum said. 'You off to this party with your friends then?'

'Yeah, the youth club – Bambers up the high street. Lacey's mum is dropping us off.'

Her mum was leaving, perfect; she could avoid the freak-out about her hair until tomorrow.

'Will Elaine drop you back after?' Her mum's voice sounded tired.

'Uh-huh.'

Minnie stood in front of the mirror, distracted by her new hair. It was *so* blonde – she looked like a completely different person.

'Minnie, you hear me?' said her mum. 'No drinking either; if I smell it on your breath tomorrow you won't be allowed out again, we clear?'

'Yes, Mum.'

A few minutes later she heard the door slam. Minnie walked over to the flat window with her towel wrapped around her. She looked down to see the hunched figure of her mother walking towards the Tube station, pulling her coat up around her ears against the cold.

They'd had a good day today, she and Mum. Will and Dad had been out at a car boot all day and Mum had been batch cooking for the Salvation Army bake sale tomorrow. She'd made a dozen chicken and veg pies and she'd let Minnie help. Baking was one of the few activities Minnie and her mother did together. Mum patiently taught her how to knead the pastry, then roll it out with just the right amount of flour. Today, Minnie had been in charge of the casings while Mum stewed the filling. 'Well done; good, even thickness,' her mother had said over Minnie's shoulder. Her mother rarely gave compliments. Minnie had glowed with pride.

Her mum was softer somehow when she cooked, too busy in her own head to criticise. Sometimes, she even sang as she baked, she sounded happy. Today, while they were baking all those pies together, Minnie hadn't thought about Hannah Albright once. Baking was like a holiday for her head from all the bad stuff.

As she stood by the window she felt nervous about going out. The knot in her stomach was still there. What if blondes didn't have more fun? What if Hannah turned up? What if her new hair just drew more of the wrong kind of attention?

Up in the sky a single firework exploded, tendrils of light hung in the air leaving a shadow of brilliant white behind it in the grey, cloudy darkness. Something about that firework made Minnie feel hopeful; it wasn't supposed to be there. Maybe it was planned for a bigger display at midnight and had been let off by mistake. That lonely firework, all the brighter for going out alone.

'What is this place we're going to?' asked Bev.

'Hair by Clare,' said Leila. 'They do your hair in the proper fifties style, with curlers and a set.'

It was Saturday morning. Leila had booked for Bev, Minnie and Fleur to all have a hair trial ahead of the wedding in December. She had decided if they were going to be her bridesmaids, they would all have to embrace her favourite decade.

Fleur planned to meet them at the salon, and Minnie, Bev and Leila were walking together from the Tube station. Getting off at Chalk Farm made Minnie feel she was stepping back in time, as though she was seeing the world through a sepia lens. She looked up at the window of the flat she'd grown up in; it looked just the same. Now, as they passed the railway bridge, which led to Primrose Hill, her eyes found themselves drifting in a new direction. Quinn's flat must only be a five-minute walk from here.

It had been six days since the kiss and there had been just one text exchange between them. She'd hung around all morning on Monday, waiting for him to come back and collect his car. Eventually, some guy in a peaked hat had turned up, who turned out to be Quinn's private driver. His driver? He'd sent his driver.

Minnie had felt something was off as soon as he left that day. Maybe it was her parents arriving, maybe he'd sobered up, maybe it was the zoo all over again. When she still hadn't heard from him by Tuesday evening she'd sent him a text.

'You have a driver?'

She'd deliberated for hours over what to send. In the end she'd just gone for those four words, something simple to remind him she existed. His reply had been cold and underwhelming.

'Yes. Sorry, crazy week at work. Maybe see you at the ponds.'

No kiss. No jokes. No sense of him at all. Reading it late that night made Minnie's insides tense up into a familiar grinding knot and she couldn't sleep for thinking about it.

The next day she'd tried to be positive. Maybe he really did have a crazy work week? What did she expect – that after kissing her he'd suddenly want to spend every minute of his time with her? She noticed he'd said 'maybe' see you at the ponds. Would he even be there tomorrow if she went? However much she went around in circles thinking about it, something about the silence from him this week just didn't feel right.

'Walking down the street with Leila is like going out with a celebrity, isn't it?' said Bev, interrupting Minnie's spiralling thoughts.

Leila was wearing a bright green 1950s dress with yellow roses all over it. She had freshly coloured rainbow-striped hair, and wore bright red lipstick. Bev was right; Leila was drawing the heads of everyone they passed.

'It's nice to be noticed,' said Leila, doing a little skip along the road.

Bev was wearing black jeans and a T-shirt that said: 'Straws Really Suck'. Minnie didn't even know what she was wearing; with all the talk of clothes she had to look down to check she had actually got dressed this morning. Jeans and a blue T-shirt, phew.

'Can I just say, you are looking so well, Minnie. All this swimming you're doing clearly suits you,' said Bev.

'That's nice of you to say, Bev. You're looking lovely too.'

'Don't you love August? The warmth in the air, the flowers in the park. London looks so beautiful at this time of year,' Bev said, taking a loud inhale.

'Bev, you're sounding very upbeat,' said Leila, reaching out to squeeze Minnie's hand as she said it. 'Is this Minnie's influence, sending you out campaigning with all the do-gooders?'

'Oh, I've met so many wonderful people, so inspiring. I've also joined this brilliant group called "Pick Litter, Have a Witter". They coordinate groups of people to go litter picking and you can chat to like-minded people on any given topic while you collect rubbish. There was a bit of a mix-up when I first joined, they put me in a group of people suffering from PBA – Post-Brexit Anxiety. I was talking at cross-purposes with this lad for hours about the trauma of separation – I thought his wife must have left him!' Bev laughed.

'Well, I'm so pleased you're feeling better about everything,' said Minnie.

'My GP also started me on a course of anti-depressants, but I don't think that's what's making the difference to my mood. I think it's more likely to be the litter picking.'

'Well, you're feeling better, that's the main thing,' said Leila.

They arrived at the hair salon, which was tucked away down an unassuming side street. 'Hair by Clare' was run by two ladies who were both in their eighties and both, unsurprisingly, called Clare. Leila had known them for years and was a regular client. Walking into the salon felt like stepping back in time. The walls were covered in old prints of vintage cosmetic adverts; there was a gramophone in the corner playing jazz music, and two of those old-fashioned-style hairdryers, with large pink plastic helmets. Even the magazines laid out on the coffee table were from a different era, and the two Clares wore vintage pink and grey smock shirts over their clothes. Fleur was already there. She was scrolling through her phone with one hand and holding a flowery teacup in the other.

'At last,' she said, looking up as they came in.

Leila hugged both of the Clares, and then turned to introduce everyone.

'So Fleur you've met. Bev, Minnie, this is Claire and Clare. One with an "i" and one without.'

The Claire with an 'i' wore glasses and had neat brown hair set into a wave. The Clare without had grey hair styled in a short bouffant bob.

'So, how did you decide whether Hair by Clare should have an "i" in it or not?' Minnie asked.

'Don't mention the name,' said Leila dramatically, shaking her head.

'It's a long story ... ' said Claire.

' ... involving a great deal of sherry, and a game of gin rummy,' laughed Clare.

'Which I won,' said Claire. 'There used to be an "i" on the sign, you can see the gap where it used to hang. This old crone pulled it down with her stick one day. I watched her do it, then she blamed it on pigeons. Pigeons my arse!'

'It was pigeons. Don't listen to a word of it,' said Clare, shaking her head, and they all laughed.

'So what are we doing for you lovely ladies today?' asked Claire.

'Well, I'm getting married in December, as you know, and I wanted my bridesmaids to go a little fifties in the hair department. We thought we'd have a trial, make sure they can pull it off,' said Leila.

'I don't want too many weird chemicals on my hair,' said Fleur, firmly.

'Don't worry, the chemical hallucinations usually stop once the hairspray dries,' Clare said, revealing a mouthful of crooked teeth as she grinned. Fleur narrowed her eyes suspiciously.

Minnie perched next to Leila on one of the button bar stools by the counter, and they watched the Clares set to work on Bev and Fleur's hair. Minnie was feeling nauseous. She hadn't slept properly all week. The situation with Quinn had cast a cloud over everything and the effort it took to appear fine was exhausting. Leila had planned this day out weeks ago. Minnie wanted to be upbeat and enthusiastic for her friend, but she felt like curling into a ball on the floor.

'Hey, you OK?' asked Leila, reaching out to put her arm around Minnie.

Minnie clenched her teeth and gave Leila a beaming smile.

'Sure, of course. Sorry, just tired.'

Sometimes she wished her friend didn't know her so well. Sometimes, she just wanted to pretend to be fine, and for Leila to just pretend right along with her.

'Still nothing from Quinn?' Leila asked.

'Have I missed something happening with love twin?' asked Fleur, her eyes darting up to look at Minnie.

'Nothing, let's not—' Minnie protested weakly.

'Minnie has liked this guy for ages,' Leila explained to the Clares, 'and then finally they got it on and now he's gone quiet on her.'

'Oh dear,' said Claire, giving Minnie a sympathetic look through the mirror.

'They kissed last Sunday, and now he's fully Charlie Chaplined her,' said Leila.

'Charlie Chaplined?' asked Bev.

'Gone silent,' said Leila.

'Well, not totally silent. He has sent me a text,' said Minnie, shifting her weight awkwardly on the stool.

'What did the message say?' asked Clare.

'Some bullshit about a busy week and maybe he'd see her at the ponds sometime. They swim together,' Leila explained.

Clare screwed her face up into a grimace.

337

'Maybe he really is busy,' said Bev, giving Minnie a long, sympathetic look.

'Maybe he's married,' said Fleur with a shrug.

'He's not married, Fleur,' said Minnie irritably.

'Maybe he's a secret agent then' said Fleur, 'he could be working undercover for the Russians. You can't form attachments if you're a spy.'

'Maybe he's a homosexual,' said Clare. 'My first husband was a homosexual.'

'He and Minnie have become friends and I doubt he's ever started a relationship with a friend before. He's scared of intimacy,' said Leila.

'You want my advice?' asked Claire.

'The Clares give good advice,' said Leila, slowly nodding her head.

'If you kiss a man and he runs a mile, he's no good. Life is full of times you have to turn towards the storm, and life brings many storms. Sick children, parents dying, cancer, just the challenge of building a life together and not driving each other completely nuts. You need a man who'll turn into the storm with you when it comes, doesn't she, Clare?' said Claire, as she pulled Fleur's hair into rollers.

'She's right. When life gets stormy, a man afraid of commitment will be off in a flash, looking for calmer shores with some flibbertigibbet called Kimberley,' said Clare. 'He won't be up in the night when you've got a bubba to feed; he won't be at your bedside after a double mastectomy.' Clare paused, leaning over to pat Claire's hand as she worked, 'Your best friend will be there.' A look of deep understanding passed between them.

Minnie watched this moment between the two older women. She wondered if she and Leila would still be friends when they were that age. Maybe this was the important thing; maybe this was the love that truly endured.

'And if he asks you to bleach your love glove, he's a miscreant to boot,' said Clare, tapping two fingers against her pubic bone. Then Fleur sprayed a mouthful of tea across the room and slapped a hand over her mouth, which broke the sombre tone and made everyone laugh.

Minnie moved the conversation away from men and onto Leila's wedding. Part of her knew they were right, but another part, perhaps it was the ever-hopeful owls, wanted to go swimming tomorrow and find him there, and all would be as it had been before.

Once the Clares had set Fleur and Bev in rollers, it was Minnie and Leila's turn to have their hair styled.

'So, when's the big day, Leila?' asked Claire.

'Thirtieth of December,' said Leila with a sigh.

'Oh. Well that's … unusual.'

'We wanted New Year's Eve but my maid of honour is superstitious about that date so we had to shift it twenty-four hours,' said Leila.

'That is not the reason,' Minnie said, talking to her friend in the reflection. 'They couldn't afford New Year's Eve and they got a great deal on the thirtieth. No one else is having a big party the night before New Year's Eve.'

'*And* you wouldn't have come if it was New Year's Eve,' said Leila.

'But mainly you got a good deal,' said Minnie.

'Plus you wouldn't have come.'

'But mainly the deal.'

'And you wouldn't have come.'

'The deal.'

'You.'

'The deal.'

Minnie's phone started to ring, which saved the discussion from escalating further. It was her mother.

'Hi Mum.'

'Minnie, now, I'm at Tara's house,' she said. 'I'm setting Tara up on a blog page, she wants to write about gardening for anxiety, but I'm struggling to work out this site. Do I want a banner? And would the standard design be OK or should we pay for a theme? And how do we get photos of her garden out of the phone and into the website?'

Minnie closed her eyes, overwhelmed by the barrage of questions.

'I'm not an expert on blogs, I'm afraid,' she said. 'Oh wait, I'm with Fleur, she'll know.' Minnie covered the receiver and held out the phone to Fleur. 'Will you talk to my mum about setting up a blog?'

Fleur clicked her fingers, then pushed up the giant pink cylindrical heater she was sitting beneath and took the phone from Minnie. 'I swear that thing is frying my brain. Hi Connie, yes – what do you need?'

A very confusing conversation followed, where Fleur attempted to talk Minnie's mother through the options she needed to click, screen by screen. In the end Fleur had to give up.

'Listen, you're just in Primrose Hill, aren't you? We're all in Chalk Farm at some weird hairdresser's. I can just nip down there when we're done, it will take me two seconds to set this up for you if I can see the screen ... yes, we can all come ... sounds good ... I'll tell Minnie.'

Minnie shook her head wildly and flapped her hand for the phone, but Fleur had already hung up.

'What?' Fleur said to Minnie.

'We can't all go down there!' said Minnie.

'Why not?' asked Fleur.

'This is Quinn's mother's house, what if he's there? Plus Tara won't want a load of strangers coming by.'

'Who's Quinn?' asked Clare.

'The guy she likes – storm avoider,' said Leila.

'Well he's not going to be there, is he?' said Fleur. 'Your mum said Tara wants us all to see the garden or something, said they had a gooseberry tart that needed eating.'

Minnie frowned; she couldn't go to Tara's house. What if Quinn popped in and found her there? It would be too awkward. She called her mother back.

'Mum, we can't come over to Tara's,' she said firmly.

'Oh Minnie, don't be ridiculous, Tara wants to see you, and she said to bring your friends, didn't you Tara? ... Oh, well she wants to know how many of you are there?'

341

'Four of us,'

'Four of them, Tara ... yes, that's fine, she says come.'

Minnie felt her skin getting hot. Clare pulled the last curler into place and sprayed a cloud of setting spray over her head.

'Is Quinn going to be there?' Minnie asked quietly.

'I don't think so, why? Do you want to see him?' Connie asked.

'No, I just wouldn't want him to think I was – um, following him around London.'

'Tara, Minnie wants to know if Quinn's coming over?' Connie yelled.

'Oh god, don't ask her!' Minnie sank down into the chair and put a hand over her eyes. Pleased as she was that her mother had a new friend, it wasn't ideal that this friend happened to be the mother of the man she'd just been ghosted by.

'No, he's at some conference all day. So you don't need to fret about running into him without your lippy on, Minnie.'

Half an hour later, the four of them were standing outside Tara's house, each modelling impressively bouffant 1950s hairstyles.

'Jesus – this is her house?' said Leila. 'It's bigger than my whole block.'

'You know, if I lived somewhere like this, I'd probably never want to leave the house either,' said Bev.

'Shhh,' Minnie hissed as they stepped up to the front door and rang the bell.

Tara answered the door.

'Minnie, well look at you? You look gorgeous. I used to wear my hair that way once upon a time.'

Tara was wearing gardening gloves and a green apron over a grey shift dress. Her skin was sun-kissed and her eyes twinkled with life.

'Are you sure we're not intruding?' said Minnie. 'We won't stay long.'

'No, no, come in, come in. Oh my, how colourful!' Tara said, on seeing Leila and her rainbow hair. 'What a jolly way to be.'

Minnie introduced Tara to her friends and they all followed Tara through to the kitchen where Minnie's mother was scowling at a laptop. Leila and Bev both gawped at Tara's palatial interior with undisguised awe. Minnie mimed closing their gaping mouths at them while Tara was looking the other way.

'Oh Minnie, you look like a young Elizabeth Taylor,' said her mum. Minnie did a double take at such a compliment from her mother. 'And Fleur, a touch of the Bette Davis. What's this all in aid of?'

'Hair trials for Leila's wedding,' Minnie explained.

'Right, show me this blog you need setting up?' said Fleur, pulling up a stool next to Minnie's mum.

'Well, we haven't got past the first page,' said her mum, shaking her head.

'I don't think I'll be able to manage if it's complicated, Connie,' said Tara, clasping her hands together, her brow knitted in consternation.

'It's not complicated, don't worry, I'll walk you through it,' said Fleur, dismissing Tara with a wave of the hand.

'Show Minnie the garden, Tara, I'm sure she'd like to see,' suggested her mother.

'Oh, it's nothing remarkable,' said Tara quietly, shaking her head, 'but it's something of an achievement for me.'

Tara led Minnie, Leila and Bev down a flight of stairs into the basement, where there were French windows leading out to the back. The garden was huge by London standards, stretching off to a wall of trees a hundred and fifty feet away. Nearest the house was a cobbled patio with wicker table and chairs, then beyond, an arc of flowerbeds full of white roses, purple foxgloves and orange dahlias – a wild array of colour.

'This is all the gardener, I can't take credit for the flowers,' Tara explained, 'but this I can – this is our little project.'

She couldn't hide the pride in her voice as she showed them the vegetable garden beyond. Four neat squares of soil, all planted with rows of leafy vegetables, herbs, climbing beans and tomato plants.

'Wow, you've been busy,' said Minnie, kneeling down to smell the thyme.

'Your mother drove me to the garden centre last weekend. I got out and bought those myself,' said Tara, pointing to the row of herbs. Then she turned to Leila and Bev. 'I know that doesn't sound particularly impressive,' Tara clasped her hands again, rubbing the back of one hand with the other palm, 'but I sometimes have trouble getting out, I get a bit overwhelmed.'

'We've all got our demons to fight, hey,' said Bev heartily, and Tara nodded.

'Your mother is such a wonderful woman, Minnie. She's pushed me to make a small step every day. Doesn't take no for an answer, does she?'

Tara spoke with such warmth in her voice, it caught Minnie off guard. She rarely heard anyone talk about her mother like that. She hadn't often considered that her mother's stubbornness could be such a positive trait.

'Well, I'm glad she's been helpful,' said Minnie.

She could see Tara's hands begin to shake; she was clasping them together so tightly her knuckles were turning white. 'Please, we don't want to overwhelm you, Tara, if it's too much us being here,' said Minnie softly.

'Please stay,' said Tara, 'I need to push myself to do more.' She blinked quickly, her eyes darting back towards the house. 'Would you all have tea if I made a pot?'

They all agreed that they would.

As Tara hurried back inside, Bev, Leila and Minnie sat down on the chairs around the patio table.

'Jeez, I need the toilet, but I'm scared to go,' said Bev. 'This place is like Buckingham Palace or something.'

'Bev, if you need the toilet, go,' said Leila. 'It will be more embarrassing if you wet yourself.'

'I won't be able to go. My bladder seizes up in fancy places.'

Tara returned five minutes later with a tray of tea things and a gooseberry tart. She had a phone balanced beneath her chin.

'Yes, Minnie and her friends popped in … her friend is helping me set up a blog page … no, I'm not overdoing it, darling. Here, Minnie was wanting to speak to you,' Tara said, laying down the tray and passing the phone to Minnie. 'It's Quinn, checking up on me.'

Minnie felt the blood drain from her face; the knot in her stomach twisted uncomfortably. Of all the ways she wanted to hear from Quinn, this was not it. She shook her head weakly, but Tara kept thrusting the phone at her.

She finally took it and walked down the garden with it. If she had to talk to him, it wouldn't be in front of everyone else.

'Hi,' she said.

'Hi Minnie,' said Quinn. He cleared his throat. 'So you've been roped in to helping with the gardening?'

'Something like that,' Minnie said.

The line was silent for a moment, then Quinn spoke.

'I'm sorry I haven't called you, I know I should have. I've ... none of this isn't straightforward for me.'

His voice was awkward, embarrassed. Minnie squeezed an earlobe with her free hand, the pressure distracting her from the horrible realisation of what she had suspected.

'Why are you being like this?' she said quietly. 'I thought ... I don't know what I thought.'

'Minnie,' his voice softened, 'I ...' He let out a sigh. 'I can't just jump into something like this. I'm not sure I can handle disappointing someone again, and I know I can't be what you need me to be.'

'How do you know?' she said, her voice catching in her throat. 'I don't want you to be anything.'

There was silence on the line. She thought maybe he'd gone.

'I've already disappointed you. I can hear it in your voice.' They were both silent for a moment. Minnie stood shaking her head. 'Please don't think it's you, Minnie, you're so ...' Quinn took a sharp inhale of breath. 'Do you remember that penguin we heard about at the zoo, the one in Japan who was in love with the cardboard girl?' His voice sounded hoarse, broken.

'Yeah,' Minnie said, closing her eyes.

'Well, I'm the cardboard girl. I don't have the capacity to be a living, breathing penguin. I think Lucy was right – in what she wrote about me.'

Minnie felt tears welling in her eyes and she wiped them away furiously; she didn't want the others to see her crying. 'Maybe we'll see each other at the ponds?' he said softly.

'I don't think so, Quinn.'

She hung up the phone and gritted her teeth, willing the tears not to come. She took a minute to compose herself and then headed back towards the house. At least she knew now, at least there was no more deluding herself, no thinking of excuses for why he'd gone quiet. A cardboard girl was definitely not someone to weather the storm with.

She walked back over to the others and handed Tara the phone as cheerfully as she could. She got through tea and then, finally, once Fleur had finished setting up Tara's blog and shown her how to use it, they were able to leave. As Tara thanked them and said goodbye at the door, she pulled Minnie aside.

'I know I've made life difficult for him, poor boy,' Tara said, her voice shaking. 'I tried not to lean on him so but ... when I was at my lowest, I didn't even realise I was doing it.'

Minnie squeezed Tara's hand. She didn't know what to say. Tara pulled Minnie into a hug and spoke quietly in her ear. 'Don't give up on him, Minnie. You're what he needs, I can see it.'

Minnie didn't want to tell her that it was too late, she had already given up.

'Where have you been hiding, Quinn? I've hardly seen you all night.'

Lucy walked towards him, her hips swaying hypnotically as she sashayed across the room in stiletto heels. She planted a firm kiss on Quinn's lips then took him by the elbow, escorting him over to the far end of the room, away from the volume of the band. The party was in full swing; there were over two hundred people here. Quinn didn't know he had this many friends. Lucy had arranged it all – the venue, the band, the private catering.

'Have you talked to Rupert yet?'

'Rupert …' Quinn's eyes hovered up and to the right betraying the fact he had no idea who Rupert was or why he was supposed to speak to him.

'Oh Quinn,' Lucy gave a delicate foot stomp. 'Rupert! The Lexon guy, he's a great business contact for you. He's also desperate to employ me. I keep telling him I'm happy at the paper, but you never know when these contacts are going to come in useful.'

Quinn nodded, as though it had been a case of temporarily forgetting the guy's name, rather than having no memory of the conversation.

'Can we step outside?' Lucy said, lifting her glass towards the balcony behind the sliding glass door. Quinn pulled the door open and a sharp blast of cold air hit them both. He took off his jacket to wrap around Lucy's shoulders.

'Listen, I know we said we wouldn't talk about it tonight, but I haven't been able to stop thinking about what Carol said,' Lucy said, hugging his jacket.

Carol was the relationship counsellor Lucy and Quinn had been seeing for the last month. Lucy's idea. She decided Quinn had a 'fear of intimacy, stopping him from taking their relationship to the next level'. She thought he needed therapy to 'unpack unresolved issues about his childhood'. This was the problem with the internet; everyone fancied themselves amateur psychologists.

He and Lucy had been together for a year and three months. Lucy expected 'I love you' by six months, preferably three. Fifteen months meant there had to be something wrong with him. She had said it at six, to the day. He didn't know many women who would drag someone to couples therapy just to get him to say those words, but she clearly thought he was worth trying to fix. Lucy was solutions-based; it was one of the things he liked about her.

The therapy with Carol was a warning siren pulsing through his temple, yet for some reason he had muted the sound for over a month. Why hadn't he just ended it? He would never have tolerated such scrutiny or interrogation from past girlfriends. One answer could be that he did in fact love Lucy; perhaps he didn't want to leave? She was beautiful, bright and confident – what was not to love? She had even been accommodating about his aversion to phone calls, something other women had never been able to tolerate. She didn't need him, she wanted him – it was a dynamic that worked.

And yet, in the dimly lit periphery of his subconscious, Quinn was aware of a darkness lurking. If he ever shone his attention towards it, it would skulk back into the shadows, ungraspable. And yet. Only yesterday he had stared down that shadow for the first time. He had seen it for what it was and he had formulated it into words. Ever since Polly, he had been subconsciously attracted to women with unappealing qualities. It didn't make sense, he didn't understand it, but once he'd thought it, he couldn't help looking back at his relationship history through this strange, murky lens. Jaya had been a narcissist, Eddie a compulsive liar, Anna hated dogs and Lucy was a snob who was rude to waiting staff. All these traits had been immediately visible to him and yet, strangely, were part of the attraction.

Why? When he tried to peer into this rabbit hole he started to feel anxious. What kind of psychopath would actively choose to go out with women who possessed traits he disliked? The anxiety made him feel as if he was his mother, that it was in his DNA, that he was not in control.

Back to the question in hand: why hadn't he ended things with Lucy? The idea he might love her appealed to him. If this was love, this was manageable; this was not an earthquake waiting to destroy his foundation. If something went wrong in the future with Lucy, he would be sad, but he couldn't imagine locking himself away for the rest of his life.

There might be another explanation for this stay of execution; that he had started to see value in the sessions with Carol. Growing up, Quinn came to think of therapy as akin to fixing bomb damage with wallpaper – it was something to take your mind off the fact that the walls of your house had been blown to bits. In the sessions with Carol, he'd found himself talking about his mother and father's break-up, about his mother's condition, his father's disappearance. What had made him unload like that, heaping emotional coal into the filthy engine of therapy? Carol just listened, nodding in comprehension; she did not try to wallpaper anything.

At their fourth session, Carol said, 'Now I know you have booked this as couple's therapy, but if I'm honest, I feel Quinn could benefit most from some one-to-one sessions. You should only embark on one course of therapy at a time, so you'd have to do one or the other.'

Lucy looked disappointed. She liked being involved; she liked nodding sympathetically, as though if only he could unload all these words about his past, then at the bottom of the pile of words would be the three she was looking for.

'Well,' Lucy frowned, looking back and forth between Carol and Quinn. 'We'll have to discuss it. I felt we were making progress?'

Lucy leant forward in her chair, her usually taut face creasing into frown lines. She clasped her hands together and nodded both forefingers in Carol's direction. Carol responded with one of her neutral, dental-advert smiles.

'I think you were right to want to talk this through,' she said to Lucy, 'but what is becoming clear to me is that Quinn needs a lot more time to work through some issues independently.' Then Carol gave Lucy one of her encouraging nods, the nod that made you feel you'd given all the right answers and were winning the therapy game show. 'You're doing a fantastic job being a supportive partner, Lucy.'

'Well, I have a very secure attachment style,' said Lucy, keen to out-therapy the therapist.

That had been over a week ago. They had said they would discuss it. Now Lucy was bringing it up at the party.

'So what do you think we should do?' Lucy asked, reaching out to hold Quinn's hands. 'I think you should ask to be referred to someone else. Carol's supposed to be the best when it comes to relationships, so I'd rather we saved her for us, don't you agree?'

'It's freezing out here. Let's go back in and enjoy the party. We can talk about it tomorrow,' Quinn said, pulling Lucy towards him and kissing her on the forehead.

Lucy forced a smile and then turned to open the sliding door back to the party.

'Fine, but we need to decide. Now, make sure you mingle, you should talk to everyone here for at least three minutes, then everyone feels that they've seen you.'

Quinn looked around the room. Who did he want to talk to? Over by the bar were the few school friends he still kept up with: Matt, Jonesy, Deepak. On the dance floor, his work colleagues and a handful of faces from UCL and Cambridge days. Mike was busy chatting up Lucy's friend, Flaky Amy. Three minutes. Could anyone really see him in three minutes? Would anyone see him in three hundred minutes? In a room full of his friends, Quinn didn't think he'd ever felt so lonely.

Quinn watched Lucy strutting over to reprimand a waiter for standing idle. The man looked terrified and launched into action, knocking straight into a girl walking towards him. The girl had brown curly hair and was dressed in a strangely casual tank top. The plainness of her clothes only made it more apparent how striking she was. The waiter dropped his tray and the canapés flew into the air. Quinn watched the girl with the curly hair stop to help the waiter pick them up, apologising as though it was her fault. She got down on her hands and knees and helped brush off the goat's cheese stuck to the waiter's tie. Then she cleaned his glasses on her top. Quinn smiled to himself as he watched the scene. He didn't know anyone here who would help a waiter like that.

The girl stood up and brushed herself down, then picked a piece of goat's cheese from her hair. The waiter scurried away and she stood there, alone, watching the party as though she wasn't a part of it. Something about this girl didn't fit here; she stood out like a swan in a pond full of geese.

Quinn turned his head to see Lucy letting out one of her overblown, mirthless laughs, and he knew then – whether it was to do with his past, their present, or something else entirely – he did not love Lucy. He was going to choose Carol. He wanted to get out of this rabbit hole.

Minnie was in the garden helping her parents knock down her father's shed. Now he'd turned the loft into a fully functioning, damp-proof repair studio, he didn't have any need for the shed, which was taking up valuable space that could be used for her mum's vegetable project. Minnie's mother had caught the vegetable growing bug from Tara.

'Global warming means we should all be growing our own,' she said by way of explanation.

'What's global warming got to do with it, except things grow quicker?' asked her dad.

'Well, when tomatoes go up to ten pound a punnet because there's no land to grow food on, you'll be glad we got some in our back yard won't you?' said her mum, wiping strands of sweaty hair from her eyes with her free hand.

'If we're all gonna to be living underwater, you'd be better off learning how to build submarines or growing gills,' said her dad.

'It's strange taking the shed down, the house looks so different without it,' said Minnie, taking a step back to survey the scene. She was wearing blue dungarees and had a shoebox-sized mallet in her hand. 'I never realised how much light it was blocking. Look how much sun you've got going into the kitchen now.'

'Perfect for growing things,' said her mum, eyes wide with delight.

'I'm going to miss that shed. You know how many clocks I fixed up in there?'

'You're just as happy in the loft,' her mum said quickly.

'There's not as much light in the loft though,' her dad grumbled.

'Well, you were hogging it all down here, weren't you?'

Once the shed had been dismantled and the wood piled high in the back of her dad's van, Minnie went inside to boil the kettle and cut up the fruitcake she'd brought. As she stood waiting for the kettle to boil, her eyes wandered along the shelf, scanning her mum's cookery books. Stashed between Nigella and Jamie Oliver she noticed her mum's old grey file of clippings. She pulled it out, absent-mindedly flicking through the contents. She'd never looked through it herself. She'd only been shown the odd article or certificate when her mum brought it out at special occasions.

Minnie flicked through Will's Spelling Bee certificate and the article he wrote for the local paper about the resurgence of Drum and Bass. Minnie shook her head and smiled. There was the newspaper article about Quinn being the first nineties baby, then the next piece of paper in the file made her freeze – it was the menu from Victor's, the first one she'd cooked. Behind it was the Christmas Day tasting menu from Le Lieu de Rencontre; Minnie had brought it home to show her parents what she was working on. Then there was the first flyer they'd designed to advertise No Hard Fillings, and some pie recipe ideas she'd brought home to show her parents. Minnie flicked through the rest of the file – everything she had ever worked on was here, her mum had kept it all. Minnie quickly covered her mouth with her hand to stop a sob from escaping. Maybe her mother wasn't so disappointed in her after all.

'You bringing us a cuppa or what, love?' came her mother's voice from the garden.

'Yeah, I'm coming,' she said, her voice coming out at a peculiar pitch. Minnie quickly stuffed everything back into the folder and returned it to the shelf.

'Heaven's pyjamas, this is a hell of a cake, love,' said her dad, as they all sat on the back step with thick slices of fruitcake.

'Thanks. I put extra cherries in, just the way you like it, Dad,' said Minnie, then she turned to look at her mother, her eyes flushed with affection.

'What you looking at me like that for?' her mother asked suspiciously.

'Nothing.' Minnie smiled, reaching out to squeeze her mum's hand. 'It's just nice being here with you both.'

'Well, I'll say this is one of your best, Minnie. Do you miss baking all day?' asked her mum, collecting crumbs in her palm as she took another bite.

'Yeah I do,' Minnie said wistfully. 'I miss baking, but I miss my customers more. I had a day off last week so I popped up to the social club to see everyone. Old Mavis Mahoney died; I didn't even know she was ill.'

'Well, at least she had a good innings. A woman on my ward died yesterday, she was twenty-four, poor love. Life's a precious gift, there's no time to waste in regrets.'

Minnie's dad choked on his piece of cake.

'You've changed your tune, Con,' he coughed. 'What's come over you?'

'She's "gardening her way through anxiety", Dad,' said Minnie, sucking her cheeks together to stop herself from smiling.

Her dad laughed.

'Next thing she'll be saying she's off on some yoga camp to have her Jackras cleansed.'

'Chakras,' said her mum with a smile, making a meditational pose and clasping her hands together in prayer.

'Oh, here we go,' said her dad, shaking his head. 'Well, I'm not sold on this new "no time for regrets" woman. I thought you had a list of regrets tattooed to the inside of your eyeballs, Con? Marrying me being top of the list.'

'No,' her mum shook her head, and let out a sigh. 'Best thing I ever did, Bill – you and my kids. I wouldn't change you for the world.'

Minnie's parents both reached out to squeeze each other's hand.

Minnie looked back and forth between them. She couldn't remember a time they'd been like this: teasing each other, laughing, being affectionate. As a teenager Minnie thought adult conversation revolved around lists; one person would list the jobs they had done, then list the jobs the other had not done. If her dad laughed, her mum would snipe at him for making light of something. When her mum finally got to sitting down in the evening, her dad would choose that moment to go and start some crucial piece of clock maintenance. She had rarely witnessed this kind of companionship between them. It was as if her mother had taken the antidote to some bitter pill she'd been swallowing all her life.

Maybe this was what her parents' relationship had been like before they had children? Maybe the stresses of family life had knocked the love out for a while. Last time she was here, she saw her mum rub her dad's back when she was standing in the kitchen next to him – Minnie had never seen her do that in thirty years.

'Anything you regret, Minnie Moo, or are you going in for this "no regrets" way of thinking?' her dad asked.

'I regret you calling me Minnie bloody Cooper,' Minnie said, elbowing her dad gently in the ribs.

'Oi, I still say you'll get a sponsorship deal off them one day.'

Minnie looked up at the clear blue September sky and thought for a moment.

'I guess I regret giving up on No Hard Fillings like I did.'

'You had your reasons. I'm sure you did the right thing, love,' said her mum.

Minnie wasn't used to this reassuring, sympathetic version of her mother. She did a double take, looking over at her, turning to her dad and then looking back again.

'Are you sure she's hasn't got a brain tumour or something?' she said to her dad in a stage whisper. 'She doesn't seem like herself.'

Her dad shook his head in mock solemnity. 'My working theory is alien body snatchers.'

'Oh, shut it you two,' said her mum, swiping an arm in their direction.

'Seriously though,' said Minnie, 'I think I was too quick to give it up. I even thought of an idea for how I could make the finances work without needing funding from charities. It's no good thinking of these things six months too late though, is it?'

Minnie had been in the chemist buying shampoo when she'd had the idea. There was a 'buy one get one free' offer on haircare products. It reminded her of a silly pun Greg had pitched for the business last year – Pie One Get One Free. Then it hit her – what if she got the corporates to fund the pies for those in need? For every pie they bought for themselves, they'd buy another one for someone in the community who needed it. Businesses were always looking for ways to bolster their corporate responsibility, right?

She'd been frozen to the spot in the aisle, with Coconut Bliss in one hand and Passion-Fruit Explosion in the other. She'd felt that fizz of excitement that only comes with a genuinely good idea. Then she remembered the minor obstacle to enacting this genius plan; she'd dismantled the business, sold all her equipment and given up the kitchen lease. Even if she wanted to, she'd never get another loan to start all over again.

Minnie found herself telling her parents about the idea, even going into detail about how she would make it work. She didn't usually talk to her parents about ideas like this; normally she wouldn't be able to get to the end of a sentence before her mother pointed out a flaw in the plan. But today, sitting on the step in their garden, both her parents listened to her talk until she had finished. When she ran out of things to say, she looked back and forth between them.

'Sorry, was I going on a bit?' she said.

'Sounds like you have to do it, Minnie,' her mother said softly. 'I'm sorry if I wasn't supportive enough before. I didn't see how important it was to you.' Her mother reached over and put her hand on Minnie's knee. 'Maybe I didn't always say the right things, you know. No one gives you a manual on how to be a mother.'

She looked pained at the effort of getting the apology out. Minnie patted her hand.

'I know, Mum, it's OK.'

'So, you're going to do it then?' her mum asked, wiping the corner of her eye with a finger.

Minnie wrinkled her nose as she shook her head. 'I should have thought of it earlier. I couldn't get the funds together now.'

'Couldn't you get an investor, someone who believed in the idea?' asked her mum.

'*Dragons' Den*,' said her dad, his eyebrows shooting halfway up his bald forehead.

'I didn't invent pies, Dad.' Minnie pushed her hair back behind her ears. They were both egging her on now, making her think it might be possible. 'Even if I could persuade some investor to come in, I'd need some seed capital myself. I'd have to be invested too.'

'How much we talking?' asked Dad.

'How much what?' said Minnie.

'For this seeding capital?'

Minnie shook her head. 'At least ten grand, I don't know. More than you've got lying down the back of the sofa, Dad, but thank you.'

She leant into his arm, resting her head on his shoulder. It didn't matter if the new pie plan didn't happen. Just talking like this with her parents, where they both listened, and believed she might be able to do something – that meant so much.

'Come on,' said her dad, removing her head from his shoulder so he could stand up.

'We're done, are we? You're not going to help me dig that concrete base out?' asked her mum.

'Not today, my love, we need a drill to break it up first. Minnie Moo, I want to show you something.'

'Take your shoes off!' her mum cried as they made to go in through the kitchen.

Dad led Minnie through to the lounge and pointed up at her favourite clock, the one she had given him – Coggie. Minnie looked at him, perplexed.

'I remember the day you bought this for me. You lugged it back in your school bag all the way on the bus, must have weighed a ton. I bet there were a million other things you could have spent your pocket money on back then.' He looked up at the clock with rheumy eyes.

'Well, it looked like a piece of junk then. You polished it up, Dad.'

'Only four like this left in the world, according to the internet. Apparently it's worth four thousand quid now I got it working.'

'No!' Minnie cried, flinging a hand over her mouth.

'And there's a few others around the house that collectors would like to get their mitts on.'

'You can't sell your clocks, Dad, not for me.' Minnie shook her head slowly. 'You spent so much time on them.'

Her dad nodded solemnly.

'Maybe I spent too much time on them, didn't spend enough time on what's important.' He stretched his large hand around his chin and squeezed his cheeks together. 'No regrets though, hey.' He paused. 'I see so much of myself in you, Minnie Moo,' he said, putting an arm around her shoulder. 'If you've got a chance, I want you to have it.'

They stood watching Coggie for a moment.

'Does Mum know they're valuable?'

'Does she heck!' her dad laughed. 'I always told her they were junk. She's going to go category nine ballistic.'

He rubbed both palms up and down across his eyes. Minnie couldn't believe her dad had been sitting on a small fortune all this time, or that he'd just offered to give it to her. Her heart swelled with affection for both her parents.

'We'll just make sure Mum's in one of her "gardening moods" before we say anything, shall we?' said her dad.

Her laptop was charged, the presentation loaded, and Minnie was wearing a new black jumpsuit paired with red lipstick. One of the Instagram influencers she followed had worn an outfit just like this. She'd decided at 2 a.m. last Monday that this was the look that was going to win her the investment.

She'd spent the last few weeks racking her brains as to how she could raise the rest of the money needed to set up her 'Buy a Pie, Give a Pie' scheme. It was Greg's words that rang in her head – 'Contacts, contacts, contacts.' Who did she know who was well connected in the corporate catering world? Lucy Donohue, that's who.

Greg had told her that, since leaving the newspaper, Lucy had a new job running corporate catering for Lexon, one of the biggest banks in London. She was exactly the person Minnie needed to get behind her idea. In the past, Minnie would have just assumed that someone like Lucy would never give her a meeting, would never take her seriously. She would have been too intimidated to ask. Now Minnie felt differently. It would probably come to nothing, but she had to try. No regrets.

Greg and his flatmate Clive had helped her put together a PowerPoint presentation with statistics and graphics.

'Don't be too effusive,' Clive prepped her. 'Don't act like she's doing you a favour. You're doing her a favour by bringing her the idea.'

'And put your hair up,' said Greg. 'Don't hide behind your hair – you always do that, it's annoying.'

'And take a business plan printed out to leave with her. She'll want to look at the numbers once you go,' said Clive.

'And take a pie,' said Greg. 'That's your product, that's important.'

'And testimonials,' said Clive. 'Everyone loves a testimonial.'

'Oh god,' said Minnie, trying to take it all in.

Greg put a hand on each shoulder. 'You can do this Minnie, I know you can.'

Since they broke up, Greg had finally decided to start work on the book he'd always wanted to write: Jennifer Aniston's unofficial biography. The process of writing it had led him to reassess his priorities in life. He'd called Minnie a few months ago to say that, like Jen, he was happy being single, that he didn't need a partner to define him, and that he wanted to champion the women in his life, so if she ever needed championing, he would be there. Minnie hadn't realised how deeply his passion for Jennifer Aniston ran, but this new, supportive, Jennified Greg was definitely an improvement.

*

Walking into the shiny Lexon offices, Minnie felt like Sheryl Sandberg and Hilary Clinton rolled into one. Katy Perry's

'Roar' played in her head and she was definitely strutting as she walked – Minnie never strutted. Lucy and a man in a pinstripe suit with dark, slicked-back hair welcomed her into their boardroom. There were miniature bottles of water lined up in a row along the enormous boardroom table and huge shiny wall-mounted TV screens at either end of the room.

'Thank you for meeting with me,' Minnie said, shaking Lucy's hand while fastidiously keeping eye contact. She wanted to say that she knew Lucy was busy, that she wouldn't keep them long, but she stopped herself – that would be old Minnie talking.

'We've met before, right?' said Lucy, squinting, trying to place her. 'Greg was rather vague on the phone.'

'Yes – last New Year's Eve,' Minnie said. 'At the Night Jam.'

Lucy cocked her head to one side and then slowly looked Minnie up and down.

'Oh yes ... ' A glimmer of recognition. 'I hardly recognised you, have you changed your hair?'

Minnie launched into the presentation. She'd rehearsed it so many times over the last few days. She had all the stats and figures. She'd even made a short video of her old clients explaining what a difference it made to their lives, having her pies delivered.

It went without a hitch – well, except for a glitch with the PowerPoint where the screen froze. When she tried to reset it, a picture of her and Leila on a beach in Goa popped up instead. She was holding Fleabag dog with one hand and a cocktail in the other – she looked sunburnt and happy.

'Sorry, technical difficulties,' Minnie blustered.

Lucy and her colleague Rupert asked questions and listened politely. They both tasted samples of the pies she had brought and Minnie left them with a bound presentation of her proposal.

'Well, thank you for coming in, we'll be in touch,' said Lucy. 'Great jumpsuit, by the way.'

Minnie skipped all the way home. She wasn't sure, but it felt as though the pitch had gone well. If Lexon said no, she would try someone else – she was going to make this happen. On her phone, she had a text from her mother: 'I hope it went well love. I've got my course this afternoon, but call me later and let me know xxx.'

Her mother was retraining to be a midwife. She'd surprised them all at dinner the other week by saying it was something she'd always wanted to do. Tara had researched a course for her online, specifically for nurses wanting to retrain, and she'd signed herself up. She made Dad sell another of his clocks to pay for it. Number thirteen was getting quieter and quieter with all the family's changing career plans.

Back at her flat in Willesden, Minnie let herself in and flopped on the sofa. She took out her phone. She should reply to Jake, one of the chefs from the catering firm she'd been on a date with last week. Jake was attractive, kind and popular with the waitresses. He'd surfed his way around Mexico in a van last year, and was off base-jumping in Yosemite once he pulled some more cash together. He was the kind of happy-go-lucky adventurer it was impossible not to like. There was no reason not to go on another date with him. Minnie's owls were not overly enthusiastic, but the owls had not proved helpful in the past.

Just as she was typing out a reply to Jake, a text came through on the No Hard Fillings WhatsApp group. It was a link from Fleur. Her producer friend who'd filmed the video of Leila's engagement had finally sent through an edit, and she'd uploaded it to her YouTube channel. Minnie watched the video and laughed out loud; it perfectly captured the joyful madness of the occasion. Minnie watched the close-up of Leila's delighted face and kissed the screen.

'We've gone viral!' read Fleur's message beneath the link. 'We've 60,000 views and counting!'

As she was watching the video a second time, her phone began to ring.

'Hello, Minnie? It's Lucy Donohue.'

'Oh, hi Lucy.'

Lucy coughed on the line. Oh god, what if Minnie had given her food poisoning? Did that sound like a food poisoning cough? What if Lucy had just spent the last hour on the toilet, Rupert vomiting next to her or holding her hair back? What if she was calling to say she planned to sue?

'We loved your pitch, Minnie. We want you to cater for all our London offices if you think you could develop that capacity? And we'd like Lexon employees to help you deliver the pies to the community as part of our "giving back" initiative. We can pick over the finer details later, but I wanted to give you the good news before you pitched the idea to someone else.'

Minnie wanted to squeal down the line, 'Thank you, oh thank you Lucy! You don't know what this means to me!' but she contained herself – pushing away Lucky, who was pawing at her leg and meowing for attention – and she thanked Lucy as professionally as possible. They arranged a follow-up meeting for Monday.

As she hung up the phone, Minnie heard a scratching noise and walked through to see Lucky scrabbling at the front door. Minnie had forgotten to keep the bathroom door ajar so that he could get to his cat litter.

'Don't scratch, Lucky! You'll lose me my deposit again,' she said, pushing the bathroom door open, and trying to pick up the cat. Lucky sprang forward and Minnie watched in horror as he started peeing all over her doormat. 'Eugh, Lucky! What are you doing? Bad cat!' Minnie scolded.

She picked up the mat to rinse it out in the kitchen sink. As she did so, she noticed an envelope on the floor. It must have come through the postbox and slipped beneath the mat. She picked it up – the letter was soaked in cat urine. On the front, the name 'Minnie' had been handwritten.

How long had this been here? She opened it quickly, grimacing at the smell. 'Lucky, what the hell have you been eating?'

Minnie quickly scanned the writing down to the end – it was from Quinn. The ink was starting to run so she read the note as fast as she could.

Dear Minnie,
I tried to call you, but I think you've blocked my number.
You've also blocked me on, well everywhere else, and I don't

blame you. So I've reverted to the old-fashioned form of communication. I have behaved ... (Minnie couldn't make out the next word, it was either 'terribly' or 'teriyaki' – 'terribly' probably made more sense.) *I'd like to see you, to explain. I know you might not want to see me, but I'll be at our pond on Sunday at ...*

And then the rest of the words had dissolved in the acidity of the cat pee and the letter began to disintegrate in her hand.

'Oh, for fuck's sake,' Minnie cried. She hardly ever swore. 'Lucky, you've peed on the most important part of the letter!' Then Minnie remembered she might never have found the letter if it hadn't been for Lucky peeing on it, so she couldn't be too cross.

She went to wash her hands, scrubbing them with Brillo pads until she was confident they were cat-pee free. Why did Quinn want to see her? It had been months. How long had that letter been there? Maybe weeks; maybe he'd been to the pond and she hadn't been there? Had there been a date on the letter?

Minnie pulled the letter out of the bin. There was a date, but it was now covered in peanut butter, the remnants of her pre-presentation snack. She tried to scrape it off but the letter was too far gone.

Maybe the rest of the letter just said something like, 'you've still got my favourite T-shirt, so can you meet me at the ponds to return it?' Maybe it said, 'I'm still not into you, but I wanted to apologise in person for being a dick about it.' Maybe it said a lot of things.

Would she go on Sunday? Did she even want to hear what he had to say? After that excruciating phone call at Tara's house, Minnie had made a pact with herself – no more mooning over Quinn Hamilton; in fact, no more mooning over anyone. She needed to take back control of her life, of her happiness. She resolved to be more Leila, to stop letting other people mess with her self-esteem.

The letter put a cloud over Minnie's week. She had been in such a jubilant mood after the pitch with Lucy, and now she was spending all her time speculating, weighing up whether she should go to Hampstead Heath on Sunday. She could just unblock his number and text him. 'Hey Quinn, thanks for the letter, I don't know when you sent it because it's now covered in cat piss and peanut butter. I know, it's disgusting – clearly I live like an animal. Anyway, could you recap the content over text? Ta.' What would Meg Ryan do?

She went that Sunday. Of course she did. Her curiosity got the better of her. At seven thirty she was on Hampstead Heath, skulking in the bushes near the entrance to the mixed ponds. It was a cold, crisp morning and this pond was now closed for the winter. No one was around. Eight o'clock came and went. Minnie sat down on a bench nearby and kicked a pile of autumn leaves at her feet. The letter must have been sent over a week ago. She could unblock him, call him, but she didn't want to. She'd already spent too many hours fixated on this particular cardboard girl.

She strolled up to Parliament Hill, wrapping her scarf tighter around her neck and tucking her hands deep into the pockets of her new woollen coat. She hadn't been back here since that day in August; she'd taken to swimming at the indoor pool instead. The heath looked so different with its autumnal clothes on. An orange carpet of leaves covered the footpaths and a crisp, low light shone through the tangle of tree boughs above her head. She picked up a perfect red leaf from the ground, examining the intricate pattern of vessels mapping its thin surface. So beautiful, yet only created to last such a short time before its role on this planet was over, and it would decay into mulch. An unremarkable existence, and yet to look at it – how remarkable.

'Minnie?'

Minnie jumped, dropping the leaf. She looked up to see Quinn standing in front of her.

'Oh, you scared me,' she said, clutching a hand to her chest.

Quinn wore a thick green woollen jumper, a camel coat and dark navy jeans. She hadn't seen him for months. When you see someone often, you can forget to take in what they look like – they just become a configuration of features and foibles. Then, after an absence, you see them again as though for the very first time. With Quinn, this was like a sledgehammer hitting you with how handsome he was.

'Sorry, you were looking very intently at that leaf,' said Quinn, with a cautious smile.

Minnie looked for the leaf she had dropped. She picked it up and put it in her pocket.

'It's a great leaf,' she said, then berated herself for saying something so stupid.

'I didn't think you'd come,' said Quinn.

'I got your letter,' said Minnie, 'but I didn't know when you'd sent it. It got a bit ... damaged.'

'Oh,' Quinn looked relieved. 'I sent it three weeks ago, but I still come here every week, on the off-chance I might run into you.'

He fell into step next to Minnie as they walked down the tree-lined avenue.

'I tried to call you, then I couldn't get through. I didn't want to turn up on your doorstep but I ... I needed to explain ...' Quinn paused; he was nervous.

Minnie scuffed up a pile of leaves with her feet and it gave a satisfying crunch. She stayed quiet, letting him talk.

'I guess I'm a bit of a screw-up, Minnie. I have issues with feeling needed,' Quinn blinked and thrust his hands into his pockets. They both walked with their eyes on the path ahead. It was sometimes easier to speak when you weren't looking at someone. 'I think I've grown up with a messed-up view of what love is. I thought it was love that destroyed my mother, but I realise now, it wasn't that.' Quinn shook his head.

'Sounds like you've been doing a lot of soul-searching, Quinn,' Minnie said.

'I have,' he frowned. 'I started seeing a therapist at the beginning of the year, started talking through some stuff I've never talked about before. I quit after a few months, though; thought I could handle it myself. Then, running out on you like that, I knew I had to go back. I don't want to be that person, Minnie, not any more. I've finally come to a few important decisions.'

'Like what?'

'I need to move away from Primrose Hill. I need to apologise to you for the way I behaved. I need to start being open to letting people in.'

In her peripheral vision, Minnie could see him looking sideways at her with hopeful eyes. She kept her eyes on the path ahead.

'Is this some therapy thing where you go around apologising to all the girls you've ghosted?' Quinn made a short 'huh' exhaling sound. 'I understand if you need to get on. It must be a very long list.' Minnie elbowed him gently.

'That's not what this is. I meant every word I wrote in that letter. I knew I'd done the wrong thing the second I left your flat, but I couldn't start something with you, Minnie, not until I knew I could do it properly.' He stopped in his tracks and she turned to face him. He tapped a fist against his chest. 'From the minute I met you, you've burrowed your way in here like a song stuck in my head. I can't get you out.'

'That must be very annoying,' said Minnie with a little shake of her head.

'It's not annoying.'

'Well, that's not a good analogy then, because getting a song stuck in your head is incredibly annoying.'

'Not if you like the song.'

'Especially if you like the song. Best way to ruin a good song, having it go round and round in your head all day. It ruined Pharrell's "Happy" for me.'

Quinn reached out to take Minnie's hands. 'OK, it's a bad analogy. Look, I'm clearly no good at this.' Quinn let out a sharp exhale of frustration, then took a breath and tried again. 'Minnie, you were like this light coming into my life – you dazzle me. But your light also made me see all these shadows in my own life, shadows I finally realised I had to deal with.' He frowned. 'You see how I've moved from song to light analogies?'

'Better,' Minnie nodded, her mouth twitching into a smile.

'I've only ever kept people at arm's length before. With you, as soon as we talked, you refused to be arm's length, you were right here.' He put a palm over his chest. 'Look, I don't know what I'm asking. I guess I'm saying I might screw up, but I want to give it a chance. I think I love you, if that doesn't sound too nuts.'

He looked up at Minnie – his eyes meeting hers, willing for her to say something.

Minnie felt her stomach tense. This was everything she'd wanted to hear – two months ago. He was saying he was ready to take a leap off a high board with her, but for some reason, she no longer felt prepared to jump. She squeezed her hands into balls. Hadn't she expected this? Didn't she know from the letter that he'd changed his mind? But when she heard him say it out loud, her first instinct was to step back, not leap in.

'I'm glad you've worked through some things, Quinn, and it doesn't sound nuts – I felt the same about you.'

'Felt?' Quinn said, the fire in his eyes already dampened by disappointment.

'I'm sorry, but things have changed for me since I last saw you.'

'Oh.' Quinn hung his head.

Minnie wrapped an arm through his and pulled him into stride next to her. It was easier to talk while walking.

'Not like that. I've just been doing a lot of soul-searching too I guess. What you said about being the cardboard girl ...'

'I'm not the cardboard girl, I don't want to be the cardboard girl.'

'Maybe not, but I think I've always been that penguin, always looking beyond the penguin enclosure for someone else to make me happy.'

They walked a few steps in silence. Minnie loved the feeling of his arm in hers. Physically it felt so right to be here next to him, but she had to fight that feeling – she needed to think with her head. It was something Fleur once said to her, which stuck in her mind: 'You need to be a "me" before you can be a "we".' It sounded twee, but Minnie felt it to be true. This last month she'd felt more 'me' than she'd felt in her whole life: more contained, more comfortable in her own skin. She had a new confidence, an inner fire, and she didn't want it to go out. It was that quote on the back of her print: 'Be a good companion to yourself and you will never be lonely' – that had to be the aspiration. She wanted to fuel her own fire. If you got your fuel from men, they could leave, and you'd be left alone in the cold.

'I've been getting on with my parents,' she said. 'I have you to thank for that. My mum is a different person since she's been spending time with yours.'

'The vegetable project,' Quinn said with a nod.

'"Gardening their way through anxiety",' said Minnie, making air quotes with her free hand.

'Yes, she told me about their blog project, it's all she can talk about,' Quinn smiled.

'I can't describe how much she's changed, Quinn – it's like she's put down this sack of resentment she's been carrying around for decades. And when she put it down, for some reason it made me feel so much lighter.' Minnie shook her head. 'I know it sounds ridiculous.'

'It doesn't,' said Quinn.

'I pitched this new business idea to Lucy Donohue last week, a way to get my pies funded again. She loved it; Lexon are going to sponsor the whole thing. We'll cater for their staff canteens, and they'll subsidise pies for people in the community.'

'Lucy? Wow.' Quinn gave a perplexed smile, his eyebrows knitting in confusion. Then he nodded, 'Minnie, that's great, I'm so impressed. Lucy's got a great eye for business.'

'I know you didn't end things on the best terms with her,' said Minnie.

'I owe that woman a lot – I'll always be grateful to her for dragging me to therapy in the first place.'

'This year, turning thirty, I don't know – I feel like I've finally been given the keys to my own car and I just want to drive. I'm happy to be me, and I've never felt like that before.'

Quinn took a loud, slow inhale. 'And you're not ready to take any passengers in this new car of yours. Especially not messed-up weirdoes who'd scuff the interior and play all the wrong music on the radio.'

Minnie looked over at him, biting her lip. 'I don't think so, I'm sorry.'

Quinn let his head fall backwards and looked up at the sky.

'Not the weirdo bit, just the passenger part,' she said.

They'd walked right to the bottom of the hill now. Barney's van had been moved for the winter. A large square of dead grass was all that remained, like the chalk outline showing where a body had been.

'We'll still be friends?' Minnie asked, her voice breaking slightly. 'I would like you in my life, Quinn, and with our mothers hanging out so much now ...'

'Sure,' he said softly, though something in his voice made her think they would not.

'How's your mum doing?'

'Good, actually. Better than she's been in years. Your mum is incredible, she just bulldozes in and ... Well, she's managed to do in a few months what I failed to do in decades.'

'You didn't fail.'

Quinn looked across at her and sighed. Minnie couldn't quite read his expression – he looked tired.

'Well she's a force of nature. We're both very grateful to her.'

'I'm so pleased, Quinn.'

She squeezed his arm. He slowly unlinked his arm from hers and thrust his hands back into his pockets.

'Just tell me one thing before I go. This car you're driving alone into the sunset – it's a Mini Cooper, right?'

She smiled. 'Actually, I was imagining more of an open-top Mustang – the kind they drive in *Thelma and Louise*.'

'You know they drive off a cliff in that film, right?'

'Thanks for the spoiler, Quinn – I've never seen it.' She pretended to be angry, giving him a gentle punch on the arm.

They both laughed, a half-laugh half-sigh – a laugh that signalled an ending.

'Goodbye then, Minnie,' he said, leaning in to kiss her on the cheek.

She inhaled the smell of his neck, and the angry owls in her belly started to flap their wings and cry, 'What have you done, Minnie? What have you done? Take every word of it back while you can!'

But she did not.

Leila clinked her champagne glass with a fork and stood up to address the long trestle table of guests. She was wearing a wedding dress made of feathers and tulle. The dress had a fitted corset and a flowing skirt – it was a pretty conventional wedding dress design, if you ignored the huge feather shoulder pads thrusting upwards like some angelic Boudicca, preparing to charge into romantic battle.

'I just wanted to say a few words,' Leila said, 'because it's my wedding and I can do what I like.' There were a few whoops and chuckles from the table. 'First of all, I want to thank my *husband* ...' Leila said it in that way brides do when they expect a cheer for simply using the word. The wedding guests obliged. 'Ian has made me so happy these last four years – mainly because he lets me have all the cupboard space in our flat, and he knows never – ever *ever* – to wash any of my underwear at more than thirty degrees. He learnt that the hard way.'

Minnie was seated next to Leila at the table. She looked along the row of familiar faces laughing at Leila's jokes. Dotted amongst Leila's friends and family were all their regular customers from No Hard Fillings – Leila had invited them all. Fleur, Alan and Bev were there, so were the two Clares. Poor Bev was sandwiched between deaf old Mrs Harris and Terry Piper who suffered from dementia.

Leila turned to look at Minnie as she went on with her speech.

'But before I bang on about Ian, I have to talk about the other love of my life, my first wife – my Minnie.' Everyone cheered. Minnie blushed and covered her face with a napkin. 'Minnie, who has been my best friend since we met at summer camp when we were fifteen. The second I saw her on a bench eating the Penguin biscuit out of her packed lunch at nine o'clock in the morning, I knew we were going to be friends.'

Minnie lowered the napkin and shrugged as people laughed at her.

'Minnie, who has been on so many adventures with me – to India with suspicious luggage . . . ' Leila gave Minnie a wink and left a pause long enough to have Minnie worried she was about to launch into the Rampant Rabbit story in front of both sets of parents. 'Adventures with pies – so many pies; adventures with men, I'm sorry to say so, Ian, but there were a few before you.' Ian played along and gave a comical scowl. 'But the biggest adventure of all has simply been being your friend.' Leila turned back to Minnie with a tear in her eye. 'I know there's nothing you wouldn't do for me. This is the woman who I called three days ago in tears, explaining that our wedding venue had been flooded. She only went and volunteered to cater the whole thing here in her brand-spanking-new kitchen, before she'd even worked out how to turn on the ridiculously high-tech ovens.'

Everyone cheered and clapped, there were whoops of 'go Minnie!' from around the table.

'She saved the day, for someone else – as she always does. And I hope you'll take this the right way,' Leila looked pensive for a moment, gazing slightly off focus into her champagne glass, 'if I steal a Cooper family adage to say – all this, these wonderful people here today, this amazing new business, this would never have happened to a Quinn Cooper. Some things are all Minnie, and I wouldn't have you any other way.'

'To Minnie!' everyone cheered, raising their glasses high in the air.

*

Alan turned out to be surprisingly adept at the accordion. After dinner, he launched into a traditional Irish wedding dance and everyone helped push the tables back to make room for dancing. Mrs Mentis pulled out her harmonica to accompany him and a few guests started clapping along to the beat.

'We do have a professional band waiting to play,' Fleur said irritably, cocking her head at Minnie and then pouting in Alan's direction. Clearly she was not a fan of accordion music. 'I had to call in some serious favours to get this band in from Zurich. I don't think you realise what a big deal it is for Green Marmite to play a private gig.'

'Fleur, I need to hear more about your new business,' said Minnie, putting an arm around her shoulder. 'How is it going?'

Since the engagement video had gone viral, Fleur had been inundated with requests from people to help them stage their own elaborate proposals.

'I'm calling it "Proposals by Fleur",' said Fleur, handing Minnie a pink business card. 'I'm flying to Cairo next week, to produce a proposal in the tomb of Tutankhamen with loads of dead mummies running about. This guy wants to scare the shit out of his girlfriend and then pop the question. People are so weird.'

'Wow, that's so exciting, Fleur. I'm glad it's all taken off. What about the dating site you were designing?'

'Oh, it's going to be a whole franchise, Minnie – this year we're focusing on Proposals by Fleur, then we'll do Dates by Fleur, Weddings by Fleur – who knows, I hear the funeral market is due a shake-up.' Minnie laughed. 'Oh, and my Instagram feed has now officially reached Influencer status, so let me know if you want me to do any influencing for you.' Fleur turned to look at the dance floor. 'Is this harmonica woman still going? Sorry, Minnie, I'm going to have to intervene.'

Minnie crept away from the dancing to have a moment alone. The last week had been intense. She'd only had the keys to this kitchen a week. And then, with Leila's wedding venue falling through, she'd had to get everything set up and working in twenty-four hours. She didn't even have staff yet, except Bev and Alan. She'd worked all night to get the space ready and pulled in a lot of favours from catering contacts to find people who would work last minute. Looking back across the room at everyone dancing and singing, she realised something; she had pulled it off. This industrial kitchen in Old Street wasn't quite the romantic stately home that had been booked, but Leila was happy, and something about doing it this way felt so perfect. Now, Minnie couldn't imagine the wedding party being any other way.

Fleur, to her credit, had done an amazing job with the decorations. She had turned the kitchen into a winter wedding wonderland, full of fairy lights and garlands of silver bells strung up between the steel girders. Bev had sourced all the linen, crockery and chairs for dinner and Alan had spent the last few days picking up everything they needed in the new van. It was so good to see so many old friends, people she was going to start delivering to again as soon as next week.

Minnie stroked her hand along the jars lining the shelves, taking a moment to breathe in the familiar floury smell of her baking apron which hung ready on a peg. She turned the gooseneck tap on and off at the sink – she'd always wanted a gooseneck tap. She couldn't believe this kitchen was hers and that in a few weeks' time she'd be coordinating hundreds of pies a day being delivered all over London.

Bev clocked Minnie alone by the sink and came to stand beside her. They both had fifties hair and wore outfits that had 'bridesmaid' written up the side in italic gold writing. This had been Leila's solution to the perennial problem of finding bridesmaid dresses that suited everyone.

'Are you hiding from Fleur?' Bev asked.

'Kind of.'

Bev laughed. 'I can't believe we pulled this off.'

'Me neither.'

'And I can't believe we're going to be doing all this for real in a few weeks. Just like the good old days, hey?'

'Except no Fleur, and no Leila,' Minnie said, watching Leila throw some shapes on the makeshift dance floor, as the band started to play.

'They'll always be there,' said Bev, putting her arm around Minnie's shoulder. 'Life is change – if nothing's changing, you aren't living.'

Minnie looked sideways at Bev. 'That sounded profound.'

'It did, didn't it?' Bev grinned. She looked down at the silver dress she was wearing, and at Minnie's dark blue silk jumpsuit. 'Do you think we can wear these again?'

'Sure, we'll have dress-down Fridays at work.'

'Minnie, while I've got you here, I had an idea I wanted to mention,' said Bev. 'Do you remember that friend of Fleur's who invented the seaweed packaging?' Minnie nodded. 'Well, Fleur got her along to one of my Pick Litter, Have a Witter groups. She's an incredible woman; I think we should use her packaging for all our pies. Do our bit to be green, you know?'

Bev looked at Minnie nervously; this clearly meant a lot to her.

'You know what, Bev,' said Minnie, 'I think that's a wonderful idea. I think our clients will love it too.'

Bev beamed and started jumping up and down on the spot.

'And can we do more jump meetings? Honestly, I think Leila was onto something, it really gets my brain jelly moving.'

The party went on all afternoon and into the evening. It only ended because Leila and Ian had to leave to get the

Eurostar to Paris that night. As Green Marmite played their last song, Leila found Minnie on the packed dance floor.

'I'm going to wear my dress all the way to Paris,' Leila said, pulling Minnie into a tight hug. 'I'm not going to take it off until I've climbed to the top of the Eiffel tower tomorrow.'

'I look forward to seeing the photos,' said Minnie.

'I wish you were coming too,' Leila whispered, swaying slightly on her feet.

'I'm sure Ian doesn't,' said Minnie.

'This has been the best day ever, all thanks to you,' Leila gushed. 'I want you to be this happy, Minnie.'

'I am happy,' said Minnie.

'I know you are,' Leila paused, as though weighing her words. 'Do you still think about love twin?'

'Leila, please,' Minnie said, shaking her head. 'It's been months.'

'That's not what I asked.'

'You're the one who said I needed to put myself first, channel my inner Leila, refuse to compromise.'

Leila pulled her friend in tight and whispered in her ear. 'If he's still in your head, it's worth taking the risk. You never know just how perfect it might turn out to be.'

And before Minnie could reply, Ian stepped in and swept Leila away.

Minnie sat on her sofa with a large bag of Maltesers, wearing her favourite owl pyjamas. Leila had given them to her for Christmas three years ago. The bottoms were covered in pictures of real owls dressed up as the characters from *Friends* and the T-shirt top had 'Owl be there for you' written across it in the *Friends* font.

She had been shopping yesterday and stocked up on all her favourite food. Bev had offered to keep her company this evening, but Minnie said no, she was happier holed up in her flat alone. To be clear, this wasn't a fearful hiding-from-the-world kind of bunking down; this was simply an I'd-rather-be-at-home-watching-Netflix-in-my-owl-pyjamas-because-I'm-exhausted-after-yesterday kind of bunking down. On one of their park walks, when Minnie had told Quinn about her New Year superstition, he'd called her 'selectively agoraphobic'. This wasn't that, this was hashtag self-care. Loads of people stayed in on New Year's Eve, it wasn't a big deal.

This time last year she'd taken a sleeping pill just to get through her birthday. That wasn't going to happen this year. Tomorrow she had plans; she was going for lunch with her family.

Was she anxious about it, already catastrophising about all the things that might go wrong at such a lunch? Yes, OK she was, but that didn't mean she was going to cancel. It didn't mean she was going to stay in and hide. So much had changed for Minnie this year, but facing the New Year's jinx was the ultimate test.

One thing at a time, she thought. Get through tonight, then get through tomorrow, then she could stop just trying to get through. She could start living.

She scrolled through the list of films she had flagged as possible downloads to watch tonight; *Working Girl, Erin Brockovich, The Iron Lady* – OK, so maybe she'd gone too far with a theme here, but she didn't want to sit here on her own watching *Sleepless in Seattle*.

She was fine. She was fine on her own. She didn't need a man to make her life complete. She didn't want the cliché 'you complete me' ending. She was finally on an even keel and someone like Quinn would definitely rock the boat. She smiled, imagining what Quinn would say about her matching boat metaphors.

No, it wasn't worth the risk. Sure, they'd have amazing sex for a few months – Minnie cleared a frog from her throat as she imagined it. Right here where she was sitting, this is where they had almost... she bit her lip thinking about it. Yes, of course it would be mind-blowing, life-affirming, house-screaming-down-to-the-point-of-the-neighbours-complaining sex, but then what? Her mind went to Lucy's article in the paper. All his old commitment issues would creep back to the surface; he'd feel awkward about ending things; she'd have her heart broken and this safe new life she had built for herself would crumble like crops after a nuclear catastrophe. No, it was safer to leave things as they were. In any case, she had no reason to believe he was still even an option. Just because she still thought about him, didn't mean he felt the same as he had a few months ago.

And yet.

Leila's words banged against the inside of her skull, 'If he's still in your head, it's worth taking the risk.' Clearly Minnie still thought about him. She noticed things she knew he'd find funny. With all the new ideas for the business, it was his opinion she craved. Whenever her mother talked about her trips to see Tara, she found herself angling for news of him.

The time she had spent with Quinn had changed something. It was as though in all her previous relationships she'd been wearing a suit of armour, this barrier skin. With Quinn she felt laid bare, he saw who she really was. Yet she also remembered how low she'd felt when he'd bailed on her, how fragile and vulnerable. When she felt emotions like that, she was transported right back to those hellish years at school.

Minnie wondered what Quinn was doing now. Maybe she could call him. She could just be friendly; he'd said they could be friends. She could just call him, perhaps invite him over, just see. It was nine o'clock on New Year's Eve; he would be out at a party. Before she could talk herself out of it, she scrolled down to his name in her phone and dialled his number. He'd get a missed call and then he'd know she'd tried to—

'Hello?'

'Oh, hi,' she said, surprised he had picked up.

'Minnie?'

It sounded loud where he was, windy or aeroplanes overhead. Music was playing.

'Yeah, I just – um – I thought I'd call you to say Happy Birthday, even though I'm a few hours early. I didn't know where you'd be tomorrow and—'

Why had she called without working out what she was going to say? What *did* she want to say?

'I'm so glad you called,' he said. It sounded as though he'd walked away from the source of the noise.

'I've been thinking about what you said,' she said.

'You have?'

'I don't know.' Minnie pressed her eyes closed. 'I still don't know. I just – I miss you ...'

'Minnie, my battery is about to go, it's bleeping at me. I'm getting on a boat with some friends – a party on the Thames, we leave from Westminster Pier in an hour.' He paused. 'Come, jump in a cab and come join me.'

'I can't.'

'I'm not asking for you to decide anything. Let's just spend New Year with each other, let's do the countdown together.'

'Not tonight,' she said, 'but maybe we could hang out on the second when all this New Year stuff is over?'

The line went quiet for a moment.

'The jinx is still keeping you indoors.' He sounded disappointed.

'Kind of,' she winced.

'You know there have been studies, right? That bad luck happens to those who believe in it. If you still believe, what hope do I have of ...'

Then the line went dead.

'Hello? Quinn?'

She jumped off the sofa. She tried calling back – it went straight to answerphone. What hope did he have of what? Had he changed his mind? Would he say he couldn't be with someone who couldn't leave the house like his mother?

Then Minnie knew what she had to do. She had to take off her owl pyjamas and get herself to Westminster Pier in less than fifty-nine minutes. She had to find Quinn Hamilton and prove that he did have a hope, that she knew the jinx wasn't real. She had to tell him that she didn't want to live in a suit of armour any more, whatever the risks might be. She might not say those exact words – they wouldn't make much sense to anyone, but she could finesse the wording en route.

Minnie buzzed with excitement as she pulled open her wardrobe to find something to wear. Anything, anything, she didn't have time to plan an outfit, any clothes would do. She picked up some jeans. Not those, they were too baggy for her now – in fact not jeans at all – what if it was a dressy boat party? She'd stick out if she went too casual. She only had a few smart tops and none of them went with the flowing blue trousers she liked that made her bum look good – gah! She did not have time for this. *Anything*, just put on anything, Minnie.

Four minutes later she was out of the door wearing three-quarter-length green Capri pants and a crocheted top she'd bought from a beach vendor in India. It was supposed to have another layer underneath it, so she threw on a neon exercise bra. Only when she got to the main road did she realise she'd have looked less ridiculous leaving the house in her pyjamas. She'd also failed to grab a coat and it was freezing outside.

The Underground would be the quickest route to Westminster. She ran along the pavement, her limbs flailing like a baby giraffe's. Outside Willesden Tube station was a large white sign: 'Transport For London regrets to inform you that due to an incredibly pungent sewage leak, the Jubilee Line is not in operation tonight. Happy New Year folks!'

Great. She carried on running to the bus stop; there was a bus in eleven minutes but she didn't have eleven minutes to lose. She'd get a cab and blow the expense, but on New Year's Eve she wouldn't have a hope. Her Uber app said twelve minutes. Suddenly out of nowhere, like a mirage on wheels, a black cab with its light on drove around the corner. She sprinted up the street towards it, only to have a man ahead of her on the pavement flag it down moments before she got there.

'Oh no! Oh please! I really need that cab,' she said, breathless, catching up to the man as he opened the car door.

He turned to look at her and scowled. This was not how London worked – black cabs were first-come, first-served; they didn't work on a 'who needs it most' basis. His look informed her that she wasn't abiding by the rules.

'If I don't get to Westminster Pier in forty minutes, I'm going to miss proving to the man I love that I've changed. He'll set sail and it will be too late!'

The man looked her up and down, taking in her outfit. He glanced at his watch then sighed, 'I'm headed as far as Charing Cross – we can share and split the fare?'

'Oh, thank you!' Minnie clasped her hands together and jumped up and down on the spot before ducking into the cab after him.

The man was in his twenties, with dark curly hair that tumbled down from the top of his head but was cut short at both sides. He wore jewellery – rings of silver and gold on every finger.

'So your fella's in the navy, is he?' asked her cab mate as the car pulled away from the kerb. 'Funny time to set sail.'

Minnie looked confused for a minute, rewinding their conversation in her head.

'Oh no, he's not in the navy, he's going on a boat party,' she explained.

The man frowned. 'You made it sound like he'd be at sea for months, like it had to be tonight?'

'It *does* have to be tonight,' said Minnie. 'If I don't show him I can go out on New Year's Eve, he'll think I still believe in the jinx, and then maybe he won't be able to love someone like that, someone scared and superstitious—'

'The jinx?' asked the man.

Minnie shrugged and gave a little shake of her head. 'Bad things seem to happen to me on New Year's Eve, so I usually try not to go out.'

'What kind of bad things?' The man narrowed his eyes at her from the other side of the cab.

'Nothing particular, it just feels like I'm unlucky this time of year. Logically, it must be coincidence or—'

Before she could finish her sentence, the cab jerked into the air, throwing her into the man's lap. The car screeched to a halt with an alarming crunching sound.

'Gah! Sorry, are you OK?' Minnie asked, as she found herself sprawled against him.

'Tyre's blown,' the cab driver shouted back to them. 'Are you all right?'

They both made noises that they were. Minnie felt her skin getting warmer and warmer as she realised the man's rings were attached to her, an insect caught in her weird webbing top. They climbed out of the cab in conjoined crab-like unison and Minnie tried to untangle herself with as much dignity as possible.

The cab driver stood on the kerb inspecting the blown tyre. He gave a weary groan. 'Looks like you'd best find another way of getting where you're going.'

'What were you saying about bad luck?' groaned the man.

'Coincidence,' said Minnie.

They both stood awkwardly together on the pavement, and a few minutes later the man managed to hail another taxi.

'Maybe we could—' Minnie edged toward him hopefully.

'No,' he said, 'I don't need your bad luck following me round tonight, lady.'

Minnie ran south. She could see the number eighteen bus pulling in ahead, if she could just get on that bus, if there could be no traffic on the roads, she might just make it. She had to try.

'Wait, wait!' she cried, willing the bus to pause a moment longer. Thankfully the driver waited and waved her on. He was a broad-shouldered man in his thirties, with a heavy beard and tattoos down both arms.

'Oh thank you, thank you,' she said, out of breath as she paid her fare.

'Always room for one more,' said the driver in a broad Scottish accent.

Minnie took a seat in the middle of the bus. She was definitely testing the limits of London's transport network tonight.

The bus contained the usual smorgasbord of London nightlife: an elderly man in a battered duffel coat with a tinsel-collared Jack Russell on his lap, a group of teenage girls all in short skirts, long boots and fake eyelashes, laughing over their phones, and a middle-aged couple having a disagreement about the best route to Covent Garden.

'Your lucky day,' said the man with the dog, giving her a wink. He had kind, creased eyes and a pointy face that reminded Minnie of a leprechaun.

'Sorry?' Minnie said.

'Making the bus,' he said.

'Oh yes, well I won't count myself lucky yet, I'm trying to get to Westminster Pier by ten o'clock.' Perhaps it was the man's bright, curious eyes, or perhaps it was the adrenaline of making the bus, but she found herself saying more. 'There's a man I'm in love with who's leaving on a boat in thirty minutes.'

What was it about tonight, and oversharing with complete strangers?

The man ruffled his dog's head. 'Well that's a reason to run for a bus if ever I heard one,' he said. 'Boris here thinks so too.'

The bus pulled in at the next stop, and the engine went dead.

'Sorry folks, just pausing for a change of driver,' came a voice over the tannoy.

Everyone groaned. Minnie jumped up and ran to the front.

'Sorry, sir, but can you tell me how long that will take, please? It's just I'm in a real rush.'

'Aren't we all luv,' said a blonde woman in a high-visibility jacket, white shirt and bus driver's hat. She was holding a clipboard in her hand, and she looked Minnie up and down as she got onto the bus.

'Oh great, are you the new driver?' Minnie asked.

'She needs to get to Westminster Pier to tell a guy she loves him,' shouted the human leprechaun from further down the bus.

'Well, we'll get there when we get there. Move yourself, Hamish,' said the woman, moving to one side so that the large, bearded Scot could get out of the driver's seat. Then she called out to the whole bus, 'The bus will be waiting here for ten minutes to regulate the service on this route. If you are in a hurry, you should get off and catch the bus behind, which will be arriving in seven and a half minutes.'

She gave Minnie a tight grin, flashing a gold tooth, and took her seat in the driver's cabin. People on the bus groaned and started to disembark.

'Oh no, can't we just have an unregulated service tonight?' Minnie pleaded.

'Shaylene's a stickler for the rules,' said the burly male driver, who was filling in some kind of log on the clipboard.

Minnie decided she would need to appeal to Shaylene's romantic sensibilities.

'Look, Shaylene, I'm sure you've seen *Sleepless in Seattle*? You know that bit where Meg Ryan is supposed to meet Tom Hanks at the top of the Empire State Building on Valentine's Day? Well, I'm in a situation a bit like that, except instead of the Empire State Building, it's a party boat, and instead of Tom Hanks, it's this guy I like, but I have to get there before it leaves at ten. That's why I'd really appreciate it if, on this one occasion, you didn't try to regulate the service. It is New Year's Eve after all,' she gave Shaylene her most pleading face, clasping her hands together in prayer.

'You know that saying about how you wait ages for a bus and then two come along at once? You know why that happens?' Shaylene said, pulling a Snickers bar out of her bag and opening it noisily. 'Because someone didn't regulate the service.' Then through a mouthful of Snickers she added, 'and I don't like romcoms.'

'I love *Sleepless in Seattle*,' said Hamish, shaking his head and grinning to himself as he handed the clipboard back to Shaylene.

'Oh, you've seen it?' Minnie squealed. 'Then you know what I'm talking about. Oh Hamish, have you ever just had that feeling about someone – that sudden realisation that whatever the risks of getting hurt, whatever the odds of failure, you just have to give it a go? Before I met this guy my expectation of what love could be was like a five. A five! And then with him, when we're together, it's like ten – a *ten*! And maybe I'm scared about having a ten and then losing it and never being happy with a five again, but if there's a chance for a ten, I've got to go for it, right?'

Hamish looked up at her with a serious expression, his eyes welling up.

'I had a ten once,' he sniffed. 'His name was Roger and he moved to Amsterdam. He said I should move with him, give up my job on the buses, learn Dutch. I can't even roll my "r"s.'

'You never told him how you felt?' Minnie asked.

'No, I let him go. I never met a ten since.' The man looked up at Minnie, he scratched his stubble with a knuckle, a new resolve filled his eyes. 'Out of the way Shaylene, I'm pulling a double shift tonight.' He waved her out of the way, and she and her half-eaten Snickers bar clambered out of the driver's seat.

'You want to do my shift, be my guest,' she said, waving a hand in his face.

Hamish pressed the tannoy button. 'This is now a non-stop, *unregulated* service to Westminster Pier. Anyone not going that way, I suggest they disembark immediately.'

Minnie turned around. Everyone else had long since disembarked. It was just her and the human leprechaun who was now clapping his dog's paws together in excitement.

'Let's get the lady where she needs to go!' he yelled.

Hamish pulled the bus away from the kerb and the bus bumped along at a rollicking pace.

'Buckle your seatbelts!' he cried. 'Make way for the number ten love bus!' yelled Hamish, as he sped out, overtaking the car in front.

'I don't think we have seatbelts on these buses,' said Minnie, clinging on to the pole for dear life, while she tried to get herself into a seat, 'and isn't this the eighteen?'

'Now it's the ten. We're going to get you your ten, hen, if it's the last shift I do!'

As the bus screeched up the kerb at Westminster Pier, Minnie could see the boat was still there; she had made it with a minute to spare.

*

'Thank you, thank you so much,' she yelled to Hamish and the human leprechaun as she leapt through the double doors.

'Go get him, kiddo!' shouted Hamish.

'Call Roger in Amsterdam – tell him how you feel! It's never too late,' Minnie yelled back as she ran across the road to the pier.

It was one minute to ten. She jumped over the turnstile and ran up the ramp onto the boat. It was surprisingly quiet on board – no music, no people for that matter; maybe the party was below deck? She ran around to the front, trying to find a way down, where she found a solitary woman quietly sweeping the deck.

'Is this the party boat?' Minnie asked, trying to catch her breath.

'No,' said the lady sweeping. 'This boat's not in service. You shouldn't be on here. Party boat left five minutes ago.'

She pointed to a boat out in the middle of the Thames. It was four times the size of this boat. Lights flashed from the interior and music boomed out over the water. Women wearing sparkling dresses and men in black tie were out on deck laughing and dancing with drinks in their hands.

She had missed the boat. She was too late.

Minnie took the night bus home. She sat dejected, staring out of the window, watching Londoners preparing to celebrate. A group of girls wearing hairbands with glittery pom-poms tottered down the street, and a couple wearing matching red and green jumpers stumbled out of a pub kissing, as a swaying man urinated against a letterbox.

She could call Quinn tomorrow, of course she could. Logically she knew this, but she still felt that she had missed something important tonight. She'd missed the chance to prove she wasn't the superstitious, fatalistic girl from a year ago. She'd missed the chance to prove to herself that the jinx wasn't real.

As she got off the bus near her house, a car driving past opened a window and threw out a polystyrene container. It bounced off the kerb and spattered her green Capri trousers with a warm yellow gunk, something that smelt like curry sauce.

As she turned the corner of her street and got closer to her front door, she saw that it was hanging open. Oh great, she'd been robbed. The perfect end to the perfect evening. She walked cautiously towards the doorway and heard a noise inside; whoever had broken in was still there. Oh god, where was Lucky? Would he have escaped through the open door? She should call the police; she shouldn't try to confront the intruder alone. She paused, conflicted. Her warm, hooded parka was just there on the peg, visible through the open door. She was freezing; she could grab it and then run and call the police. She reached out to take it, just as a figure emerged from the kitchen. Minnie screamed and threw the coat she was holding over the figure's head.

'I've called the police!' she yelled, running back out into the road.

'Minnie?' she heard a muffled voice calling after her.

How did the burglar know her name? She slowed down and turned to see Quinn, in black tie, holding her parka in his arms.

'It's you? Oh god, I thought someone was robbing my flat,' she said, holding her chest, breathless with the adrenaline.

'The door was wide open,' said Quinn. 'I was worried something had happened so I went in to check. Sorry I scared you.'

Minnie looked at him and blinked, she couldn't believe he was here.

'You're shivering,' he said, wrapping her coat around her shoulders and guiding her inside.

Minnie quickly checked the flat but nothing looked to be missing. Lucky was sitting contentedly on the sofa licking his paws, and she rushed over to pick him up, nuzzling her face into his fur.

'I guess maybe I didn't shut the door properly when I left,' she said with a frown. "My dad warned me the door had a dodgy lock.'

Quinn stood in the hall, as though waiting to be invited in.

'Where did you go?' he asked.

Minnie came to stand opposite him and he reached out to take her hands in his.

'Westminster Pier – I missed the boat.'

'I wasn't on it,' the dimple on Quinn's cheek creasing into life.

'I can see that,' she said, biting her lip. 'You came all the way up here, you missed your party.'

'If you want to stay in and hide from the jinx, I will stay and hide with you.'

'I thought I might have missed the boat with you too …' She paused awkwardly. '… I didn't know if you'd still feel the same.'

'Minnie Cooper, I think it's time I showed you exactly how I feel.'

He put his hands gently on her face, and Minnie had that funny feeling she'd had so often before, that Quinn Hamilton might be about to kiss her. This time she was right. He leant over and gently pressed his lips to hers. His mouth was tender but firm; his hand stroked her hair down around her cheek. Her skin fizzed with electricity and Minnie had to reach backwards for a wall to support herself.

After a few blissful minutes, Quinn pulled away, sniffing the air, his nose wrinkly.

'Do you smell curry sauce?'

'It's me. It's all over my trousers – it's been an eventful evening.'

Minnie shivered. She'd got so cold her body was finding it hard to warm up. Quinn rubbed his hands up and down her arms.

'Maybe I'll just have a quick shower to warm up and de-curry? Then I'll be right with you. Hold this thought!'

The hot water scorched her skin and she watched her belly go pink under the stream. The heat was heavenly. Quinn knocked on the bathroom door. Minnie turned, nervously clutching her hands around her body. Was he coming in? Would he be that bold?

'Oh I, er, I just wanted to check you didn't actually call the police,' Quinn called out.

'Oh, no,' she called back. 'I didn't. That's just what I shout when I think a burglar is chasing me down the street.'

'OK, good, just checking. Sorry to disturb.' His voice sounded nervous. Minnie smiled to herself.

What was going to happen now? Was she going to go out there, kiss him again and pick up from where they'd left off the last time he'd been in her flat? She closed her eyes under the water. She wanted that, of course, but she also felt nervous – could anything live up to the expectation?

She dried herself in the shower and crept through to the bedroom. She wanted to get changed rather than talk to him with nothing but a towel between them. She threw on her warmest clothes; a green polo neck and yesterday's jeans, then she went through to the living room. Quinn was sitting on the sofa with Lucky on his lap.

She sat down next to him, suddenly acutely aware of the empty Malteser packets, and the looming face of Margaret Thatcher on her TV screen where she'd paused *The Iron Lady*.

'Minnie, I am so glad you called tonight. These last few months without seeing you ...' He trailed off and put a hand up to her face, pulling her gaze to meet his.

'I promise you, I'm never going to stop you from having that Mustang moment when you need it. And I'm sorry I hurt you, I was scared to feel like this – to not be in control.' He took a breath. 'It took me all these months to realise I wasn't scared of you needing me, I was scared by how much I needed you.'

'I'm scared too,' she said quietly. 'It's overwhelming.'

They looked into each other's eyes and in the stillness of the moment, beyond the owls communing with each other, a new dialogue opened up between them. They held hands in the semi-darkness. Suddenly, Minnie knew what she wanted to do.

'What time is it?' she asked.

'Nearly half eleven,' said Quinn.

'Let's go out. Let's take a picnic to Primrose Hill and watch the fireworks. I've always wanted to do that.'

'Go out? what about the jinx?' he asked, raising an eyebrow at her.

'What jinx? I make my own luck these days.' Minnie cocked her head at him. 'I just want to do one New Year right, one New Year where I'm not stuck in a toilet or an airport or A&E or hiding at home watching TV. I just want one proper midnight, to start this year right.'

She said it tentatively, not sure if he'd understand. Quinn smiled, something behind the liquid of his eyes flashed in comprehension. Minnie's owls were not happy about what she was saying; the owls wanted her to get naked with Quinn as fast as possible, but she overruled them – the owls were short-termist creatures.

'Let's go find ourselves a midnight,' he said, standing up and reaching for Minnie's hand.

Minnie rummaged around her kitchen cabinets and pulled out a picnic blanket. She threw a few picnic supplies into a canvas bag and then they were out of the door and into an Uber.

*

Primrose Hill was packed. They wouldn't be able to push their way up through the crowd to get the best view from the top. It was four minutes to midnight – they'd made it just in time. Minnie laid the rug out on the only piece of grass that was free. It was near the bins at the bottom of the hill, next to a group of teenagers drinking beers and playing the guitar. Quinn opened up the bag of picnic supplies she had brought.

'Milk?' he said, laughing, as he pulled out a carton.

'I didn't have anything else to drink in my fridge,' she laughed.

'Weetabix and a banana,' he said, pulling out the remaining contents of the bag.

'They go with the milk,' she laughed again. 'Look, a picnic's a picnic.' She elbowed him gently. 'We don't keep champagne and canapés on tap in Willesden.'

Quinn took a bite of dry Weetabix and a swig of milk from the carton, then made an overblown 'hmmm, delicious' face.

They both grinned. All around them, people started yelling out the countdown.

'Ten, nine, eight ...'

In the sky there were a few early explosions, light streaming across the sky in bursts of colour. They could just see the top of the BT tower, shining brightly on the horizon.

'Three, two, one, HAPPY NEW YEAR!' cried voices all around them.

'Happy Birthday, wonderful, beautiful Minnie,' whispered Quinn, leaning in to kiss her.

'Happy Birthday to you too.'

The teenager on the guitar started playing 'Auld Lang Syne' and people began to sing along. As Quinn and Minnie kissed, the sky erupted in fireworks from all around the city. Light blazing and bursting high into the air, floating down again in a twinkling canopy of burnished rain.

Then Minnie's phone began to ring. She pulled back from Quinn, took it from her bag and looked at the screen.

'Unknown number,' she said, making a puzzled face. 'Hello?'

'Hi Minnie, it's Tara. Is Quinn with you?'

'It's your mum,' Minnie mouthed to Quinn.

'Yes, he's here,' she told Tara. 'I'll put you on ...'

Quinn closed his eyes and held out his hand to take the phone.

'No, no, I don't need to speak to him,' Tara said. 'I just wanted to check that he'd found you. He called me looking for your number earlier, and I only just managed to get your details from your mother. I'm glad you managed to find each other.'

Quinn was still holding out his hand for the phone, his brow furrowed in confusion as to why Minnie was still talking to his mother.

'We're on Primrose Hill,' said Minnie, standing up and waving at the blue house across the road. 'I'm waving now, I doubt you can see me. We could come and say hello in a bit?'

'No, don't. Go and enjoy yourselves,' said Tara. 'Oh, and Minnie?'

'Yes.'

'Happy Birthday, sweetheart.'

Minnie said goodbye and hung up the phone.

'What was that about?' asked Quinn.

'You called her earlier looking for my number, she just wanted to check you'd found me.'

Quinn nodded and rolled his eyes to the sky. 'I called her from a friend's phone when my mobile died. I hoped she might have your number.'

'Well, she says Happy Birthday,' said Minnie.

Minnie leant back against Quinn's chest. He wrapped his arms around her and kissed her neck, setting off a whole new wave of fireworks. Streams of light crackled on the horizon and Minnie let out a contented sigh. As they gently swayed to the music of the guitar, Minnie's head resting on Quinn's shoulder, he said, 'In the morning, shall we go to the heath and watch the sunrise from our hill?'

'Our hill? I like the sound of that.' Then, after a pause, Minnie said, 'Quinn, can I ask you something?'

'Sure, anything.'

'It's a silly question Leila always asks on New Year's Eve. It's kind of a tradition – where do you want to be this time next year?'

'Where do I want to be?' Quinn paused for a moment. 'I want to be right here, with you, on Primrose Hill, having a Weetabix picnic.'

She smiled, the kind of smile where you feel your muscles might soon tire from smiling so much. She turned her head to kiss his mouth. Kissing for Minnie usually came with a degree of self-consciousness. Beneath the physical connection there was always an awareness of what the other person might be thinking, of where it might lead, or that you might need to leave soon to get the bus. It was like reading subtitles while watching a film – your focus wasn't always entirely in the right place. With this kiss, there were no subtitles. Her thinking mind surrendered to the pleasure of the moment.

'What about you?' he said eventually, his breath hot on her cheek. 'Where do you want to be?'

'I don't mind where I am,' she said softly. 'As long as it's you I'm kissing at lemming o'clock.'

She saw his eyes grow wide and he said in a strange voice, 'Lemming o'clock? You? … I knew it was you …'

And in the time it took her to realise what he meant, she leant in to kiss him again and the whole world folded into this small patch of grass on Primrose Hill.

Acknowledgements

They say it takes a village to raise a child. Well, I think it takes a small town to publish a book. There are so many people I need to thank for their role in bringing this book into your hands. Firstly, to my wonderful, talented agent Clare Wallace at Darley Anderson, for helping me to become the writer I always wanted to be. I couldn't ask for a better, more supportive co-pilot on my writing journey. Secondly, to my editors Sonny Marr at Arrow and Margo Lipschultz at Putnam Books, whose insight and input have elevated this book from a shop-bought ham sandwich, to a slow-roasted ham hock with all the trimmings. It has been a joy to work with such brilliant people, who care as much about my characters as I do.

I would also like to thank the whole team at Penguin Random House, especially the Rights team and the PR and Marketing teams. They have done a fantastic job putting this book out into the world. Without them, you would not be reading this.

Closer to home, my husband Tim, who, even though he said this book was "not really his thing," still read it (twice) and held the fort with the domestic load while I scurried upstairs to write another thousand words. It's no easy task to write a book on top of having a job and two small children – life around the edges gets squeezed so, for supporting me as tirelessly as you do, I will always be grateful. To ArtHouse Jersey, for allowing me time off when I had an edit due. (If you are an artist look them up, they do wonderful things.) To Strawberry Laces, for fueling the majority of this book. To my first readers – Rids, Nat, Sarah and Traci – your input on various drafts was hugely appreciated. Rids – you will *always* be my first reader. To all my female friends – who inspired the character of Leila – this book is as much a love story about friendship as it is a romance. AHAS, JANSS – *you* complete me. To my parents, who built my foundation, allowing me to believe I might do anything I put my mind to in life.

Finally, and most importantly, to you, for reading this book to the end! I really hope you enjoyed it. If you did, I would love you to leave a review online – it helps other readers discover me. And please do get in touch on social media:

@sophie_cousens on Instagram

@SophieCous on Twitter

#ThisTimeNextYear

P.S. This book was written in a pre-COVID world. The 2020 of Minnie and Quinn's world now only exists in some parallel universe. Whatever the year ahead might bring for us all, let's keep reading. Books free us from isolation. Stories unite us. We've all had to play in One Player mode for a while – but we're all still in this game together.